GLOBAL STRIKE

BOOK 6 IN THE WAR PLANNERS SERIES

ANDREW WATTS

Severn River
PUBLISHING

Severn River Publishing

ISBN: 978-1-951249-84-7 (Paperback)

ALSO BY ANDREW WATTS

Firewall

The War Planners Series

The War Planners

The War Stage

Pawns of the Pacific

The Elephant Game

Overwhelming Force

Global Strike

Max Fend Series

Glidepath

The Oshkosh Connection

Books available for Kindle, print, and audiobook. To find out more about the books or Andrew Watts, visit

AndrewWattsAuthor.com

Therefore he who desires peace, let him prepare war.

— VEGETIUS

History teaches that wars begin when governments believe the price of aggression is cheap. To keep the peace, we and our allies must be strong enough to convince any potential aggressor that war could bring no benefit, only disaster.

— PRESIDENT RONALD REAGAN

1

The inverted bow of the *USS Michael Monsoor* cut through the dark waters of the Pacific Ocean, the ship's distinct silhouette nearly invisible on the moonless night. A thin layer of scattered clouds allowed the occasional window of starlight to illuminate patches of sea.

"Any sign of them?" Captain Harris asked.

"Nothing yet, sir," replied the officer of the deck.

The captain stood in the center of the dark bridge with a small watch team. They were surrounded by flat-panel video feed that provided them with an artificial 360-degree view of the outside world, dimmed down to the lowest level so as not to affect their night vision. Two petty officers steered the ship with a trackball, keyboard, and the click of a button.

The officer of the deck touched his headset. "Captain, the TAO requests your presence in combat."

"On my way."

Captain Harris hustled into the ship's combat information center, the envy of most modern warships. Nearly a dozen personnel sat in four rows of multi-screen computer terminals, monitoring the electronic signals, passive sonar, and communications. The captain and XO had hand-picked the combat watch team, and the varsity players were on duty tonight.

As the captain entered the space, someone announced his presence. "Captain in combat."

Captain Harris approached the Tactical Action Officer, or TAO, who managed the ship's combat systems and sensors. "What's up, TAO?"

"We're starting to get some ESM hits. Chinese commercial surface search radars."

"Got any fixes yet?"

"Not yet, sir. They just started showing up."

"Bearing?"

"Two-four-zero to two-seven-zero. Sure would love to illuminate with the SPY, make sure no surveillance aircraft are out there..." The TAO gave him a frustrated look.

"You know we can't."

"I know, sir."

All electronic emitters, including radar, had been powered down. Task Force Bruiser, which included both the *Monsoor* and its embarked special operations team, was a covert assignment. However much the captain would love to use his surface search radar to detect contacts in their vicinity, he wouldn't risk it for fear of detection. Their destroyer was well below the equator, further into the Chinese-controlled South Pacific than any American ship had operated for more than a year.

"How are we doing on fuel?"

"Getting close to our bingo, sir, as the aviators like to say."

"Might have to move our RAS further to the south if these guys don't show up today. Talk to the Navigator. Have him come up with a plan and run it by me tonight."

"Roger, sir." The TAO looked up. "Sir, the SEAL commander has an update for you."

Captain Harris glanced up at the second-level balcony, where a row of men were overlooking the combat information center. The SEAL commander and a few intel officers were embarked with them. Usually the SEALs would run this type of mission off a submarine like the *USS Jimmy Carter*, but in the year since the war began, US submarines had more missions than they could handle. And their reconnaissance deployments were significantly closer to Chinese shores than the *Michael Monsoor* could get.

But the *Monsoor*, one of only three stealthy Zumwalt-class ships ever made, was almost invisible on radar. And when she went dark, she could be forward deployed to places like this, where the Chinese were suspected to be operating, but not in such significant numbers that the American stealth ship couldn't avoid detection.

Captain Harris climbed the ladder to the upper-level combat space, where the SEAL team commander and a DIA officer stood behind a mustached submarine tech rep. The submarine expert was monitoring a dashboard of numbers and technical data.

The SEAL commander turned to face Captain Harris. "Sir, good evening. We just received a short-range burst transmission. They're on their way. Should be about thirty minutes."

"Excellent. Please let the TAO know to prepare for recovery."

A half-hour later, the captain watched from the internal bay's peripheral platform at the ship's aft. The massive, cavernous space had a central track normally used to deploy and recover the ship's rigid hull inflatable boats. Waves sloshed up onto the angled deck below.

A silent, black monolith surfaced from the deep, barely visible at first but growing larger as it drove up the ship's wake.

Members of the ship's crew, the SEAL team leader, and intelligence personnel watched as the newest mini-submarine lodged itself onto the rear of the ship's ramp. Specially trained enlisted men attached lines and then used electronic devices and the moving tracks to pull the submarine into the bay.

The whole operation took about twenty minutes, as fast as they could safely go. When they were finished, the rear bay door closed, the submarine's hatch opened, and four SEALs exited. One of them handed an object to the SEAL team leader.

Moments later, the captain, along with the SEAL commander and intel officers, listened as the SEAL team reviewed the reconnaissance data.

"That's the first rocket, right there," one of the men said, pointing at the image on the screen. "The next one comes a few minutes later. They recovered about twenty of them, I think. One crashed into the water."

The DIA officer said, "That's their new series 8 rocket. They're launching about forty mini-satellites from each one of these babies. Times twenty..."

"That's a lot of satellites."

"Why are they recovering them here?"

"Based on the trajectory, this must be the optimal spot. Then they'll have about a fifteen-day haul back to Hainan. Their space launch facility is right near there."

A phone on the wall rang. Captain Harris picked it up. "Captain."

"Captain, TAO, sir, we've got a problem."

Captain Harris looked out the glass window and onto the watch floor below. The TAO was holding the phone to his ear, looking up at him.

"Sir, we now have at least twenty electronic fixes on what I think are Chinese warships. Sonar is picking up corresponding noise. Some merchants. But also what we think are Type 52 destroyers. Sir, if those are here, they'll be flying surveillance helicopters..."

The captain hung up the phone and headed toward the ladder. "Make a hole!" Two seamen scattered from the ladderway. The captain slid down on his palms, his steel-toed boots landing with a thud, and then headed over to the TAO's station, glancing up at the tactical display at the front of the room. Nearly two dozen red tracks were dangerously close to their position, the speed indicators all pointing toward the *USS Michael Monsoor.*

"What's their ETA?"

"About thirty minutes until they're in visual range, based on our tracks, sir. Hard to say without radar..." The watchstanders surrounding the TAO glanced up, listening intently to the conversation.

"Any indication they've detected us?"

A chief manning a nearby display said, "TAO, ESM hit bearing two-six-zero. Looks like a Chinese helicopter radar."

The TAO looked at the captain in alarm.

"Maneuver us northeast. Give me twenty-five knots."

"Aye, sir."

The TAO relayed the command to the bridge, and the ship's deck listed beneath the captain's feet as it turned.

The captain walked over to the air defense team. "Do we have a track on that helicopter?"

"Yes, sir, but it's pretty sketchy since we don't have radar up. It's somewhere over in this area." The petty officer pointed at the red hostile air track on his display.

Captain Harris felt his pulse racing as he calculated a half-dozen options. He had a lot of firepower on board, but he wanted to avoid detection...

"Sir, the helicopter looks like it's headed our way. The electronic fixes are getting closer."

Captain Harris said, "Ready the laser. No radar. Use visual aiming only."

The TAO looked at him. "Sir?"

"Hurry."

"Yes, sir."

The TAO ran over to an Operations Specialist manning the newly-installed laser weapons system.

"Throw the video feed up front, please."

"Aye, sir."

The right front screen flashed to a green image external of the ship. A small dark object was visible in the distance. A white reticle centered over it.

"Power coming online. Ready to lase, sir."

The *Michael Monsoor's* electric drive and integrated power system generated over seventy megawatts of power, enough for a small city. Now, that power was about to be directed into a small, focused energy beam aimed at the Chinese helicopter heading toward their position.

Inside the helicopter, the Chinese aircrew studied their tactical display, trying to determine if the small radar return to the northeast was really a ship, or merely a pod of whales breaking the surface of the ocean. It was too small to be a ship, wasn't it? They decided to fly closer to gather infrared video imagery to be sure.

On board the *Michael Monsoor*, Captain Harris said, "Open fire."

The men and women in combat fell silent, staring at the screen, as thousands of watts of power flowed through the laser weapon and focused on a moving target.

The helicopter's silhouette on the monitor exploded into a liquid-black ball of smoke, flame, and metal remains now tumbling to the sea. The approaching Chinese fleet, still unaware of the American ship's presence, knew only that they had lost communications and radar contact with their helicopter.

The *USS Michael Monsoor's* inverted bow continued cutting silently through the water, speeding away from the Chinese in stealth as it headed northeast.

2

David Manning walked down the steps of a CIA Gulfstream IV jet and onto the hot tarmac at Ronald Reagan Washington National Airport, the Washington Monument and Capitol Building visible in the distance. He flanked his boss, Susan Collinsworth, head of Joint Task Force Silversmith, as they walked toward a waiting black Chevy Suburban.

The SUV was escorted by two armored US Army security vehicles, blue lights flashing, as they took the Arlington Memorial Bridge across the Potomac River. What little traffic was on the roads quickly moved out of the way as they passed. That had been one of the few good things about the war. Less traffic, everywhere. Thanks to Russia and China flexing their muscles in oil-rich countries, gas prices had skyrocketed and few could afford to drive to work anymore. The war had decimated international trade, and the country was still reeling from the effects of Chinese cyber and EMP attacks during the conflict's opening days. The economy had tumbled, and never fully recovered.

Most people now worked remotely via the North American Secure Internet or took lower-cost public transportation to the office. Many of the new jobs supported the war in some way or another, and those employees were the lucky ones. Others didn't have work. Movie theaters and restaurants had shut down, and small businesses declared bankruptcy in droves. The times were tough.

The war had several names. Most Americans called it World War Three, or simply The War. The "neutral" international community often referred to it as the Chinese American War. To Chinese state-sponsored media, and the news organizations wishing to receive favorable treatment from China, it was known as The War Against American Hostility. David and his colleagues at the CIA sometimes used that term tongue-in-cheek. Dark humor to get through dark times.

Susan glanced at him from across the SUV. "Nice to be back in DC. I was getting tired of Raven Rock."

David hummed agreement, studying his notes before the brief. Within twenty-four hours of the Chinese EMP attack that kicked off the war, the Washington DC-based government leadership was physically decentralized. Congressmen and generals alike were shipped off to a pre-identified collection of bunkers and military bases across the nation. But people hated living like that, and now that the hot war had cooled, the power players who controlled America's military, intelligence, and political leadership were returning to their original locations.

The highly secretive Silversmith task force remained at Eglin Air Force Base near Destin, Florida. Silversmith was a joint CIA-DOD organization tasked to analyze Chinese military strategy and lead covert programs designed to counter Chinese activities. While the number of personnel involved in Silversmith was small—only a few hundred—its output was very influential in shaping US war policy.

A fusion center for the vast American and allied intelligence collection organizations, Silversmith was made up of elite military and intelligence personnel. Top-level experts on technology and China. Spies. Strategists. Special ops. Susan and—until recently—General Schwartz led them all.

David had become one of her most prized team members. She realized early on that he had a talent for strategy and analysis that few others could match. And having lost his own father in the war, he was highly motivated to perform.

Susan glanced at David. "Try not to give the president too much detail. Just enough to make a decision. Keep it short and sweet."

"I'll do my best," he said.

David hated these types of meetings, where he had to speak to a bunch of high-ranking politicians and flag officers. The type who often came with massive egos and hardened points of view. They would second-guess his facts and make decisions based on ulterior motives. Sometimes they would just try to crush the briefer to make themselves look smart and score points with the boss. It was even worse when the boss happened to be the President of the United States. Higher stakes. Olympic-level boardroom battles. But David had learned long ago that the most powerful weapon in the world was information in the hands of someone who knew how to use it.

The column of vehicles came to a halt under a long security tent designed to obstruct the view of snipers and surveillance. US Secret Service agents directed David and Susan through security before escorting them into the West Wing and, finally, the Situation Room.

Most seats were already filled. The CIA Director nodded to David and greeted Susan by name. David greeted General Schwartz, now the Director for Operations, J3, of the Joint Staff at the Pentagon. General Schwartz had been promoted out of Silversmith after they'd successfully orchestrated the Battle of

Johnston Atoll. David recognized the other faces around the table as cabinet members and intelligence agency heads.

The President of the United States walked in, and the group stood. He sat in the conference table's head seat and the others followed his lead. James Roberts, age forty-five, had been considered a rising star in his party, picked as vice president in an attempt to bolster the late President Griffin's appeal to younger voters.

President Griffin died when Air Force One was shot down by Chinese special forces. The assassination sewed chaos in the US chain of command during a brutal first strike. In the fog of that opening salvo, EMP weapons detonated across the US and over American naval fleets. Thousands of Chinese missiles were launched at American aircraft carrier strike groups in the Pacific. Simultaneously, North Korea invaded South Korea, using poison gas to devastate civilian and military targets alike. And a Chinese cyber-attack, using deep fake technology to simulate a US Presidential national TV announcement, deceived most Americans into thinking that nuclear ballistic missiles were hurtling toward the US.

That was the moment when President Roberts was sworn in.

During the opening hours of his presidency, President Roberts learned that his predecessor had ordered a limited nuclear strike on Chinese targets, and that missiles were already airborne. The order had been issued under the false belief that Chinese missiles were headed toward the United States. What he didn't know was that China was trying to get the US to launch a limited number of nukes.

And they succeeded.

American ICBMs hit dozens of Chinese targets, eliminating their land-based nuclear capability, while American fast-attack submarines simultaneously sank the majority of Chinese nuclear ballistic missile submarines. Chinese nuclear offensive capability was severely depleted.

But the political fallout America suffered after using weapons of mass destruction was severe. The unthinkable infliction of self-harm on his own country had turned out to be one of Chinese President Jinshan's best strategic moves.

The week after America used nuclear weapons, Russia announced the infamous "Russian Ultimatum." Any further use of nuclear weapons by the United States would henceforth trigger Russia to enter the war, fighting on behalf of China. The Russians then led a multi-nation coalition calling for an economic embargo on all US goods. America, already struggling to recover from the Chinese's devastating attacks, watched as much of the international community turned their backs on them right when it mattered the most.

Several nations continued to provide support. But with the Russian ultimatum, even the staunchest American allies had to hide their assistance, lest Russia have more of an excuse to spread its wings.

"Good morning, ladies and gentlemen," said the president.

"Good morning, Mr. President," came the scattered replies from around the table.

David had only met the president a few times, but he approved of him. A veteran himself, the president had spent five years as an Army JAG after law school, deploying to Iraq twice. He was analytical and decisive. And as far as David could tell, he did things for the right reasons.

The Director of National Intelligence motioned to the screen at the far end of the room. It displayed reconnaissance imagery that David had reviewed the previous day.

The DNI said, "Mr. President, these are self-landing rockets. Approximately twenty-four hours ago, the US Air Force detected a mass-launch of Chinese satellites from their

Wenchang Space Launch Facility. We had intelligence that they were trying something new with this launch and had a reconnaissance team waiting."

"A reconnaissance team?" the president asked.

"Yes, sir. Task Force Bruiser. A SEAL team operating from one of our stealth Navy ships, the *USS Michael Monsoor*, forward deployed to the South Pacific. Shortly after the US Air Force detected the Chinese satellite launch, the SEAL team observed two dozen rockets landing on platforms in the center of this uninhabited atoll." The DNI motioned to the screen, where a thin, circular sandbar surrounded several platform barges floating in the water. "The Chinese had a ship-based team collecting the rockets after they landed. We estimate it will take them two weeks to transit back to the Wenchang Space Launch Facility. Maybe another week to load up for their next round."

The president rubbed his chin. "What's the significance?"

"Two things, Mr. President. One, this is a new space warfare capability. And a distinct Chinese advantage for the moment. With these reusable rockets, the Chinese can greatly reduce the cost and cycle time of launching new satellites into space. As you know, sir, after the war began, maintaining space-based systems has been a major challenge for all countries. The US has attempted to replenish our satellite reconnaissance, communications, and navigation systems, but the Chinese are launching attacks on every new satellite we send up. Usually within a matter of hours."

"Their anti-satellite capability has really improved, Mr. President," the National Security Advisor chimed in.

The president sighed. "I recall you saying that our anti-satellite capability is on par with theirs."

"That's correct, sir. We shoot down theirs about as quick as they shoot down ours. But right now, we're only able to launch one or two satellites at a time. And without a reusable rocket system like this, it takes us much longer and costs a lot more money."

The president frowned. "You said this new data meant two things. What's the second?"

General Schwartz leaned forward. "Mr. President, the Chinese have executed a mass satellite launch from their Pacific space launch facility. We estimate their new mass-launch capability has a three- to four-week reload time. These mass satellite launches may cost less per rocket, but when they're launching twenty of them, each carrying dozens of mini-satellites...well, sir, it turns into a big bet. One they can only make every so often."

President Roberts said, "The implication being..."

General Schwartz placed his hands flat on the table. "That they would only do it for an important reason. They'll likely be timing these mass satellite launches with something else. Think of it like a war drum."

"How big was this launch?"

General Schwartz turned to one of the Air Force officers sitting in the outer row of seats. "Approximately one thousand mini-satellites in the constellation, sir," the officer replied. "Oriented north-south in geosynchronous orbit over the Pacific. As per our standing orders, we're engaging them with our anti-satellite weapons. But..."

General Schwartz turned to face the president. "That's a lot of targets, Mr. President. It's going to take a few days, at best."

The president looked around the room. "Let's hear it. What do we think they're up to?"

The CIA director glanced in their direction. "Sir, Susan Collinsworth and David Manning are here from the TF Silversmith team. Would you two like to add something?"

Susan nodded for David to speak.

David wiped his sweaty palms on his pant legs under the

table. "Good morning, Mr. President. Sir, as stated, the Chinese would know that those satellites will get shot down. China wouldn't have launched that many unless they were planning something very big, and very soon. This provides them with a robust ISR picture of the Pacific theater, but it gets less accurate after the first day or two. So, I would expect the Chinese to take action within the next few hours or days. The *USS Michael Monsoor*, the destroyer that deployed the SEAL recon team, observed a very large number of surface contacts in their vicinity. They were forced to shoot down a Chinese surveillance helicopter to avoid detection."

The president nodded. "I've been briefed. What's your point, Mr. Manning?"

"Sir, based on the position, heading, and speed of those unknown surface tracks, we think the Chinese may be mobilizing a large-scale transit of the Pacific. This correlates with HUMINT we've received from inside China."

General Schwartz said, "What Mr. Manning said is precisely correct."

"So China is launching their fleet across the Pacific?" the president asked. "Where are they headed? What's the target?"

The National Security Advisor stammered, "Sir, it would be much too early to guess…"

The president pointed at David. "You. What do you think?"

David didn't blink. "Sir, for a coordinated space launch and fleet movement this big, my guess is that this is the push further east we've all been waiting for. Their target could be the Hawaiian Islands, or our new bases at Midway or Johnston Atoll. The Chinese have already planted a small number of troops on every land mass in the South Pacific, transforming them into PLA Navy outposts. It's even possible they're making a push toward South America. That's a very real objective for Jinshan, and one I don't think we should rule out."

The SECDEF looked skeptical. "Mr. President, I don't think anyone can say with certainty. It's also possible the Chinese fleet is just moving to increase their numbers around South Pacific islands they already hold. After all, it's been nine months since the last major military engagement. Why would they make such a bold move now?"

David looked at Susan, who nodded. He said, "Sir, we know with certainty that the Chinese Ministry of State Security has operatives in Ecuador, Venezuela, Peru, and Bolivia. Their infrastructure won't be starting from scratch."

The SECDEF said, "Having spies in a country is one thing, but having the necessary infrastructure to move a massive military throughout the continent is an entirely different matter."

David said, "Sir, for years, Chinese businesses, which are all monitored and controlled by the Chinese government, have been building up infrastructure in South America. They've been investing in railway lines and roads across the continent. Chinese companies have been opening manufacturing facilities in South American nations, selling to their consumers, and using their raw materials. Before the war began, we thought they were only making these investments for profit. If you're going to ship more goods and products across the continent, then building railways and highways makes sense. But these investments also provided the infrastructure to efficiently move troops, tanks, and supplies around the continent."

"This is conjecture," the SECDEF declared.

The president said, "Based on China's actions last year, his argument appears to be on solid ground."

The SECDEF frowned.

David said, "Sir, there is something else. Cheng Jinshan is dying of cancer. And our sources tell us that he's taken a turn for the worse. He has a successor in place, but he's very young. The PLA has been massing troops near Chinese ports for months.

We believe Jinshan's ultimate goal is to defeat and occupy the US. If Jinshan has received new medical information indicating that he won't be around for much longer, that may be his motivator for taking action now."

The president cleared his throat. "How long until we know for sure?"

General Schwartz turned to an admiral sitting in the back row, who said, "Sir, based on the position of the *USS Michael Monsoor's* surface contacts, it would take about a month for them to cross the Pacific and reach South America. Maybe two weeks if their destination is Hawaii. But that doesn't include delays if they face US resistance along the way, or if they take a longer route to try and avoid such resistance. They also might move slower to conserve fuel."

"Three to four weeks." The president stood up, and the rest of the room followed. Leaning forward on the table, he met the eyes of everyone in the room as he spoke. "Our country has been waiting too long for progress. It's been eighteen months since the war began. I'm pleased that open combat has all but ceased. I'd rather have a cold war than a hot one. But I can't help but think we're stuck in a castle while the Chinese armies put us under siege politically and economically. I've got unemployment up another three percent this quarter. GDP is in the red like it's never been. And our increased military budget is burning a hole in the deficit. I can't keep asking our citizens to grow patriot gardens and buy war bonds. I only have so much political capital left." He paused, standing straight and folding his arms. "We need a way to improve our situation."

Then he turned and left the room, followed by a few of his staff.

General Schwartz turned to Susan. "We need that scientist."

"Our best men are on it, sir."

3

Lima, Peru

Chase Manning stepped onto the cobblestone road of *Parque el Olivar de San Isidro*. To his left, a duck pond was lined with a natural stone retaining wall. A light wind blew through the trees, ruffling the hair of the few locals sitting on a bench overlooking the pond. His eyes scanned them as he walked. Split-second discreet glances at each possible threat. Chase turned down a narrow path lined with tall trees, passing a large home with German architecture. He was almost finished with the surveillance detection route that would ensure he was clean of any observers.

Chase was still relatively new to these spy games. While his background in Navy special warfare had allowed him to transition pretty easily into the CIA's Special Operations Group, shifting over to the world of espionage was an adjustment.

Susan Collinsworth, head of the Silversmith task force and a seasoned CIA operations officer herself, sought to expand Chase's skill set by sending him to a months-long training course on counter-surveillance. In her words, "You are a talented operator, Chase, but a piss-poor spook. I'm merely trying to increase that classification to adequate."

After several months of the CIA's denied areas operations training, Chase saw suspicious-looking eyes everywhere he went. Possible Chinese agents on the park bench. Maybe a Russian operative pushing a stroller in the park. But Chase had to admit, he was a hell of a lot better on the streets than he used to be.

His brother David had undergone similar upgrades, although his training was designed to improve his abilities in intelligence analysis and strategy rather than street tactics.

Like most wars, this one was lasting longer than any of the "experts" had predicted, morphing into a cold-war-like stalemate, with neither side advancing to attack the other's home turf. Minor skirmishes still flared up every so often, but both sides kept their moves quiet.

China was winning the political and economic war. The US had been forced to cede its presence in Asia within the opening weeks, which China used to spread its sphere of influence. Chinese diplomatic, military, and economic interests began to dominate the world stage.

Twelve months ago, Chase wouldn't have needed denied areas training to operate in South America. Now, Chinese operatives were everywhere. Venezuela, Ecuador, and Bolivia had each welcomed the Chinese military to station a small contingent of special operations troops within their borders. Russian and Chinese military aircraft were increasingly spotted on the military base runways of sympathetic South American nations. For months, Chinese intelligence agents had seeped throughout Latin American streets and institutions like termites boring their way into a wood house, destroying the foundation. Together, these moves paved the way for a future invasion that the intelligence analysts had been describing as "imminent" for months.

Chase checked the time on his Omega wristwatch and turned down the final street of his route. He was within two minutes of his expected arrival time. The safehouse was a nondescript two-bedroom home with a yellow exterior, small wrought iron gate, and a single bush out front, smushed between two nearly identical homes.

As he walked closer, he took in every inch of the neighborhood. Telephone and power lines spread out overhead like a spider web. The CIA techs at Lima Station had taken measures to disable many of their connections, a precaution meant to prevent China's cyber operators from discovering or eavesdropping on the meeting.

An elderly woman watered her plants on a second-floor balcony next door. The CIA surveillance asset didn't glance down as Chase walked past. A red rose plant rested on her outdoor coffee table. The *all-clear* signal telling Chase that she had observed nothing unusual. Only the normal pattern of life for this time of day.

A small Toyota sedan sputtered along the road and turned down the alleyway next to the house, parking in the lone covered space. The CIA officers inside the vehicle quickly moved their guest into the house through the side door. Chase remained outside for another few minutes, watching for any foot traffic or tail vehicles. None showed, and so he entered the home from the same door.

Now standing in the security room just inside the entrance, Chase recognized the guard on duty as one of the local CIA ground team members. Former Air Force pararescue, Chase was pretty sure.

He nodded a greeting. "Mike."

"Chase, good to see you, man." Mike held a relaxed grip on his H&K UMP-45.

"You too. Everyone upstairs?"

"Yup. Homeboy brought some local food. He gave me a sample. Hope he's not a Chinese double operative because I'm a sucker for spicy food. Consider it worth getting poisoned for. You like spice? This shit'll put hair on your chest, hombre. Although you were with the SEALs, right? So you'd probably just wax any chest hair right back off."

Chase laughed. "Ah yes, Air Force jokes. The lowest form of humor."

"Oh whatever. Everybody wishes they were Air Force, man. Don't lie. You know our secret, right?"

"What's that?"

"You Navy guys, when you build a base, you start with the harbor, then you go build the runway. Then you build the barracks and the squadron buildings and all that crap. Then you run out of money and there's nothing left so you have a lousy time. In the Air Force we did it the right way, see? First thing we build is the bar. Then the *golf course*. Then the bowling alley. *Then* we run out of money for the runway and go back to Congress, and hell, what are they going to do, say no to a *runway*? See how it works?"

Chase nodded. "You guys certainly have your priorities straight."

Mike smiled. "And good looks. Well, not me personally. But my kid apparently has my wife's genes, thank God. Check it out. My wife just sent me this. Kiddo turned five last week."

Mike took a picture of his wife and son out of his breast pocket. It looked like it had been printed from home. Folded creases and grainy. This was what we were reduced to, Chase thought. No more using cell phones, which could be tracked and tapped into. And the world's free web capabilities had been dramatically reduced. Each continent now had their own tightly controlled internet.

Chase admired the picture. "They look great, buddy. And you're right, he's sure lucky he doesn't have your genes."

"Damn straight." Mike folded up the picture and stuffed it back in his breast pocket. "All right, have fun, traitor," he added, teasing Chase for no longer working exclusively within the CIA's paramilitary group.

Chase just smiled as Mike typed in the code that unlocked the door behind him.

"Later, bud."

"See ya."

Chase could hear bits of conversation as he walked up the narrow stairway and the security door shut behind him. The Lima CIA station chief and his deputy sat around a dining room table with a third man. The scientist.

The scientist was a plump Latino man of about fifty, clean-shaven and tan. The wrinkles around his eyes creased as he smiled. "Ah, another one," he said as he spotted Chase. "Good. I've brought lots to eat."

The two CIA men nodded at Chase. The deputy station chief said, "Chase, allow me to introduce Doctor Oscar Rojas."

The scientist extended his hand and Chase shook it.

Chase said, "And here I thought we were meeting with an esteemed physicist. But I see you're a chef?"

"My friend, cooking is a science. My wife and I love to cook. She actually made these for you today. They are a Peruvian specialty. We wanted to treat you right. Our American *friends*." Chase noticed the look the man gave the station chief at that last word. A hint of conflict? Were there already problems? Chase and the station chief had received the unusual orders to take this guy back to America by force if need be, but he hoped it wouldn't come to that.

The plan was to get Rojas to agree to work with them today. Then Chase was supposed to escort him from Peru through Colombia, then Panama, and eventually to the US, ensuring they didn't get spotted along the way.

Rojas handed Chase a paper plate. "This, my friend, is called *Rocoto Relleno*. Stuffed spicy peppers. Here, sit. Take a fork."

Chase noticed the hint of a smile on the CIA men's lips. Never good, when one was about to try new food in a foreign country.

Chase used a fork to cut through the small stuffed red pepper, ground meat and a layer of white cheese oozing out. His mother used to make stuffed bell peppers at home all the time when he was growing up. This looked the same. And his brain told his mouth to expect it to taste that way too.

Then, as the food entered his mouth, a liquid magma of spice hit the inner lining on his cheeks and gums, and his teeth went numb.

"Wow." He coughed and wiped the tears from his eyes as the CIA men laughed. Soon the heat melted away into a delectable sweet and savory flavor. Chase fanned his mouth. "Delicious."

He drank some water and the conversation resumed. They spoke briefly about the technical aspects of the technology. The CIA men verified a few facts and figures that had been cabled to them from the analysts at Langley.

After answering their questions, Rojas said, "We need to discuss something. I must tell you that last week I was approached by a Chinese recruiter."

The room went silent. Chase looked at the CIA officers to gauge their reaction. Each maintained a solid poker face, but Chase could tell it was forced.

"When was this?" asked the deputy station chief.

"Last Wednesday."

"Do they know you are here?"

"With you? No."

The hair on the back of Chase's neck began to rise.

"What did they ask you, Mr. Rojas?" the station chief asked.

"They were interested in learning more about our research."

"Did they ask you to work for them?"

"They offered to invest in our research and said they are building a facility in Ecuador that we can move to."

"And what did you say?"

"I politely told them that I was not interested." He frowned. "I prefer not to work with them."

The station chief said, "We also prefer that you not work with the Chinese."

Rojas smiled knowingly. "Yes."

Chase said, "How did they take your answer?"

Rojas said, "It was only one man. He didn't seem to understand the technology. He seemed like he was just following orders. He said he would relay my answer to his superiors."

The station chief's voice was soft. "Mr. Rojas, it's time for me to ask you to work with us."

Rojas's face was serious now. Sad, even. "I know." He sighed. "I told my wife this is what would happen. I need to say that we have concerns."

"If we can address your concerns, will you agree to work with us?"

Rojas shifted in his chair. "Yes."

Chase knew the game at this point. Let him talk, address every issue, keep him saying that magical word...*yes*. These CIA men were both salesmen and purchasers. Buying information. Selling whatever the asset required: money, ego, peace of mind.

Rojas said, "I know the technology that I have developed is extremely valuable. If the world was not consumed by war, maybe I could have patented it and licensed the rights to a large company. My wife and I could have lived off the profits, sipping drinks on a beach for the rest of our lives." The scientist looked off into the distance. "Alas, we do not live in the world of the past."

"We will pay you handsomely for your work, Mr. Rojas," said the deputy station chief.

"The Chinese said the same thing."

The station chief spoke in a soothing tone. "Mr. Rojas, I understand your concerns. There is a big difference between the two sides of this war. Chinese soldiers are currently marching in the streets of Caracas. It's possible that someday soon they'll be all over South America, including here. Let me ask you a question. Do you think that if the Chinese ruled this country, you would be able to patent and license your work? Sip piña coladas on a beach somewhere? No way. It would go to the Communist party technology inspection division, and four factories would be producing identical materials within a year. All of your hard work would be wasted. Any claim to ownership would vanish as the Chinese government comes to control more and more territory."

The deputy station chief chimed in, "The irony of communism is that it's the least fair system there is."

Rojas nodded. "Yes, yes. I understand this. And I want democracy to survive." Then he shook his head. "But it's not just about the money. It's about how my discovery will be used. Your country and the Chinese will bring war and all the horrible things that come with it to the world. You have already launched nuclear weapons."

"Mr. Rojas, that was defensive in nature..."

He held up his hand. "I have read American accounts about what happened. I understand your argument. But I also understand the enormous potential of what I have developed. My ceramic coating has the ability to more than double hypersonic weapon speeds as they reach their point of impact, while protecting the internal components from overheating. This, as you say, is a game-changer. I know this. I am proud of my work. And I am worried. I do not want to be known for ushering in the next era in warfare. There are many applications for this technology beyond military use. Killing on a mass scale is not what I want to be remembered for."

Chase leaned forward. "If I may say something, Mr. Rojas. I've seen war on several continents now. Eighteen months ago, I watched as North Korea invaded South Korea. I flew out just as the North Koreans began using poison gas weapons on civilians. I was lucky to survive. In Japan I watched as Chinese missiles hit targets in and around Tokyo. These so-called precision-guided missiles destroyed military and civilian targets alike. I agree with you that war should be avoided at all costs."

"Exactly." Rojas's eyes were transfixed on Chase. "Yes, you understand."

"But I also know that there is justification for war, in some circumstances. This is one of those times. America is a freedom-loving nation. For our country, this war is a last resort. We fight not for the expansion of our economic well-being, as China now does, but for the preservation of justice. All sides are not equally just. There is right and wrong in this world. There is good and evil. I promise you, the technology you developed will someday be used in hypersonic weapons. Now, whether it is you or another research team who makes that happen, is up to you. Your research can't prevent the war from spreading. But you have a unique ability to help speed up the war's end, and reduce the number of deaths. You have a chance to help choose the outcome of the war. And if you work with us now, you will do so knowing that you gave your life's work to the right side of history."

Rojas remained silent, looking at the Americans.

Then he took a deep breath. "If I agree, I will need to take my wife with me to America."

The CIA station chief nodded. "Done."

Rojas said, "It is not so easy for me. I will agree with you now. But I will need to speak with my wife. She doesn't want to go. She and I must discuss this together, but I think I can convince her. Give me the evening to speak with her. We can travel back here first thing in the morning."

Chase looked at the two CIA men.

The deputy station chief said, "I'll go with him and take Mike. We'll provide security and meet back up here tomorrow morning."

The station chief nodded. Then the group stood, shaking hands.

4

Victoria's helicopter flew racetrack patterns on the port side of the *USS Ford*. She glanced out her window as they passed the massive ship. Through her tinted visor, she could just make out her father, standing upright in his admiral's uniform on vulture's row. A pair of F-35s screamed overhead. The fighters performed the break maneuver, banking hard to the left, then slowing, their landing gear and flaps coming down as they circled to land on America's newest aircraft carrier.

Her radios blared a warning from the other submarine-hunters a few miles away. The American anti-submarine warfare personnel calling out information about the threat.

Bearing and range to the contact. Up-doppler.

Victoria tried to talk but couldn't. Her lip mike wasn't working. She shouted out but couldn't hear her own voice. She tried to maneuver the aircraft, but her hands were stuck in a cement grip on her flight controls.

She looked down at her display screen, seeing the enemy submarine closing in. Five hundred yards from the carrier. How had it gotten so close? Moments earlier she had dropped her torpedo in the perfect position. They had heard a detonation. She had executed a textbook attack.

But it wasn't...

The radio called out more warnings. Victoria turned to look out her cockpit window again, only this time she saw something different.

The New York City skyline at night.

A bright white flash burst in the sky overhead, and the lights of the world went out.

Victoria looked back down into her cockpit. She tried and failed to move her hands on the controls, then gazed once more out her helicopter window. The city was gone, but she could still see her father standing on the aircraft carrier's highest bridge wing.

He was staring up at her.

More radio calls from the maritime patrol aircraft nearby. She glanced at the ASW information on her tactical display. The submarine was hiding underwater, right next to the carrier. Hunting her father.

From the back of the helicopter, her aircrewman cried out for her to look to her ten o'clock. White streaks of smoke raced across the sky, arcing overhead and slamming into the aircraft carrier, detonating in the place where her father stood...

And she could do nothing but watch.

———

Victoria woke up to the sound of her stateroom phone ringing. She reached over and pulled the black plastic receiver off the wall mount and held it to her ear.

"Commander Manning."

"Skipper, your brief is in thirty minutes, ma'am."

"Roger. Thank you."

Victoria hung up the phone and sighed. Her palms were sweaty.

She kicked her legs over and rolled out of her rack. She flipped on the LED light above her sink, and the room illuminated. Victoria zipped herself into her dark green flight suit, wrapped the laces of her steel-toe boots once around her ankles to take out the slack, and then double-knotted them. She splashed water on her face, looking at herself in the mirror.

Her watch alarm began beeping, and she tapped it off before checking the time. Zero-four-thirty. She let out a breath.

"Yeah, I know. Time to go fly."

5

Six hours later
100 nautical miles west northwest of Lima, Peru

The shadowy silhouettes of two US Navy destroyers appeared on the horizon.

Victoria said, "*Stockdale* in sight."

"Roger, Skipper," replied her copilot. He was a freshly promoted lieutenant commander, and a new arrival to Victoria's squadron. On paper, he was one of her most promising department heads. The perfect choice to replace someone getting fired.

A ship controller spoke over the UHF radio. "VIXEN seven-zero-five, *Stockdale* control, radar contact, ten miles out. Flight quarters is set."

Victoria keyed the microphone. "Roger, Control. Kicking to Deck."

Her copilot reached over and changed the UHF frequency, giving her a thumbs up. This allowed her to keep her hands on the controls while she flew.

"Deck, VIXEN 705, how copy?" By now the ship's aviators should be manning the Landing Signals Officer shack, checking their own communications.

"Lima Charlie, VIXEN. Have numbers when you're ready."

"Send 'em," Victoria said. Her helicopter was close enough that she could make out the wake of the ship, and she maneuvered to follow the trail of white water toward her landing spot.

"VIXEN, Deck, numbers are as follows..." The pilot manning the USS Stockdale's LSO shack passed the ship's course and speed, pitch and roll, and winds. He then said, "You have green deck for landing."

"Roger, green deck for one approach, one landing." Victoria switched to the internal communications circuit. "Landing checks?"

"Complete," her copilot responded, followed shortly by the aircrewman stationed in the helicopter's rear cabin.

She scanned her instruments, maintaining her speed until the distance measuring equipment indicated she was half a mile away from the USS Stockdale. Then Victoria began pulling back on the cyclic with her right hand while lowering the collective power lever with her left. Her scan switched to mostly outside the aircraft, only spot checking her instruments every few seconds. The aircraft pitched up, bleeding off airspeed while keeping its altitude as she drove up the ship's wake.

Her copilot called out, "Point-four. Fifty knots. Point-three. Thirty-five knots. Twenty-five knots. Altitude fifty feet."

"Crossing the deck edge," called out her aircrewman.

"Roger, radar altimeter hold off."

Her copilot depressed the switch and gave her a thumbs up. He had the good sense to keep his hands near the controls without actually touching them.

Victoria felt the helicopter's vibrations grow more intense as it slowed below translational lift and came to a hover over the destroyer's flight deck.

The ship heaved, pitched, and rolled in the ocean below them. Victoria kept her aircraft in a steady hover over the center of the flight deck. She was aware of, but not reacting to, each movement of the flight deck. Her landing spot would never remain still, and chasing it was the worst thing she could do. Instead, Victoria used her peripheral vision to monitor the horizon, making nonstop micro-adjustments to her flight controls as she inched forward in a slow hover-taxi. Her job was now to maneuver the 20,000-pound helicopter precisely over the trap, lining up the one-foot-long metal probe extending from the bottom of her helicopter.

Her aircrewman began guiding her toward the square metal trap that would lock her helicopter into place.

"Easy forward five... easy forward four... three... two..."

A constant flow of wind whipped around the superstructure, kicking her aircraft with turbulence as the ship's steel flight deck took another big roll beneath her.

"Little squirrely today," was all Victoria said as she maneuvered the aircraft to a rock-solid hover right over the trap.

"In position," called her aircrewman.

Victoria kept her head on a swivel as she crouched forward while holding the controls, keeping her yaw steady with her foot pedals, and patiently waited for that perfect moment. Timing the roll of the waves. Wait for it... here it comes... She started her arm movement when the ship was still angled in a roll. To the casual observer, it would look like the worst time to land. But Victoria knew that the ship was about to swing back the other way like a pendulum.

She reduced power by lowering the collective lever all the way down, making rapid, precise inputs with her right hand on the cyclic as she did so. Each movement of her cyclic transferred inputs to the rotor disk above her, correcting for drift in the seconds that mattered most. As a result, her aircraft came straight down, landing on its large wheels with a thud like a pickup truck coming down hard over a grassy hill, the helicopter's shock struts earning their keep.

"In the trap...trapped," the LSO called over the radio. The beams' metal jaws closed on the helicopter's probe.

"Chocks, chains," said Victoria. Her copilot made a rolling motion with his fists, followed by inward-pointing thumbs joining together. The plane captain, one of the ship's sailors who bravely stood just forward of the spinning rotor, acknowledged the signal and then directed the flight deck crew to put chocks and chains on the aircraft. They immediately began running into the rotor arc from either side, helping to further secure the aircraft to the rolling ship.

As she waited for the crew to tie her aircraft down, she felt two familiar but uncomfortable sensations. One was the roll of the ship. These smaller warships rolled a hell of a lot more than the big deck she was currently deployed on. The second was being angled down toward the hangar. The Arleigh Burke-class destroyers were great ships, but aviators hated their flight decks' forward angle. In a hover, your nose was angled up. When you landed, your nose was actually pointing down a few degrees. Victoria once heard that the designer wanted to make sure the helicopter didn't fall off the ass end of the ship if the parking brake slipped. She guessed no one worried about the rotors chopping through the hangar if that happened.

Victoria and her copilot requested permission to shut down the aircraft and then went through their checklist to do so. Within minutes, the aircraft engines were off, and she had applied the rotor brake, bringing the four rotors to a stop.

"We'll ask the 2-Ps to get the water wash," she said to her copilot, snapping the black cord that connected her helmet to the helicopter's internal communications system. Carefully swinging her right leg around the flight controls so she wouldn't accidentally kick them, she inched out the door, one hand on her seat for balance, the other on the door so it wouldn't blow off its hinge. The doors were made to come off easily, in case of a crash.

She closed and locked the door, still feeling the waves rolling beneath her feet. After being aboard a big deck ship, the *USS Wasp*, she needed to get her real sea legs back. Balancing herself, she walked slightly aft, scanning every inch of the aircraft from the tail rotor gear box then forward along the tail boom, bending down to check underneath, then up to scan the main rotor, and on and on. Her eyes took mental snapshots of every section, checking every rivet, every inch of metal and comparing it to what she had seen during her thousands of previous helicopter inspections. Good aviators didn't pass on a chance to evaluate their aircraft, even post-flight.

Victoria walked forward on the flight deck, saying hello to the maintenance men, aircrewmen, and junior pilots from her squadron that she hadn't seen in months.

They were all smiles, happy to see familiar faces after months away from their team. Victoria, meanwhile, couldn't help but inspect everything she saw. Like a mother visiting her kids at school, she intended to use this as an opportunity to spot check everything from uniforms to helicopter maintenance to the junior pilots' knowledge of the anti-submarine warfare. This air detachment and its ship hadn't seen battle yet, and she wanted to do everything in her power to make sure they were ready. She of all people knew what they would face.

As the Commanding Officer of Helicopter Maritime Strike Squadron 74 (HSM-74), the "Swamp Foxes," Victoria was embarked on the *USS Wasp* with only half of her subordinates. The other half of her men and helicopters were scattered across a half-dozen destroyers and cruisers. Some of her detachments were embarked on nearby escorts and remained close enough for her to meet with for an hour or two. Other ships, like the *Stockdale*, were thousands of miles away on expeditionary missions. It was much easier to communicate before China destroyed most of the US satellite communications capability. But even in the good old days, some conversations needed to be held face to face.

Like when the ship's commanding officer demanded that his helicopter detachment's Officer in Charge be replaced.

Victoria walked inside the hangar, removing her helmet, the inner liner soaked with sweat. Her hair was matted and equally wet. Her eyes searched the hangar until she found the three senior officers on board. The *Stockdale's* captain, XO, and the man of the hour, the ship's helicopter detachment Officer in Charge. Lieutenant Commander Bruce "Plug" McGuire. Or, as her own XO had referred to him before she left the *Wasp*, Lieutenant Commander Numb-nuts. Victoria had deployed with Plug, and knew that despite his many faults, he could be a great asset. It remained to be seen whether she could convince the ship captain of that.

"We're honored to have you, Commander Manning," the captain said, shaking her hand.

The ship's CO looked happy to receive her. Victoria's role in the Battle of Johnston Atoll had been all over the news, even the text-only Early Bird version they got on deployment. Now, everywhere she went, Victoria was preceded by her "living legend" celebrity status. A status she did not care for.

"Thank you for having me. I hope it won't be a problem to give me an airlift to Lima tomorrow? With the ESG going through the ditch today, I didn't see another way to make this happen."

"It's no problem at all," replied the captain.

Orders came for the ARG to proceed toward the Panama Canal Zone for immediate transit east through the canal. Victoria would be helicoptered to Peru tomorrow, and get transportation back to the States. Her admin folks were still working on how exactly she would re-join the *Wasp* after it transited east through the Panama Canal.

None of this would be required if the ship's captain hadn't been determined to fire Plug. Victoria wanted the chance to speak to them both face to face before agreeing to it. The ship's captain was giving her that courtesy. Plug, to his credit, stood quietly, looking like a teenager about to get his butt chewed.

The captain clapped his hands together. "Well, Commander Manning, why don't you join me in my stateroom for some coffee? We can have our discussion."

They both glanced at Plug, and then at the other Lieutenant Commander, Victoria's copilot. One of them was flying off the ship with her tomorrow. The captain would decide.

"I would be delighted, Captain."

Plug said, "I better run. I want to make sure the maintenance team is getting those new radar parts installed as soon as possible. Excuse me, sir, ma'am."

The XO said, "I gotta run too. Meeting time. Planning board for planning."

Victoria inwardly smiled at the meeting name. A meeting to plan for other meetings. When she was young and naïve, she thought that Navy deployments would all be like the movie *The Hunt for Red October*. She was surprised to find out that, in actuality, most days resembled the TV series *The Office*. Until the war began.

Victoria followed the captain through the ship's passageways and into his stateroom.

Chatting along the way, she tried to cover as much ground as possible. The easy items. Victoria let him know that she came bearing gifts. An additional helicopter, which he, of course, knew about, but the reminder wouldn't hurt. Some much-needed radar parts. And a new, very experienced Aviation Electrician's Mate. Together, these should solve most of the maintenance issues plaguing this particular helicopter detachment.

The captain listened, nodding politely as they walked through the ship's rolling passageways. Members of the ship's crew, seeing two O-5s coming at them, attempted to melt into the bulkhead as they passed.

Once in the captain's stateroom, both seated and sipping bitter black coffee from the captain's china, the two commanding officers got to the harder discussion.

The captain said, "Commander Manning, I..."

"Please, call me Victoria."

"Sure. I'm Jim. Victoria, I'll cut to the chase. Look, Plug just isn't working out."

She crossed her legs and placed the coffee cup down on the table. The coffee sloshed to either side with the waves.

"I got your message and was hoping to hear more details. I would very much prefer *not* to swap out one of my OICs in the middle of a cruise. That being said, I have come here prepared to do so. If it's not too much trouble, could you please describe the problem?"

The captain shifted in his seat under her stare. "Well, obviously, the aircraft has been flying much less than it should. We've got two destroyers out here, alone and unafraid, in what's supposed to be the southernmost guard for the fleet. But the other destroyer is a Flight One, so they don't have a helo. And we've only got one bird."

"Now you've got two."

"Yes, and we thank you and the rest of the chain of command for that. But I worry it's more than just bad luck. I mean, our air det has suffered mechanical problem after mechanical problem. I'm getting my ass chewed by my boss for something that is out of my control. Because even when our helicopter *has* flown, its radar is broken. So our surveillance flights are much less effective."

Victoria understood the situation. Not only was the ship captain worried about actually having the dead weight of a non-flying helicopter detachment, he was getting flak from above.

"Jim, I don't argue with you there. You need to have reliable surveillance coverage. Trust me when I say that the Strike Group folks are aware of this and pushing us hard to make sure you've got a long-term fix. That's why I'm here. How *have* you been getting ISR out here?"

"The VP squadron out of El Salvador. Flies a route every day and gives us an update. But..."

Victoria nodded, knowing what he would say. "That's not good enough. Not in this environment."

"Right."

"You've seen the intel estimates about possible South American landings?"

"I have. That's why we need a change."

Victoria crossed her arms, nodding. "Sure. I understand. But, Jim, I think we can solve that without swapping out OICs, don't you?"

The captain frowned. "Well...there's more."

Victoria raised an eyebrow.

"Look, I didn't want to get into this. I understand that Plug is decorated and all. But...he's just not meeting the standard required for an officer of his rank. He comes to meetings late. His flight suit looks like a bag of shit. More importantly, he has gotten blackout drunk at every liberty stop we've had."

Victoria suspected this might be coming. "I understand."

"...Multiple liberty incidents. El Salvador, Panama, Colombia. As an O-4? Come on."

Victoria's face remained impassive. "I agree that this is unacceptable."

The captain frowned and lowered his voice. "And as I understand it, there are rumors that he's had overly familiar relations with two female junior officers on the ship."

"I see."

"I don't want to make a big deal about this, Victoria. But if it's all the same to you, I'd just assume you give me a new airboss and we call it a day."

Victoria sighed. "There's a famous quote from a football player my dad used to like."

At the mention of her father, the captain said, "I'm sorry about the admiral's passing."

"Thank you." She paused. "The quote. I'm going to butcher it...but it went something like...'On third and ten, I'll take the whiskey drinkers over the milk drinkers every time.'"

The captain smiled. "You trying to tell me I should be happy Plug drinks so much?"

"Jim, I've flown with him for several years now. He's got flaws. Bad ones. But when the rubber meets the road, he's the guy you want to be fighting with. I've flown in combat with him on multiple occasions. He will make sure that..."

The captain snapped his head to one side, looking alert. At first Victoria didn't understand why, but then she felt it. The ship's engine vibrations had picked up. They had changed speed, and now the deck was listing as the ship turned hard to port.

The captain lifted his phone just as it began to ring. "Captain. Uh-huh. When? Very well, go to GQ."

A jolt of adrenaline shot through her veins. GQ. General quarters. Battle stations. On the overhead speaker, the ship's 1MC, whistles and bells began blaring. A voice called the ship to general quarters.

The captain stood. "ESM. We just picked up a Chinese periscope radar."

Victoria followed him out of the stateroom and into the ship's combat information center, a dark room illuminated by dim blue lights and a dozen digital screens. Radars, tactical displays, and weapons systems. The ship's Tactical Action Officer began bombarding the captain with information.

"Bearing cut from zero-three-five, approximately three minutes late…"

"No range?"

"Negative, sir, we weren't able to triangulate the position."

Victoria silently cursed. The submarine must have popped its periscope up, conducted a sweep, and submerged.

The captain turned to Victoria. "Can the helicopter you just landed perform ASW right now?"

She nodded. "Give us fifteen minutes and we'll be ready and airborne."

The captain nodded and turned back to his crew, rapid-firing orders.

Victoria began jogging aft, her steel-toed boots joining the rest of the ship's crew pounding through the passageway.

The entire ship was a mass of men and women hurrying to close hatches and man their battle stations.

Victoria's mind raced through a dozen different scenarios and memories. She thought about the last time she had flown an ASW mission. They had just participated in sinking an enemy submarine stalking the *USS Ford*. Or so they thought. Victoria had spotted her father on the admiral's bridge aboard the carrier. Then a submarine-launched missile detonated a few yards from where he stood.

As she reached the hangar, she felt her legs grow heavier.

Was this Chinese submarine getting ready for an attack? Or had it been there all along, silently following its target?

Plug said, "Skipper, we'll get a Mark-50 and sonobuoys loaded. You and I are flying." He was standing next to the maintenance chief, both men issuing orders and cracking the whip. The ship was maneuvering wildly now, and Plug's team was working fast to get the aircraft ready. Seeing this, Victoria felt a bit of reassurance. At least she had trained him well.

She threw on her helmet and flight gear as ordnancemen rolled a six-hundred-pound "lightweight" torpedo toward the aircraft.

Some of the men wore the proper general quarters attire while others looked like they had just awoken in their racks. Messed-up hair, T-shirts, and sneakers. One of Victoria's first actions as commanding officer was making sure that her squadrons understood the importance of being battle ready at a moment's notice. She held mock alerts at all hours, wanting the aircraft to be ready to fight and launch without error. That decision was paying off now. An evolution that she had seen take hours would now take minutes.

"Sonobuoys loaded!"

The ship turned hard to starboard. Victoria saw the panicked ordnancemen and other maintenance personnel leveraging their bodies against the torpedo trolley like football players leaning into a sled.

Plug yelled from inside the cockpit, "Boss, we gotta go!" He was already linked into the ship's communications system, hearing whatever was going on.

A loud bang, and then the thunder of a rocket engine emanated from the destroyer's forward section.

Through the sun's glare, Victoria could see white smoke streak upward and away from the USS Stockdale. She could barely make out a tiny parachute and a splash of white water in the distance.

Their ship had just fired an ASROC torpedo.

Plug was screaming bloody murder, trying to get her attention. She looked at the ordnancemen. They were fast, but no one was that fast. The helicopter's own torpedo still wasn't attached. They would need more time. Time they didn't have. She started to connect her helmet communications cord to hear what Plug was yelling about.

But she didn't need to. The ship's alarm rang out as a terrified voice on overhead speaker yelled, "All hands, brace for impact!"

An earthquake hit, and Victoria's legs buckled beneath her.

White and gray smoke and water rose up from the ship's forward section as the deck pitched up and then fell back down. The back of her helmet hit the flight deck, and everything went black.

6

Chase rode in the passenger seat of a small Toyota sedan as it raced through the streets of Lima. They were headed toward the CIA safehouse, checking their mirrors for any possible tails. No time for a surveillance detection route, after the news they'd just received.

The driver, a CIA ground team member, said, "Any luck?"

Chase looked down at his mobile phone. "No joy. Cell signal is down."

The car radio, which had been broadcasting the local news a few minutes earlier, had transformed into a static hissing. Chase tried to find another station. Nothing.

It had already started.

"Turn right here," Chase said.

The car lurched to the right, and soon they were driving up curvy dirt roads on the outskirts of town, kicking up clouds of dust behind them as they sped past neighborhoods built into hills that surrounded the city. Kids playing soccer in the dusty street stared at them as they drove by. Chase looked back at them through his wraparound sunglasses.

The CIA emergency flash cable had been issued less than thirty minutes ago. It read:

INDICATIONS OF IMMINENT CHINESE MILITARY OPERA-TIONS IN THE VICINITY OF COLOMBIA, ECUADOR, PERU, AND CHILE. ALL EMBASSY-BASED PERSONNEL ASSIGNED TO THESE STATIONS MUST EXPEDITE DESTRUCTION OR REMOVAL OF CLASSIFIED MATERI-ALS. BEGIN IMMEDIATE PREPARATIONS FOR CHINESE OCCUPATION OF HOST NATIONS.

The driver made another sharp turn and Chase saw a group of locals standing on a balcony, pointing at something on the horizon. They were shouting, and their faces were twisted with concern.

"What are they pointing at?" the driver asked.

"I can't tell." The two-story townhomes and mountainous roads blocked Chase's view. The buildings on their left rose up like the face of a cliff as the road curved up a small mountain.

They passed several more homes and shops before turning a corner, where dozens more people stood in similar fashion, staring at something in the distance. They made another turn and their line of sight cleared. Their right side held an expansive view of the cityscape and ocean.

And then Chase saw what everyone was pointing at.

"What the hell is that?" the driver asked, hunching low to see.

Chase watched in horror as six large shadows from the west began a steep nose-dive toward the ocean, one after the other.

"Stop the car."

The driver brought the vehicle to a skidding halt where they could get a better look.

"What kind of planes are they? They look like Air Force C-17s, right?"

Chase shook his head. "Naw, man. Those are Chinese Y-20s. Long-range military transports. Same kind they had in Ecuador last year. Looks like they're diving toward the airport."

As the two CIA men watched, each of the six aircraft pulled out of its dive, leveling off at about one thousand feet over the water. As the transports crossed the coastline, their noses pitched up. They slowed, flaps coming down. Chase could barely see their rear doors opening.

"Shit..."

Now the aircraft were flying slow in single file. A trail formation, about a half-runway separation between each bird.

And they were dropping gray puffs in their wake. Hundreds of them.

The first wave of paratroopers.

"Come on, man, let's roll," Chase said. The car accelerated again, and the driver began taking turns with increased speed, bouncing along the uneven roads.

"So much for a month to prepare while the Chinese sail across the Pacific."

Chase removed an M-4 from the duffle bag at his feet, throwing the weapon's sling around his neck. He had no way to contact the safehouse remotely. Standard operating procedure for Lima was radio silence lest a foreign signals intelligence agency locate the safehouse's position. He had hoped that the deputy station chief would have his burner turned on, but his inability to even get a signal made Chase think that the Chinese might have disabled all cell phone networks.

"That air drop was definitely by the airport."

"Yup."

"Estimated strength?" Chase would need to send out this

information as soon as he picked up the team at the safehouse.

"Battalion size, by the look of it. Six aircraft. Probably two platoons per bird."

"Those'll be their version of Rangers," Chase said.

"Yup. So expect a second wave at T+4 or so."

Chase felt the hair on the back of his neck rise. The driver was exactly right. The first wave would be ground troops. Specialists with a mission to take out any enemy personnel and defenses that could be a threat. The second wave would bring in heavy equipment and extended anti-tank capabilities.

Resistance would be minimal here in Lima. But if the Chinese were seizing control of the airport, Chase's primary evacuation route for Rojas was compromised.

"Take this right. The safehouse is on this street," Chase said. "We'll need to switch to one of our alternate exfiltration plans. There's a—"

Chase went silent as the car navigated the last bend and the safehouse came into view.

Smoke was pouring from the second-story window.

"That it?" asked the driver. He was hunched forward, scanning the rooftops and second-floor balconies along the street.

"That's it."

They parked the car two houses away, threw on the parking brake, and got out, heading cautiously toward the home. Chase kept his M-4 trained forward, its stock positioned against his shoulder blade, jogging heel to toe to quiet his steps.

The rattle of machine gun fire echoed in the distance, miles away. The first sounds of the country transforming into a war zone.

As they approached the safehouse door, Chase caught something out of the corner of his eye. He glanced up and saw the old woman on the second-floor balcony of the townhome next door. The surveillance asset.

She was slouched against the two-by-four wooden beam holding up her porch overhang. Lifeless. A small trail of crimson streamed from a hole in her forehead.

Chase stepped into the safehouse's security entrance. The half-shredded front door lay on the ground, blown off its hinges. Mike, the CIA security team member Chase had been joking with only yesterday, now lay dead on the floor. A scattering of bullet holes marred his neck and head.

They raced past the body and through the second security door, also blown wide open. Chase crept up the stairway, his weapon aimed ahead of him, clearing the stairway corner and then taking in the scene.

The Lima CIA station chief and his deputy were sprawled out across the floor and living room couch, their service weapons at their side. Bullet holes riddled their clothes. The couch was smoldering, and the room smelled of gunfire.

Chase and his companion continued clearing each room of the house in silence until they were sure the threat was gone. No sounds except the now-constant crackle of gunfire miles in the distance.

After a minute, the CIA ground guy announced, "It's clear."

Chase nodded, forcing his emotions into a box for later. Right now, he had to move. "Help me get their bodies into the car."

As they began carrying the first corpse down the stairs, Chase said, "We'll need to go to the port at Callao."

"Not the embassy?"

Chase shook his head. "We should assume it's compromised by now. I need to get information back to the States. My contact at Callao will get us out of the country, but we need to move before the Chinese take the port."

"Where's the scientist? Rojas?"

"The Chinese have him."

7

USS Stockdale

Victoria sat up, dazed, looking around the chaotic flight deck. A torpedo must have hit the ship. Dark smoke billowed from somewhere forward of the hangar. Through the ringing in her ears, she heard the shipboard speaker, the IMC, announce a series of alarms.

"FIRE FIRE FIRE," followed by "FLOODING FLOODING FLOODING."

The ship's damage control teams raced through the various compartments, trying to save the ship, while others continued the fight.

Through open hangar doors, she could see sailors running inside the skin of the ship. She winced in pain as she stood, using the helicopter's nose for balance. She almost fell back over, and realized she was leaning heavily to one side. A standing angle normally reserved for the maximum roll of a large wave.

But the ship wasn't taking heavy rolls.

The ship was *listing*...and dead in the water.

Not good.

She looked into the helicopter cockpit. Plug sat in the right seat, waving and yelling to get her attention. Victoria walked over to the cockpit door and opened it.

Plug said, "We're offline. No one in Combat is talking on the radio anymore. Boss, we gotta lift off now. We're a sitting duck here."

Victoria looked around the flight deck, still getting her bearings. The flight deck party was scattered, the maintenance chief yelling at his men to get on their inflatable life vests. The aircraft was still chocked and chained. It would take a few minutes, but it still might be possible to get airborne...

Victoria felt a shudder beneath her feet and heard an explosive rumble somewhere in the ship. Plug's eyes widened. Soon the deck began pitching downward at a slow but alarming rate.

She said, "We can't take off. We won't make it."

He nodded and began unstrapping with the urgency of a man possessed. The flight deck continued pitching forward. Soon it would transform into a giant ramp, its steepening angle forcing everything and everyone on it to slide down into the hangar.

Victoria instinctively ran to the side of the flight deck and gripped one of the rails. The ship's aft end was beginning to rise out of the water. Sailors scrambled toward the sides and jumped overboard. The center of the ship had buckled and snapped, its back broken. The bow was moving upward, angling itself opposite the stern. Everything amidships was already underwater.

Victoria recognized the frantic voice now on the 1MC. It was the XO, whom she had met less than an hour ago. He called out, "ALL HANDS, ABANDON SHIP! I SAY AGAIN, ALL HANDS ABANDON SHIP!"

Her grip on the flight deck rails tightened. She was now

looking *down* through the open hangar door. Dark gray water flooded in through an open hatch, with a pair of sailors surfacing and heading toward daylight.

She heard dozens of splashes in the ocean as sailors began jumping overboard en masse. Victoria found herself recalling stories of Pearl Harbor and the people trapped in compartments and spaces below the waterline as the ships sank.

She felt conflicting impulses. The intense fear of her survival instinct, followed by an illogical but overwhelming urge to dive into the rising water. To swim into the flooded passageway of the sinking warship. The urgent need to find someone—anyone—to save. She couldn't leave without trying...

"Boss! Let's go! Jump!" Plug was screaming from the other side of the flight deck. Then he leapt off and fell, legs and arms flailing, into the ocean.

Victoria began backtracking on the flight deck, heading higher and aft...climbing toward the stern, which was now up and out of the water.

A distant thunderous boom broke the sound of rushing water. Her eyes snapped toward the starboard horizon and she saw a geyser of seawater, metal, and fire. The other destroyer. Another torpedo had hit its mark.

"JUMP!"

Her vision shifted to port. A few sailors were floating in the water, buoyed by their inflatable vests. Others were treading water nearby, yelling for Victoria to jump. The water was rising faster by the second, the ship making impossible dull creaking noises under the strain—a metallic warrior giving herself up to the sea.

"MA'AM, *JUMP!*"

Victoria edged to the side of the ship, climbing over the flight deck nets. She pulled the black beads around her flight vest and heard a pop as it filled with compressed air. Then she

jumped, plunging into the water, the weight of her heavy boots
and flight gear momentarily pulling her under. She rose up to
the surface, buoyed by the inflatable vest that formed a horse-
shoe around her neck.

"SWIM AWAY FROM THE SHIP, MA'AM!"

Twenty yards away, the group of survivors floated in the
water, watching the ship sink. She recognized one of them as
one of the ship's senior enlisted, a chief. He was waving his arm
to get her attention, and motioning for her to swim to them. He
was right. She needed to get away from the ship. The destroyer's
cavities were now filling with water, and soon the massive metal
object would plunge into the depths. This would create
powerful eddies that would act like a rip current, dragging its
victims into the deep.

Victoria heard someone shouting behind her. She turned
and risked a glance, swimming sidestroke. She now had a better
view of the bow and stern, each angled upward like Poseidon
himself had snapped the ship in half.

A sailor fifteen yards behind her thrashed around, his
screams muted by large gulps of seawater. Victoria almost
swam back to him but stopped as she realized what was
happening.

A few sailors were there, in no man's land. They were being
dragged toward the sinking ship like it was a whirlpool or black
hole. The last visible pieces of the superstructure, bow, and
stern disappeared beneath the waves. The handful of sailors
who had been too close soon followed.

Victoria watched in horror as at least a dozen young men
went under. An incredibly powerful undertow pulled anything
and anyone nearby into the death trap, only to be replaced by
oil slicks and loose gear.

She turned and swam as hard as she could toward the group
of sailors in the opposite direction. Hard strokes, cupping the

water with her hands, pulling and kicking. Swallowing gulps of ocean and cursing and coughing.

A few moments later, she reached the group of survivors and allowed herself to rest, floating in the waves. The chief took a muster.

She looked back toward the now-empty sea. A few other groups of sailors were scattered in a wide area around the remnants of the ship.

Helmets and vests and papers and...and a few bodies, floating face down. No lifeboats. Just a few people who had jumped off in the chaos.

Plug was on the other side of the oil slick. Eventually, he and the others swam to join Victoria's group, about three dozen of them in all. A few didn't have life vests. They were treading water, using the dead man's float. Plug shimmied out of his vest and flight suit. Then he placed his vest back on and created a makeshift inflation device by tying the flight suit's arms and legs together to capture pockets of air in the legs. He handed it to one of the vest-less survivors.

Some were crying. Some were hysterical. Some were quiet, in shock. Many were bleeding from wounds received during the attack. As they floated in the rolling Pacific, Victoria thought about all of the shark attacks during World War Two. Many crew members had survived being sunk by torpedoes only to live short, hellish existences while packs of hungry sharks tore them and their shipmates apart. Would that happen to them?

One of the young sailors pointed to the west. "Hey, here comes a SAR bird!" His voice was filled with hope.

Victoria turned, squinting to see through the sun's glare. The dark silhouette of a helicopter made its way toward them.

"It doesn't sound right."

Plug twisted around in the water to face her. "Chinese?"

She didn't respond.

The helicopter looked similar to the French Dauphin. It approached with speed and then turned and began circling their group at low altitude. The cabin door opened, and a crew member trained his machine gun on them.

A bright red star was painted on the aircraft's tail.

8

David sat at the head of the table during the Silversmith team's morning intel brief. Susan was absent, working on the other side of the base on her special program again. More and more lately, David had been taking her place as the senior member of these meetings. His ascension over the past year was lightning-fast. One of the ex-military officers joked that David was on the wartime promotion track.

The initial suspicion David received after the Chinese red cell incident had faded. Over the past two years, David had earned his chain of command's trust and admiration through repeated contributions to the Joint Task Force Silversmith. His experience as a technologist, and his natural flare for strategic planning, made him a valued addition to the war planning team.

Over the past several months, David had attended intense training sessions throughout the country. Most of his classmates had been new CIA recruits, future case officers and analysts preparing for a life of clandestine operations. Outwardly, David and his classmates were thrilled by the excitement of their work. Inwardly, each worried about the dangers they would soon face.

Now, sitting in Susan's chair, David wasn't just acting as an analyst. He was making decisions on how Silversmith would use their intelligence information, deciding what would be kept secret, what would be disseminated, and what would be leaked. This level of security preserved the future flow of intelligence.

David and the other members of the intelligence community played a dangerous game. They carefully curated a tapestry of truths, half-truths, and utter deception for their Chinese counterparts. Human penetrations and cyber-warriors on both sides of the Pacific attempting to steal secrets each day. The penalty for being caught was death. The penalty for failure was defeat and dishonor.

David listened intently to the morning brief being given by one of the intelligence analysts.

"They launched the attack from Easter Island. We estimate about twenty to thirty Y-20 transport aircraft were used."

"How were they able to execute so quickly?" David asked. "We only discovered their fleet movements a few days ago."

"The PLA Navy has been on an island-hopping campaign in the South Pacific. They've lengthened runways to support their transport aircraft and reinforced them with SAM sites. The entire South Pacific is now a Chinese air defense zone, and a denied area to our surveillance flights."

"We've had some maritime patrol aircraft sanitizing..."

"Those patrol aircraft are stretched too thin. It was down to one flight every few days in the area south of the Galapagos."

David turned to another analyst. "What about our other naval assets in the vicinity?"

"The initial attack was by submarine. We think the Chinese had two fast-attack subs in the area. They used one as a decoy, drawing our Los Angeles-class submarine away from our destroyers ahead of the attack."

David looked at the map of the Pacific. "Drawing it away from our ships?"

"Yes. The Chinese snuck two frigates up..."

He shook his head, folding his arms across his chest. "How the hell were PLA Navy warships operating that far out without us knowing?"

"A gap in surveillance coverage. They must have known our flight patterns and timed it accordingly. We think they resupplied at Easter Island. The ships were probably low on fuel by the time they got there."

"And our ships didn't detect them?"

"Supply chain problems. The Navy says that their organic air assets on those destroyers had been out of commission, unable to get spare parts since they were operating so far south from the rest of the fleet. If the maritime patrol aircraft hadn't made a run in forty-eight hours prior...fifteen knots times forty-eight hours...that's a lot of distance they can cover, if our fly is down."

David shook his head. This was a similar pattern around the world. Everyone was spread too thin.

"And satellite reconnaissance?"

Marcia Shea, the representative from the National Reconnaissance Office, said, "There is no change to our capacity issues, I'm afraid. We're able to get about one bird up per week right now, with an average life of thirty-six hours before they get shot down by Chinese anti-satellite weapons. Priority has been surveillance around Hawaii and North America. Secondary is for the Chinese convoys now crossing the Pacific."

David tried not to lose his temper. His sister Victoria had

been aboard the *USS Stockdale* when it sank. Signals intelligence indicated that a few American survivors had been picked out of the water and taken prisoner by the Chinese. As of yet no names were listed on the prisoner roster.

David said, "These ISR limitations are absolutely killing us."

Marcia replied, "Surveillance inadequacies are hampering the Chinese, too. That big satellite launch they just made has been completely shot down after three days. It gave them a snapshot, but that's it."

"It gave them exactly what they needed." David stood and walked toward the wall, taking a few breaths to calm down. "As long as China's new Space Warfare Center is operational, they have a capability we don't. They can launch hundreds of mini-satellites into orbit at a much lower cost. The Chinese advantage is too great."

The room was silent until a woman spoke from behind David. "You're both right."

David turned to see that Susan had entered the briefing room. "Both sides are suffering from a lack of surveillance information," she continued. "But the system of reusable rockets the Chinese have developed at their Beishi facility *is* a game changer. It allows them to overcome the advancements we've made with our anti-satellite weapons. They can launch a few hundred satellites, knowing that they will be shot down. But the rocket launch's cost is a fraction of what it once was, with the self-landing reusable capability. We are still trying to catch up. And from what I understand, we've got months until our own similar program is ready. Is that accurate?"

Marcia nodded. "Yes, it is."

Susan said, "The result of this shift is that China gets to use modern satellite imagery and communications for a day or two, every three to four weeks. Then we shoot down their satellites, and they start over. It's costly, but it gives them a next-generation

C4ISR capability while our military is fighting a Vietnam-era mechanical war."

An Air Force officer in the room chimed in, "That's a bit of an exaggeration, but the situation is pretty painful compared to what we used to train for."

Susan tapped the tips of her fingers together. "So where does this leave us?"

David said, "The old-fashioned game our intelligence services have been playing for decades."

Susan agreed. "Precisely. Neither side knows what cards the other is holding. Neither we nor the Chinese can see everything via satellite like we could two years ago. We can't see their military movements."

David said, "But they can see ours...if only for twenty-four hours."

Susan held up a finger. "Can they, though? Even if they launch at their max capacity, my understanding is that they must still make choices."

Marcia nodded. "That's correct. Even with all of those satellites in orbit, they still have to focus on certain regions. Most of those satellites are for GPS and datalink. Only a few dozen are for surveillance. So they have to prioritize."

Susan said, "So they can't simultaneously look at our Air Force bases in the Nevada desert, our naval submarine pens in Kings Bay, and how many helicopters have just landed at Camp David. They have to *choose*. What's the most important target? Always remember that."

She made eye contact with everyone in the room, but David suspected she was mostly talking to him. His continuing education on high-level war strategy.

A chime sounded on the wall clock, signaling the top of the hour. David said, "All right. Thanks, folks. That's all for now."

People stood and began funneling out to their next meeting. When the door shut, he and Susan were alone.

David massaged his temples as he spoke. "We believe that the scientist, Rojas, is being forced to work for the Chinese. NSA signals intelligence indicates they are moving him to a secure research facility somewhere in the region."

Susan nodded. "I saw that."

David said, "If the Chinese get that technology..."

"I know."

"Should we speak with General Schwartz? See if JSOC can draw something up? Chase can link up with them and..."

"Chase is flying up here," Susan interjected.

"Eglin?"

"Yes. He'll be arriving shortly." Seeing the surprised look on his face, she added, "I need his help with a recruitment."

"Who's the target?"

"Someone I think can help us get our scientist back."

David frowned. "Who?"

"Lena Chou."

9

The C-12 military transport aircraft taxied up to the base operations building at Eglin Air Force Base and came to a halt. Chase looked out the window, seeing his brother David waiting for him on the tarmac. A few moments later they embraced, and both men slid inside the back of a waiting US Air Force sedan. The car sped off to the opposite side of the base.

David said, "You heard about Victoria, I assume."

Chase's jaw clenched. "Yeah."

"A Red Cross observer was allowed to inspect the POWs at one of their camps. According to that inspection, the prisoners are being treated appropriately."

"We have to get her out of there." Chase looked at his brother. "Will there be any prisoner exchange? Or a rescue op?"

David glanced at him. "I haven't heard anything being discussed yet."

The car drove through a security gate, and the driver and both passengers were made to show IDs. They drove past a large hangar with multiple cameras and security personnel positioned outside.

"Susan still running her show from in there?" Chase said.

David nodded. "Yup."

Susan spent most of her time inside the hangar, which housed a system of prison cells, interrogation rooms, and communications equipment. Part of Silversmith's charter was to mislead the Chinese political and military apparatus through a robust counterintelligence operation. Susan had compartmentalized this effort, personally supervising the program out of the old hangar.

The US had several POW camps for captured Chinese combatants, but this one was different. The prisoners here were officers and assets of the Chinese Ministry of State Security. The MSS was China's version of the CIA, FBI, and NSA all rolled into one.

The highly classified prison was hidden among acres of Florida swamp and wilderness, far from the more interesting parts of the sprawling Eglin Air Force base. Even inside the American military and intelligence communities, very few people knew this program existed. Inside the hangar, groups of experienced American interrogators extracted information from Chinese spies, and recruited double-agents. Those who turned assisted in the deception programs. This was one way the CIA influenced the river of Chinese intelligence that flowed back to their mother country.

Their car came to a stop outside a small single-story building next to the hangar that held only one prisoner. The most important one, in Chase's opinion. The one who started it all.

Lena Chou first came to the United States as a teenager after completing several years at elite MSS training schools. Lena was one of Jinshan's top sleeper agents. Her identity was changed upon entry into the US. A series of Chinese penetrations in the US government enabled administrative string-pulling. This eventually led to Lena being selected as a CIA officer, where she naturally excelled. Chase had met her while they were both stationed in Dubai.

Their relationship extended beyond work. They'd spent many nights together, sipping champagne while overlooking the beaches of the Arabian Gulf and making love atop the plush white sheets of Dubai hotel rooms.

All the while Lena had been spying for China. And using Chase like she had so many others.

"Right this way, sir." A security guard led them through a full-body scanner.

Once through security, Chase followed David down the hallway and into a darkened room, stopping on the observer side of a two-way mirror. Chase's heart beat faster when he saw Lena in the other room. She was doing pull-ups on a wall-mounted bar, her muscles flexing like the elite athlete she was. Sweat dripped from her forehead. The burn scars were healing, but they would still draw stares, especially the one that ran down the side of her face. Chase wondered if she blamed him for that.

Her cell had a twin bed with a nightstand. Paperback books. A toilet. And some sort of empty roller cart with a cloth interior. For laundry, maybe? Chase wasn't sure.

"Welcome back, Chase," Susan said quietly. The lone observer on their side of the room, she was sitting on a plastic chair, reviewing handwritten notes. She gestured to the chairs across from her. "Have a seat, gentlemen."

Chase sat down, planning to tell Susan he was sorry about Rojas slipping away. But then he found himself distracted by something going on in the next room.

Susan studied his face as it happened.

On the other side of the mirror, Lena's cell door opened and three people entered: two security guards and someone who appeared to be a nurse.

And she was carrying a baby.

The nurse handed Lena the baby, whom she took without hesitation. Then Lena began nursing the child while the others waited.

Chase's mouth dropped open. He couldn't speak. His face was contorted as he tried to make sense of it. He hadn't seen Lena since the day he helped capture her in Maryland, a little over eighteen months ago.

Susan finally said, "When Lena arrived here, she was pregnant."

Chase turned to look at Susan.

She examined her fingernails. "The timing suggests that she got pregnant in Dubai."

Chase blinked.

"You were in Dubai around that time, right?"

Chase felt his jaw sliding open further. His palms grew sweaty. "Are you saying..."

"Yes," Susan said.

Chase kept shaking his head. He tried reviewing the timeline but found that his brain cells weren't functioning. "I just...I had no idea..."

"Gentlemen, I've worked for the CIA for over thirty years. There is one axiom that holds true all over the world. People can be idiots sometimes. You are no exception."

David let out a small cough.

Chase looked at his brother. "You knew about this? Are you guys actually saying that I'm the father of that child? And you didn't tell me for what...how old is it?"

Saying the words aloud made it all the more real. Chase stood, peering through the two-way mirror, feeling the urge to examine the baby.

Susan said, "This child's existence is known by only a select few. You of all people were not to be told. I made sure David knew that."

Chase shot them both a disapproving look, then looked back at Lena and the child. Lena had finished breastfeeding, and the nurse was patting the baby on the back. He got a glimpse of its tiny face. As the nurse rested the baby down in the cloth cart next to Lena's bed, Chase realized it was a portable crib. Curiously, Lena was looking away from the baby, her arms folded across her chest.

"Why is she doing that?"

Susan said, "This is her normal behavior. She agreed to feed the child, but wants nothing to do with it other than that. Three nurses rotate shifts, and we've had two psych evals performed on Miss Chou over the past six months. Her disinterest in the child likely means one of two things." Susan began reading from her notes. "... either a stubborn unwillingness to be leveraged by her captors. Or a genuine distaste for a half-breed with the enemy."

Chase's face contorted. "You're kidding me, right? She's that brainwashed that she..."

David said, "We don't really know, Chase. That's one of the reasons we brought you in."

"You should have told me about this. Did you have the baby tested?"

Susan nodded.

"And?"

She nodded again.

Chase sat back down. "Holy shit."

They sat in silence a moment. Chase rubbed his eyes with the palms of his hands, then looked up. "You said that's one of the reasons you brought me here. What else?"

Susan said, "You saw the intel reports that Rojas is still in the region?"

"Near Peru, yes."

"We think that Rojas is being taken to the Chinese base in Manta, Ecuador. It's been built up quite a bit. This is the same camp you assaulted with a Marine special operations team. They are forcing Rojas to work there, at a Chinese research facility."

"You want me to lead a hostage rescue."

"No. The Chinese have a substantially larger footprint there now, and it's growing by the day. We have very little intel about the base. Without more intel, it's too risky. He would likely be killed, as would the assault team."

"So, what, then?"

"From interviews with our captive MSS prisoners, we have deduced that the Chinese military team overseeing the project is one that Lena has worked with before. We want to explore the possibility of her assisting us on this. If she can use her past status to gain access to the base, she can verify Rojas's location and provide us with the intel we need to get him back. She may even aid his escape, if the situation presents itself. Our ultimate goal is still to retrieve Rojas and transport him to the US."

Chase shook his head. "Susan, with all due respect...look at her. Why would Lena ever volunteer to help us?"

Susan held up her notes. "Because this psych eval is bullshit. I think she does care about that child. And we're going to leverage the hell out of it."

10

The security guards and nurse left the room, nodding to Chase as they passed him outside Lena's door. One of the guards said, "We'll be observing from the hallway."

Chase nodded and walked into Lena's cell. The baby slept in the portable crib next to her bed. Lena sat on the floor, stretching. After a momentary flash of surprise, her eyes remained steady as she took Chase in. His own gaze passed between her and the child. He moved a few steps closer to the crib, watching the baby's tiny chest move up and down as it slept.

Lena shook her head, clicking her tongue. "Shameful they didn't tell you." She was reading his face, he realized, and getting to work. Probing for weaknesses.

Lena rose from the floor, her athletic five-foot-ten frame only a few inches shorter than Chase. She took a step toward him, and he instinctively tensed. She cocked her head and smiled, then sat down on her bed.

Lena said, "So, they want something from me?"

Chase stood over the crib. He knew that Susan and his brother were watching from behind the mirror, along with the Army psychologist and two other CIA observers. But seeing this tiny child in person had floored him. Chase had trouble remembering the coaching he'd received only moments earlier.

Chase looked up at her. "What's his name?"

"Did they tell you to lead with that?"

Chase frowned. "Why won't you name him?"

"We can do it right now. Let's name him together, darling."

Venom in her voice. She wiped back a lock of her long black hair, then ran the tips of her fingers along the scar on the side of her face, studying him for a reaction.

"I don't believe your act," Chase said.

She shrugged and leaned back on the bed, resting on her elbows. She crossed her legs, which hung off the end of the bed. Her foot rhythmically stirred in the air. Chase thought her eyes resembled those of a large predatory cat.

He realized that she drew energy from his presence. Moments ago, through the glass, she looked uninterested. But now, she had a companion. Or an opponent. Or prey.

Lena said, "Cut to the chase, Chase. What do they want me to do?"

"Help us locate someone in Chinese custody and bring him to the US."

Lena said, "Who?"

"A scientist."

"How would I help?"

"They want you to travel with me and a small team. Make contact with some old PLA colleagues. Provide us with some information and help in any way you can."

Lena arched her eyebrows. "You must be kidding."

"We're not."

"Then you must be quite desperate."

Chase smiled. "It's very important."

"Important enough to risk my escape?"

"Obviously we would be taking precautions."

Lena studied him. "A tracking device? I'll get rid of it. An implant? I'll cut it out. Or have a Chinese surgeon remove it."

Chase looked down at the child, and then back up at Lena.

Lena sat up and shook her head. "Stop. I told you, that won't work."

"You aren't worried about his well-being?"

She leaned forward, giving him a deadpan stare. "No. I'm really not."

Chase could feel his face redden. "Then why do you nurse him?"

She shrugged. "A transactional arrangement."

He forced himself to breathe, trying to remain composed.

Lena said, "So you have nothing to offer me, and your only leverage is some sort of pathetic appeal to my non-existent motherly instincts. If your superiors allow me to go on an operation with you, I'll likely escape. And I'll let the Chinese know just how important this scientist is to you. You must already know that." Lena nodded toward the mirror lining the side of her room. "Collinsworth certainly knows that, watching us from behind the glass. So then why are you really here?"

Chase was beginning to wonder the same thing.

Before he could answer, Lena said, "Ah. You're here because you guys are *losing*. Something big happened, didn't it? That's what you haven't told me. And whatever this scientist has can change your fortunes. Or so you think. Chase, you should know that nothing you do will matter. We've gamed out every scenario. You're just delaying the inevitable."

"Still a believer, eh?"

Lena narrowed her eyes. "Yes, I am. Don't waste any more of your time. It's finite."

Chase took one more look at the child and sighed. Then he walked to the door and knocked. It opened and Chase left, shutting the door behind him.

Chase walked around the corner and entered the observation room.

The psych evaluator said, "Look, folks, we've been over this. She's like a robot. She hasn't named the child. Doesn't look at him. Just feeds him and hands him back to the nurse. You're barking up the wrong tree."

Chase said, "If she doesn't care about the baby, why does she agree to feed him?"

The psych evaluator said, "It was one of our initial bargains after the birth. Lena said she wanted books to read and exercise equipment. We told her that she would have to nurse the child. Her idea." He pointed at Susan.

Chase said, "She really doesn't care about her own child?"

David said, "I'm not so sure. If she really wanted out of here, why would she have been so eager to point out our risk? If she wanted to escape, or wanted freedom, she should play the part. Lena's always been deceptive. Why would this be any different?"

"So, what, then?" Chase said. "She wants to stay here?"

Susan and David both nodded.

David said, "I think we should…"

Chase held up his hand. "Shh! Wait. You hear that?"

The room went quiet.

The distant whining of a siren was barely audible over the hum of the air conditioning unit.

"Is that…is that the air raid siren?"

The attack was launched from Chinese stealth bombers and submarines.

Three Chinese H-20 stealth bomber aircraft had taken off

from China two days earlier. Their last stop was a refuel at the Chinese-held base in Manta, Ecuador.

The H-20 was an ambitious and highly secretive project modeled after the American B-2 and B-21 stealth bomber programs. Slower than supersonic bombers such as the American B-1, the H-20 was stealthy and capable of carrying a large payload of long-range cruise missiles. These particular aircraft carried the newest generation of electronic attack cruise missiles, which the Chinese launched from a position one hundred miles north of Venezuela.

In the years before the war, the targeting data for these incoming missile tracks would have been detected by signals intelligence satellites and relayed to all American air defense forces via encrypted satellite datalink communication. But in the war between China and America, the days of uninhibited satellite communication were over. Now, US military datalink existed through a patchwork of semi-reliable drones and line-of-sight links.

The electronic attack cruise missiles jammed radars and executed offensive cyber-attack measures. The effect was similar to linemen on a football team protecting a running back, creating a black hole of disabled radars and air defense networks, and making way for what came next.

The second wave of cruise missiles launched from another section of bombers south of Cuba. After launching, the stealth aircraft turned around, their part of the mission completed. Joining the air-launched attack were missiles fired from two Type 093 Shang-class submarines, each positioned in water space south of Panama City, Florida. Twelve cruise missiles were fired from each submarine's vertical launch system. The noise alerted nearby sonar monitoring stations, as well as a patrolling Los Angeles-class submarine. The Chinese submarines, by launching, had signed their own death warrant.

But it was too late to stop their cruise missiles from reaching their targets.

The twenty-four submarine-launched cruise missiles joined the dozen fired from the H-20 bombers in a race toward Eglin Air Force Base, each programmed to attack a specific target. Three of the missiles had cluster-bomb payloads and were used to attack the runways. Other missiles struck hangars, command centers, weapons bunkers, and fuel depots.

Half were saved for the most important target. A group of old hangars and buildings on the far side of the base.

Chase and the others jumped out of their seats and raced into the hallway. An Air Force security guard jogged toward them, his steps echoing on the linoleum floor.

He waved as he shouted, "Incoming attack! Get back in the room."

A thunderous rumble in the distance turned into two...then three...then the giant booming noises could be heard outside every few seconds. The group ran back into the observation room just as an explosion shook the building's foundation. Dust sprinkled down from the ceiling. An internal fire alarm sounded, and the sprinkler system kicked on. The detonations were almost continuous. Deafening. The ground shook. Chase fit himself under the wooden bench.

The attack lasted about three minutes, and then stopped as suddenly as it had begun.

"Is it over?" David asked.

Chase got up and dusted himself off.

Susan picked up a phone in the corner of the room, then placed it back down on the receiver. "Nothing. Lines must be damaged."

David waved to get their attention. "Guys. Hey. Look at this."

All eyes turned to where he was pointing. Through the two-way mirror, Lena was visible in the corner of her room, holding the baby in her arms. She was shushing the crying child, rocking him, their faces close together. Her eyes were filled with tears.

11

The van traveled west along I-10. The group was escorted by three unmarked security vehicles, one belonging to local law enforcement, the others a combination of CIA ground team members, USAF security forces, and one nurse.

They were conducting a prisoner transfer while emergency services were still dragging bodies out of smoldering buildings. But this couldn't wait.

The safehouse was a large hunting lodge tucked away in the Alabama pine forest. The vehicles parked on the gravel driveway, and security forces began walking the perimeter.

The nurse took the baby while Chase, Susan, and Lena gathered around a small kitchen table. David was not present. His family lived on base, and he needed to make sure they were okay after the attack.

A single incandescent light bulb hung above the table, flooding the room in a warm yellowish glow. Chase made them coffee and handed Lena a cup.

After taking a sip, Lena said, "I need you to promise me that the child will be safe and cared for."

Susan said, "Of course. We..."

Lena glared at Susan. "Not you. I don't trust you. *Him.*"

She looked at Chase.

He nodded. "I'll make sure."

Lena said, "If I do this, I will likely never see my child again." Her voice was soft.

Susan and Chase remained silent.

Then, like a switch had been flipped, Lena's face grew hard. She placed her elbows on the table, pressed her fingers together, and said, "Let's get to it, shall we?"

For the past few months, Lena had been kept in the dark about geopolitics and the war's progress, being fed only what Susan's team had wanted her to know. Now Susan brought her up to speed on the state of world events. Lena listened with an intense expression.

When Susan was finished, she asked, "The attack on our base today. Why would they do that now?"

Lena shook her head. "What else are you running out of this base?"

Susan didn't answer.

Lena rolled her eyes. "Fine. Make me guess. My thought is that you are playing the double-cross game. If you're here, you wouldn't waste all your time on just me. So you've probably got a shitload more MSS operatives in some other buildings."

Chase raised his eyebrow and looked at Susan, who remained quiet.

Lena smiled. "I hit the nail on the head?"

Chase said, "The question remains: why would Jinshan choose to target this base now?"

Lena shook her head. "He wouldn't."

Chase frowned.

Lena looked at Susan. "Jinshan wasn't involved in planning this attack. He would have made sure it was executed properly. Appropriate employment of weapons by type and volume."

"It wasn't appropriately planned?"

"No."

"What makes you say that?"

Lena said, "I'm still alive."

They went quiet.

Lena said, "If Jinshan is not involved in planning, that means one of two things. Either he is dead, or weakened. Which is it?"

Susan said, "Our sources say that he's been undergoing intense chemotherapy treatments, and that his cancer has progressed despite them. Expectations are that he'll be dead in three to six months."

Lena leaned back in her chair, her eyes softening.

"You were close with him?" Susan asked.

Lena ignored the question. "There is a power struggle beneath him."

Susan said, "There is a power struggle. But not to be Jinshan's successor. He has named a successor."

Lena looked skeptical. "Who?"

"A politician named Ma Lin. He's young. Only forty-five. Jinshan's new apprentice, they say."

Lena searched her memory. "I know this name. His father is on the Politburo Standing Committee."

"Not any longer. His father retired. Now Ma the son is on the standing committee. He has found favor with Jinshan."

Lena shook her head. "There will still be a power struggle. Perhaps not for succession, but for influence."

Susan nodded. "You are correct. We have information that suggests Ma will name a vice president."

Lena said, "For someone so young and inexperienced, that advisor will likely have a lot of control. There are only two men with enough power and influence to serve in that position. I assume they will be competing with each other for that spot."

Susan said, "Who do you believe they are?"

"One is the Minister of State Security, Minister Dong. You know him?"

"Of course," replied Susan.

Lena said, "He was another favorite of Jinshan's. He is loyal, but only because he is smart enough to know to appear that way. I suspect his motivations are more complex."

"Who is the other?" Chase asked.

"General Chen."

Susan let out a hum of interest.

Chase turned between the two women. "I'm sorry, why is that significant?"

Lena looked at Chase. "General Chen is my biological father."

Chase raised his chin. "*Oh*."

Lena turned away, lost in thought. "This attack has General Chen's fingerprints all over it. Unpredictable. Painful for the US, but not particularly strategic or completely effective. My father is better at backroom dealing than military tactics. I suspect that this attack was on General Chen's orders, and without Jinshan's knowledge."

Chase said, "Why would he do that?"

"General Chen is driven only by personal gain. He will understand the political shift that will take place after Jinshan's death. General Chen will take risks to impress the young princeling Ma." Lena paused, then said, "Jinshan is an intellectual. His moves are strategic. He will avoid the use of weapons of mass destruction. And he will want to do the least harm possible on the American populace while still achieving his goals. If this young politician Ma is his chosen successor, he will likely have a similar temperament."

Chase said, "Jinshan started World War Three. That doesn't sound like someone who's concerned with reducing casualties."

Lena gave Chase an icy stare. "Things could always be worse. Jinshan sees every action he has taken as necessary toward achieving his end goal."

"And what is that?"

"Jinshan wants a new global government, led by China. He will do everything he can to avoid an oppressive military occupation. He wants a peaceful American surrender. He will not approve of any destructive attacks on the American populace. If his plans come to be, the Americans will one day welcome the end of the war, whatever concessions they must make. Think of Germany and Japan after the war. American military bases in each country. Both countries prohibited from having standing military forces. Jinshan wants a similar outcome, only with Chinese forces in the US. Eventually, the country will be transformed into his desired image."

Chase said, "I don't see Americans welcoming surrender, ever. Those EMPs blacked out half the country. Hundreds of thousands are dead, and we're very lucky it wasn't more. How is that not harming the American populace?"

Lena said, "He could have used nuclear weapons on cities. And his disinformation campaigns likely have many in your country questioning American leadership. Eventually, the popular sentiment may shift. Would it really be so bad to have a benevolent Chinese leader, if food was back on the table?"

Chase's face was red.

Susan said, "Lena, how do you think Ma will be affected by who's behind him?"

Lena smiled. "This is the right question to ask. If I was to guess, Jinshan has chosen Ma because he has the qualities of an idealistic leader. He will make utilitarian decisions, and not be susceptible to bribery or corruption. But his honor and innocence are also his weaknesses. Minister Dong and General Chen are too strong. I suspect Ma will become the puppet, and either Secretary Dong or General Chen will become the puppet master."

"Our analysts say Dong has the inside track."

Lena nodded. "This is good. If Dong becomes Ma's number two in command, they will likely seek to follow Jinshan's plan for ending the war. China will continue to move to a position of power and create a siege. They will capture as much territory surrounding America as possible. Eventually, America will voluntarily surrender."

Chase said, "What about General Chen? What if he is chosen as vice president and becomes Ma's main advisor?"

Lena said, "That would be a much more volatile scenario."

12

Beijing, China

General Chen sat down at the dinner table across from Minister of State Security Dong. Neither man spoke.

There were four place settings, one for each of the most powerful men in China. The door opened and Chairman Jinshan, the Chinese president, hobbled into the room, his bodyguards taking up station nearby. His apprentice, Secretary Ma, walked behind him. General Chen still couldn't believe Jinshan had chosen this young politician to be his successor. It was such an unworthy choice.

General Chen studied Jinshan and his apprentice as they approached. Cancer would take the old man soon. He looked more pitiful each day. Ma, on the other hand, looked sprightly, carrying himself with dignity and grace. The innocent eyes of a lamb before the slaughter.

Jinshan's chemotherapy was failing. General Chen knew that this was the reason for China's recent waking from hibernation. The attack on South America came after a year of slumber, a cold war that made American-Soviet hostility look mild by comparison.

Jinshan wanted to see his ambitious quest accomplished before he passed on. How long did he have? Another month? Two, at most?

Politicians had been sharpening their knives for the past year now, waiting for the power struggle that would follow Jinshan's demise. Even with his successor named, things were uncertain. Ma was but a young man. Naïve to the ways of the world. If a leader of sufficient power and influence stepped in as his vice president, Ma would become but a figurehead. There would be so much opportunity...

General Chen and Minister Dong rose from their seats as the group approached the table, bowing politely and offering warm greetings to Jinshan. Neither man's smile reached his eyes as they greeted Ma.

After they sat, the conversation began with normal courtesies, but that didn't last long. Minister Dong didn't like to waste time.

"Your attack was clumsy," he said, looking at General Chen.

"I solved a problem," General Chen replied.

"Without consulting anyone else?"

"Chairman Jinshan has provided leeway for my battlefield commanders to make quick decisions, should it become necessary."

Minister Dong said, "Ah, so your subordinates launched the attack on the Florida base? Not you? My operatives were engaged in important intelligence gathering. Preparatory actions that will be crucial to the war effort. You've ruined several operations with this haste."

General Chen said, "Your spies were being captured and interrogated at that American prison camp. We discovered their location during the most recent mass satellite launch. I had to move fast to clean up your mess. Would you have continued to allow the Americans to deceive us?"

Dong looked exasperated. "*Yes*. That's how the game is played."

General Chen laughed, tapping Ma on the shoulder. "You see, Secretary Ma, all intelligence officers know this trick. They like to pretend that their failures are actually calculated traps for the enemy. It relinquishes them of all blame."

Ma looked mildly amused. "I see."

Chairman Jinshan said, "General Chen, you are not without past mistakes."

Minister Dong nodded. "Quite true. Secretary Ma, surely you remember when the general's haste cost us two carriers in a failed attack on Hawaii?"

General Chen bowed his head, glancing at Secretary Ma. "Under my leadership, Chinese military transport ships are landing in South America at this very moment."

Dong grunted. "My organization was instrumental in laying the groundwork for the South American occupation. You can't possibly be taking credit for it."

General Chen said, "And regarding our setback in the Pacific, it would not have happened without our Minister of State Security having been so careless, speaking our plans within earshot of your secretary's mobile phone?"

"You know that's not the way it transpired."

Secretary Ma looked confused. "Your mobile phone, Minister Dong?"

General Chen grinned, delighted for the opportunity to twist the knife. "Ah, yes. Secretary Ma, you were not yet privy to that information. You see, American agents had hacked into the mobile phone of Minister Dong's secretary, turning it into an electronic eavesdropping device. By the time our military cyber operations team finally uncovered the penetration, the damage was done."

Ma glanced at Minister Dong. "I see."

General Chen said, "It was most embarrassing."

Minister Dong shook his head. "Yes, and it had saved General Chen from being the sole scapegoat after his defeat at the Battle of Johnston Atoll."

Chairman Jinshan raised his hand. "Gentlemen, enough." He waved to one of his servants, who opened the door to the kitchen. The cook's staff rolled in trays of food. Chilean sea bass, roast duck, sautéed vegetables, and chilled white wine. General Chen had grown accustomed to eating well over the years. Jinshan's personal chefs, imported from all over the world, didn't disappoint.

After one of the servants filled their wine glasses, Ma raised his for a toast. "Gentlemen, I believe congratulations are in order. South America, and all of its resources, is now under Chinese control."

Minister Dong and General Chen carefully clinked their glasses in a toast, eyeing each other as they sipped their wine.

Jinshan placed his glass down on the tablecloth, and the men began to eat. They spoke of strategy and status reports. General Chen knew that despite the fine china and Michelin-star-quality food, this dinner was really just a tryout for the position of vice president. Jinshan was giving Ma facetime with the two candidates who would be most helpful in wartime.

Chairman Jinshan said, "What were the results of our satellite launch?"

General Chen set down his fork. "The mass launch went very well, Chairman Jinshan. The imagery provided us with a much-needed update of American forces. Accurate intelligence and reconnaissance have been hard to come by of late." He looked at Dong, who glared at him.

"Our space launch facility near Wenchang is, as you predicted, Chairman, a source of great advantage," Dong said. "We are now able to launch large-scale surveillance mini-satellite constellations at much lower costs. And we are continuing to improve this capability. Under my oversight, we soon shall be able to provide China with a reinstatement of satellite datalink. Global positioning, targeting, and communications will all be available to our military partners when they enter combat."

General Chen said, "Yes, but the problem remains: the Americans destroy these satellites within days."

Minister Dong said, "And we destroy theirs within hours. We have the communications and surveillance advantages, General. As our forces advance north through the Americas, they will fight US troops on the ground. But our PLA forces will be armed with enemy targeting information, beamed down from above. On that same battlefield, the United States will be in the dark."

General Chen snorted. "They aren't in the dark. They have drones and surveillance aircraft, just like we do. And they are working on the same ISR satellite capabilities."

Minister Dong said, "We are much further ahead of them in that regard, thanks to the investment we made at our Wenchang space facility."

Ma looked inquisitive. "And what makes this new capability so potent, Minister Dong?"

"The new space facility uses dozens of reusable rockets to lower the cost per launch. Each rocket can carry racks of mini-satellites. As our forces in the Americas advance, our advantage will be significant, and sustainable."

Jinshan nodded. "The tipping point. Good work."

Dong lifted his glass and drank. "A pity that our submarines near the US coastline won't be able to participate."

Ma said, "What do you mean?"

Dong feigned surprise. "I am sorry, I thought you knew. The attack that General Chen ordered used the only two submarines we had placed near the United States. Because they were ordered to fire their cruise missiles, they gave away their positions. The American Navy has destroyed both vessels. All of our other submarines are busy protecting our convoys now traveling across the Pacific."

Jinshan flashed a rare look of anger and turned toward General Chen. "Your haste cost us the only two submarines we had positioned near the US? You are aware of how challenging it will be to successfully place more submarines that close to US bases?"

"A regrettable setback, Mr. Chairman." General Chen glanced at Dong, fuming.

Jinshan said, "What was the result of the attack?"

"Sir, we estimate that particular American base is out of commission for a month. The POW camp was destroyed."

Ma covered his mouth. "Our own people?"

Jinshan said, "I admire your compassion, Secretary Ma. However, we must continue to make these difficult choices for the greater good." Jinshan's face went dark. "Lena? Is she dead?"

The room quieted. This was a delicate subject between Lena's biological father, General Chen, and the man who became her mentor, Jinshan.

General Chen shrugged, looking at Dong.

Dong said, "No word just yet."

Jinshan said, "Tell me about the scientist in Peru. Progress?"

Dong nodded. "Things have been going well, sir. Our researchers are now attempting to replicate his methods. The technological improvement in hypersonic weapons capability shows incredible potential."

"Good." Jinshan placed his knife and fork down on the white tablecloth and turned to General Chen. "General, tell me, how would you use this new hypersonic weapons technology?"

General Chen recognized the tone. Jinshan was famous for testing his subordinates. During his first few months as the head of the People's Liberation Army, he had been battered many times by such lines of questioning. But eventually his survivalist instincts took over, and he was able to better anticipate the tests, leaning on his staff to prep him for whatever Jinshan might ask.

"Due to the cost and limited launch capacity of these hypersonic weapons, I would use them in a strike on American naval and air force bases, destroying as many air defense stations as possible. After this is accomplished, we will be able to use conventional air strikes to soften American ground forces. As tactically important targets present themselves, we would employ the remaining hypersonic weapons as needed."

Jinshan nodded approval.

Ma said, "General, excuse my ignorance. But could you explain what makes these weapons important?"

General Chen took a breath, summoning patience. "Of course, Secretary Ma. Due to their great speed, hypersonic weapons can travel uninhibited by enemy interference, and destroy long-range targets with great precision and lethality. Air defenses are made useless, due to the speed and maneuverability of hypersonic missiles."

Ma said, "But what makes them more important than nuclear weapons? How do they help us strategically?"

General Chen kept his face still, trying not to show annoyance by the question's simplicity. "They allow us to defeat our enemy, obviously."

Jinshan turned to Dong. "What do you say, Minister Dong?"

Dong looked thoughtful. "Hypersonic weapons technology tips the scales of power. The Russians claim to have these weapons operational, but our operatives know that they, like the Americans, have faced technological hurdles." Dong leaned forward. General Chen was sure that the man practiced speaking in front of a mirror. "Now that China has successfully landed in South America, we will slowly and methodically move our forces up through the continent. Our military reach will spread into Central America and the Caribbean. We will strangle the United States economically and politically. We will use our growing international influence to pressure the US. In a year's time, our military will be built up to levels never before seen in the world, and they will be waiting at America's weakened border."

Ma said, "And that is when you will use hypersonic weapons? When the Americans are at their weakest?"

Dong shook his head. "That is when the Russians will become a threat."

Jinshan looked intrigued. "The Russians?"

"Sooner or later the Russians will see that America will fall, once and for all. Up until this point, they will be happy to see Chinese and American militaries fighting each other. They will gladly ally themselves with the Chinese cause. But right before the final stage begins, after General Chen's strikes on America's military bases and air defense stations, as our PLA is readying for massive paradrops into the central US, as our amphibious landing on the American coastline is being readied, that's when I would order the use of hypersonic weapons on Russian targets."

Jinshan said, "And what exactly would your targets be?"

"I would consider a preemptive hypersonic missile attack targeting the Russian president. He is an unpredictable man. I would want to ensure the Russians are not able to order a nuclear strike."

Jinshan took a sip of wine. "But what of the Russian successor? Wouldn't he just pick up the mantle and have renewed incentive to attack Chinese interests?"

"No, Chairman Jinshan."

"And why not?"

"Because if the Russian successor is not openly allied with us, he will fear the same end."

Jinshan cocked his head. "An interesting thought. But too great a gamble, I think."

General Chen smirked.

Jinshan turned to Secretary Ma. "Still...Minister Dong has a point. We allowed the Americans to destroy the vast majority of our nuclear capability. This makes us overly reliant upon the Russians serving as our nuclear deterrent proxy."

Secretary Ma nodded. "We need our own deterrent."

Jinshan said, "That would be better. The balance of power will continue to shift. As Minister Dong suggests, the Russians could become unstable. Unpredictable. The Americans themselves could even get desperate."

"What is the solution?" Ma asked.

"We will need to develop one..." Jinshan said.

A knock at the door, and then one of Minister Dong's assistants entered. "Excuse the interruption, sir, but you asked for any information regarding Miss Chou. We have some. It appears that Lena Chou escaped during the attack on the Florida base."

Jinshan said, "Very good. Where is she now?"

"She sent a signal to one of our embedded agents and then went underground. We don't know, sir."

13

Lena and three CIA ground team members waited on the small plane. She looked out the aircraft window and saw David speaking with his brother Chase. She could guess their words by their body language: David was telling Chase not to trust her. Chase looked over his shoulder at the plane, seeing Lena staring back at them both. His eyes said, *Don't worry, brother, I don't.*

Chase boarded the US Army C-12, and the twin turboprop engines started up. Within a few moments they were airborne and flying southwest over the Gulf of Mexico.

Lena sat alone in her row, those in the rear no doubt watching her every twitch from behind. She understood their lack of trust. Lena hadn't pledged loyalty to the United States. They simply had leverage over her. Everyone involved understood that the child—she still couldn't bring herself to name him—was all that really mattered.

During the missile attack, Lena thought the end had come. She knew the game was up when they saw her hugging her boy. But she couldn't help it. She needed to hold him. To let him feel her compassion, for once. She would do whatever it took to protect her child. And he certainly wasn't safe living near her on some American military base.

They'd spent two days at a hunting cabin in the Alabama wilderness, where Susan went over the terms of their agreement in great detail. Lena's child would be moved to safety. Lena would travel to South America with Chase and a small CIA team.

There she would make contact with the Chinese, help Chase smuggle the scientist out of the country, and return with them to the US. She would then be moved to a safehouse where she could be with the child, under the CIA's "protection."

"And what will I do?" she had asked. "Live out the rest of my days in peace? Picking flowers and raising my child in the American countryside?"

Susan shrugged. "If that's what you want, yes. You'll be taken care of."

Lena didn't point out that this part of the deal assumed that the United States still *existed* in the near future. She could feel their uncertainty when proposing the arrangement. From their preparatory brief, Lena now knew that the Chinese military presence in South America was growing by the day. Within a matter of weeks, the first ships in a massive convoy would arrive, and then the real threat would begin.

Ships could transport incredible amounts of troops and tanks. The Pacific Ocean had served as the moat keeping the US and China in a stalemate over the past year. But that was quickly changing.

The Americans were terrified of what would happen if the People's Liberation Army began transiting up through Central America. Their economy strangled, their political allies isolated and neutered...America was losing. It would take time for this Chinese strategy to work, but they all knew it was coming.

The fact that the CIA would risk allowing Lena to betray them or escape told her just how valuable this technology was.

They might have leverage. But they were still sure as hell trusting her.

Chase had said, "We'll keep the child safe; I promise. He will have a good home. David and I will make sure."

While none of them knew it, those words had sealed the deal for her. Despite her continued loyalty to China, she believed that Chase and his brother would keep their word. She had spent enough time in the United States to understand the code of honor these men lived by.

"Mind if I sit here?" Her thoughts interrupted, she turned from the blue water outside the aircraft window and watched Chase sit beside her. The small propeller plane was very noisy, keeping their conversation private.

Chase said, "I'm sorry about that." He indicated her scars.

"You should be," Lena said, a hint of playfulness in her tone. "Is that why you don't trust me? You think I'll take revenge for letting me burn?"

"I don't trust you because I saw you kill innocent people."

Lena's smile faded. "There are no innocent people. We are all sinners."

"The occupants of that limousine near Bandar Abbas. The ones you killed with sniper fire?"

Lena shrugged.

"I saw you shoot an Ecuadorian officer at point-blank range in front of his men."

"I'm not sorry about that one. That man *deserved* it."

"Last year. Beijing. Rooftop garden. Televised all over the world. The Chinese president, his wife, and his daughter."

Lena's face grew darker. She didn't say anything.

Chase nodded. "So, you do have regrets. Interesting."

Lena began to respond but the words wouldn't come.

Chase said, "I'm not trying to pick a fight. I just want you to know that I intend to hold you to your promise. You do your part. Make contact. Extract the information. We'll take it from there. We will be watching you every step of the way."

Lena said, "I trust that you'll keep your promise, too."

"You know I will."

"I do."

Chase rose and returned to the seat behind her. Lena leaned into the seat cushion and resumed staring out over the ocean.

She toyed with the idea of not honoring her contract with the Americans. She could warn the Chinese in Ecuador. Help them capture Chase and his team. Lena played out the options in her mind. What would happen if she betrayed them? Even if Lena went against her word, the Americans would still take care of her child. She was sure of that.

And Lena didn't want to betray China. She hadn't stopped believing in Jinshan's vision for the future. She still wanted China to prevail. But the stronger motivation was to make sure her child wouldn't be harmed as the war progressed.

So...would she betray Chase? Street work could be very dangerous. No one would know what really happened if he were to meet an untimely end. She could stick a meat cleaver into his neck while he slept. Then she could walk right out the door and onto the Chinese base. Her life would start again.

She turned and snuck a look back at Chase. He was staring at her, speaking quietly to one of his men. She felt the slightest tug of affection for him. Nothing like the tsunami of motherly instinct that gripped her when she looked at her child. At *their* child. Maybe that was the odd feeling of loyalty she felt? The bond of parenthood? She shook away the thought.

Lena made up her mind. She would keep her word to the Americans. It was her parting gift to Chase, her down payment for a lifetime of taking care of their child.

But her decision didn't mean she wouldn't ditch the Americans the moment the mission was complete. Lena felt a rush of adrenaline just thinking about it. She wanted back in the game. Maternal instincts aside, she needed to get her fix. Her life's work was coming to a climax. And she needed to do what made her a star. She needed to kill.

14

The major was starting to like this assignment.

His vehicle came to a halt outside the riverside bar. Muddy water flowed by, and lush green vegetation surrounded the two-floor establishment. Latin dance music echoed in the surrounding jungle.

And those stiletto-heeled beauties strolled in, eyeing him, sizing him up.

"Sir, they look like they remember you," the Chinese officer's driver said.

The major looked at his driver, a corporal who'd entered the service only a year ago. China's military was growing fast, and some of these new recruits still didn't know when to keep their mouths shut.

"They remember my wallet is all," he replied.

"Stay with the vehicle, Corporal," the veteran sergeant said, hopping out and pounding the hood in excitement. "Major, we will be out back securing the perimeter."

"Fine." The major knew the sergeant and two other veterans were going to drink and talk up whores at the bar. He couldn't care less. They would all be in combat in a few weeks anyway.

The major walked into the brothel. A plump older woman serving as the house madame gestured for him to take a seat on a worn velvet couch. The major placed his arms back on the couch as a column of barely clad women lined up before him.

In broken Spanish, he said, "This one...and that one there." He pointed at the ones trying not to make eye contact. The others seemed too desperate.

"Move along, ladies," the madame called. The girls scattered. Turning to the major, she said, "You can go upstairs to your room. The girls will join you shortly. First door on the right when you get up the stairs."

The major cracked his knuckles and rose from the couch. He walked up the creaking wooden stairs, entering the first door on the right. He began unbuttoning his shirt, stopping when he heard the knock at the door. Turning around, he expected to see his two evening companions.

Instead, he saw a ghost.

"Hello, Major. Good to see you again." Lena Chou shut the door behind her. "Have a seat. And keep your clothes on, if you please."

"Miss Chou..." The major sat down on the bed, stunned. "I was told that you had been captured."

She arched her eyebrows. "I escaped."

He was dumbstruck. "Why are you here?"

Lena said, "I need your help. I will need you to transport me onto base."

He began to stand. "Of course."

Lena took a seat on the single cot across the small room. "But I need to ask you a few questions first."

The major appeared confused. "Of course, Miss Chou. But would you like me to get my battalion officer? I'm sure he can..."

She held up a hand. "Listen and answer me precisely. Before I escaped the Americans, I learned that they were very interested in a certain scientist. They believed him to be held at our base in Manta. Are you aware of such a man?"

"Yes. Yes, I know him. He was here. But they moved him."

"To where?"

"I don't know. They flew him out on a transport aircraft days ago. A different base. He needed a bigger research facility to support his work. What does this have to do with..."

"Which base?"

The major paused. "The MSS was overseeing the project, along with our engineers. I wasn't involved." He shook his head. "Why are you..."

A knock at the door. Lena rose.

"Sir, we have a problem. Please open up," a gruff voice yelled in Mandarin.

Lena watched the major closely. The first hint of suspicion flashed across his eyes as he yelled, "Come in."

The door burst open. Two PLA soldiers marched Chase Manning into the room at gunpoint. The soldiers each wore the uniform of the major's special operations unit.

"Sir, this man was sitting down by the bar," one of the soldiers said. "The locals didn't know him. I think he's an American. He had these."

He tossed a mobile phone and a 9mm handgun, magazine removed, onto the bed.

Lena cursed to herself. Chase was not supposed to be in this building. The microphone clipped to her bra would have transmitted the fifty yards to where his team was waiting in the jungle. He was here because he didn't trust her. And now he'd pay the price, unless she did something about it.

Lena said, "You are correct, Sergeant. This man works for the Americans. He has been following me. Take him down to your vehicle and keep him under guard. Once we are at the base, I will want to question him."

The two soldiers looked at the major.

He looked between Lena and Chase. Finally, he nodded to his men and they walked out of the room. When he and Lena were alone again, the major said, "We need to take this to the battalion officer immediately. I can't..."

A string of gunshots erupted from somewhere outside. The major's eyes widened, and he began heading toward the door.

Lena's blow came quick and strong.

She rotated her body, snapping her arm around and catching the major's trachea with her knuckles.

He fell to his knees, gripping his throat, his face turning blue. Lena removed his sidearm from the holster at his waist. She placed the weapon's barrel into his mouth and pressed the trigger.

The loud gunshot exploded the back of his head.

Lena moved into the hallway and then down the stairs. She held the pistol casually at her side so it wouldn't draw attention. Somewhere in the house, women were screaming. Then Lena heard the sound of more gunshots outside. Both American- and Chinese-made rifle fire. Lena reached the bottom of the stairs and peered out the open front doorway.

A Chinese military jeep was parked in front of the brothel, smoke rising from bullet holes in the hood. A streetlamp bathed the jeep in yellowish light as bugs swirled around in the humid air. Two dead Chinese soldiers lay face down in the mud. A third was slumped over the steering wheel.

Chase stood a few yards away beside a Chinese special operations soldier pressing the barrel of his long gun into Chase's side. Another gun lay in the dirt near Chase's feet. A thick concrete wall stood between them and the Americans in the jungle.

Lena assessed the scene. Chase, possibly with the assistance of his gunmen in the nearby jungle, must have killed his captors before he was recaptured by the lone remaining soldier. Neither Chase nor the soldier were looking in Lena's direction.

Lena slid her blood-soaked pistol into her waistband at the small of her back. She felt the cool metal on her rear as she headed outside, into the American field of fire, betting they wouldn't open up on her.

She kept her voice calm as she said in Mandarin, "Sergeant, do you have a radio?"

The startled soldier turned his gaze and weapon toward Lena as she approached.

Her hands slightly raised, she said, "Careful, Sergeant. I am not the enemy."

She stepped closer. Now ten feet away.

"We already made the radio call," he said, studying her. "Where is the major?"

The crackle of the radio in the jeep. Lena heard the frantic words of an incoming Chinese security team and then the distant rumble of large military trucks heading their way.

"Sergeant, you need to secure the prisoner. Here, I will do it."

She took a step closer. Then the shadows lit up. Two flashes as she fired into the soldier's body. He dropped to the ground.

Lena turned to Chase. "I spoke to the major upstairs. The scientist was here, but they have moved him. I don't know where. He may be in China. Tell your team that you were too late."

Chase looked at her, stunned, his face red and sweaty from the action.

Her tone was firm. "You need to go now, Chase. When the PLA soldiers arrive, I'll tell them you headed south. If you wait, they'll see you and kill you."

Chase picked up the weapon on the ground. "You need to come with me."

She shook her head. "That's not going to happen."

Lena was careful to keep her pistol pointed toward the ground. "I've fulfilled my part of the bargain. I did what I could."

Chase stared at her. He was weighing his options. Kill her or leave her. They both knew he wouldn't be able to drag her with him alive.

Chase said, "What about the boy..."

She leaned in. "Make sure you take care of him. I no longer can." Their eyes locked together in a moment of understanding. Then Chase turned and ran across the street, disappearing into the jungle.

15

Victoria and the other Americans spent weeks as prisoners aboard the Chinese warship. They slept on the cold floor of the center passageway, near the ship's aft end. Their captors kept them blindfolded most of the time, with zip ties around their wrists. Going to the bathroom and eating was an ordeal, each activity carefully observed by frowning guards.

As Victoria sat on the rolling deck, her fear turned to anger. She had plenty of time to think. The few conversations between the men were met with swift physical punishment. Victoria would hear the crack of a baton followed by moaning or spitting up blood. Or sometimes silence. That was the worst.

The American prisoners learned it was best to keep quiet. Over the past twenty-four hours, the rolling of the deck died down as the seas grew calm. They could hear the familiar cadence of ship bells and whistles, of 1MC calls and stomping boots.

They were approaching port.

Soon Victoria heard the Chinese sailors calling to each other as they tossed lines on the pier. The sounds of men hurrying through the warship, refilling stores. Cleaning for inspection. Paying little attention to their American prisoners of war as they sat bound and silent on the rough deck. Tired, hungry, and listening intently for any sign of what was to come.

While she waited, Victoria's thoughts kept wandering back to the darker moments of her past. Her recurring nightmare. Images of her father's death, as witnessed from the cockpit of her helicopter a year earlier. Waves of guilt washed over her as she replayed the scene. The voices on the radio were still fresh in her memory. The crews aboard the other anti-submarine aircraft all thought they had destroyed the Chinese submarine circling the carrier. Victoria was now pretty sure they had actually destroyed a decoy, allowing the attack sub to launch its anti-ship missiles. Then Victoria watched them explode into the *USS Ford's* superstructure, ripping her father apart.

The same feeling of survivor's guilt overwhelmed Victoria as her memories shifted to recent events. She thought of her fellow sailors aboard the *USS Stockdale* and its sister ship...of all those...

"Get up!" A shove snapped her back to the present.

Chinese guards pulled on her arms, forcing her off the floor. Beneath her blindfold, she could see that they were being marched single file amidships. The guards removed their blindfolds as they made their way to the gangplank. A bright scene lay before her. Seagulls flying. The smell of the shore.

Victoria heard diesel truck engines rumbling on the pier. Glancing to her right, she saw what must have been fifty trucks, all lined up. Chinese troop transports, with uncovered flatbeds. Metal rail guards and aluminum benches. One of the Chinese soldiers shouted at the prisoners to head into the trucks. The other soldiers used hand gestures to get them moving. Soon they were seated in the rear cargo compartments.

No sooner had Victoria sat down than her vehicle jolted and they began driving forward, bouncing and sliding. The smell of the sea faded as they traveled through a dusty third-world city. Victoria guessed they were in Peru. She'd been to Lima once, and this looked similar. Arid, mountainous terrain with small huts pressed together.

Several PLA soldiers sat near the rear of the vehicle. The Chinese guards looked scared, Victoria thought, even as they held their rifles. They were green, she realized. How long had these boys been in military service? A world at war, sucking everyone into its vacuum.

"No talk," one of them yelled, and the few whispered conversations ceased.

The truck ride lasted a few hours, ending at a train station surrounded by jungle. The ground rumbled beneath her feet as a train moved slowly down the tracks, the cattle cars finally coming to a halt in front of them.

Troops unloaded the prisoners from the trucks. Victoria saw Plug and the chief who had been in the water with them. She took a quick headcount. There were at least one hundred men. A handful of women. A handful of officers. No pilots other than Plug. They all were wearing the same outfits they'd been captured in, flight suits or Navy working uniforms. Their faces were a mix of scared, shell-shocked, tired, sick, and pissed-off.

PLA soldiers angled their rifles toward the gaggle of Americans as they waited by the train. They looked like cattle, standing there on flat brown dirt. That's exactly what they were, Victoria realized. And what happened to cattle?

She heard a whisper from a nearby group of Americans and then three of the prisoners began pushing and yelling at each other. Their argument was preposterous. Something about rival football teams.

"The only reason Green Bay even has a team is because of Brett Favre. And where did he end up? That's right, Minnesota. You see, you dumb bastard, even your hero knows where it's at..." The men were moving their zip-tied hands and getting in each other's face.

Based on the animated way they were yelling, Victoria could see they were up to something.

One of the guards shouted, "No talk. NO TALK!" As the group of PLA soldiers moved closer to the prisoners, the guard looked nervously between his comrade and the shouting Americans. He kept his weapon trained on them.

"You know what? You can have him. Brett Favre sucks! But the Green Bay Packers are the goddamned best team in the NFL!"

Out of the corner of her eye, Victoria saw one of the petty officers, an operations specialist, creeping toward the far edge of the group of prisoners.

"NO TALK. STOP. NO TALK."

The PLA guard prodded one of the instigators with the barrel of his weapon.

"Okay, okay! Jeez!" The lead actor held up his bound hands and sat back down.

Twenty feet away, the petty officer bolted down the train track.

A guard's whistle blew, and all eyes snapped toward the now-sprinting escapee.

One of the guards stood high above the others on the truck bed. He held his rifle up to his shoulder, raising it to the firing position, taking aim...

"Wait!" Victoria called out, joining the others' shouts.

Crack. Crack.

The loud echo of gunfire reverberated throughout the train loading area. Jungle birds flew away in fright as the echoes reached the nearby rainforest. Yells and screams and swearing as the group of American prisoners, still bound, began to riot.

More Chinese soldiers now raised their rifles at the Americans. More whistles blew. Victoria felt a wave of fear and revulsion mixing inside her. She saw the crazed rage in the eyes of the Americans, having just witnessed one of their shipmates gunned down. And the horrified fear in the eyes of the young Chinese soldiers pointing their weapons at the Americans.

Whispers from around her. "We should just rush 'em right here. Screw it, man."

"Fucking commie bastards..."

Victoria felt that same anger. For a brief moment, she almost allowed herself to succumb to it. A final stand. The mob unleashing itself on their guards. They could kill them all, maybe. They had numbers.

But then what?

What was her duty?

"Hey! Stand down," she said. Then, louder. "Stand down!"

"Get back." The chief and Plug, seeing Victoria take the lead, got up in front of the mob of prisoners and began restoring order.

Soon Victoria heard more whistles in the distance, joined by the clap of boots running on pavement. She turned her head to see dozens of additional PLA soldiers now running their way. A reserve unit stashed in one of the trucks further back in the convoy.

The additional Chinese troops broke off in pairs and surrounded the American prisoners.

A short PLA soldier—this one with the shoulder boards of an officer—appeared, flanked by several guards who looked distinctly more experienced than the other soldiers.

He searched the faces of the American prisoners, saw Victoria, and yelled something out. The guards nearest to her began shouting in Chinese, hurrying her along. Her fellow POWs, seeing an officer and one of the only females in the group being taken away, began to protest.

"Calm down, everybody," she said. Some instinct—whether it be maternal or command—told her that she needed to help save her men from themselves. Otherwise, they would throw themselves into a furnace to protect her.

She walked toward the PLA officer. He wore a pressed light green uniform shirt with jump wings above the right breast and several rows of ribbons above the left. Dark green shoulder boards with gold embroidery and tiny stars, gold lapels on each collar, and a dark green cover with a red star surrounded by a gold wreath. He was skinny, with pronounced cheekbones and a thin neck, but his eyes were confident and serious.

"You are Commander Manning?" he asked in perfect American-accented English. The guy could have been from Ohio.

"Yes, I am."

"I am Captain Tao. I have been appointed to oversee American prisoners here. You are the senior prisoner. I would like to apologize for the loss of your man."

Victoria did not reply.

Captain Tao motioned to his men and issued a command in Mandarin. Victoria saw the Chinese guards open the train's cargo doors and begin moving the Americans into the empty carts. No seats, lights, or bathrooms, by the look of it.

Soon all of her fellow Americans were inside, peeking through tiny window holes with metal bars.

Captain Tao said, "There were one hundred and six prisoners when you left the docks. Now there are one hundred and five. I don't wish for anyone else under your command to be hurt. Please ensure there are no more escape attempts."

Victoria recalled her training. Every member of the military was taught The Code of Conduct. *Article II: I will never surrender of my own free will. If in command, I will never surrender the members of my command while they still have the means to resist.* She didn't want anyone else hurt or killed. Was she allowed to tell her men to sit tight and not try to escape? *Article III: If I am captured, I will continue to resist by all means available. I will make every effort to escape and aid others to escape. I will accept neither parole nor special favors from the enemy.*

Her men were not in a good position to escape. And she didn't want to see anyone else killed.

"I'll do my duty."

Captain Tao frowned.

One of the PLA soldiers standing behind him was holding a mobile phone, recording video of the scene. He was now focused on the petty officer's corpse.

"What is he doing?" asked Victoria.

"He is documenting the incident," the captain replied. "If a prisoner is killed, we must file paperwork. I'm sure you have similar requirements. We will be reprimanded for this."

Victoria shook her head, mouth half-open.

The Chinese officer nodded for his men to take her onto the train.

As soon as she was aboard, the doors slid shut behind her, and she was trapped in the cramped, humid compartment. She looked out the small window at the Chinese soldiers. They were moving supplies onto the train, and after the trucks left, several platoon-sized groups of PLA soldiers embarked on a passenger car to their rear.

The train engine rumbled and they began moving forward, slowly at first and then at a good clip.

"Ma'am." It was Plug's voice. She turned, barely able to make him out in the shadows. He squirmed through the crowded car, then took his place next to her, looking out the window.

"They're taking us south."

"Yes, they are," she replied.

The chief moved next to her. "Ma'am, you all right?"

"Fine."

"What'd that Chinese guy say?"

"He said not to try to escape anymore."

The chief snorted.

"Chief, let me know if I'm wrong, but I think you're the senior enlisted here. I need you to get a muster. Let's divide into four platoons and set up a command structure. Find out everyone's military occupational specialty and any other talents that might come in handy, such as Spanish-speakers."

"Yes, ma'am."

She turned to Plug. "Plug, you'll be our escape officer. I don't know what conditions we'll face when we get to where we are going, but from what I've seen so far, we won't have many opportunities during the transit. Prove me wrong if you can. If you can't, start coming up with escape plans the second we reach our destination."

"Got it, Skipper."

The train traveled for three days, stopping six times along the way for bathroom breaks, food, and water. During each stop, the prisoners were kept under close watch.

The scenery shifted from shaded rainforest to vast, verdant farmland. Tunnels were carved in the mountains. They transited through several thunderstorms, downpours of water hammering their car's rooftop. The prisoners cupped their hands to gather rainwater to drink.

Victoria knew they had arrived when she saw the waiting trucks. They were ferried out of the train and onto the flatbed troop transports, then endured a twenty-minute ride bouncing through the jungle.

"Shit." Plug swore softly next to her as the prisoners were taken off the truck and marched into the prison camp.

Five guard towers stood above two layers of razor wire fencing that stretched ten and fifteen feet tall, respectively. Guards with dogs patrolled the ten-foot-wide path between the two fences.

Men and women were not separated before they were forced to strip down. Victoria tried not to feel humiliated as she stood in a single-file line with her men, walking into a building under guard as the Chinese soldiers smirked and leered at her. Inside the building, she walked through a human assembly line. She was hosed off in a shower area, then deloused with powder. Her hair was cut down to a buzz, and she was issued drab prison garb consisting of gray tunics and matching baggy pants. Victoria put on the clothing and then rejoined the line of prisoners leaving the building.

In the center of the prison yard were rows of what looked like tiny doghouses made of cinderblock, each containing three concrete walls and a four-foot-high ceiling.

Jail cells.

A door made of iron bars completed each structure. One by one, the prisoners were stuffed inside their new cells. The doors slammed shut. Guards locked each one as they passed. Victoria barely fit. She could only imagine what some of the taller men were dealing with. Her men whispered to each other at first, then one of the guards began beating a prisoner for talking, and they fell silent.

The cells faced each other. Three cell doors were in her field of view, on the other side of the dirt pathway. Hands gripped the bars. Emotionless faces peered out. Someone was talking again, and Victoria watched as one of the guards dragged the kid out of his cell and into the center area where everyone could see. The guard lifted his baton into the air and came down hard, repeatedly.

"No talking," he yelled. Then two of the guards dragged the boy's limp body back into his cell and locked the door.

The bugs came out in force that night. Victoria was sweating profusely in the humid air. She could see the jungle less than a football field away, bird calls and all sorts of other animal noises emanating from inside. Mosquitos swarmed around her, and other insects crawled around the floor. She forced herself to breathe...to be calm. She tried to meditate. To pray. To be at peace, even in this world of pain and suffering. She promised herself that she would prevail.

16

Chase arrived at NAS Pensacola via an Air Force U-28 turboprop to find the base was a flurry of activity, with giant C-17 and C-5 transport jets landing every few minutes. Army Patriot missile batteries were being set up throughout the base, and grass fields transformed into tent cities. Trucks, tanks, and uniformed personnel headed every which way.

A blue government sedan pulled up to the base ops parking lot near the airfield. David opened the door and helped Chase throw his duffle bag into the trunk before the brothers got in and David drove them away.

"Quite the show out there," Chase said, gazing out the window at NAS Pensacola's new military buildup.

"No one wants to get caught off guard when the Chinese try again," replied David.

"Silversmith is here?"

"Until further notice." David parked his vehicle outside a building labeled "United States Navy Flight Demonstration Squadron."

"The Blue Angels?"

David smiled. "They didn't need the space anymore. Those guys are all with fleet squadrons now."

Chase looked at the sign as the brothers walked into the main entrance. "I always wanted to be a Blue Angel."

They headed to the second-floor offices of Silversmith's senior members.

"Is she in?" David asked a secretary when they arrived.

The woman nodded and the brothers entered Susan Collinsworth's office. While speaking into a landline phone, she signaled them to sit before ending the call and looking up at Chase.

"Lena's in China."

Chase cursed. "That was fast."

Susan glanced at David and then back at Chase. "I read your after-action report. It sounds like you made the best decision you could, given the situation."

Chase said, "My assignment was to bring back Rojas and Lena. I have returned with neither. I'm sorry."

"I imagine you are beating yourself up about it. Don't. We don't have the time."

Chase nodded.

Susan said, "With our changing scope of Silversmith mission sets, we'll be sending you to serve as our liaison to JSOC. They'll have you working with DEVGRU."

Chase was intrigued. When he was a SEAL, he'd applied to the unit twice but was turned down each time. DEVGRU, known by many as SEAL Team Six, was the US Navy's most elite special operations unit. If there was ever a pointy end of the spear, they were it.

"Understood. What will I be working on?"

Susan glanced at David, who said, "You'll be training for a variety of potential missions that will be vital to future plans."

"Right..."

David said, "Sorry. You'll get more info when it's ready to share."

Susan clasped her fingers together. "Let me ask you something, Chase. You witnessed Lena operate more than anyone else. What was her state of mind when she left? Do you think she would continue to work for us in China, given that we have her child?"

Chase was embarrassed at the mention of the child, and strangely thankful that Susan hadn't said *your* child. He was going to need to start seeing a head doctor before long...

Chase let out a long sigh. "She could have come back with me, but she left us. She made her decision. I think her loyalty is split between China and the child. But the impression I got was that she thinks she fulfilled her end of the bargain and believes that the child is safe now. So she's free to pursue other interests, so to speak."

"Do you think she betrayed us in the field?"

"No."

"You don't think she warned Chinese soldiers that you were trying to get Rojas?"

"I watched her kill a PLA soldier. I might not be alive if she hadn't."

"But she still didn't come back."

"No, she did not."

"Why?"

"If I had to guess? Cheng Jinshan. She worships the ground he walks on. She's a true believer. She's cut the ties of motherhood to go back and be a warrior for his cause. Then there's her father, the most senior military officer in China. I assume there is some loyalty there as well."

Susan and David exchanged looks.

Chase frowned. "What am I missing?"

David said, "What if she *didn't* worship Jinshan? And what if she had reason to betray her father?"

Susan slid a manila envelope across her desk. "Read."

Chase removed the documents inside and looked them over.

David watched Chase closely as he read. "We may be able to take advantage of her entry back into China."

Chase thumbed through the two-page report. "She was a teenager when this happened?"

David nodded. "Chinese high school students have a mandatory military training they must fulfill called Junxun. It's usually done during the summer months. Local Chinese military units teach the students how to march, salute..."

"...how to be good communists," Susan said.

David waved his hand, offering, "It's sort of like a Chinese patriot boot camp. But it's also where the Ministry of State Security scouts and recruits young agents."

Susan tapped the documents. "This is how Lena was recruited. She got plucked from one Junxun school and sent to another for the top-performing MSS recruits."

Chase continued reading, then briefly looked up from the document. "Holy shit, man."

David nodded knowingly. "Pretty screwed up, huh?"

"The MSS arranged for her to be sexually assaulted by a male student at the school?"

David said, "Look at the recruiting officer's name. It's not just anyone. Lena caught the eye of a former MSS officer. One with lofty ambitions."

Chase whistled. "Cheng Jinshan."

"Unbeknownst to anyone, Jinshan arranged for a male student to pay her an unwanted visit one night. The operation was supposed to compromise her. The Junxun cadre were to discover them together and accuse her of impropriety. Her father was a colonel in the PLA at the time, and if his only child was kicked out for sleeping with..."

"She wasn't sleeping with the guy voluntarily, though," Chase interrupted. "This was...this was fucked up is what it was..."

David made a sympathetic face. "It didn't matter what actually happened. Only what it appeared to be. Lena's father was a colonel. To the upper-crust society that her parents lived in, Li, as she was then known, would have been a disgrace to her family. Jinshan would then swoop in and offer her a way out."

"Joining the MSS."

"Exactly. She would disappear and become one of his spies. A sleeper agent, to be inserted into the US under a new identity."

Chase held up the document. "It says she practically killed the guy who came into her room."

David said, "Yeah. I don't think they knew who they were messing with. Apparently, she waited until *after* he was done having his way with her. Then she went into his room and cut out his tongue."

"Holy shit..." Chase shook his head, looking away.

Susan said, "This is why I am curious about her current psychological state. You see, Chase, Lena Chou doesn't know that Jinshan orchestrated her assault. She thinks he just came in afterwards and helped her out of the kindness of his heart. He offered her an honorable way out of trouble, after she so violently took matters into her own hands."

Chase said, "This is crazy."

"What you'll also read in that document is that Jinshan consulted with Lena's father, General Chen, prior to her recruitment. It doesn't say whether Chen knew how Jinshan would orchestrate the event. And surely no one foresaw Lena's violent reaction. But it certainly appears as if General Chen sold his daughter to Jinshan in exchange for career enhancement. Jinshan began string-pulling on the good general's behalf shortly after. Lena doesn't know any of this."

Chase shook his head in amazement, then turned to Susan. "So, you're going to...what? Release this? Let Lena see it? To what end?"

"I want to diminish her loyalty to China. I want her further motivated to spy for us. Internally motivated."

Chase said, "How long have you had this information?"

"You're wondering why I didn't use it before?"

"Yes."

Susan said, "Because I didn't want to play my full hand if I didn't need to. I had you. And the child."

After their meeting with Susan, David drove Chase to the NAS Pensacola Bachelor Officer Quarters. He checked into his room, and then the brothers went to grab a few subs for lunch. Thanks to the war rations, the shop was out of most ingredients, but they managed to put together a halfway decent turkey sandwich.

Chase and David ate at a waterfront picnic table overlooking the sound. A weeping willow tree provided shade overhead.

"Anything on Victoria?" Chase asked. Both brothers knew what Chase was asking for—David's inside knowledge of US intelligence reporting.

David's face grew somber. "Nothing good."

"Anything bad?"

"She's on the manifest at a Chinese POW camp near Manta. About twenty miles from where you were that time."

Chase said, "Any plans to..."

"I can't say."

Chase stared at his brother, trying to decide if he should be pissed off. A lot had changed for David in the past couple of years. He'd gone from being a technology expert to an intelligence analyst, and now he was working on higher-level operations. A real spook and acting the part, keeping his cards close to the vest just like all of the others Chase had worked with.

It was annoying as hell. But he understood.

Chase changed the subject. "How's my...how's the boy?"

"Lindsay says he's doing well." After Eglin had been attacked, the families of Silversmith employees living on base were moved away. There was too much risk, and too much distraction. Lindsay, David's wife, had volunteered to take temporary custody of Lena's child. With Susan's approval, she had relocated to a remote site in Colorado. They were under military guard and being assisted by one of the military nurses who had been looking after the child.

"Please tell her I said thank you."

David nodded. "Of course." He put down his sandwich and looked out over the sound's white beach and calm water. "Susan is going to use the information in the document."

Chase said, "I am not sure how that's gonna go. Lena won't respond well to coercion. I know her. This could backfire."

"We're willing to accept that risk."

"We?"

"I had a hand in the decision analysis."

Chase said, "I read that Chinese forces are moving north through Colombia now. That a land battle is imminent."

David didn't say anything.

Chase said, "I also heard that most of my San Diego buddies are going to be busy real soon. Sounds to me like things are about to get real?"

David said, "I'm not supposed to discuss it."

Chase snorted. "I get it. I'm a mushroom now."

David looked around, and then headed toward the sandy beach. "Come on over here."

Chase followed. David knelt down, picking up a twig and drawing an outline of North, South, and Central America.

"Dude. You suck at art."

David smirked. "You get it, right?"

"Yeah."

David said, "So here's me saying a few things without saying anything. I've been asked to work on a few projects, one of which is contributing to Pentagon war planning. I'm intimately familiar with a lot of these rumors you are speaking of."

David used the twig to begin tracing a few arrows within his outline. The drawing was very crude, but Chase understood. The Chinese were advancing north through Colombia, into Central America. David pointed at that part of the map and said, "Big numbers. Really big numbers."

"Shit."

He then began tracing arrows in the eastern Pacific Ocean, pointing north along the western edge of South America. "Support elements." He drew arrows from the coast of California and marked a big X to the west of Panama. Chase understood. The US military was about to have a big land battle in Colombia or Central America, and another naval battle in the Pacific. David looked up at his brother to make sure he understood before wiping the drawing from the sand.

Chase said, "You don't look happy about it."

David shook his head. "I'm not. We have a few new tactics that should work. But the numbers don't add up. Sooner or later..."

"The lines are going to break."

David nodded.

Chase said, "So have you said anything?"

"To the Pentagon planners? Brother, I'm a nobody there."

"Didn't you come up with the plans for…"

"Yeah, they don't care anymore. That was last year. And besides, to them, it was mostly General Schwartz. You can't throw a stone around the Pentagon without hitting three flag officers. And whether we're at war or peace, some things never change. Everyone wants to make their own mark. Everyone wants their idea pushed to the top. I can't get heard. And frankly, I am not sure it matters. I don't have a solution right now. I thought I did, but…"

"Hypersonic weapons. That's what you kept telling me."

David nodded. "Yeah, well. There's a missing link there. If we could make the Rojas tech work, that could potentially give us a huge tactical advantage. But without it, we're left fighting a modern war without GPS or reliable ISR."

"Is it really that bad?"

"Hell yes it's that bad. We shoot down their satellites and drones, and they shoot down ours. Both sides are lucky to get a sneak peek for a few hours before their multi-million-dollar birds get shot out of the sky."

"Even the little drones? Stealth drones? Micro-satellites?"

"A lot of that stuff is just a bunch of buzzwords. Yes, we have a few reliable tricks. But nothing for this." He pointed at the dirt. "In a large-scale attack, or battle, you need reliable datalink for targeting, navigation, and communications. Without it, we're back to Vietnam-era tactics with more expensive weapons."

Chase put his hand on his brother's shoulder and squeezed gently. "Relax. It'll come. You're the idea guy. The ideas always come."

David gave a weak grin. "Maybe. Look, I should probably get back."

Chase gathered his trash and began walking with his brother. "David, one thing I don't get…what's the big push to get

Lena to work for us? I mean, we've got other ways of gathering intel, right?"

David stopped and looked around before answering. "It's not just about gathering intel."

"What is it, then?"

David said, "Let me ask you something. Do you think we would have risked Lena escaping if we didn't have a lot to gain?"

Chase went silent.

David said, "We expected Lena could very well end up back in China. Before you got on that plane, what did I tell you?"

"To make sure she lived, whether I was able to bring her back or not."

"And you did that."

Chase said, "Yeah, but I was still supposed to bring her back."

"If you could, yes. But these operations are a game of chance. We need to plan for multiple outcomes, and a big one is this: Jinshan is sick. One day soon, he's going to die. And when that occurs, we want his successor to be our ally."

"And Lena?"

David arched one eyebrow. "We think Lena can help make that happen."

17

Lena barely recognized Beijing. As she rode from the airport, she witnessed a city transformed by war. Tanks and anti-aircraft weapons were positioned every few blocks throughout the city. Gone were the extravagant stores and glamorous lifestyles of Beijing's elite. Gone were the vibrant street markets and modern bustle of the business district. Men and women hustled down the streets wearing uniform gray tunics with red patch insignias on every right shoulder.

Propaganda posters hung on the exterior of most buildings. Some reminded citizens to register for government service. Other urged the public to report anyone who looked suspicious to the MSS website. Billboards that once advertised luxury goods were replaced with patriotic artwork. Digital ads on mobile phones all showed different flavors of state-sponsored media, carefully tailored by Chinese psychological operations teams to appeal to different demographic targets.

Lena's car turned toward the Zhongnanhai government headquarters.

"They are here?"

"Yes, ma'am," replied her escort.

"Not in the mountains anymore?" She was surprised. The mountain fortress had been built in secret, intended for use as a command and control center throughout the war.

The PLA officer in the passenger seat turned to glance at her. "Our leadership has not been in the mountains for some time. The war is going well for us now. There is no need for them to hide. Our leaders are well-protected in Beijing."

"I see."

She decided on the plane that she would keep two things to herself: her limited cooperation with the Americans, and the child. Regardless of how fond Jinshan was of her, her friends in the MSS would look at her with suspicion. If they found out she had aided Chase's CIA team, she would be branded a traitor.

Lena went to see Jinshan first.

Chairman Jinshan was in his private quarters, getting treatment. His room was a palatial chamber overlooking a spectacular private garden. A drip IV fed medicine into his veins. Two aides sat in chairs next to his bed, scribbling notes as they listened to him issue orders. Jinshan stopped speaking when he saw Lena, and a warm smile spread across his face.

"Sir, Miss Chou has arrived," announced her military escort with a bow.

Jinshan looked at his aides. "Please leave us."

Lena waited as the room emptied. Even his personal bodyguards moved to the balcony, shutting the French doors behind them. Jinshan gazed out the window overlooking the garden. Bright white sunlight shone over a dark pond. Carefully manicured trees lined a stone path. It looked peaceful.

Jinshan said, "Secretary Ma, you stay, please."

Lena realized that one of the aides was not an aide at all, but Jinshan's apprentice. He didn't look to be too many years older than her.

"Lena, this is Secretary Ma," Jinshan said. "He will take over for me, when the time comes."

"A pleasure to meet you, sir."

"The pleasure is mine, Miss Chou. Chairman Jinshan has informed me that you are an irreplaceable asset."

She bowed her head in thanks, then turned to Jinshan. "Are you all right, Chairman Jinshan?"

His smile broadened. "Only you would return from captivity and ask that. My end is near, I am afraid. But it will not be today."

He indicated for her to take one of the chairs beside his bed.

"We have made great progress during the time you have been away."

Lena said, "I am most proud."

"Minister Dong and your father will be here soon. Have you seen them yet?"

"Not yet."

A knock at the door, and then the clatter of footsteps as General Chen and his entourage of staff officers marched into view. When he saw Lena, General Chen's expression flickered to shock, and then feigned pleasure.

"I heard you were coming back to us, daughter. Welcome. Are you well?"

Before she could answer, another group of men rounded the corner, this time led by Minister Dong.

"Hello, Miss Chou," Dong said. "I read your report earlier today. A miraculous escape."

Lena said, "The credit belongs to my Ministry of State Security training, sir."

Dong's gaze was piercing, as if he was trying to read her thoughts. Lena sensed danger there. It made sense for him to be suspicious. Any high-level prisoner returning to the motherland unharmed would be looked at this way. She realized that her military escort and the driver were probably counter-intelligence. They too would be watching her closely.

Jinshan said, "We should all be grateful for Lena's return. I look forward to you providing me with the details of your escape. Alas, time is of the essence and we must get to business. Please proceed, gentlemen."

General Chen began summarizing PLA movements in South America. China's progress was impressive. Whole divisions of PLA troops and armor had been moved across the Pacific.

"We're consolidating our forces in Colombia and Venezuela. The rail lines are working well. We expect to be pushing north to Panama by the end of the week."

"Excellent, General."

General Chen looked at Dong. "I am concerned that our intelligence support is still lacking, however. My battlefield commanders have repeatedly stated that they need better information before our northward push."

Dong cleared his throat. "General Chen will remember that our capacity for mass satellite launches is limited, and the timing is crucial to his men's success. If we launch too soon, the Americans will destroy the satellites."

Lena watched as the two men verbally jousted, their barbs fiercer than when she had last seen them. As she looked at Jinshan, the reason became evident. He was literally on his deathbed. It would not be long until he was gone. The rivals were not speaking for Jinshan's benefit, but for Ma's.

Dong was clearly annoyed. "And what about your organic drones?"

General Chen said, "We do not want to use them before we need them. You know this."

Secretary Ma said, "I'm sorry, General, but could you remind me why that is?"

Lena hid her amusement. She was sure the question irked her father.

General Chen said, "Of course, Secretary Ma. You see, we can't send our drones deep over enemy territory. American cyber and electronic attacks make drones very high-risk assets unless they are close to the control station, and sending them to do longer-range reconnaissance means they could be destroyed. The longer-range surveillance was something we thought Minister Dong's satellites would be taking care of by now."

Dong rolled his eyes. "Well, you could at least have your submarines near the American coast provide you with signals intelligence. But you've wasted them on a spontaneous attack. Poor judgment, I think."

Lena registered the comment. So, her father had ordered the attack. Had he known she was there?

General Chen said, "We have more submarines en route…"

Jinshan frowned, holding up a shaky hand. "I've heard enough for today, gentlemen. General, continue to be aggressive in your push to the north. Consult with me the moment you reach the American front lines."

"Yes, Chairman."

Jinshan said, "Now, Minister Dong is correct. We do have a capability gap. Our strategic missile force is depleted. And only a few of our nuclear ballistic missile submarines are in position. Much of this was by design, but we must make improvements. We need the help of an ally."

Dong said, "Russia?"

Jinshan nodded, then turned to Lena. "Lena, you will meet with the Russian ambassador tomorrow. We need to further our military alliance. It is not good enough to have them standing by as a nuclear deterrent anymore. Our bargaining position with Russia has improved. We must change our terms."

Lena bowed. "As you wish, Chairman."

Jinshan dismissed them, and the group left his chambers.

After they left, General Chen cornered her in the hallway. "Will you join me for tea, daughter?"

Daughter? He wants something, Lena thought.

"Of course, General."

A few moments later they sat in his private office. One of the general's cooks brought them a tray with tea and left.

"Minister Dong doesn't seem to trust you," her father said.

Lena was surprised that he had noticed. Or would state such a thing. She remained quiet.

"It's no secret that we are both vying for the same position. Whenever the chairman succumbs to his cancer, Ma will need a vice president. It will be Dong or me. Everyone knows it."

Lena sipped her tea. "I see."

"My surgeon tells me it could be a matter of weeks. It's a miracle that Jinshan has made it this long." Lena thought her father looked giddy while saying this.

Her father placed his cup on his desk and leaned back in his chair. "I am very impressed with your accomplishments...Lena." She noticed that he called her Lena, the name she had gone by since she became an MSS operative. Not her childhood name, Li, as he always had. He must really want something.

"Thank you, General."

"Jinshan certainly favors you, giving you such an important assignment as soon as you are back. Special envoy to the Russian Federation, perhaps?"

"Whatever I can do to serve."

"I believe the Russian contributions will be minimal. We should be focusing on other areas of strategic importance. Not a simple military alliance with Russia. I am not suggesting that you should disobey Jinshan. By all means, meet with the Russians. Ask for what he wants. But in the end, it is not going to be the difference maker, I suspect."

"And what will make the difference, may I ask?"

"Weapons innovation."

Lena's face betrayed nothing.

General Chen said, "When we break through the American lines, they will be faced with a decision. They will either use their arsenal of nuclear weapons to regain the tactical advantage on the battlefield, or face defeat. Jinshan gambled away our own nuclear ability during the first days of the war."

"But the Russians' ultimatum already took care of..."

General Chen scoffed, waving away her comment. "What do you think will happen when we *really* tip the scales in our favor? When we're rolling our tanks north through Mexico and into United States territory? Do you think the Russians will still be cheering us on then?"

Lena realized he was right. The Russians were enamored with the idea of the United States being torn down. But they would be horrified at the thought of such a powerful China, owning all of Asia and the Americas. She was surprised her father had thought of this all by himself.

Lena said, "The chairman instructed me to convince the Russians to assist us during the coming military assault on the US mainland."

"And you will do that." The general nodded. "But China also has another requirement. Jinshan himself has said that we need an organic means of nuclear deterrence."

Lena waited for him to continue.

General Chen said, "I want you to ask the Russians to share certain weapons research. Jinshan's strategy created a severe depletion of our nuclear capability. I have been working on a solution. An unrestricted warfare program that shows much promise. My scientists tell me the Russians have made a breakthrough in this area. I want the Russians to share some of their information with our scientists. If China is able to develop a new deterrent to American nuclear weapons, we will no longer be reliant upon the Russians. Only then will we achieve true power."

Lena said, "This is very interesting, General." Unrestricted warfare. He was talking about biological or chemical weapons.

"It is the type of progress that Secretary Ma would be impressed by, is it not?"

Lena nodded. "Yes, it is. May I ask why the Russians would agree to share this information?"

General Chen said, "When I am in power, I will ensure the Russians get better trade agreements. This is what you should offer."

"When *you* are in power?"

General Chen raised his chin. "If I can show my value to Jinshan and Secretary Ma, then it is only logical that I will be chosen as Ma's future vice president and chief advisor. Minister Dong's contributions pale in comparison to my own. Establishing this new unconventional weapons program will further cement my advantage."

"This is well thought out, General."

General Chen frowned. "This request for weapons research information is something we can only ask of the Russians now, when they do not sense its importance. When our military advantage over the Americans is not so great that they feel threatened by us."

"I will lay the seeds during my conversation. Such a request will need to be put delicately, and to the right Russian officials. There may be alternative channels we would need to take."

"Good."

The general shifted in his seat, wringing his hands.

"Is there something else?"

He lowered his voice. "Yes. There is. You are an officer of the Ministry of State Security."

"I am."

He stood and walked close to her, whispering, "Minister Dong, the Minister of State Security, does not trust you."

Lena looked up at him. "Is that so?"

He gripped her shoulder, and she forced herself to remain still. "*We* are blood. I suggest we act to our mutual benefit. Dong has his allies in the politburo. I have mine. I can ensure that Dong does not move to reduce your influence with Ma."

"Could he really do that?"

General Chen released his grip from Lena's shoulder and walked back to the other side of his desk. He placed his hands down on the desk and leaning forward, towering over her. "It is the time after Jinshan passes that we both must focus on. When that time comes, I will need something to use against Dong. Otherwise, neither of us will remain standing. Can I count on your loyalty?"

"Of course you can, Father."

18

Victoria awoke to the sound of one of the American prisoners screaming and pleading for the guards to stop torturing him. Then the voice seized and grunted, followed by cries of pain.

In the darkness, Victoria could barely make out the faces of the prisoners in their cells across the way. Faces pressed up against the bars, they looked like dogs in a kennel as they listened to the same sounds that had awoken her.

She could hear the men whispering to each other, trying to figure out who was being tortured. Then came the sound of a wooden door creaking open and slamming shut. Boots on gravel. A crew of PLA guards dragging the prisoner's limp body back to his cell.

Then the guards moved to the next cell. This time she recognized the prisoner's voice. "Hey, fellas. Hoping you'd show up." It was the chief. The PLA guards took him into the wooden building. Within minutes, the prisoners could hear his screams.

Victoria wondered what they were doing to cause such pain. And who would be next. The fear of the unknown was what drove you crazy.

The whispers between cells died down as the chief's

screams grew louder. The sailors looked up to him because of his seniority, and the sounds were horrific.

By the next morning, everyone was sleep deprived, starving, and wondering when their own turn would come. The soldiers placed loudspeakers outside the interrogation hut, facing the rows of prison cells, and blasted an English-language propaganda recording on loop. Despite the ear-shattering volume, Victoria could feel the rumble of heavy vehicles nearby and hear the occasional roar of jets overhead.

They were served one small bowl of rice and some water each day. Unless being interrogated, they were mostly kept in their cells. The interrogations always happened at night. Eventually people began to break.

The Chinese interrogators wanted information. But also propaganda. Signed and video-taped confessions. When prisoners confessed, they were given rewards, usually in the form of hot plates of food served to them in their cells so everyone else could smell it.

While the prisoners ate, their confessions were broadcast on the loudspeakers for the whole camp to hear.

One week in, losing weight and starting to hallucinate from lack of sleep, Victoria began fantasizing about what might be on those plates.

Eventually she found out. It was the chief, two cells across from her to the right. She could see his face when they put the plate of steaming chicken, vegetables, and warm flour tortillas in front of him. Victoria's mouth watered.

Then they played the recording of his confession. It was the standard stuff announcing to the world that he was a war criminal, and that he and his ship were engaged in illegal activity attacking a peaceful Chinese people.

At first the chief didn't touch the food. The plate lay outside the metal bars of his cell. But after a moment, he stuck his hand through and began eating, bringing bits of chicken to his mouth. After the first few bites, he began vomiting. Then he stuck out his hand and flipped over the plate, trying to get it as far away from him as he could manage. The chief began to sob, his confession still playing on the speaker system.

Victoria snapped her fingers, trying to get his attention. He looked up, his eyes red and moist. She couldn't speak. She didn't want to risk bringing the guards' wrath down on them both. But she gave him a thumbs up and a look that told him it was going to be okay. She wished she could talk to him. Tell him to shake it off. Everyone was bound to break.

"Commander Manning."

A female PLA soldier stood over her cell door, two guards flanking her. "You have been summoned."

The jingle of keys. Her cell door swinging open. It was her turn. They pulled her out and marched her away.

Until now, Victoria hadn't been interrogated. She'd hated herself for feeling relieved each time the Chinese had taken someone else away. Now, though, she was actually glad to get the first interrogation over with. Let them do what they will.

She tried to make herself believe she really was this brave.

———

Victoria sat on a metal chair in the center of the interrogation room. The cement floor was wet. A fresh spray of water to wash away blood or bodily fluids was still dripping down the metal grate drain in the center of the floor. Outside she could hear guards barking orders, followed by the footsteps of her men being moved throughout the camp's central yard.

The door creaked as it opened. Victoria's pulse quickened as she saw a man's silhouette surrounded by bright daylight. The crisply starched uniform. The tall, ornate military cover atop his head. Shoes shined to a reflective, polished black. He radiated intensity and precision.

Captain Tao. The same Chinese officer who had spoken with her at the train stop. He appraised her from just outside the door. Her hands were bound in front of her. He smiled cordially as he entered the room.

"Good morning." His polished shoes clicked on the floor as he made his way toward the table in the center of the room.

He sat down across from her and spread out his papers, then removed a felt pen and placed it beside them.

"Commander," he began, "I must say how refreshing it is to be sitting across from you. It's such a welcome change. For the past year I have been relegated to interviewing low-level soldiers in East Asia. The work had become so routine. There was no challenge. Do you ever feel that way about your work? Like it's always just the same old thing?" He motioned with his hand while he spoke, his palm facing the ceiling.

Victoria didn't answer.

Captain Tao said, "Routine interrogations on such men got to be mind-numbingly simple for us. You put three soldiers in a room, you tell them the one who talks first lives, shoot one of them a few seconds later, and voilà! You get a confession. Two, sometimes."

His eyes glowed. He removed his cover and placed it down, parallel to the edge of the table.

Victoria remained silent. She forced herself to control her breathing and keep a calm demeanor.

He studied her, cocking his head to one side. "Commander Manning, it is an honor to be sitting here with you. You're a decorated officer. Quickly promoted after a series of incredible victories in battle. Well, until you were captured by an enemy force."

He paused, looking at her. Giving her the opportunity to speak.

Satisfied that she wouldn't, he said, "But this shall give you another opportunity, no? Prisoners of war are celebrated in your country?" He changed his tone. "Hmm. Well, they *were*. Although I'm not sure what will happen once the PLA begins marching down Pennsylvania Avenue. Do you know what happens to the prisoners of a losing nation? Have you given much thought to that?"

Victoria shrugged.

Captain Tao said, "Do you think about what will happen when this all ends? I'm sure you do. You're in a prison cell all day long. You probably think about the end *a lot*. You must think about returning to your home in..." He looked down at his notes. "Jacksonville, Florida? That is your home, correct?"

He paused, offering her a chance to reply. After a moment of her silence, he continued. "Do you know what happened just a few days ago? We attacked an American military base in Florida. The week before? We conquered an entire continent by driving the last remaining Americans out of Colombia."

They stared at each other in silence. Victoria willed herself to show no emotion. But her mind raced, wondering if he was telling the truth. He was attempting to break her. To remove hope. To strip it away, thread by thread.

"Was Florida really attacked?"

"Oh yes."

"I don't believe you." She wondered if she could coax out more information.

He shrugged. "It doesn't matter whether you believe me."

Victoria said, "Your English is very good."

"So's yours." He smiled, then changed the subject back to her. "You are a woman in a man's profession. And an *admiral's* daughter..." He lowered his voice. "I see here that your father passed away. My condolences."

She dug her fingernails into the wooden seat beneath her.

Captain Tao said, "You are the senior prisoner in this camp. That means that you will be responsible for the behavior and well-being of its prisoners. I will, from time to time, call on you to make sure everything is running smoothly."

Victoria said, "My men need better living conditions. They need more food and water than you are giving them. They need to be let out of those cages you have us in so we can walk around. And we need to bathe."

Captain Tao said, "We can do all of this."

Victoria was startled by this reply.

"In return, you will provide me the names of everyone in the camp, as well as their occupational specialties. Each one will sign a confession. And there can be no more resistance to interrogations. If we ask a question, I expect your men to answer. In exchange, your men will be moved to barracks suitable to their rank and stature. They will have exercise privileges in the central court, under the close supervision of our guards. Food, water, and hygiene concerns will also be addressed."

"I can't order my men to sign a confession."

Captain Tao frowned. "Fine. Then *you* read a short statement. And all your troubles go away."

Victoria knew that they would use whatever she read as propaganda. Perhaps doctor it up to make it look worse than it really was. She also knew that she had a responsibility to take care of her men. She thought of the chief, vomiting up food because he couldn't live with his shame. They needed their living situation improved.

"Let me see the statement."

Thirty minutes later, Victoria was brought back to her cell. It was dusk, and the bugs were out again. As soon as the bars closed on her cell, she began swatting away giant mosquitos and God knew what else.

"When will we be moved out of here?" she asked the female PLA guard standing in front of her.

"Captain Tao said tomorrow. You must stay here at night."

"That's not what we agreed to."

The guards walked down to a cell on the end of the next row as Victoria's confession blared on the speakers. She leaned back against the concrete wall, her feet pressed up against the other side, angry with herself for allowing them to take advantage of her. Humiliated that her men were now witnessing her dishonor. They hadn't even tortured her. Instead, they used her desire to take care of her men as the dangling carrot. She hadn't been thinking straight. She was dizzy from the sleep deprivation and hunger pangs in her belly.

"Oh yeah! Party time!" a familiar voice said.

Plug was being marched to the interrogation building.

Victoria yelled, "Hey! Hey! Captain Tao said that the interrogations would stop..."

One of the guards ran over and opened her cell door. He dragged her out onto the gravel and took out a night stick, then swung it rapidly at her face.

A searing white-hot pain exploded on her cheekbone.

Stars and dizziness and then another eye-popping wallop of pain, this one near her kidney.

She was lifted up and slung back into her cell, landing like a sack of potatoes. After a moment of agony, she began taking stock of her injuries. She touched her face. It was already swelling, and still oozing blood.

Yells of protest from nearby prisoners who had witnessed the attack on their senior ranking officer. Then whistles and more guards coming out of the woodwork and boots marching on gravel. The sound of iron cell gates swinging open on creaky hinges. More intense beatings and groans.

After a few minutes, the punishment had been properly doled out, and the guards shut the prisoners back in their cells. Then the POWs were treated to the loudest screams yet from the interrogation room. Plug was putting on some sort of performance, and getting punished for it. The interrogation lasted for an hour, and then he was dragged back to his cell.

After the guards left him, the rows of cells were completely silent. Victoria thought they might have killed him.

Then Plug broke the silence with, "This prison has the worst conjugal visits *ever.*"

Laughter filled the prison cell courtyard but died down as a few guards made the rounds again. They pulled her out again, but Victoria's beatings felt good this time, like they were washing away her sins. Plug's comic relief also felt good.

Her men's spirits were still strong.

19

Camp David
  Maryland

David sat in a chair along the outer wall of the conference room. A hush fell over the room as the president and his entourage entered. The president nodded to General Schwartz, who was standing near the presentation screen.

"Good morning, General."

"Good morning, Mr. President."

"Sir, this brief outlines our plans for Operation CENTER SHIELD."

The screen flipped to a map of Central America. "We are positioning American forces in three defensive belts: belt one is Panama, belt two is Costa Rica—the Puerto Limon-San Jose-Caldera corridor—and belt three is Mexico City."

The president said, "Why Panama, General? We had military in Colombia. Why didn't we move our forces there?"

"Sir, frankly, the Chinese moved faster than we expected. Panama is a great choke point, small and narrow. Think a stretched-out Delaware with jungle-covered mountainous terrain. The Panama Canal is the treasure. It presents enormous strategic advantage if one side controls both bodies of water around it. In the Panama operating area, heavy tanks are less useful, so we've deployed helos and Stryker brigades."

"Very well. Continue."

General Schwartz said, "Belt two: Costa Rica. Also mountainous, and the last geographic choke point before the terrain widens and the enemy can flank, infiltrate, and continue northward movement. Helicopters are coin of the realm here."

General Schwartz pointed to the screen. "The final belt: Mexico City, a major population center. There are hills and desert, especially north of the city, where our mechanized infantry and armored units can maneuver and cut off or destroy vast enemy formations in a Desert Storm-type counterattack. Warfighting here will be very different than what went on in Central America. If the enemy gets this far north, my counterattack plan, focused in Mexico, also involves an airborne and seaborne invasion to seize Panama and cut off all land-based escape/resupply. Think MacArthur's amphibious op at Inchon that virtually destroyed the entire North Korean army."

The Chairman of the Joint Chiefs of Staff, sitting next to the president, said, "What would prevent the Chinese from using the same tactic to flank our forces?"

A Navy four-star admiral sitting near the end of the table leaned forward. "Third Fleet is deploying both Carrier Strike Groups to the area for supporting operations in the eastern Pacific. Second Fleet will provide a Surface Action Group in the Gulf of Mexico."

The president said, "What's the latest update on Chinese PLA Navy movement?"

The Navy admiral said, "Sir, their Jiaolong-class battleships and two carrier groups are headed north along the western side of South America. We anticipate they will be supporting PLA ground forces as they move north through Panama."

The Chairman of the Joint Chiefs of Staff asked, "Do they have amphibious capability?"

A few of the senior officers glanced at each other. "We don't think so, sir," one of them answered.

David could see faces around the table contort in disappointment. The Chairman of the Joint Chiefs of Staff said, "I prefer not to hear what you think. Tell me what you know."

General Schwartz, still standing for the brief, said, "Sir, our ISR capability is struggling to meet all of the requirements. We've had to make tradeoffs. We don't have a good look at the PLA Navy's approaching fleet."

The president waved him on. "Keep going."

General Schwartz clicked a button and the presentation screen zoomed in on Panama. "The 25th Infantry Division with its Stryker brigades has been deployed to Panama. There they will defend and, if necessary, withdraw north up the Pan-American Highway corridor." He clicked to the next slide. "The 101st Airborne, 10th Mountain, elements of 2nd Infantry Division, and remaining Stryker brigades are now deploying to Costa Rica. This movement had been ongoing since the Chinese began landing in South America and should be fully complete by early next week. If this belt gets overrun, the light infantry units may need to be evacuated by helicopter or sea."

The Chairman of the Joint Chiefs of Staff turned to the Pacific Fleet Admiral. "That's you, Bob. We need those sea lanes and airspace clear. Understand?"

"Yes, sir, absolutely."

The president turned to General Schwartz. "What happens if they get to Mexico City?"

"Sir, if the Chinese get that far north, we'll have 1st Armored Division, 1st Infantry Division, 3rd Infantry Division, 4th

Infantry Division, and 1st Cavalry Division move to defend Mexico City. The 82nd Airborne and 1st Marine Division are in reserve, and CONUS based. Elements from the 7th Special Forces Group and 75th Ranger Regiment will go to ground in Nicaragua, Honduras, El Salvador, Panama City, and Guatemala. If the ground war moves north into Mexico, we envision small-unit ambushes and raids along the Pan-American Highway to disrupt enemy logistics, and strategic reconnaissance within Panama to inform future contingency planning."

The National Security Advisor said, "I assume most of this will fall under Southern Command? Where does Northern Command come into play?"

General Schwartz said, "US Southern Command will be responsible for the first two defensive belts, Panama and Costa Rica. We've pushed them additional rotary-wing lift assets, artillery counter-battery radars, and tactical unmanned aerial vehicles for reconnaissance and surveillance. US Northern Command owns the Mexico City defense. We're massing rotary-wing attack assets and logistics commensurate to an extended defense or large-scale maneuver operations."

"If the Chinese make it that far, where will they most likely maneuver?"

"Sir, the Pan-American Highway is really the only high-speed maneuver corridor in much of Central America."

"Any rail they can use for supply chain and logistics?"

"Negative, sir. Central America's rail is a mess of small, disconnected lines. The Pan-American Highway can be interdicted by artillery or air assets by either side. We've allocated our air defense artillery, artillery counter-battery radars, and Javelin antitank missile systems accordingly."

"Status of the Panama Canal?"

"All transits have ceased. The locks have been rigged with

explosives and are set to detonate if it looks like the Chinese could take that territory."

The president said, "I would like to emphasize that destroying the Panama Canal is to be done only as a last resort."

"On-scene commanders have been briefed, sir."

The president crossed his arms, gazing down at the floor like he was calculating something in his head. Then he looked up and said, "When will it begin?"

General Schwartz said, "Sir, our SIGINT reports indicate that China is preparing another mass satellite launch. It's possible that they will begin their expected northward thrust prior to that happening. But if they do, they'll be flying blind, and attacking without their major advantages: GPS guidance and satellite datalink. So, we suspect that we'll get a warning—albeit a very short one."

"When, General?"

"I'd say within the next forty-eight to seventy-two hours, sir."

The president looked at the Chairman of the Joint Chiefs of Staff. "Anything to add?"

"We need to hold the line in Central America."

The president said, "Godspeed." With that, he stood, and the conference room stood with him. Then he and his aide departed.

One of the officers said, "Dismissed." David watched the tired-looking officers shuffling out of the room.

General Schwartz nodded for David to approach. "Come with me, please, Mr. Manning."

The general began walking down the Camp David hallway, two armed guards following close behind. This particular building was large, reminding David of a major conference center. Dozens of meeting spaces and conference rooms, all set up for this. The president reviewing war strategy with his key advisors.

Many of the conference rooms had been transformed into command and communications centers. Everywhere he looked, David could see uniformed men and women motoring along through fatigue and stress. Many of these Pentagon planners had been on the front lines themselves over the past year. Now their job was to plan out each detail of the war and give the troops in combat the best chance they could. Their brothers in arms depended on this work. Sleep, food, and any ounce of personal comfort could all wait, if it meant adding one iota of efficiency to the plan.

They walked into General Schwartz's makeshift private office, which wasn't much more than a closet with a desk and window. The general's bodyguards took their posts outside his door, standing at parade rest. General Schwartz waved David into a seat, then said, "What did you think?"

"Sir, the plan is well thought out. I don't pretend to have your knowledge when it comes to..."

"Say what's on your mind, David."

David hesitated, then said, "The numbers are not in our favor. The estimates I've seen put the number of Chinese troops currently in South America at just under eight-hundred thousand. Significant air and sea warfighting assets have all been deployed there. They are forming and improving supply lines as we speak, with scary efficiency."

"So you think we'll be overrun."

"In Panama? Yes. Beyond that, I don't know. But again, sir, I defer to you on this."

General Schwartz nodded. "Sure." He looked over to his bookcase. "This is the office where they stick us military flag officers whenever we get invited up to Camp David. They stock it with books for ambiance. At least they get the books right. You read any of these?"

David glanced at the titles and authors. Stephen E. Ambrose. James D. Hornfischer. David McCullough.

"Yes, sir, I think I've read most of those. My father was a big fan of Hornfischer. *The Last Stand of the Tin Can Sailors. The Fleet at Flood Tide.*"

General Schwartz said, "You're a student of military history, and you know how to strategize. My guess is you picked up a few things from your father. You have an unparalleled knowledge of the latest military technological capabilities. And you're smart enough to go to the experts when you don't know something. Say what's on your mind."

David said, "Sir, it's our overall situation that concerns me. We got sucker-punched on the first day of the war. Our allies have a gun to their head, and they can't help us. And our nuclear deterrents are useless, unless we want to end the world. We've ramped up production and recruiting. Many of our consumer factories have been transformed into military manufacturing facilities. We've drafted millions into service, and by all estimates, our warfighting capability is the best it's been since 1945."

"But..."

"But you and I both know that it won't be enough."

General Schwartz cracked his knuckles. "David, I used to play football. If a one-hundred-pound guy is lined up against a two-hundred-pound gorilla, guess who's gonna win?"

David thought about his crowning achievement while assigned to the Silversmith team, planning the Battle of Johnston Atoll. Looking back now, that plan seemed like a whole lot of luck. A confluence of events lining up for the perfect deception. What did the Americans have now? Lena Chou had escaped to China, and David wasn't confident they would ever hear from her again. The Rojas hypersonic technology had gone to the Chinese. The

Pacific had all but fallen. The only remaining bastion of American naval might was Hawaii. Thank God they had held Hawaii. But China was pouring men and military might into South America each day. If they breached Panama, it could get ugly.

David continued turning the problem over in his head. Finally, he said, "No. I don't think our current plans will be enough. We need a new way to attack the problem."

"Say more."

David's eyes scanned the ceiling rapidly as he thought, synapses firing. "Sir, I used to work for In-Q-Tel. It's essentially the CIA's private equity firm."

"I'm familiar, David. Get to your point, please."

David cleared his throat.

"Okay. At In-Q-Tel, I used to work on a lot of different projects. Explore new and upcoming military technology. Most of those projects didn't pan out. But you needed to seed them with funding to do the exploratory work."

"I'm familiar with the concept of R&D. It sounds like what you're trying to say is that we need a Manhattan Project."

"That, sir, but I was also thinking we need something closer to an Operation Bodyguard. Are you familiar?"

"The deception plan, correct?"

"Yes, sir. Operation Bodyguard was a collection of operations, each one meant to deceive Germany prior to the Allied invasion of Europe. I think we need to come up with multiple options for something similar, prior to a Chinese invasion of North America."

"David, despite what Hollywood suggests, the Pentagon isn't full of idiots. They are definitely working on deception plans..."

"I understand that, sir. But I worry about how realistic it is to keep something like this under wraps when operating on our homeland, at this scale. When Silversmith suggested plans for the Battle of Johnston Atoll, you were able to give us cover at the

Pentagon. Now you're at the Pentagon. And to give you an idea, we need to go through three layers of staff. It's slow and inefficient. And the more eyeballs that see this stuff..."

"The more chance that the Chinese find out about it. I get it, David. So how should we proceed?"

"Silversmith should create a special project team to begin game planning ideas that the US military and intelligence organizations will need to execute. Some of these recommended actions would require massive investments of time, money, and resources. This will require political muscle in the DOD and White House. Somebody needs full authority to move mountains."

"I can speak to the White House and CJCS. Rumor has it I'll be getting a fifth star. POTUS is sending me to run SOUTHCOM."

David said, "Congratulations, sir."

General Schwartz nodded. "Okay, I'm sold. Gather your team and start working on your ideas. Assuming that CJCS and the White House approve, Silversmith should report only to me on this."

20

China

Lena met her Russian contact in a street market one kilometer north of his embassy. They offered greetings and then walked in silence to a nearby gastropub. Once inside, Lena ordered them drinks as they sat in a poorly lit corner table.

"Kostya, you are moving up in the world. Ambassador? Last time I saw you working in an embassy, your title was quite ambiguous."

"Last time you saw me in an embassy, you were an American citizen."

"We are all deceptive creatures."

The Russian grinned. "Yes. But I am getting older. I no longer play the young man's game. Now I serve at the pleasure of the tsar."

Lena shot him a knowing look. "Sure. If it suits you."

He shrugged. "And you? Do you still serve your tsar loyally?"

Lena's face grew serious. "I do."

"And how much longer will he be in charge?"

"No one really knows."

"Who will succeed him?"

"Ma. You must know this already."

"We like to confirm our SVR reports. Your country has not made that public yet."

"Jinshan doesn't want to be a lame duck, as the Americans say."

Kostya said, "I read another report about the transition. There is a competition for the number two spot, and it's down to General Chen and Minister Dong. Is that true?"

Lena held up her hands. "Perhaps."

Kostya said, "I think it is. Where will your loyalty lie, when that transition occurs?"

"Where do you think?"

"General Chen is your father. I would assume with him."

Lena offered him a Mona Lisa smile.

Kostya said, "Okay. Enough of this. Time for a joke."

"Ah, yes. Your legendary jokes."

"Two rabbits are hopping along the Russian road during Stalin's reign. The first rabbit says to the second, 'Comrade, comrade, have you heard? They are castrating all the camels. We must hurry out of here at once!'"

Lena listened with amusement.

"The second rabbit looks at him like he is crazy and says, 'Why are you so concerned? You are not a camel.' The first rabbit replies, '*You* try proving that you are not a camel once they catch you.'"

Lena allowed herself a polite laugh. She liked him. He saw the truth in people and institutions. The Chinese knew he was a spy first and a diplomat second, and the Russians knew they knew it. The SVR and MSS both believed he was a loyal patriot to the Russian Federation.

But Lena knew what really made him tick. Kostya, like many

Russians, was a cynic of the system he served. She could accomplish a lot with such men. When a transaction served both of their needs, he was a willing trade partner. Sometimes the deal was in the best interests of his country. Other times it was in the best interests of Kostya.

Kostya sipped his drink. "Lena, it is good to see you again. I hope your time away wasn't too difficult." He was eyeing the scars on the side of her face.

"My time in America was not pleasant. I am very glad to be back in my mother country." The image of her child flashed through her mind.

Kostya said, "How may I be of service?"

"I have been asked to speak with you about a delicate matter. As you must be aware, our military is making excellent progress in Latin America. Soon we will be marching through Mexico and then on to the continental US."

"The Russian Federation applauds your great military achievements." His tone was dry.

Lena said, "My leadership considers the Russian-Chinese partnership to be its single most important strategic alliance."

Kostya raised an eyebrow. "Until it's not..."

Lena dipped her head. "My leadership acknowledges that there will come a time when our strength may be...intimidating."

Kostya laughed. "I will certainly refrain from using that word when I write up my report to the Russian president."

Lena said, "Chairman Jinshan recognizes that Russia needs assurances. We must have continued stability in our relationship."

"Russia welcomes any Chinese action that keeps our relationship mutually beneficial."

"Is your country worried about what will happen in the future?"

"Between friends? Yes. Absolutely."

Any other Russian diplomat or intelligence officer would have denied it. But Kostya didn't bother with that nonsense, knowing she would see right through it. This was why she liked him. A mutual respect, and a logical response.

Lena said, "You are worried that China will become too powerful, and you will have gone from a manageable American foe to a gargantuan Chinese ruler."

"Again, not the way I would word it in front of our president. But yes."

Lena said, "If things keep progressing the way they are, we will eventually reach that imbalance of power. But right now, you have leverage. And China has a military requirement that would best be served with Russian assets."

"Our nation is not supposed to be involved in your war with the Americans. We made a deal to provide deterrence, not for the use of force."

Lena said, "The Americans have built up their defensive capabilities in the Atlantic. It would be in our best interests if Russian forces assisted us in defeating these defensive systems, prior to a Chinese attack."

Kostya looked at her sideways. "Atlantic bases? But your navy is moving northward in the eastern Pacific. The People's Liberation Army is headed to Panama. Every intelligence service...hell, every newscaster in the world knows this."

"Jinshan wants us to plan long-term. Plan for success. When we defeat the Americans in Panama, we will eventually need to invade their homeland. Russia has submarines and hypersonic cruise missiles that could be used to give a massive blow to critical American military installations at just the right time. The Americans will see us coming. And they will prepare. But a *Russian* attack..."

Kostya folded his arms, leaning back in his chair. "I suspect that my president will not be comfortable with this. As things stand, we have vastly improved our bargaining power with Europe, Africa, and the Middle East. Our economy and political strength has never been of higher standing. If we were to overtly take such an action, world politicians might turn against us."

Lena flashed a seductive smile. "Who said anything about overt action?"

Kostya narrowed his eyes. "But you just said..."

"China could take credit for any military moves you made. General Chen would be more than pleased with that, actually."

Kostya stared at her thoughtfully. "I see. Hypothetically, if we were to do this, what would Russia get in return?"

Lena crossed her legs and shook her head. "Kostya, my friend. You should know better than to give us your price at this stage. I tell you this because I like you. Make your military preparations now. Then, when we need it most, that is when you give us your asking price. China will have to pay it."

Kostya sniffed, studying Lena. "You never fail to impress me."

She took a sip of water. "Now, about the other things I asked you about."

"Quite a list of requests."

"The special weapons research..."

"Officially, the Russian government denies all knowledge of the biological weapons program you mentioned."

"Unofficially?"

"It will cost you. And the idea that we would share such valuable classified military research in exchange for the promise of a future trade agreement is laughable."

"I thought that might be a stretch. I'll let my superiors know that you aren't interested..."

Kostya said, "Well, I didn't say that, did I?"

"Stop playing. What's the ask?"

"Singapore."

"What about it?"

"You have seized control, yet still hold back on exerting much influence on their governance."

Lena said, "The frog won't jump if you boil it slowly enough."

"China hasn't made it easy for international companies to compete. Singapore isn't China. But its business enterprises have a disproportionately large share of the Asian market in some industries."

"It is now Chinese-controlled. I would expect change."

Kostya held up his hand. "Hear me out. If Russian businesses were able to gain equity positions in Singapore-owned companies, that could provide us with a strong economic return in Asia. It could be just the type of change needed to strengthen our relationship."

Lena knew that the Russian businesses chosen to benefit from this arrangement would be sending huge kickbacks and dividends to the oligarchs, and to the Russian president himself. This was how the world worked.

"I will make the proposal to my leadership. What about the other request I sent you? Were your people able to find anything on him?"

"As a matter of fact, they were." He checked his watch. "And if you hurry, you'll be able to see for yourself."

Lena left the meeting location and followed Kostya's directions, walking as fast as she could without drawing attention to herself. She was making her way past a crowded subway exit when she spotted her target. Two black SUVs came to a stop one block ahead.

Minister of State Security Dong exited the rear vehicle, his security escorting him into the side entrance of a commercial building.

The SUVs then departed, and the building's entrance door swung to a close.

Lena found it somewhat unsettling that Russian intelligence services would know his intended meeting location with such certainty. She would need to look into that. But what really made her curious was why the head of the MSS was alone in this part of town. At his level, people came to see him...unless he didn't want to be seen. The location was only blocks from most of the international embassies. Kostya only gave her tidbits of information. The rest she must discover on her own.

Her father's words passed through her mind. *Find information we can use against Minister Dong.* While she certainly didn't feel loyalty to General Chen, her training as an intelligence operative told her that something about Dong's current actions was off. And if he was doing something unscrupulous, it was in her best interests to get leverage on him, whatever she chose to do with it.

Lena walked past the subway entrance and into what used to be a Starbucks coffee shop. All American-owned restaurants had been renamed when the war began, their corporate ownership transferred to the Chinese government. The place was mostly empty. Lena ordered a cup of coffee and sat at a table by the window.

She waited for thirty-five minutes before Chairman Dong reappeared at the building entrance across the street. Almost instantly, the two government SUVs rounded the corner, picked him up, and departed.

After Dong left, Lena rose from her chair and walked toward the building. She headed down the adjacent alleyway to check for alternate building exits, finding three, and frowned. She wouldn't be able to visually cover all four exits. On instinct, she moved to a park bench with a view of the alternate exits. If it were her, she wouldn't use the same door as Dong to leave. She was counting on whoever met with him to behave the same way.

She removed her smartphone from her purse and powered it on. She always made sure to keep it powered off whenever she was doing street work to reduce the chances she could be tracked. Over the next twenty minutes, she took pictures of no less than eight people leaving the building.

The ninth departure was her mark. Lena knew this because she recognized the man. Oddly, she couldn't place his name.

Asian male. Medium height, medium build. Jet-black hair. He matched the description of several million Beijing men his age. But with China's growing facial recognition capability, discovering his identity would be relatively easy.

Still, Lena wanted to gather more information while she had him in her sights. She followed him through the city streets, careful to stay far enough back that he wouldn't notice. It didn't take her long to confirm he was a professional. When he did a reversal, she just barely escaped his view by slipping into a clothing shop. After fending off a pushy salesperson who was thrilled to finally get a customer, she departed the store and frantically searched for the agent again.

There. He was backtracking, and Lena was on him.

Until she wasn't.

He disappeared right outside the Japanese embassy.

No, Lena realized.

He had gone inside.

———————

Lena was one of the few people in the world who could be

granted an audience with Jinshan at her leisure. Each of his security men and handlers knew her well.

Now she stood next to Jinshan as he took his tea on the balcony outside his bedroom, looking down at the quiet garden where security guards with automatic rifles patrolled under the shade of the manicured trees.

"You are sure it was Minister Dong?"

Lena nodded. "Yes."

Jinshan frowned. "There could be a number of reasons for the meeting. You've taken such meetings."

"As a field operative, yes. Not as the most senior official in the MSS. It seems odd."

"And you say you have images of the man he met with."

"Yes. I was hoping to bring them to someone who will be discreet. Obviously, I don't want to use MSS resources to avoid someone finding out I was looking into this."

"I will put you in touch with someone you can trust." Jinshan shook his head, muttering under his breath. He was clearly disappointed in Dong.

Lena said, "You favored him as Ma's vice president? After you..."

The words didn't quite make it out of her mouth. Very few things could make Lena emotional. But the future death of the man who had shaped her life since she was a teenager was one of them. She cursed herself inwardly. Motherhood had made her soft.

Jinshan looked up at her. "After I die."

"The rumors are that Ma will be your successor. And Dong or my father will be Ma's vice president and main advisor."

"The rumors are true. I want Ma to make this decision, but I have offered him my thoughts. Your father has proven to be a surprisingly adept politician. He has members of the politburo backing him now."

Lena looked at the floor, unable to meet his eyes. "This decision needs to be made and announced soon."

"I am well aware that if a succession plan is not in place before I am gone, it will be a chaotic mess. But if I announce it too early, then I am neutered. And I can't be. Not yet."

"Hence the delay."

Jinshan said, "Yes. Dong has shown good judgment until now. Much better than your father. I recommended that Ma choose him, when it is time." He paused, peering into her eyes. "It is too much of a coincidence for *you* to be the one to bring this to me. You didn't just stumble onto this now, on your own."

Lena didn't flinch. "My father asked me to look into Dong."

Jinshan looked amused. "Of course. He sees you as another pawn. Does your father think you will be loyal to him?"

"I serve our nation."

"But you did your father's bidding, in this instance?"

"You taught me to always keep my eyes and options open."

Jinshan looked back out over the garden. "There is a man at my cyber security firm. I will give you his name. He will help you with this name identification."

"I will go immediately."

Jinshan sighed. "I want you to continue to look into Dong. Quietly. See where it takes you. You will know what to do, I think. Now, tell me how it went with the Russian."

———

Two hours later, Lena stood in a private office at Jinshan's cyber technology firm, one of the businesses that had made him wealthy.

She looked over the shoulder of Jinshan's trusted cyber operations specialist. The man was a former member of the 3PLA cyberwarriors, an elite Chinese military cyber operations group. He now worked exclusively for Jinshan's firm, which specialized in providing the government with facial recognition software. While the firm was closely tied to the Chinese government, Jinshan still commanded loyalty among its elite members.

"Is it finished?" Lena asked.

The cyber operations tech had uploaded Lena's picture of the suspect. The software program compared the image to over one billion faces in the registry. Results took only seconds.

The tech said, "We have a ninety-five-percent match with this man." An image popped up next to hers.

"You have his bio?"

"Right here."

Lena scanned the information. "Hmm."

The tech said, "A Japanese embassy official? Low-level, by the sound of it."

Lena thought the suspect's biographical information sounded like a typical intelligence officer's cover legend. But Japanese? Japan had surrendered to China. Lena wondered if Japan still deployed intelligence officers to Beijing. It was possible, but unlikely. The MSS would be keeping a very close eye on Japanese military and intelligence operations, both here and in Tokyo. Why would a Japanese intelligence officer meet with the head of the MSS in private? The only explanation Lena could come up with was that Dong didn't want the others in his circle to know. But why? Was he planning something that Jinshan and some politburo members would disapprove of?

"Well that's odd." The tech continued scrolling across the biographical information on the screen.

Lena stretched her neck forward for a better look. "What is?"

The man typed on his keypad and a new window appeared with more of the Japanese man's files.

"I accessed some of the archived information on Japanese government servers, cross-referencing his past known images from social media, emails, and his past cloud storage accounts. When I try to match a few older pictures from the same man's file, we only get an eighty-five-percent match. Not ninety-five, like the first time."

Lena frowned. "What do you mean?"

"The first facial recognition match was based on the official picture on file here, at the Japanese embassy, comparing it to your picture. But when I match the picture you took with the older archived images, the confidence score goes down."

"And that's abnormal? What does it mean?"

"It's still a possible match, but unusual. The program is meant to account for aging. We usually see something like this if a subject has gotten reconstructive surgery."

"Can you look up that information?"

"Hold on." The tech began typing. After a minute, he said, "I did a search of Japanese medical records, and there is no indication this man ever had plastic surgery."

Lena said, "Expand your search. Cross-check my image with any known American intelligence operatives. Prioritize ones who have worked in Japan."

He resumed typing. "Of course. That search should be very quick since there are so few. See? All done. Nothing of high confidence. One is somewhat close, though. This one."

Lena recognized the face on the screen. This was who she'd been reminded of when she first saw the man on the street. She'd seen his face in Tokyo a year ago. The American CIA officer who had been working with Chase Manning.

21

Tap tap tap. Tap tap.

Victoria awoke to the sound of her cell neighbor signaling through their concrete wall. If she listened carefully, she could also hear the faint sounds of other prisoners communicating in similar fashion.

The origins of tap code dated back to Ancient Greece but were more recently used by prisoners of war during Vietnam. Every American soldier knew of this communication method. But as Victoria discovered, familiarity and mastery were two very different things.

Victoria and her fellow POWs had begun communicating to each other through tap code within the first few days of arriving in the camp, though it took her a while to get the hang of it. Five rows of letters, A to Z. C was also K, in the top row. The first consecutive taps were for the vertical row, top to bottom. The second set of taps were for which column the letter was in, left to right.

Tap tap tap. Tap tap. Three down, two across. M.

Morning. Short for good morning, in this case. Her cell neighbor was greeting her.

She responded, and then began receiving her morning report.

All personnel present and accounted for. PO Nordyke sick. Needs meds.

Petty Officer Nordyke had caught pneumonia. The poor kid had been suffering chills and a fever for the past forty-eight hours. Victoria would use her meeting today with the camp's commanding officer to ask for better medical treatment, her job for now. She was the prisoners' representative for food, water, and humane treatment.

The first week in this camp had been almost nonstop torture and interrogations, but even the guards couldn't keep up that pace. Those bastards had to sleep at some point. Victoria had negotiated with the base commander, promising him "good behavior" in exchange for better food and a few hours per day of exercise. In a moment of weakness and fatigue, she had even conducted a video confession.

Victoria was humiliated and dishonored. The prisoners' conditions improved, but her mistake only further fueled a desire to resist. She commanded her fellow prisoners to continue creating an escape plan.

South American men and women forced to work for the Chinese cooked the prisoners' food. Some were local political prisoners, held in a low-security barracks outside of the American POW camp. Others came from the nearby town. As Victoria understood it, they were paid pennies.

Several groups of non-prisoners used the mess hall as well. The guards ate first, of course, and next came a team of scientists or researchers. Some wore white lab coats. They were Hispanic, but Victoria got the feeling that they weren't local. Every time the researchers entered the mess hall, they were under the Chinese guards' watchful eyes. They didn't receive the same tender loving care as Victoria and the American servicemen, but she could feel a definite tension.

Whenever the scientists weren't eating, they worked under guard in a building half a mile south of the camp. Sometimes Victoria could hear incredibly loud rumbles coming from the facility, almost like a jet engine.

Several Chinese installations were located near the POW camp, and a lot of manual labor was required to keep everything running. Venezuelan military soldiers also ate at the mess hall sometimes. They drove their jeeps right up to the hall and looked like they were having a great time while they ate. Victoria was mainly interested in the gear the Venezuelan soldiers stored on their jeeps. The Chinese guards kept all of their communications gear in a single building that overlooked the camp courtyard from the north. Captain Tao's office was there. But the Venezuelan jeeps had UHF/VHF radios that looked similar to the standard American-issue gear, and a long HF antenna on the rear of each vehicle. She had tasked Plug and his escape committee with finding a way to get access to that comms gear.

The Chinese eventually put the American prisoners to work alongside the locals, doing laundry, cleaning, and cooking.

After a few weeks of this, Victoria ordered the escapes to begin in earnest. There were several unsuccessful attempts, one resulting in an ensign's death. The kid had actually tried to rip the sidearm out of a PLA soldier's holster. He was shot twice by snipers in two different guard towers. Some of the Americans thought it might have been a suicide attempt, but Victoria didn't want to think about that. Even though that particular escape hadn't been run by her before execution, she still added it to the pile of things she couldn't forgive herself for.

Most days were long, boring, and hot as hell. Her time was

spent staring at the thin slice of jungle she could see from her cell or tapping through the wall to the young man next to her. Sometimes they played telephone, passing information along from one cell to the next. Other times they had deeply personal conversations, telling each other about their homes.

She found herself telling her prison cell neighbor about her childhood. Reeling up home-made crab pots with her brothers in the Chesapeake. Scoring the winning goal during a college lacrosse game. Sun-filled stories of a happier time. Stories she hadn't thought about in forever. Her life had been consumed by work and purpose, her rank and title forged through years of stress and sweat. But now, looking back, she found that these simpler times were the memories she cherished the most. The ones she wished she had more of.

Victoria stopped tapping when she heard a guard's club dragging along nearby cell bars.

"Rows one and two. Morning meal."

The guards' English was getting better. Some of them regularly conversed with their American captives, and Victoria suspected they enjoyed it. Her standing orders to the prisoners were to befriend anyone they could. Forge useful connections. Find out information. Probe for weaknesses and potential solutions.

Escape. It was their ultimate objective, despite any false pretense of cooperation.

She wanted nothing more than to get all of her men out of here alive so they could rejoin the fight. As she thought of this, the ground rumbled beneath her feet. Another jet engine test from the research facility to the south.

A guard opened her cell door with a clang, and she stretched as she got out and stood up. Victoria spotted Plug in the cell row next to hers. They wouldn't be allowed to sit together at breakfast—or morning rice, as her men called it—but she would likely get a chance to speak to him in the dirt-covered exercise yard.

She walked through a meal line. A pregnant Hispanic woman served each of them a bowl of rice and a plastic cup of water. Today there was a hard-boiled egg in the bowl, an exciting addition. They ate in silence. They knew not to test the rules. Three armed Chinese guards watched over them, including the mean one with the shaved head who always ogled her chest.

After the meal, Plug and another American were chosen to stay behind and help clean up the mess hall. The rest were marched out to the courtyard for "exercise time." Soon the group of American prisoners lined up in a formation, almost like they were back on base, doing squadron PT. Victoria was happy to see the chief out with them. He seemed to be getting over his violent arrival. He even led one of their "daily dozen" exercises.

Plug, finished in the kitchen, fell into the rear of the group's formation, then traded spots with the guy in front of him so he could stand next to Victoria, watching for the guards to look away so he wouldn't attract too much attention. The chief, seeing what Plug was trying to do, turned up the volume.

"Let's count a bit louder now, eh? One!"

"One!" replied the group of prisoners in unison.

"Two!"

"Two!" replied the group.

It went on like that for a while, the group performing a simple arm stretch while Plug gave Victoria his update.

"The day after tomorrow."

"How?"

Plug shrugged. "That fat Venezuelan soldier driving the jeep has a thing for one of the laundry girls. A local Venezuelan girl."

Victoria frowned. "Is the laundry girl a prisoner?"

"No. She's just a local girl of questionable morals who happens to work here."

Victoria glanced at Plug.

"She puts out, boss."

"Thank you, Plug. I understand."

The chief switched exercises to sit-ups. The group sat in the dirt and began counting.

"One!"

"One!" the group replied.

"Two!"

"Two!"

Plug continued whispering to Victoria. "So Skanky Laundry Girl works *nights*. Apparently, her parents frown on the relationship. So Fat Venezuelan Soldier Guy and Skanky Laundry Girl are looking for somewhere to...you know..."

"Plug, what does this have to do with..."

"You know the mess hall lady? The cute pregnant woman? She's the only woman here with the research team. The Chinese have got her husband and his researchers working around the clock, so she's got her barracks building all to herself."

"And..."

"I happen to communicate with both women, when I'm in the mess hall. My Spanish is really coming in handy. My high school teacher would be proud. Anyway, I worked something out with them. Well, technically I just overheard them talking. I made my deal with the cute pregnant woman, and then let her work out a deal privately with the skanky laundry girl."

"So how's it going to work?"

Plug said, "I'll give her the message and instructions. While the two lovebirds are in her bedroom, the pregnant lady will go to his jeep. She'll broadcast on guard frequency. I gave her a sixty-second Morse code transmission to make. The one we agreed on."

"Prisoner names?"

"Yes. A few names and the total count. If the SIGINT guys are good, they'll be able to triangulate our broadcast."

"If they hear it..."

Plug said, "After pregnant lady finishes her broadcast, she's to shut down the equipment, burn the Morse code note, and sit outside her barracks until the love birds finish."

"What if she's spotted during the transmission?"

"She's willing to take the risk. Chinese SIGINT will be slow to catch on, if they even do."

"We don't really know that."

"Boss, this is the best way."

"Fine, just make sure you guys take precautions. And be sure that she's not telling anyone else what she's really up to."

"Wilco. The Venezuelan soldier guy's going to park his jeep behind her barracks, where it won't be easy to see. He doesn't want anyone knowing he's there either."

"How can you trust them?"

"Well, the only one who knows what's going on is the pregnant mess hall girl. She and I have an understanding."

"An understanding? Plug, tell me you didn't..."

"What? No. Skipper, come on. I mean, my schedule doesn't allow it for one thing. We're locked up most of the day. Besides, I have my chivalry to uphold. She's obviously in love with her husband, the head scientist."

"Her husband is the head scientist?"

Plug looked at her like she was living on another planet. "Yeah, you know. She has been trying to convince all of us that he's super-valuable to the American military or something. How have you not heard about this yet? Jeez. Our tap code telephone game is failing."

Victoria said, "Plug, can you find out what her husband is working on over in that building?"

"Maybe, why?"

"I might want to change the Morse code transmission."

22

PLA Headquarters
Beijing

Lena walked down the hallway toward her father's office.
Armed guards stood at attention on either side of the entrance.
Seeing Lena, one of them held open the door as she passed into
the waiting area. Inside, multiple secretaries and staff officers
hustled every which way, making phone calls or speaking
urgently.

The waiting area was crowded with military personnel,
each nervously awaiting his meeting slot. Doors opened and
closed in the outer offices. The comings and goings of round-
the-clock appointments with the senior staff. Or, if the patrons
were *very* important, they might just have an audience with
General Chen himself, the highest ranking general in all of
Asia.

"Hello, daughter."

General Chen stood in his inner office doorway. Lena
noticed that everyone in the waiting area was standing at atten-

tion in silence, respect and fear reflected in their eyes. Her father was becoming more powerful. She must remember that.

"Good morning, General." She stood at attention as she greeted him, fingers straight, in the fashion of the Chinese military.

"Come," he called, and turned to enter his private office.

She nodded and followed, closing the door behind them.

"It is so good to see you." General Chen gave a rare smile.

Lena remained stone-faced. His motives were transparent to her. Any affection he displayed for her now was a charade. She had become important to him, maybe for the first time in her life.

But the moment that changed, his false affections would end. Men like her father didn't care about anything, even their only child. General Chen was consumed with self-aggrandizement and the need to amass power. In her experience as an intelligence operative, such men made excellent targets.

"Chairman Cheng is pleased with your progress with the Russians."

"I serve China, General."

"The Russian president has asked to meet. He wants to discuss terms."

Lena raised an eyebrow. "Is that so?"

General Chen continued. "We must send a representative. I am delegating that task to you."

Lena's mind raced. Her father watched her reaction.

"The chairman wants me to go?"

"I said I am delegating the task to you."

Jinshan would have given her this information in person. He must have given this assignment to her father.

"As you command, General. Will anyone be accompanying me?"

"You are not a child anymore, Li. You should not require an

escort." He shuffled papers on his desk, looking away from her piercing eyes. "And I am not a servant, sent to do the bidding of a dying man. And I haven't the time to negotiate with that Russian egomaniac."

The last part was quickly muttered, but it explained everything. This was classic behavior for her father. He didn't like being told what to do. Jinshan's short time remaining was no longer sufficient to command his fear, and fear was her father's only true motivation. Right now, he feared the Russian president defeating him in a diplomatic negotiation.

General Chen snapped, "You must make sure we get the Russians to share the weapons research I have requested."

Lena said, "I understand, General. Chairman Jinshan has military objectives he wants the Russians to assist us with. Given the importance of the meeting, I request some time with your senior staff to go over our military details so that I may better serve."

General Chen waved his hand. "Yes, yes. Of course."

Lena said, "Then I shall be going..."

"Wait. There is another matter we must discuss. Dong."

Lena's heart skipped a beat. Did her father already know what she had seen?

"Well?" he asked. "What have you found out?"

Lena felt her father studying her face, gauging her loyalty. She knew that one day soon, Jinshan would die and she would be forced to choose a side. General Chen or Minister Dong. The two factions of power beneath Jinshan were both licking their lips, waiting for his death so they could transform Secretary Ma into their figurehead puppet.

Her father wanted Lena to remain in both blocs. He wished to use her as his spy, and her actions over these next few weeks would decide her fate. The image of her child once again flashed into her mind's eye. A child she had left behind in a land that China could soon invade.

She looked at her father and said, "Minister Dong met with someone recently. Someone he shouldn't have."

The next day, while on a flight to Russia, Lena pondered her predicament. She had decided to give her father only a partial summary of her discovery. A breadcrumb that would give her wiggle room while she decided which road to take.

She looked out the aircraft window, thinking of where this left her. Thousands of feet below was Siberia's taiga forest, a vast land of tall pines and spruce trees. Mountains, lakes, and streams as far as the horizon. It was beautiful, and part of her wished to be there, clean and free.

"We will be landing soon, Miss Chou," said the military aircrewman as he walked down the aisle.

She acknowledged him and checked her seatbelt, her thoughts returning to the binding chains of duty and honor.

Lena knew that it was dangerous to give her father *any* information suggesting Dong might be working for the Americans, unless she was certain how he would use it. So she hadn't told him that she believed Dong was meeting with an American agent. She hadn't even said that the person of interest worked in the Japanese embassy.

Lena had informed her father that Dong was meeting with someone in secret, and that she would have the person's identity soon. General Chen was understandably dissatisfied with that level of detail, but she had promised him that she would meet with Dong in person and gather more information upon returning from Russia.

A personal meeting with Minister Dong would give her a

chance to probe him. Lena would have to invent an innocuous reason to be granted an audience with him. She could say Jinshan wanted her to personally brief him on the outcome of her Russia visit. Before Lena decided what to do next, she wanted to find out whether Dong was working for the Americans or running one of them as a double agent of the MSS.

Lena felt the wheels skid as the aircraft touched down on the runway, a remote airfield in Siberia, mostly used by the president and oligarchs for luxury getaways. Moments later she was riding in the back of a four-wheel-drive truck as it headed up a winding mountain road. Gargantuan pine trees provided shade overhead as they drove.

The Russian president's hunting cabin was magnificent. Spectacular mountain views. Ornate decorations. A mansion fit for a czar.

Upon arrival, Russian security forces searched Lena and escorted her into the home. Kostya met her on the back patio, where a wood fire burned in a circular pit surrounded by cushioned outdoor sofas. A wheeled food cart with drinks and covered platters rested nearby. Two waiters stood out of earshot, and dozens of security guards patrolled within sight. Many more out of visual, she was sure. The Russian military presence at the airfield had been impressive. A message. The Russian president projecting strength.

Kostya looked nervous when he saw her.

"Where is your father?"

Why would he ask that? Had he not been told she would be taking the general's place? Lena felt the heat of embarrassment and anger rise up inside and silently cursed her father. His lack of thoughtfulness and poor communication might ruin the meeting, costing their nation an important military alliance.

She gathered her composure. "Unfortunately, General Chen had an unmissable operational responsibility come up. I assure you that I have all the necessary authority and knowledge needed to..."

"Lena, are you fucking crazy?"

She glanced over at the mansion doors. Some of the security men were now scurrying about.

Kostya said, "Our president came out here with the expectation that he was meeting China's senior military commander. The only reason he agreed to that was because there is a *chance* your father might become vice president when Cheng Jinshan passes away. The moment you stepped off the plane by yourself, my president was notified. He almost left for Moscow right then and there. I did everything I could to convince him to stay, but now my reputation is at stake."

"I understand."

Outwardly Lena remained calm. She ran through her options. Her leverage hadn't changed.

"Here he comes."

Lena turned toward the cabin. The president and a few bodyguards walked toward them from the north wing. As they approached, Lena casually removed the pin holding her hair in a bun. She brushed her hand through her hair, allowing it to fall over her shoulders and hoping she wasn't being too obvious. She also unzipped her jacket and discreetly unbuttoned the top of her blouse. Just a bit of cleavage. The Russian president was a man of virility. He appreciated beautiful things. Then she remembered the scars that ran from the side of her face down her body. They were healing, but still unsightly. She sighed.

"Mr. President, may I present to you Lena Chou, of the People's Republic of China."

The Russian president, his lips pressed together in an expression of boredom or frustration—Lena couldn't tell which —nodded once. His eyes ran over her face, and then her body, if only briefly.

He spoke to her in Russian. Lena spoke several languages, but Russian was not one of them. A translator stood between them, relaying the conversation in Mandarin.

"The president wants to know why General Chen has not shown up."

Lena explained and apologized profusely, then said, "I have been given full authority to speak on my nation's behalf."

The Russian president spoke more, and the translator said, "How much longer until China gets a new leader?"

Kostya looked at her.

"Soon," she said, staring into the Russian leader's blue eyes.

The president began speaking in heavily accented English. "You were an intelligence officer. You were the one who was placed in the CIA, yes?"

Lena nodded. "Yes, Mr. President. Like you, I was an intelligence officer." A stroke to his ego.

A glimmer in his eye. His chin rose up a touch more as he said, "It is cold. Let us sit by the fire and discuss how we may work together."

They ate as they spoke. Servants brought trays of tapas and expensive wine, but Lena refrained from the latter. The more the Russian president drank, the more his eyes slipped to her cleavage. But it was her words that truly helped her cause. She was an expert at manipulation. Convincing men of power to do things for her.

Two hours later, the Russian president finished his drink and stood. Lena and Kostya stood with him.

The president said, "I am pleased with our discussion. I see that there are ways in which our nations can work together for mutual benefit. But the fact remains: General Chen was supposed to meet with me. He chose not to, and that is a sign of disrespect."

He stared at her, and for a moment Lena thought he was

going to say the deal was off. But then he continued, "If your country wants to send you as its representative, fine. So be it. From now on, Russia will work with China through you, and only you. No matter who is in charge of your country, all Russian assistance will now flow through you, Miss Chou. Is this clear?"

Lena said, "Absolutely, Mr. President. I will pass along your message to my leadership."

23

Chase traveled by C-17 from the US to Mexico City International Airport. For all intents and purposes, Mexico's four largest airports had been handed over to the US military. Air traffic control was now run by the US Air Force, and all flights had to be approved by the SOUTHCOM Air Operations Center (SAOC) flight schedule. Very little commercial traffic existed here anymore, but the airport was filled with a steady flow of military transports, fighters, and helicopters conducting round-the-clock flight operations.

Chase was placed on a US Air Force V-22 for his next trip. As the aircraft lifted off, flying low over the airport, he marveled at the sheer number of American military aircraft and personnel below. Mexico City International Airport was now home to thousands upon thousands of American soldiers. Tanks and Stryker vehicles formed caravans, then headed south on the highways. Skies were filled with dark green helicopters, like flocks of geese heading south for winter.

But the helicopters were heading south for war.

Chase's V-22 trip lasted several hours. Eventually the aircraft began circling a small military camp tucked within Costa Rica's jungle-covered mountains. The small fort was only a football-field-sized cutout in the tree line. US military vehicles parked along a paved road running one mile to the west, providing security while another convoy of military vehicles transited south.

The V-22 touched down in the landing zone, the rotors kicking up swirls of brush. Chase exited, heading to the command tent. The camp was home to several SOF teams. Chase met up with the DEVRU commanding officer shortly after arrival, who introduced him to a few other members of the team.

"Most of the guys are in the rack right now." He nodded toward the tent city on the outskirts of the rainforest. "We'll be training tonight and then heading further south tomorrow."

"Where to?"

"Looking like Panama. Chinese airborne troops have arrived in the southern sectors there. Intel says they'll be defending SAM sites and supply depots for the larger contingent of regulars. SOUTHCOM is prepping a list of targets and future targets. I'm sure the Chinese are doing the same. Go get settled in. Brief's at eighteen hundred. Make sure to get chow beforehand."

"Yes, sir."

Chase headed over to the DEVGRU tent and threw his green nylon sea bag on top of an empty cot. The room was dark, hot, and humid. About a dozen men were inside, most sleeping, some reading or listening to music. He could hear the loud call of jungle insects and birds outside.

By eighteen hundred Chase was fed, geared up, and ready to go. A CIA man wearing a T-shirt and cargo pants was leading the intel brief. He was speaking with the CO as everyone took their seats.

"Gentlemen, we have a change of plans. We've just received

new intelligence. An NSA listening station just received a Morse code transmission. It stated the names of several American prisoners and added two words. Hypersonic testing. We think we may have found our missing scientist."

Chase said, "Who sent the signal?"

"We don't know yet. Could be a CIA asset in the country who's gone underground. Or a foreign national sympathetic to our cause."

"Could it be a trap?"

"That's unlikely. The transmission was sent in an unusual way. It was automatically relayed by multiple Venezuelan military beacons. Our guess is that this wasn't intentional. The operator might not have known what they were doing. The result was both good and bad. If the radio transmission hadn't been sent that way, we might not have detected it."

"And the bad?"

"We can't be sure of the point of origin. But we were able to narrow it down to about a dozen sites."

One of the SEALs said, "What's the mission?"

"We're going to have to search each one of the possible broadcast points. You'll hit one tonight. From the sound of it, we'll uncover American POWs and the scientists at the same site."

"Any ISR support?"

"Negative. Not tonight. So be careful when you're shooting. By next week, we'll have better aerial coverage."

The brief lasted another forty-five minutes, until the sun had fully set. The team had a fifteen-minute break before the heavy beat of rotors began reverberating throughout the mountains. The helicopters—three MH-60Ms—arrived and landed with their lights off in the dark grassy landing zone. Chase stood at the rear of the team, waiting.

On a silent signal, the team began jogging toward the birds.

Each man wore a set of four-tubed night vision goggles clipped to his helmet, fixed in the up position. Chase carried a modified M4. The weapon's upper receiver was shorter than normal, his preference in urban combat situations. The rifle also had a PEQ-15 infrared laser mounted at the end of the rail, just above the suppressor.

Their helicopter flight time was a little over an hour. The time was spent jostling in darkness, mentally walking through the mission. Eventually the guy sitting next to him tapped Chase on the shoulder, motioning for him to snap his goggles into place. Chase flipped the NVGs down and reached back to make sure the switch was on. The helicopter cabin glowed green.

"One minute out," yelled one of the Army aircrewmen. He aimed a GAU-21 minigun out the cabin window as another aircrewman slid open one of the cabin doors and began prepping the rappelling rope. Through his goggles, Chase saw the other two Blackhawk helicopters pitching up to slow. He felt a flutter in his stomach as their aircraft did the same and they all began descending at a steep angle.

Soon the helicopters were hovering over a field. Chase stood crouched and began moving toward the cabin door, following the men disappearing into the blackness as grass and nearby tree leaves were being whipped by the rotor wash below. Now it was his turn.

Swinging his legs around once to use his boots as a brake, he gripped the rope with his gloved hands and then slid down to the earth.

He landed with a thud, doing his best to cushion with his knees, and then sprinted to keep up with the rest of the team, already fanning out among the long grass as they moved toward the huts to their east.

Through his NVGs, Chase could see over a dozen PEQ-15 lasers bouncing around in the night, aiming toward the huts.

His visual scan caught rapid movement in the shadows. Men with rifles. PLA soldiers, taking cover near the buildings.

The gunfire began.

Quiet spurts of suppressed fire from either side of him. The PLA soldiers dropped.

The team of special forces operatives continued pumping their legs, moving closer. Movement. Laser on target. Fire multiple rounds until the target was down. Repeat.

Within minutes, the SOF team killed five PLA soldiers, searched the three small buildings, and recovered a hostage before hustling back toward the landing zone. The circling Blackhawks timed their landing for a simultaneous arrival, and the DEVGRU team jumped aboard with minimal time on deck.

The aircraft took off at max power, nosing over and gaining speed, but keeping their altitude low over the trees as they flew back to the north. In the aircraft, Chase could see one of the SEALs using an eye and fingerprint scanner to identify the hostage, taking pictures of his face before putting a cover back over his head. The hostage remained blindfolded, hands bound.

After landing, the hostage was taken to the CIA tent, and Chase joined the unit commanding officer for the debrief.

"It wasn't him," the CIA man said.

Chase cursed.

The next day, Chase and the CIA officer were called to Panama to brief the general in charge of US Southern Command, or SOUTHCOM. Chase was interested to hear that General Schwartz had been promoted and assigned to the position.

The general and his staff had taken up camp at a makeshift

Army airfield resting on a stretch of hill country half a dozen miles north of Panama City. From their vantage point, they could see the canal and a great deal of military movement.

"That's 25th Infantry over there. Stryker Brigade."

Chase looked out at the road. Several dozen M1126 Infantry Carrier Vehicles rolled along the road. A jet rumbled in the distance.

One of the nearby staff officers held one side of a headset to his ear. He said, "General Schwartz, sir, I think it's about time to move you north. Multiple PLA ground units have been spotted by our scouts, sir. It's about to begin."

"That's why I'm here," he replied, not taking his eyes away from his binoculars.

Chase admired the fact that the general, now the first American promoted to the five-star rank in half a century, had come to the front lines. But Chase also recognized when a senior officer was letting bravery overcome logic.

General Schwartz peered through his set of binoculars, ignoring the call to evacuate. "What happened on the raid?"

The CIA man said, "Sir, it wasn't him last night, but we have a few other possible locations. We'll need to task a different SOF team, however. The DEVGRU team has new tasking."

General Schwartz turned to face Chase and the intelligence officer.

"Why were they recalled? What's more important than retrieving that hypersonic scientist?"

Chase said, "Sir, the Silversmith team specifically requested DEVGRU for a special assignment."

General Schwartz grunted and looked back through the binoculars. "All right. Get another Tier One team on it. We need to find this damn guy…"

A flight of A-10s roared overhead, banking sharply over the mountains and leveling out in the direction of the city. Even from miles away, he could hear the *brrrrrrttt* of their GAU-8 Avenger 30mm cannons. A stream of yellow tracers fired out from each A-10's nose-mounted weapon, heading toward ground targets. This was followed by popping sounds and explosions in a distant tree line across the Panama Canal. Yellow and black balls of flame burst through the green jungle canopy that had been hiding Chinese armor.

General Schwartz wiped the sweat off his brow. "Well, gentlemen, there it is. The battle has started."

The staff officer, still holding the headset to his ear, said, "Sir, J-2 is reporting Chinese air mobilization. We have to get you out of here, sir. I must insist." The staff officer glanced at a pair of special operations troops nearby who were acting as the general's personal bodyguards.

Now Chase could hear gunfire erupting throughout the city. He turned to see a group of Chinese infantry vehicles parked across the canal. They opened up with their chain guns, and a pair of American Stryker vehicles began taking fire.

General Schwartz said, "Tell the forward air controller to call those A-10s down on that position." He pointed toward the Chinese infantry vehicles.

"Roger, sir," the staff officer called, relaying information into his radio.

The A-10s looped around, resembling flying crosses as they made their way in for another pass.

Then they were gone.

A pair of Chinese surface-to-air missiles shot up from somewhere in the city and detonated next to the aircraft. Chase watched in horror as pieces of the A-10s fell to the earth.

One of the special forces men walked up to the general, tapped him on the shoulder, and said in a calm voice, "Sir, we need to evacuate."

The beating of rotors overhead caused Chase to glance to

his left. A flight of Apache gunships hovered only half a mile away, masking themselves with the terrain before popping up for their attack. The Apaches' yellow tracer rounds began firing down toward the Chinese ground units, followed by streaks of rockets, which exploded into the Chinese infantry vehicles.

This time Chase saw the surface-to-air missiles. Barely, as they were impossibly fast.

The Chinese SAMs scored direct hits on both of the Apache helicopters. The army aircraft exploded into balls of flame and black smoke, their wreckage falling hundreds of feet to the ground only a football field distance from where Chase stood.

"Get all further air support out of here, now!" General Schwartz shouted.

One of his staffers relayed a series of commands on a radio.

Another section of Apache helicopters appeared over the mountains, heading toward the city. They fired a slew of missiles and rockets, scoring multiple hits before they began banking and diving away, letting out bursts of chaff and flares as they went. Chinese anti-aircraft guns were firing at them as they departed.

"Sir, Chinese air is a few miles away. There, at your one o'clock."

"In sight." General Schwartz picked up his binoculars again, and Chase followed his gaze. A group of Chinese attack helicopters was approaching from the south. They flew north over the beach, heading toward the Bridge of the Americas, just outside the Panama Canal Zone.

Chase watched as the Chinese helicopters began exploding, one by one, as American surface-to-air missiles launched from a nearby hillside. The CIA man next to him pumped his fists wildly.

The city was now alive with the rattle of heavy machine gun fire. Buildings smoked as troops and military vehicles from both sides began moving through the area. First-world urban combat leveling city blocks with weapons meant for the enemy.

A nearby hill where the American air defense missiles had launched burst into smoke and flame. The sound wave of the bombs detonating on their position hit Chase soon after, followed by a roar of jet engines overhead. Chase looked up, ducking instinctively. He could barely make out the dark shadows of what he assumed were Chinese attack aircraft ten thousand feet overhead.

Another shadow chased the first two. Soon the lead pair of aircraft were transformed into smoking fireballs as an American fighter jet scored two kills.

The battle was coming alive all around him. A war like he had never witnessed before. Two first-world militaries destroying each other with the latest generation of weapons technology. It was sensory overload.

A series of explosions from the Panama Canal lit off in the distance, followed shortly by the sound waves.

"Sir, the EOD team just detonated the Panama Canal locks."

"Roger." General Schwartz's face was grim.

The fighting had reached the bridge. Several Chinese tanks had formed up on the far side and were firing at American units to the north.

"Sir, we're in range of those tanks."

The general nodded. "Shit. All right, let's go." He began walking toward the Stryker command vehicle parked nearby. Chase and the CIA man joined him, and they headed to the north.

The Battle for Panama had begun.

24

NAS Pensacola

David stood on the watch floor of the Silversmith operations center, now located in the old Blue Angels building. Several rows of computer monitors were manned by Silversmith team members, a mix of military and intelligence types monitoring the start of combat operations in Central America.

"Morning, David," Susan Collinsworth said. She was standing with her arms crossed near the center of the room, watching updates on multiple screens.

"Morning, Susan. This just happen?" He pointed to a screen to his right showing video imagery from one of the American ground units. Tracers fired from across the Panama Canal at Air Force attack aircraft.

An Army officer on a computer terminal nearby said, "It's less than thirty minutes old."

Susan nodded. "China is attempting to move their forward-most infantry divisions across the canal. Fighting has erupted in Panama City."

David blew air out of his mouth. "I wish we had more time."

The Army officer turned to Susan. "25th Infantry Stryker Brigades have troops in combat now. Air assets are having a hard time getting close due to heavy Chinese air defense coverage."

"Thank you, Major."

Susan and David stepped away from the watch floor to speak privately. She said, "This is going to get ugly fast. It's turning into urban warfare in Panama City, and jungle warfare in the surrounding hills as American and Chinese units try to outflank each other. Our big moves over the next day will happen fast. But the aftermath won't be quick. Our military experts believe there will be a months-long ground standoff."

David said, "What can I do?"

"You do exactly what General Schwartz asked of us. Work on your special projects. The people in this room will keep me appraised of the status of combat operations. From here, we will look at the situation on the ground, see how it fits into the bigger strategic picture, and then feed information to the appropriate parties."

David nodded. "I'm headed down the hall after this."

"Good. I'll be down later today."

David left Susan and headed to the building's east wing, where his teams were assembled.

After his Camp David discussion with General Schwartz, David had been placed in charge of Silversmith's special projects division. Of Silversmith's several hundred members, about half knew of The Special Project's existence. And among them, the name was shortened to just The Project.

There were no computer documents describing the program. No paper trail that politicians on the Intelligence Committee could read about or Chinese operatives could hack into.

If The Project was to work, no one could know about it. Its plans would be carried out as orders issued by General Schwartz, or one of the other recently promoted combatant commanders. It was amazing how easily a fifth star could move mountains.

But first, David and his team needed to create the plan.

Two dozen men and women were working on The Project team, and they were all living on base, under heavy security, until further notice. The group included some of the best minds the country had to offer in the areas of defense and intelligence. David had also recruited top-level talent from outside the government. Six team members were brainiacs from private sector companies. The Whiz Kids of their generation.

David couldn't help but be reminded of a similar group he had been part of a few years earlier, set to work on a Pacific island under Lena Chou's supervision. With this group, he had taken a page out of her playbook.

On the first day, David had sat everyone down and asked them a series of what-if questions.

"What if China takes Hawaii? Panama? Alaska?"

"What if China perfects their hypersonic weapons program before us? What if we perfect ours first?"

"What if the Chinese army continues to move north through Central America? What if we defeat them in the Battle of Panama?"

These led to some second-level questions.

"How will the Russia-China relationship change as China gets more powerful?"

"What weapons programs do we have that would make the biggest impact on stopping a Chinese advance?"

Each question was designed to uncover new insights. To understand the situation in a deep and accurate way. To question every assumption and turn the current war strategy on its head. From these conversations, they could uncover new solutions and strategies to pursue.

After the first day, David divided the team into smaller groups, each tasked with separate objectives. The group leaders were to summarize findings on a good old-fashioned chalkboard in each room. The limited space forced them to get specific on actionable strategies.

Each day David floated among the groups, listening to the conversations and offering his own questions and ideas. He gathered the entire Project team together each day to see how their individual group plans could be intertwined and strengthened. David and Susan then passed on information and recommendations to General Schwartz so he could take action.

Now David joined the first group in their huddle room.

"Morning, ladies and gentlemen." Three engineers and a Marine colonel with a PhD in astrophysics greeted him. Three members of the group sat facing the chalkboard, with the fourth standing, leading the discussion. This group was tasked with identifying new military technology innovation that could be scaled to gain an immediate, major advantage over China. About as easy as coming up with a new billion-dollar invention.

"Morning, David," said Kathleen Marshall, the team leader. She'd been plucked from one of the big tech firms, and was arguably one of the top artificial intelligence experts in the world.

"Morning, Kathleen. Progress?"

"We narrowed it to these four." She pointed to a dozen technologies listed on the board with notes scribbled next to each one. All but four had a line through them.

David said, "You've crossed out R.O.G. Remind me what that stands for?"

"Rods of God," one of the other engineers explained.

Another said, "The tech sounds great, but there's a weight

issue. Tungsten and other heavy metals would be best, and the energy-to-mass ratio needed to get them in orbit is a major barrier."

The Marine colonel said, "Not to mention that the moment we launch en masse, Russia and China would detect it and probably see it as an ICBM launch."

David said, "Noted. But remember, the physics should be your reason for crossing it out. We have other teams working on countering enemy detection capabilities."

Kathleen said, "Hey, David, is it true that the fighting in Panama has begun?"

"Yes, it's true."

Forlorn faces around the room.

David said, "We'll give everyone an intel brief at today's team meeting. But we need to focus on this." He continued studying the board. "So, the four technologies you believe we should concentrate on are hypersonic weapons, robotics, AI, and directed energy."

Kathleen nodded. "Based on our research and team discussions, these technologies show the most promise. We've carved out specific ways we could use each one."

"I know I don't need to tell any of you this, but we have defense research and weapons programs in all of these areas," said David.

"Yes. Some of us in this room have worked on them. We've gathered the research data and status updates on all existing programs."

"If you had to pick one that would give us the biggest advantage the quickest, what would it be?"

Kathleen said, "No question. Hypersonics."

David recognized one of the DARPA scientists at the table, who said, "Your CIA briefer showed us the prototype of Chinese hypersonic cruise missiles. Six months ago, I would have said that the US was actually ahead of China on hypersonics developments. But the Rojas technology overcomes the heat issues. This will allow them to keep their medium-range ballistic hypersonic weapons and hypersonic cruise missiles at much higher speeds. And speed kills. The Rojas tech is a quick fix. The intelligence reports say that they are getting close."

David said, "What about our programs? Any progress on reverse-engineering the Rojas technology?"

"We have machinery that could spray on the new coating. But the materials science is like an art form. We need Rojas. If we had him, we could quickly upgrade our existing Hypersonic Glide Vehicles."

David pointed to the board. "What about the other technology options?"

"We have more work to do before we're ready to share anything on them," replied Kathleen.

"Keep working."

David departed the room and walked into the next. Inside, the second group stood around their own chalkboard beside a large screen showing the current positions of all US and Chinese forces in the globe.

Five men and two women were in this group, each hand-picked strategists and tacticians. Two were recruited internally from the Silversmith team, a CIA operations officer and a DIA analyst. Three were military officers sent from different Pentagon and Combatant Commander staffs. These officers were intimately familiar with the latest battle plans and organizational capabilities. Together, this group consumed intelligence reports like a bunch of Wall Street floor traders analyzing the moving stock ticker.

"Morning, team," David said as he entered the room. Nods and waves in reply. Their faces were somber. This group knew very well that American forces were now in contact with the enemy in and around Panama, adding even more urgency to their work.

The DIA analyst, PJ Everett, was their team leader. A retired Army WO5, Everett had spent six months retired before getting bored and accepting a position in the DIA, thus beginning a long and distinguished second career. He had a buzz cut surrounding a shiny bald patch, and he spoke in a deep baritone.

"Mr. Manning, we've identified four different COAs." David searched his memory for military acronyms. COA. Course of Action.

"Let's hear 'em," he replied.

"COA 1: outproduce. Similar to the World War Two transformation of American manufacturing facilities into a wartime machine."

"This is being done."

"Yes, sir, that is correct." The man was ten years his senior, and probably outranked David's own GS rating, but he used the word *sir* with punctilious courtesy. A habit no doubt developed from decades of military service. "Our nation has ramped up manufacturing. Our automobile factories are now producing tanks and Stryker vehicles. Our cargo ship builders are now making warships. The same transformation has occurred with other factories, increasing our production rate of aircraft, guns, ammunition, and missiles."

The woman next to him said, "And we've reinstituted the draft. That's helped. Ramped up military personnel training and shortened pipelines."

David could see where this was going by reading their body language and tone. "But...you are about to say that's not good enough."

The DIA man shook his head. "Not even close. The Chinese simply have too many men, too many factories, and too many resources. Their rare earth mines are years ahead of ours. Over the past few decades, China has become the world's manufacturer. They have an enormous head start on us. And their capacity is unmatched. Even if we were to cut every corner and put every able-bodied American to work in our converted war factories, it still wouldn't be enough."

"So..."

"So, we continue to do the best we can. Following COA 1 to the best of our ability will help us stay in the fight as long as possible. But it won't win us the war. So, on to COA 2: stretch out the invading nation's supply chain. Are you familiar with the name Operation Barbarossa?"

David said, "Remind me. Germany invading Russia, right?"

The DIA man said, "Originally named Operation Fritz, it was the code name for the German invasion of the Soviet Union, launched in 1941. Germany attacked with almost one hundred and fifty divisions, or about three million men. It was the largest land invasion in human history."

One of the Army officers in the room said, "Until now."

The DIA man nodded, looking between his colleague and David. "The Chinese have just made contact in Panama. That is the tip of their spear. Behind that, we estimate nearly *four million* Chinese troops are already in South America. And that number is growing every day, by sea and by air. They are expending an enormous amount of money and resources transporting their army into South America. Because they know that if they do, they will be able to move north and overwhelm us."

David said, "This is where you're going to tell me the good news, right?"

The DIA man gave a terse smile. "Back to Operation Barbarossa. The German supply line was stretched out over thousands of miles. A subzero winter brutalized German troops, many of whom didn't have winter uniforms. But Hitler was told that Moscow was within their reach. So, with the Führer demanding action, German tank divisions ran out of fuel trying to accomplish their mission."

David said, "And do you see a similar opportunity for us?"

"Weather was a major factor, and we won't have winter on the battlefield unless the PLA makes it to the continental US."

"At which point things would likely be going downhill for us."

"Yes. But the Chinese do require a massive supply line across the Pacific, and through South and Central America."

"I'm familiar with this part. The Chinese have been building the infrastructure for that supply line for decades," David said. Natesh and the other Red Cell members had reviewed the details at length. Chinese businesses, with the blessing of the Chinese government, had been investing in roads, railways, airports, and ports in Latin America for the past twenty years.

The DIA man said, "While the Latin American geography does present us with certain opportunities, we believe that cutting off their naval supply lines in the South Pacific is also an opportunity. The Chinese-controlled factories in South America won't be enough to support their massive army. The PLA will need to bring bullets and parts from Asia."

"Understood."

The DIA man said, "This is where COA 1 and 2 come together. If we're emphasizing military production, we've identified one conventional weapon that will be crucial to our strategy: the LRASM. The Long Range Anti-Ship Missile."

"We've been using them," said David.

"Yes, but right now we're planning for single battles. If we are to shut down their supply lines across the Pacific, we'll need a massive increase in production and training. And we'll need to put those suckers on everything that can carry them. Soon."

"Understood." David pointed to the display map.

"PACFLEET has gathered forces at Hawaii, Johnston Atoll, and Midway. But we have to make tough choices. The more of our naval and air units we place on Hawaii, the fewer we have available to support our forces in Panama, and the fewer we have to defend the west coast of the US."

One of the military officers, a naval submarine commander named Kristopher Frigetto, said, "As far as our naval asset allocation goes, a lot will be determined over the next few days. The PLA fleet is about to make contact with our strike groups in the Pacific. If that battle goes our way, it could free up some of our ships, allowing us to advance south and disrupt Chinese Pacific supply lines."

Everett said, "Mr. Manning, I know many of our Pentagon planners. I guarantee that they are working on this. But our military has been trained to prioritize protecting troops in combat. A lot of generals will understandably want to mass our air and sea power near Panama, to support the troops on the ground there. That may be short-sighted. We must prioritize the destruction of Chinese supply lines, even at the risk of increased near-term casualties. I ask that you use your influence to emphasize its importance."

David nodded. "I'll bring this to General Schwartz's attention and explain the thought process."

The DIA man said, "Thank you." He turned to the chalkboard. "This brings us to COA 3: destroy China's domestic war engine. We must go after the Clausewitz trinity. The government, the people, and the military. We must destroy their desire and capacity to fight. This is the messy part that we must talk about. The history books don't glorify this, but the fire bombings in Japan and Germany had a major impact on the war. So did the use of nuclear weapons."

David began to feel uncomfortable. "POTUS won't authorize any further use of nuclear..."

The DIA man held up his hand. "I understand, and that's not what I'm suggesting. But we will need to take steps to diminish their national will to fight. Fire bombings and nuclear weapons are horrible methods, but the psychological and physical impact is significant. At a minimum, we will need to develop a strategy of destroying China's strengths: their domestic manufacturing capability and national will. That means bringing a large conventional fight to their turf. I understand that this could only be achieved if we first gain advantage in the Americas."

A knock at the door and Susan entered, sitting down as the door closed behind her. Nods of greeting from around the room. She said, "Sorry to interrupt. Please, continue."

David turned to the DIA man. "So in summary, for Susan, COA 1 is to outproduce China, which we think is impossible given our structural disadvantage. COA 2 is to stretch out their supply chain, which isn't *yet* possible given their uninhibited dominance of the South Pacific, but pending a potential military victory in the coming days it may be possible soon. COA 3 is to bomb the crap out of mainland China, which we can't do until we achieve a military foothold within range of an air campaign." David sighed. "That about sum it up?"

The DIA man said, "There's one more. COA 4: kill the Great Leader. If Jinshan is the driving force behind China's war, could we replace him with someone else we like better?"

David and Susan looked at each other, but neither spoke. Then David said, "Your suggestion is noted. That's all we will discuss regarding that matter."

The DIA man met David's gaze. Everyone knew what that meant, and all further conversation came to a halt.

David said, "All right, team. Thank you for the high-level ideas. Please start building out how we might accomplish each one, and what would need to be true." David and Susan left the room, stopping in the empty hallway outside.

———————

General Schwartz's plane, escorted by two F-15 interceptors, landed at NAS Pensacola and taxied up to the tarmac where David and Susan were waiting. When the general's plane lowered the stairway, David followed his boss inside.

General Schwartz was joined by a single staff officer who was told not to take notes.

"What have you got, David?" the general asked.

"LRASMs, sir."

"Long Range Anti-Ship Missiles?"

"Yes, sir. Right now we've got most of them deployed to the Pacific. The USS Ford's air wing and the Air Force jets in Mexico City are loading up for the coming engagement with the PLA Navy fleet off Panama."

General Schwartz said, "This sounds right..."

"This is going to use up over sixty percent of our country's LRASM inventory. We need to double production. Our special project team has developed a plan that will streamline output not just on the missiles but on fully mission-capable aircraft trained and loaded with those weapons. That is the key metric we'll need to boost. Our end goal isn't just to win next week's battle. We want to increase that key performance indicator—fully mission-capable aircraft, trained and loaded out with LRASMs—to a level one hundred times our current state."

General Schwartz said, "What do you need me to do?"

David turned to Susan, who handed the general a single-page document. Susan said, "We're going to need to pull back some of the aircraft deployed to the west coast. Send them to these three bases near Norfolk."

The staff officer said, "Admiral Funk is going to cry bloody murder."

General Schwartz nodded agreement. "The Pacific fleet is about to go into combat. They're going to need these aircraft and missiles when they come into contact with the enemy."

"We tried to only list units that were still INCONUS," David said. "California- and Texas-based aircraft, and ships already in the Atlantic. We're already working with the defense contractor to increase production. The bases listed will become hubs for training and ordnance installation. A lot of these aircraft will need maintenance to make them capable of using the LRASMs."

The staff officer said, "This will still eat up the reserve aircraft numbers, sir."

General Schwartz said, "You really think this is important enough to risk that?"

David nodded. "Yes, sir. We need to think long term. The Chinese supply chain across the Pacific should be our focus."

"Very well." He looked at the document. "You've got ships listed here too. These combined numbers are quite large. You won't be able to hide this. It'll ruffle some feathers."

"We know, sir."

The general grinned. "That's what I'm here for, right?"

"We appreciate your support, General." After he and Susan stood, David looked around the aircraft and said, "Where are you heading?"

"Central America. I want to get down there and speak to my commanders before it begins."

After the general's plane departed, Susan and David headed

back into the Silversmith building to meet with another special project group.

"Any word from Beijing?" David asked.

"Tetsuo sent his latest report this morning. Secretary Ma and Minister Dong have both met with Lena. In Jinshan's presence, no less."

"This is very good."

Susan said, "Yes, it is."

They reached the conference room of David's last team and entered to find a group of exhausted men and women. Bleary eyes. Frazzled hair. Empty coffee cups strewn about. They were arguing loudly enough that they barely noticed David and Susan enter.

Susan looked at David sideways. "Which group is this?"

"These are the space, satellite, and cyber geeks. They're the ones who are supposed to figure out how to overcome the surveillance, global positioning, and communications problems." They hailed from agencies like the NSA, NASA, DARPA, and the NRO.

David whistled to get their attention. "What's the problem?"

The arguing stopped and they looked at him. Several of them began talking at once, in what sounded like a foreign language. David knew technology and acronyms, but these guys were on another level.

He held up his hands and the group quieted down. "Can someone please translate?"

Karen Baltzley, a petite red-haired woman who had come to them from NASA, said, "We have an idea how we might be able to jam the new Chinese mini-satellites if they execute another mass surveillance launch."

Susan said, "That sounds like a good thing. Why are you at each other's throats?"

"We aren't able to execute the idea," Karen said.

One of the engineers was red-faced. "We'll figure it out eventually!"

"*Some* people don't want to admit that we need another team member." She glared across the table, and an overweight man in his late thirties frowned back.

Karen said, "We have a knowledge and experience gap. We need someone who's worked with both American and Chinese communications companies in the past couple of years, including their newer projects on mini-satellite constellation WiFi."

"Like the projects that one big tech company was going to launch...connecting the world with satellite WiFi?" Susan asked.

"Yes, exactly. Only a handful of people in the world know this stuff well from both the American and Chinese side. And most of them live in China."

The red-faced engineer said, "Where the hell are we going to find someone qualified to do that?"

David rubbed his chin. "You know, I may have just the man..."

Three hours later, David stood in a sunny parking lot near the beach, one foot on the Florida state line, the other in Alabama. In front of him was a dilapidated two-story wooden building that looked like it had been pummeled by multiple hurricanes. Next to it was a liquor store.

A giant American flag hung next to a sign that read "FLORABAMA Lounge and Package Store."

David was traveling with a pair of FBI special agents who helped track down his newest recruit. Now the three men were surrounded by sunburnt locals. Most were several drinks in.

One of the FBI agents smiled as a pair of bikini-clad women

walked toward the shore. "Guess we better head to the beach," he said.

They walked into the two-story wooden building, wading through the crowded bar inside. The scene was a blast from the pre-war world. David had been here once before when his sister was winged after flight school. The Florabama was one of the most famous Gulf Coast bars, and it was covered with local charm. Men in camouflage Bass Pro ball caps. Dueling Alabama and Auburn fans. Peroxide-blond women in American-flag bikinis sloshing beer in clear plastic cups.

"I could stay in here forever," remarked one of the FBI agents as they exited the rear of the building and stepped out onto a beach of sugar-white sand.

The other agent said, "It's almost like they don't know there is a war going on."

David said, "Oh, I think they're well aware."

On the beach, a large banner read "Florabama Mullet Toss: End of the World Party."

David said, "Ah, the fabled Mullet Toss."

"The Mullet Toss. I've heard of this…"

Ahead of them, the crowd density increased. In the center of a large group of beach-drinkers was a short, shirtless man in his late fifties. His chest hair would make Magnum P.I. proud.

"Henry Glickstein," David said. "He lives."

Henry had a pair of twenty-something women on each arm, and a smoking cigar between his teeth. Someone had provided him with a butchered mullet-style haircut—business in the front, party in the back. The mullet haircut was, creatively, the official hairstyle of the Mullet Toss.

A huge crowd of beer-guzzling beachgoers were gathered around a line of people in the sand. A master of ceremonies watched as they took large fish—mullet—from a plastic bucket and hurled them as far as they could, the fish landing in the sand. Each toss was measured for distance.

David and the FBI agents couldn't help but smile at the scene. Thousands of miles away, their country was engaged in the opening salvos of a Central American ground campaign. Even the US news sources were pessimistic, suggesting that the PLA could be in Texas by Christmas. But here, on the beach that joined Florida and Alabama, a crowd of Americans celebrated. Like it was their last chance to do so.

"David! David Manning!"

Henry had spotted his friend and was now stumbling over, cigar in one hand, beer in the other. One of the women at his side was taking her turn hurling the mullet, which slipped and landed in the sand at her feet. The other woman was watching and laughing, still connected to Henry, her hand running through his excess of curly chest hair. David tried to ignore that as they spoke.

"What are you doing here?" Henry frowned slightly, looking like he was trying to get both of the Davids to stay still and in focus. Then he noticed the two men in polos and khakis next to David. "Oh. You still working for *them*?" Like they were Area 51 men in black.

David said, "Henry Glickstein, it's good to see you again. Listen, I've got something I need you to take a look at. It's quite urgent. Can you come with us?" David looked him over and smiled. "We can get you some coffee."

A silver fish landed at their feet, kicking up a cloud of white sand. They all turned to look at the thrower.

"Sorry!" A woman wearing a wet T-shirt that read "War Damn Eagle" jumped and waved at them, her bosoms bouncing.

Henry was looking at her as he said, "David, what do you want me to look at?"

"Uh-hum. Henry, this is important."

He turned to face David. "Sorry. What do you want me to do?"

"We need your expertise. We can go over the details when we get there."

"Where's there?"

"Henry, trust me. It's a very interesting problem to solve. And you'll be doing your country a great service."

Henry's chin raised a notch higher as he took a pull from his cigar. He let out a cloud of smoke, unknowingly in the direction of one of the FBI agents, who began coughing. "Sounds interesting. Like a chance at payback, maybe?"

David winked.

Henry dropped to one knee and pushed the burning cigar into the dead fish lying in the sand. "I'm in."

"Henry! They're ready for you!" A handful of young, buxom women, all clad in matching camouflage bikinis, came running up to him, interlocking elbows and guiding him away. Henry turned his head and said, "But there's one thing I gotta do first..."

One of the agents said, "Who *is* this guy?"

The other added, "Yeah, and how do I become him?"

David and the agents watched as Henry was taken onto an elevated stage near the beach. A large contraption resembling a crane was connected to one end of the stage.

"What the hell is that?"

The master of ceremonies had just put a helmet, decorated to look like a fish, on Henry's head. Henry now sat in a chair with huge rubber bands on either side. A group of large tattooed men began pulling Henry's chair—with Henry in it—backward, the giant rubber bands getting taut as they stretched.

"What the..."

David said, "Oh *shit*..."

"That doesn't look safe."

David tried to look at the FBI agents but couldn't take his eyes off Henry. "Guys...should we?"

"I know we should stop this," one of the agents said, "but I have to see what happens..."

The crowd began chanting with Henry. "MULLET TOSS, MULLET TOSS..."

A guy in a hunting cap screamed, "Screw those damn Chicom bastards! They ain't ever gonna take the Florabama!"

The crowd was chanting wildly now as Henry, wearing both the fish helmet and an expression of determination, was pulled back nearly twenty feet in a catapult.

And then the men released their grip in unison.

Henry launched into air, limbs flailing, screaming like a little boy as his body flew toward the Gulf of Mexico.

The crowd roared into a climax.

Later, some local news reports would claim Henry reached an altitude of thirty feet. *The Pensacola News Journal* recorded the tossed distance as one hundred feet into the ocean. David didn't think it was that far. But there were a few fleeting moments between Henry slamming into the water and the jet-ski safety observers pulling him out when David wondered if the Silversmith team hadn't just lost one of the world's preeminent experts on satellite communications to a Florabama Mullet Toss.

25

The next morning Henry Glickstein sat with his legs propped up on a chair, surrounded by members of David's special project team. He wore sunglasses as he sipped a cup of tea, listening to the ISR and communications team's summary.

David was pleased that Henry, after some brief medical attention, made a full recovery from the human catapult he'd undergone in the name of Florabama mullet festivities. But looking at the room of skeptical scientists and defense experts, he wondered if Henry might have done a better job ingratiating himself.

Henry said, "You guys tell me if I'm getting this right. Here is the problem statement. A large Chinese military force is fighting us in Central America, and they are growing stronger by the day. Their mini-satellite constellations allow them a significant advantage over US forces during critical junctions. These mass satellite launches give the Chinese periodic access to GPS and secure datalink."

"Yes, that's correct."

"And our own satellite capacity is limited. This is the part that confuses me. It was something I didn't have to deal with. ASAT, is that what you said?"

One of the Air Force officers said, "Yes. Both the US and Chinese shoot down reconnaissance and communications satellites almost as fast as the other can put them into space. But the Chinese have created somewhat of an engineering marvel. On a small island near Hainan, the Chinese have a space launch system far beyond anything we have operational. It is a mechanism for massive mini-satellite launches. They can launch upwards of one thousand of them at a time. Their rockets, which are reusable, land at a base a few thousand miles away and are shipped back to the space launch facility for maintenance, reload, and relaunch. Each rocket is designed to be launched over fifty times before replacement is necessary. This decreases their cost per launch dramatically. So the constraints are the time to create all those mini-satellites, and the time it takes to get the reusable rockets back and set them up for the next launch. Right now, their cycle supports one mass satellite launch per month. When that happens, it creates a mesh network of datalink communications and ISR capability."

Henry sipped his tea and removed his feet from the chair in front of him. "Why don't you just blow it up?"

"Their space launch facility? We have tried. We lost two submarines attempting to get close. It's in a very strategic location, heavily protected by submarines and air defense, and near their coast. The only submarines that can get close enough are too important to risk with an attack."

The Air Force officer said, "We do have weapons that could strike it."

The scientist added, "Nuclear weapons, he means."

David nodded. "But for various reasons, we don't want to use them."

Henry slapped his knees, looking relieved. "Oh, thank God. I'm glad to see you all have at least some sense. But humor me, what are the reasons?"

"Aside from triggering a massive nuclear reaction from the Russians, nuclear winter, and the instant mass annihilation of fellow humans?"

Henry raised an eyebrow. "Is slow annihilation better?"

One of the civilian DOD experts said, "This is a larger strategic issue that speaks to the entire reason why the Chinese are able to come over here and attack us through conventional means. The political leverage they have is significant, and with the Russians pointing their own highly capable nuclear arsenal at us, the Chinese are not deterred. The Russians would love for us to lob another nuclear missile at China. It would give them the excuse they've been looking for."

Henry looked at the speaker. "You can't be serious. You think the Russians actually want that?"

The man shrugged.

Henry said, "What about conventional ballistic missiles?"

A female Air Force officer replied, "The problem is that any ballistic missile launch will be interpreted as a potential nuclear threat."

"And you can't use..."

David held up a hand. "Henry, trust us. We've been through a million different options. We need a way to disable the Chinese satellite advantage. And we need it soon. It's like a geyser. We don't know when it will let off steam, but when it does, it's quite impressive. And it's their tell. Whenever they make one of those mass launches, it's a critical time on the battlefield. If we can disable their ability to communicate and target using their satellite network, that would at least put us on an even playing field."

Henry removed his sunglasses, folding and stuffing them in his shirt pocket. "Well, I'm not going to lie. This sounds very challenging."

The group looked at him warily.

Henry finished, "You guys are lucky you called me when you did."

The NASA woman rolled her eyes.

The next day Chase arrived from Panama.

"How bad is it?" David asked.

Chase let out a sigh. "The worst I've seen. Panama City is a war zone. The Canal Zone stretches for fifty miles. That's become the front. All of the major bridges have been destroyed. The swampy jungles and farmland, the cities in the area...they're all crawling with US and Chinese divisions on either side lobbing mortars and artillery. Missile and rocket attacks."

Susan said, "Any sense on how it's going for us? Are we making progress?" Both David and Susan read the daily intel reports, but it was best to hear it from someone who had been on the ground.

Chase looked at her. "Both sides have put up modern air defense shields. Most air cover is useless, because it gets shot down as soon as it's picked up on radar. When I was with General Schwartz, we had to drive fifty miles north just to get to an LZ that was safe enough for a helicopter extraction."

David said, "What happened with the Rojas mission?"

Chase shook his head. "I accompanied a SOF team on a snatch and grab for one of our suspected hostage sites. Turned out to be someone else. Some local politician that the Chinese had taken to a safehouse for interrogation. General Schwartz understands the importance of finding Rojas. He told me to tell you that he's still working on it as a priority."

They entered the small auditorium where the Silversmith team held its daily intelligence brief. About halfway through, the briefer showed a slide of the Mid-Atlantic coastline, with large red patches over the ocean.

Chase leaned over and whispered to his brother, "Why are we talking about the Atlantic?"

David pointed at the screen.

The briefer said, "These are our areas of uncertainty. Passive sonar and other signals intelligence suggest that Chinese and Russian submarine activity has picked up in these areas. A Russian intelligence collection ship is also operating just outside our territorial waters."

Someone said, "Increased Russian submarine activity on the east coast of the US?"

The briefer said, "Correct."

Susan said, "Has there been any coordination between Chinese and Russian naval forces?"

"It does appear that way, yes, ma'am."

"That would violate the Russians' own agreement."

"Only if they are caught."

An Army one-star sitting in the front row said, "Tell them the good part, Jim."

The briefer said, "We got a signals intel intercept yesterday that suggests the Russians may be prepping for an attack on a US base."

Susan said, "Which one?"

"We don't know yet, ma'am. We'll pass on any new information on this intelligence stream as soon as we get it."

The meeting went on for a while longer, and after the group

was dismissed, Chase turned to his brother. "I'm headed to Norfolk."

David gave him a hug. "Be careful."

After meeting with Susan, David headed back to speak with his special project teams together.

"It will never work," said the NASA woman.

"It might," replied the DIA man.

"What might work?" David asked.

The DIA man said, "We're preparing for the next mass wave of Chinese satellites. Henry thinks he knows a way to infiltrate the Chinese satellite network."

David cocked his head and grinned at Henry. "And that's why we plucked you from the Mullet Toss. Show me."

"What's a Mullet Toss?" the NASA woman asked.

Henry ignored her and walked up to one of the white boards. "The island they conduct their mass satellite launch from is also their central command and communications center."

David nodded. "Meaning that all of the datalink and reconnaissance satellites get their orders from a ground station there. So..."

Henry said, "So it turns out it was built by one of the companies I consulted with. I'm very familiar with the systems they'll use. Now I can't write the program, but I imagine the NSA will have people who can."

"We do," the NSA cyber expert said.

Henry said, "They'll need my help, of course. I can guide them to develop something that can inhibit the Chinese military's ability to use their satellites."

"How long would it take for us to execute?"

Henry held up his hands. "Hey, I only know about these satellite communications..."

The NSA man said, "Depends on the system, but a typical op like this takes about a week to draw up, maybe another to write. We'd have it ready for the field in three. But that's if it's moved to the front of the line. And I can't speak for how we would actually get it *on* the Chinese network."

"No, no, I understand," David said. "That's still great. Good work. Please make it a priority."

Henry and the NSA man nodded and began whispering to each other.

David addressed the room. "Ladies and gentlemen, I applaud this progress. But this still means that we're weeks away from a solution. Suppose China crosses the Panama Canal tomorrow? What then?"

One of the Army officers said, "General Schwartz's plan has contingencies. American troops are massed in Costa Rica and again in Mexico City."

David waved his hand. "I know, I know. I just mean...we're always playing catch-up. They're playing the long game. Even if we defeat their satellites, the US military is at a huge numbers disadvantage in Central America. We need to be thinking about what's next. What if they breach Panama? Or Costa Rica? Or Mexico City?"

One of the Navy officers said, "*If* they get that far, it means we have big problems in the Pacific. It probably means the Pacific fleet has been defeated or has retreated."

An Air Force officer said, "Even if the Panama Canal is taken, we have the Atlantic fleet, and superior air power based on the east coast of the US in reserve."

The DIA man grunted, "Don't be silly. China will hit that

too. If they get past Costa Rica, China will have to begin launching air campaigns into the continental US. If there's a target, they'll go after it."

David thought about that. *If there's a target, they'll go after it.* An idea began forming in the back of his mind.

"What if China successfully disabled our east-coast-based air forces?" he said. "If they hit our Atlantic fleet? Then what would they do, if they had that advantage?"

The naval officer snorted. "Then the east coast would be screwed. I mean, they would probably attempt an amphibious landing somewhere in the Mid-Atlantic."

"The Gulf Coast would be easier," someone said.

David said, "Maybe we should start making recommendations for defensive fortifications along the coast?"

"We would be in the death spiral, at that point," an Army colonel chimed in. "Without air superiority, or a naval fleet? The reason we have a chance in Central America is because the geography limits their options to advance. But if our air power is gone, that allows the Chinese to start paradropping troops anywhere in the continental US. If they get container ships filled with troops and tanks, then we're really screwed."

The DARPA scientist said, "This brings us back to hypersonics. The only real way to neutralize the Chinese onslaught is to use the Rojas hypersonic technology. That's the great equalizer. We could wipe out their advance."

David rubbed his chin. He was right. The math was too heavily in the Chinese's favor. Rojas's technology could allow them to precisely hit hundreds of targets with hypersonic weapons. And it would only take a few hundred targets wiped out—radars, communications nodes, or some of their Jiaolong-class ships—to allow American air power to dominate what was left.

Henry said, "Even if you attain this mythical hypersonic weapons superiority you guys keep talking about, it sounds to me like you'll still need to worry about the Russians. Don't forget, they've still got nuclear weapons. Most of our long-range hypersonic weapons use ballistic missiles as a delivery vehicle. That still will look to Russia like we're launching nukes. So unless they're bluffing, which we probably won't want to test, they would lob nuclear weapons back at us."

The group sighed in unison. Someone threw a pen at the wall.

Henry crossed his arms. "What, I'm just saying? Pretending it's not there isn't going to make it go away. You need to take out the Russian nuclear threat as well. Otherwise none of this will work. Even your hypersonic weapons plan."

The DARPA scientist said, "We can't do that. There isn't a viable option to eliminate the nuclear threat."

Henry shrugged. "Why not?"

"You'll never get all of them," said a naval officer wearing a submarine warfare insignia. "We tried to wipe out all of China's nukes during the opening days of the war. We launched ICBM strikes on all of their known nuclear missile sites, and we attempted to destroy all of their strategic nuclear bombers and missile submarines. But about ten percent of their force remained. There are always unknowns. And that's just China. Now we're talking about Russia, too? That's significantly more targets and we have a reduced ICBM capability."

The Air Force missile expert said, "We're actively working on improving our missile force. We are working round the clock on that."

The volume of voices rose as everyone began yelling back and forth.

The DARPA scientist said, "We don't have to just use ICBMs."

"...but what about the HGVs...those could replace the..."

"...submarine drones might do the trick if we..."

David slapped his hand on the table. "Okay, okay. Hold up."

The room quieted.

He looked around at everyone. "What if we are able to wipe out 99.9% of all enemy nuclear weapons?"

The naval officer said, "David, like I said, we tried. If..."

"Humor me. Hypothetically speaking, what if we were able to do it. What would be left?"

"I would say best-case scenario we wipe out about ninety-five percent."

The Air Force missile expert said, "You know, that might be enough to get us over the tipping point."

David rubbed his chin. "Say more."

"This is getting into psychology here, but if we remove enough nuclear weapons from the equation, that could be the difference that causes them to rethink using them. You also must consider that all of their weapons won't be usable."

A Marine Corps officer and jet pilot frowned. "What do you mean?"

The missile man said, "How many military aircraft are in a jet squadron?"

"About ten."

"And how many are flyable at any given time?"

The Marine nodded in understanding. "Maybe five or six."

One of the civilians held up his hand. "There's that government waste again. That's awful. Only fifty percent are available to fly?"

David said, "No, that's normal. These are complex machines that require an enormous amount of maintenance to keep them operating." He turned back to the Air Force missile expert. "Let's say we can wipe out twenty-nine hundred of the three thousand nuclear warheads in Russia's arsenal. Talk me through it."

"Well, we'd need targeting information. But assuming we get it and destroy the targets, maybe half of the one hundred warheads left over are usable right away. Now a warhead is different than an operational weapon. A warhead doesn't have to be on a missile. It might be sitting in a bunker somewhere with no way to move to a target. So really, we're talking a much lower number. But let's say we're at fifty surviving warheads. Of those, many might not be set up on missiles that are ready to automatically fire. They may require hours or days of preparation until they're ready to be used."

The Marine said, "But how could we hit so many targets so quickly?"

David said, "PGS. Prompt Global Strike. The idea is that you can hit anywhere in the world within a half-hour or so. If we can get the Rojas technology, we might be able to make it work."

"Haven't we been able to do that for the past fifty years, with ICBMs?"

"Yes, but let's look at that for a moment. What's our real objective?" David asked.

"Ending the war," the NASA woman said.

"Winning the war, and having a planet left to live on..." the NSA man added.

David pointed at him. "Exactly. The use of ICBMs was always for nuclear weapons. But what if we could use ICBMs as a conventional weapon? Military tacticians use the term 'simultaneous time on top.' The idea is that all of your weapons hit their target at the same time."

The naval officer said, "The leftovers after a global strike on all enemy nuclear weapons would most likely be the enemy boomers. The handful of nuclear missile submarines hiding off our coast. If we're lucky, it will be just one or two. We'll hopefully sink the rest. But one or two boomers still leaves enough nukes to wipe out a huge part of the population and create a disaster."

The NSA man said, "Twenty-five nuclear warheads are enough to do serious damage in the hands of an unstable madman."

David's face hardened. "Then we must kill the madman too."

26

Minister of State Security Dong thought about what the American CIA officer working in the Japanese embassy had said to him. *Lena Chou wants the war to end. She is loyal to Jinshan but she will be rudderless when he succumbs to his illness. In the interest of peace, we must be sure that you, Minister Dong, maintain influence over Jinshan's successor.*

He looked at the thumb drive in his palm, the one the CIA officer had given to him during the meeting. Dong opened up his office safe and removed a laptop maintained especially for these purposes. The computer had no wireless connectivity and was hardened against even the most sophisticated electronic attacks. Normally it was used to view the extremely sensitive reports he received from MSS agents overseas. The thumb drive message was encoded with an older version of MSS crypto, a version the Americans had, unknown to the MSS, cracked. This was clever. If Dong was caught, he could say that a Chinese agent had passed him the information. The CIA was very careful not to give him anything that wouldn't fit that excuse.

Dong attached the memory stick that the CIA officer had provided during their last meeting. There was only one file.

Within seconds, he had scanned the entire five-page document, his eyes widening as he read.

Lena arrived at her home—a luxury apartment in Beijing—to find two MSS security service personnel standing guard outside the front door.

"Good evening, gentlemen," she said.

They said nothing, but one held open the door for her. Minister Dong was sitting on a sofa inside, speaking on a cell phone. Seeing her, he held up a hand, signaling her to wait. Lena mentally prepared herself for whatever this might be.

"Hello, Lena." Dong hung up the phone and stood to shake her hand. "I hope you don't mind that I've made myself a guest in your residence. I took the liberty of ensuring it was clean of any listening devices."

And probably inserted a few, Lena thought.

"I welcome the company, Minister Dong."

"Please, sit."

Lena set down her bag and took a seat across from Dong. They were alone in the house, and the security guards had closed the door. To her left, the city lights gleamed out her balcony window.

Minister Dong said, "I heard you have a new title. Special Liaison to the Russian Federation. How has your father taken the news?"

Lena considered her response. Deciding on the truth, she said, "Not well."

General Chen fumed when he read the official Russian communication. *All Russian military and intelligence matters must flow through the new Special Liaison's office.* He had understood what the Russian president was doing.

Dong said, "We will need the Russians if we are to prevail, I think. And now you once again have leverage."

"I wasn't aware that I'd lost it, Minister Dong."

Dong's lips curled into the beginning of a smile. "Not yet. But Jinshan is almost gone."

There it was. No one would say it out loud until now.

Jinshan had been her only connection to power, and the reason her father was paying attention to her. He was also the reason Dong didn't lock her up for suspicion of cooperating with the Americans. It appeared that her favor with the Russian president was a new lifeline. But Lena had another that Dong didn't yet know about.

It was time to use it.

Lena said, "How long have you been working for the Americans?"

Dong's smile faded.

Lena could see his pulse beating in his neck. A moment of silence turned into two. Then Dong said, "Why did the Americans let you go?"

"They didn't. I escaped."

"I don't believe that..."

Lena said, "You didn't answer my question."

"I can only assume that you misunderstood something you heard. Or saw."

Lena raised one eyebrow. "I saw."

Dong hummed. "I see. The agent in question is mine. He works for the MSS."

"Not the Americans?"

"He provides information to me. Because of him, I now know where American forces plan to consolidate their military."

There was a moment of silence as they stared at each other, Lena deciding how to respond.

She said, "Perhaps I should apologize, Minister Dong. I must have merely witnessed a meeting that, as you say, I didn't fully understand. Thank you for clearing it up."

"No need to apologize."

"What would you like to discuss?"

"Your next assignment."

Here it was. The carrot being dangled in front of her.

"What would you wish me to do, Minister?"

"I plan to be Ma's vice president when Jinshan passes. I ask that you support me. And stop this ridiculous quest your father sent you on. Spying on me?"

So, he knew the truth. Of course, he did. Lena's anger was stirring again. But not at Dong. She was annoyed with herself for again allowing her father to cloud her judgment.

"Lena, I must share something with you. It may be upsetting. I'm sure that it will be, in fact. But before I show you, I want you to know that you can trust me. I see your greatness, the same way Jinshan did. If you support me, I will return the favor tenfold. I intend to let you shine. But you must stop this nonsense with your father. You need to know who you are collaborating with, whether he is your blood or not."

Dong removed an envelope from his inner jacket pocket and handed it to her. Lena took the envelope and removed a single sheet of paper of a printed image, double-sided. Several document pages had been scanned onto the paper. Tiny print, but legible.

Her childhood name and picture.

She frowned. "What is..."

Lena continued reading and caught her breath. Her eyes fluttered over words that couldn't possibly be true.

Dong leaned forward, his hands clasped tightly together. "I know it must be shocking. But you need to know the truth. Jinshan will die. And when that time comes, you will have a choice to make. Many of us will. You will have to choose where your true loyalty lies. With your father, or me. But know this. Your father betrayed you in the worst possible way."

Her hands shook as she re-read the document.

"How do I know this is true? Why should I believe you?" Lena blinked back tears.

Dong cocked his head. "You know it is true."

And she did.

It made sense. Back then, she was just a girl. In those early days, she didn't know how these recruitments and manipulations were carefully staged. But now, seeing this...everything began to fit into place. In her hand was the Minister of State Security's documentation of her own Junxun recruitment. The psych profiling conducted when she was only fifteen, a year before the incident happened. The careful selection of certain boys with certain physical and psychological characteristics to be placed in her class. The whole operation was staged. They intentionally set up the conditions for one of the boys to rape or impregnate her so they would have leverage. So she would have to turn to the MSS for a way out.

She read the last section a third time, detailing how they would build her into an assassin, or toss her if she couldn't handle it. She was floored. The report contained details that no one could have known unless they were present.

Dong's voice was a whisper now.

"Your father betrayed you. He sold you to Jinshan to help relaunch a plateaued military career. You owe *nothing* to that man. Even now, you don't use your family name. Lena, I recognize you for who you are. I will continue to empower you and cherish your contributions. But I need your help. Jinshan and the Russian president have both given you power. And anyone with power to wield will have to make a choice when Jinshan dies. You must choose me over General Chen."

A buzz, and Dong picked up his phone from his chair's armrest. "This is Dong. Yes. Good. I'm coming now." He hung up, then said to Lena, "Good news. The naval battle has begun. I must go. I suggest you destroy that document. But remember what I said."

He turned and left.

Lena stared out the window at the night sky, her jaw clenched.

27

USS Delaware
200 nautical miles west of Panama

Captain Davidson and his crew knew this might be a suicide mission.

But if the American battle plan was to succeed, the Chinese Jiaolong-class warships needed to be taken out. And based on months of probing Chinese naval operations, PACFLEET felt this was their only chance.

Captain Davidson said, "Officer of the Deck, on our depth five-zero feet."

"Officer of the Deck, aye. Pilot all ahead one-third."

"All ahead one-third, pilot aye."

Captain Davidson watched his officers and crew perform their duties in the control room of America's newest fast-attack submarine. Much had changed since he was a junior submarine officer. His officer of the deck was a woman. Physical periscopes had been replaced by joystick-controlled photonic masts. The sonar room had been eliminated, its watchstanders thrown into the control room with everyone else.

But the real change, the one his Command Master Chief might never get over, was the way they drove the submarine. Unlike its Los Angeles-class predecessor, Virginia-class submarines had *pilots,* just like airplanes. The dive, chief of the watch, helm, and outboard watch stations had been replaced by pilot and co-pilot.

Admiral Rickover was turning in his grave.

At first, Captain Davidson thought he would hate it. But after deploying on the *USS Delaware*, he had to admit that the new configuration was remarkably efficient. He could only hope that their new tactics would be as well.

"The Orcas are in position, Captain."

"Range to target?"

"Orca Alpha is forty thousand yards from CPA with the enemy surface action group. Orca Bravo is thirty-two thousand yards."

Each of the Orca Extra Large Unmanned Underwater Vehicles (XLUUV), like the *USS Delaware*, were at periscope depth.

"Slow us down and launch the UAV," said Captain Davidson.

The control room echoed his command. Within a few moments, the submarine had slowed to the minimum speed it needed to control itself. The *Delaware* released a three-foot-long buoy from a specialized compartment in the rear of the vessel. Upon release, it began floating to the surface, still connected to the submarine by a cable.

Once surfaced, the buoy opened its water-tight hatch and out flew a twenty-pound quad-copter drone containing encrypted datalink antenna and communications gear designed especially for this purpose.

"UAV deployed, Captain, standing by for link...link established. We have good up and down link with both Orcas, sir."

"Good link, aye. Let's move, folks. We're on the clock."

"Yes, sir."

Captain Davidson's Virginia-class fast-attack submarine was now communicating with the two Orca drone submarines, which were miles away. The *Delaware* transmitted its encrypted information to the aerial drone, which had established line-of-sight encrypted datalink connections with the two Orca submarine drones' periscope antennas. This allowed the two drone submarines to communicate with the *USS Delaware* in real time, but it was risky. While the electronic emissions were encrypted, any electronic signal would quickly be picked up by Chinese surveillance satellites, surface ships, and aircraft.

Within moments, the Chinese would know that *something* was close by. For an attacking submarine, that knowledge was deadly.

Captain Davidson watched on a nearby display as the Orcas beamed their sonar and electronic intelligence data to their mothership, the *USS Delaware*. "Mothership" wasn't really the right word, thought Davidson. The drone submarines never actually joined up with the *USS Delaware*. All three vessels had launched from Naval Base Kitsap, periodically surfacing their antennas for data syncs.

"Officer of the Deck, Orca data sync complete, UAV returning to buoy. UAV safe on deck, hatch closed. Ready to retrieve."

"Retrieve buoy."

"Roger, standby. Twenty seconds, sir."

Normally the data transfers were made from submarine antenna to drone antenna, at close range. During this crucial attack period, however, the transfer of information had to be executed with the UAV buoy, allowing the underwater drones to ambush their target at an increased distance from the *Delaware*.

"Conn, Sonar, new contact bearing zero-one-zero, designate track Sierra-Four-Two. Classify as hostile."

"Sonar, aye."

Captain Davidson said, "Type of sub?"

"Sonar signature looks like a Han-class, sir," replied the sonarman.

Captain Davidson swore softly to himself as he walked over to the sonar station. There, a chief and a first-class petty officer sat side by side, headphones on, studying waterfall displays on square monitors. Captain Davidson looked over their shoulder, then pointed across the room and said, "Get me a firing solution on that track. Wait for my order. Priority remains the Jiaolong-class ship."

"Aye, sir."

His heart was beating faster, and the tension in the room was palpable. On the digital readout, Captain Davidson could see that the Chinese surface group of twelve warships had closed within a few miles of their position.

The Chinese ships were headed northeast, protected by the mighty Jiaolong-class ships, only a few of which had been sunk since the war began. Their deadly ASW dirigibles were spitting sonobuoy after sonobuoy, surrounding their warships with protective barriers. Each of the Jiaolong-class ships were mounted with Direct Energy Weapons, lethal air defense weapons with giant radars that could instantly detect and focus their powerful beams of energy at any inbound missile or aircraft that came within fifty miles.

If the Chinese navy was to be defeated, the Americans needed to take out the Jiaolong-class ships. And if that could be done, it would be by using this new tactic Captain Davidson was about to employ.

"Range to target?"

"Twenty-five thousand yards."

Captain Davidson wiped sweat off his brow and looked at the clock overhead. He realized that everyone else was looking at it, too.

"Ten seconds," said the weapons officer. "Three... two... one... time."

The sonar tech said, "Orca Alpha is making way. Bravo is too, sir. Standby for confirmation. Sir, I show both vessels moving on the proper course and accelerating. Their speed is now thirty-five knots, sir, closing in on the Chinese fleet."

Jiaolong-class Battleship 332

"Captain, Sonar reports two submerged contacts approaching from the north."

The Chinese ship captain frowned at his junior officer, who was relaying information from a phone. "*Two*?"

"Yes, sir. Unknown type. ASW dirigibles have been assigned and are en route."

The captain rose from his chair. "Go to battle stations."

"Yes, sir."

An alarm rang throughout the ship. Sailors began running toward their stations, preparing for combat.

The officer of the deck looked at his captain. "Sir, shall I turn away from the threat?"

The captain frowned as he looked at the navigational chart, weighing his options.

They were almost in air defense range of the Panama coast. By the end of the day, their ship was supposed to provide

Chinese land forces with air defense cover as they surged north of the Panama Canal.

If he turned south and took evasive maneuvers, their ship would get off track, likely adding several hours to their schedule. The captain knew that PLA air force, ground force, navy, and even space-based assets were being deployed for today's offensive. It was a massive undertaking, and his ship was to be a key part of it.

The Jiaolong was unmatched in anti-submarine warfare. Only one of its class had been defeated in combat, at the Battle of Johnston Atoll, and that was due to American trickery. The ASW system of dirigibles with advanced dipping sonar, reusable sonobuoys, and AI computers guiding every decision made him confident that he was not in danger.

Still, two American submarines approaching at once?

That was quite unusual. American submarines did not usually operate in teams. Two submarines complicated his battle problem, but he still held the advantage. The Jiaolong carried eight ASW dirigibles. Six were flying right now. The ship's AI computers would place each buoy and sonar dip in the optimum position, using buoy fields to block the attackers' advance and quickly employing their lightweight torpedoes in the perfect attack location.

"Do not change our course and speed. The Americans are trying to slow us down. We can't let them. I am heading to the combat information center to monitor the anti-submarine warfare progress."

"Yes, sir."

Just before the captain walked out of the bridge, a junior officer on the phone called for him again.

"Sir, the combat systems officer is on the phone with an urgent update."

The captain walked over and grabbed the phone. "What is it?"

"Sir, we are being jammed. An electronic attack originating from the north."

The captain looked at the tactical display on the wall. "There are no surface contacts to our north."

"I believe the attack is coming from American aircraft, sir."

15,000 feet above the Pacific

LT Kevin "Speedracer" Suggs gripped the yoke and throttle of his Navy fighter jet as he gained altitude. They had just launched from the *USS Ford* and were now joining up with the other three aircraft in his section. His weapons systems officer, LTJG Norman "Root" Laverne, monitored the mission from the rear tandem seat.

"Electronic attack just started. Shouldn't be long now."

"Roger," replied Suggs.

Suggs kept his eye on the lead aircraft as it approached, making ultrafast micro corrections with his stick and throttle until his sight picture matched the perfect formation profile.

"JSTARS and AWACS are both on station," said LTJG Laverne.

Suggs looked down at the cockpit computers, using his left hand to quickly toggle to the tactical display.

Laverne could tell what he was doing. "You just fly, man. Ask me what you wanna know."

Suggs shook his head. "NFO's always trying to tell me what to do...just enjoy the ride back there, would you?"

"Look, man, you're just a monkey that can fly. NFOs are the brains behind the operation. Now shut up and drive."

Suggs laughed. "I was just checking on where everybody's at."

His rear-seater said, "You can see everybody and their mother from *Ford* stacked up outside your window…"

Suggs glanced to his left. At least sixty jets in groups of four, just like this one, were flying racetrack holding patterns at different altitudes, thousands of feet above the aircraft carrier. Burning precious fuel while waiting for permission to head south.

"The Screwtops have hooked us up with datalink from the AWACS—thank you, my brethren NFO overlords—and we now have the Air Force on the display. Holy shitballs that's a lot of planes, man."

"How many?"

"I mean…"

Suggs could hear him counting.

"At least two hundred, I think. And there's probably more still launching."

During the brief, the squadron's intelligence officer had told them this was the largest military aviation mission since the days of the Mighty Eighth during World War Two. The planning had taken weeks, and they probably could have used more time. They didn't have the number of aircraft or Long Range Anti-Ship Missiles requested by the mission planners. Rumor had it there were production and training bottlenecks. One pilot who had recently transferred to the squadron claimed hundreds of aircraft were just sitting on deck on the east coast.

But the attack order was pushed up.

The Chinese naval fleet was fast approaching, and Chinese ground forces had commenced military operations in Panama. The final reason for the "go" order was today's Chinese mass satellite blastoff from some military space launch facility in the South China Sea. By the end of the day, the Chinese would have satellite comms and datalink...at least until the Air Force could shoot them all down. But that took time. And American ground forces in Panama needed help now.

"Okay, here we go. New update from the Screwtops. Fly-to points are in. Lead should be turning soon." The E2-D radar control aircraft were using encrypted communications to task the fighters and attack aircraft with specific waypoints and targets.

On his external radio, Suggs heard, "Gunslinger bravo flight, turning south, coming down to angels four." Suggs held his position on the lead aircraft's wing as it banked left.

"Two," he said.

"Three."

"Four."

The four Superhornets turned and began descending as one. Dozens of other formation flights did the same. Gray metallic fighters, armed to the teeth, diving toward the sea. And heading directly for their targets.

USS Delaware

"Conn, Sonar, second torpedo in the water."

"Sonar, Conn, aye."

Captain Davidson announced, "This is the captain, I have the conn. Lieutenant Everett retains the deck. Pilot, all ahead one-third, come left to course one-six-zero."

"Ahead one-third, left to course one-six-zero, Pilot, aye."

Now the American submarine was speeding up and turning to better intercept the Chinese fleet.

"Conn, Sonar, transient. Fish in the water. Orca Alpha just fired on the Jiaolong, sir."

A muffled cheer from the control room. They all knew that was good news. Every one of them had been worried that the Orcas wouldn't even get a shot off. Even as expensive decoys, they might still win the day. But if one of them could get a hit on the target, that would be a huge help.

"Conn, Sonar, enemy ships are taking evasive maneuvers."

"Conn, aye."

The sonarman held his headset, his eyes widening. "Sir, I have an underwater explosion. I think Alpha just got hit."

Jiaolong-class Battleship 332

"Sir, the first submarine has been hit. Torpedo is still inbound."

"Range of incoming torpedo?"

"Ten thousand meters and closing, sir."

"Why are we headed in this direction? Turn us to the north-west, away from the threat."

"Turning now, sir."

The captain looked at the tactical display on the center table. A digital torpedo icon on the screen was heading for his fleet. Two of his smaller warships were maneuvering across the torpedo's intended expected track, just like they had been trained to do. Each of those warships towed a torpedo decoy behind them. With luck, the American torpedo would veer away from the Jiaolong and follow one of the decoys. The torpedo might even hit one of those other warships. This would be unfortunate, but preferable to the Jiaolong taking a hit.

The captain looked at the position of the submarines on the tactical display, trying not to scream. "How did they get a torpedo off so quickly?"

"Sir, their maneuvers were highly irregular. It may have been a suicide mission. The first submarine just went full speed right for us and..."

The captain interrupted, "What is the status of the second submarine's prosecution?"

The sailor looked at his monitor. "Sir, the dirigibles have triangulated its position and are about to launch their torpedo attack." A pause. "Torpedo away from dirigible five. Torpedo has acquired target and is homing."

An update from the combat information officer. "Sir, the enemy torpedo is following our decoy."

Finally, a bit of good news. The captain let out a breath.

USS Delaware

Captain Davidson gave the order to fire and his control room came alive with energy and movement. Little noise was heard as multiple torpedoes launched from their submarine in rapid succession. A deadly-quiet attack.

The *Delaware's* torpedoes raced to their targets with ferocious speed. Two of the MK-48 ADCAP torpedoes were assigned to the Jiaolong, with the others targeting the surrounding warships.

Jiaolong-class Battleship 332

"Sir, the second American submarine has been hit. Awaiting battle damage assessment."

"Very well," the captain replied.

"Sir, transients! Bearing three-three-zero, range less than three thousand meters!"

The ship lurched to starboard, the deck tilting underneath their feet. The officer of the deck was taking evasive maneuvers, per his standing orders.

"That can't be." The Chinese captain's mouth dropped as he ran over to the display. "How is that possible? There were two submarines here and here...we destroyed one and just hit the other. Even if one survived, they were kilometers away from..."

"Sir...there must have been a third."

Captain Davidson and the crew were deep in the problem now, carefully tracking the maneuvers of each surface target with mental math and computer programs. The Chinese warships carved through the water hundreds of feet above them while a single enemy submarine remained to the south.

"The Chinese destroyers are going active, sir."

Multi-frequency pings began echoing off their hull. Captain Davidson noticed some nervous faces. But this was a desperate act. Their active search was much too far from the American submarine to be useful. Still, prudence dictated action.

Captain Davidson ordered the *USS Delaware* to make a sharp turn and depth change just after they launched a second set of torpedoes. The evasive maneuvers would make it harder for any of the PLA destroyers to track them, if they even had a sniff. But that was unlikely. The Virginia-class submarine, now running at near full speed, was quieter than a Los Angeles-class running at a mere five knots.

The *USS Delaware* had launched its attack on the recently detected Chinese submarine before the Jiaolong-class battleship was even hit. The stealth and ruthless efficiency by which the American submarine crew carried out their attack gave the Chinese Han-class submarine little chance.

The Han-class submarine detected the sound of an incoming torpedo and attempted to evade, but the MK-48 ADCAP detonated under its hull within moments of discovery. The underwater explosion created an air bubble the size of a school bus that formed just under the submarine's center. The submarine's buoyant ends fought an instantaneous losing battle with gravity as its hull snapped amidships.

As this happened, the *Delaware's* initial two MK-48 torpedoes accelerated to over fifty knots, heading for the Jiaolong-class ship. Even with the PLA Navy's last-minute evasive maneuver, the total time of closure was less than one minute between launch and target impact.

The first torpedo hit the Jiaolong dead center. Its six-hundred-pound warhead exploded on contact, just under the waterline. A geyser of gray shot upward from the ship, whose massive futuristic radar towers collapsed, their foundations shredded. Secondary explosions followed.

The second torpedo hit near the stern, creating giant balls of yellow flame and the thick black smoke of burning fuel.

Crews from nearby Chinese destroyers watched in horror as the ship they were tasked with protecting sank before their eyes. At first, the Chinese escorts continued their desperate search for the American submarine now hunting them. But after American torpedoes hit two more destroyers, the group commander ordered them to turn south, away from the threat.

The crew of the *USS Delaware* had anticipated this.

They had moved two wire-guided torpedoes into position ahead of time. When the Chinese destroyers were properly herded, the American torpedoes spooled up and began homing.

Two more hits.

On board the *Delaware*, the crew was teeming with excitement and relief. The attack couldn't have gone better. The Chinese fleet was on the run, and its deadly air defense radar was out of commission.

The air attack could commence.

The Chinese fleet was massive, and the *Delaware* had been assigned only to the northernmost group. American submarines and Orca drones executed similar attacks hundreds of miles to the south, on the PLA Navy armada steaming in the vicinity of the Galapagos Islands. Here were the jewels of the fleet: four nuclear-powered aircraft carriers and four more Jiaolong-class ships. Each high-value unit had dozens of escorts and supply vessels, all coming to support the Chinese ground forces as they pushed north through Panama.

The Chinese had ramped up aircraft carrier production after the war began, outfitting them with the newest-generation fighter-attack aircraft. Now, as the Americans began jamming radars, these Chinese fighters were scrambled, along with PLA air force jets based in Venezuela, Peru, and Ecuador.

From the front seat of his F/A-18 Superhornet, Lieutenant Suggs heard his WSO say, "We have the execute order. Weapons armed and ready. Operation GHOSTRIDER is on like Donkey Kong."

"Roger." Suggs was focused on keeping in formation as his section of F-18s dove through thin layers of clouds toward the ocean. Behind them, the sky was filled with more Navy jets diving down from altitude. The aircraft would remain in formation, flying low to the water to avoid radar detection. Soon they would split up and begin attacking from multiple directions.

GHOSTRIDER was the aviation portion of the attack. If they were being given the go-ahead, that meant the US Navy submarine force had just taken out the three remaining Chinese Jiaolong-class ships. The incoming air attack force would still have to deal with the latest generation surface-to-air missiles launched from Chinese destroyers.

But those could be defeated.

He hoped.

Overhead, US Air Force AWACS aircraft directed a section of F-22 interceptors toward the recently scrambled Chinese fighters.

"Fifty miles until weapons release."

"Roger," said Suggs.

"Oh shit, look above us. The Raptors have started shooting."

Suggs glanced upward. Through his tinted visor and the cockpit glass of his F-18, he could see the contrails of F-22 Raptors, and faster-moving contrails of their long-range air-to-air missiles.

"Twenty-five miles until launch. Your exit heading is going to be zero-three-zero."

"Zero-three-zero, roger."

Suggs snuck a glance back up at the air-to-air battle unfolding forty thousand feet above them. An impossibly large number of contrails now approached from the opposite direction, scattering flashes of yellowish light. At first Suggs thought the Chinese jets had opened fire, but he realized that he was witnessing the F-22's missile explosions as they reached their targets. The distant explosions reminded him of fireworks ripping into a thousand little bursts during the grand finale. Beautiful violence.

On the external comms, Suggs heard his squadron commanding officer, the rear-seat aviator in the lead aircraft, say, "Gunslinger flight, fire at will."

His weapons systems officer depressed the weapons release button, saying, "Bruiser one away."

He felt the aircraft shudder as the heavy weapon fell off the wing mount.

"Bruiser two away."

Another shudder.

Two missiles fell from each aircraft, momentarily keeping speed, suspended below their jet. The missiles then extended winglets as their engines kicked on. Suggs watched as hundreds of missiles fired ahead of the Navy jets, streaking above and below his altitude. The weapons accelerated and disappeared over the horizon.

The Long Range Anti-Ship Missiles dropped down low, skimming the ocean's surface as they headed toward their targets.

"Gunslinger flight, coming left."

"Two."

"Three."

"Four."

The Superhornets banked hard left and headed back toward the *USS Ford*.

28

Lena walked into the military command center located adjacent to the Zhongnanhai governmental offices. The entire space was electric with energy. Something big was going on. Her father was there, looking frustrated as he spoke with the senior military leaders.

A colonel on her father's staff saw her standing near the entrance. "Hello, Miss Chen." He looked embarrassed. "I apologize. Miss *Chou*. Did you need something?"

"I was supposed to see the general, but he wasn't in his office. What happened?"

"You haven't heard? The Americans have attacked us near Panama. A massive submarine attack on our PLA Navy fleet near Peru. Half of our Jiaolong ships were sunk, and we lost three aircraft carriers. Now the American Air Force is battling with ours."

Lena's eyes drifted to the display of digital maps in the front of the room. Hundreds, no, thousands of digital tracks scrambled about over the land and sea near Panama.

"How goes the battle?"

The colonel shook his head. "It is too early to say. But I am afraid that your father will be indisposed for the rest of the day. I would interrupt him, but…"

"Don't bother. Where is Jinshan? I would think that he would be here…"

The colonel said, "The chairman is recuperating from another treatment. He has delegated all military decisions to General Chen."

"Thank you, Colonel."

Lena turned and walked toward the presidential quarters.

The guards allowed Lena into Jinshan's chamber without question and closed the door behind her. The cavernous space was lit only by Jinshan's bedside lamp. Darkness outside, except for a sliver of moon. She could hear her footsteps on the marble floor as she approached Jinshan's bed. An overhead speaker played Chopin. "Nocturne in C Sharp Minor." Violin mixed with piano.

Jinshan lay on his bed, reading glasses on, a thick stack of papers in his lap. He looked up when he heard her approach.

"Ah, my dear Lena. I hope you bring good news. General Chen senses my health, I'm afraid. He is bringing me less and less information at the most crucial time."

Lena reached the foot of his bed and stood in silence. She studied the face of a man she had spent a lifetime admiring. A lifetime of deceit.

As their eyes met, Lena observed a flicker of confusion in his.

"What is wrong, Lena? Have the Americans defeated us at Panama?"

She took a step closer. The bedside lamp illuminated the scar tissue on her face.

"I must speak with you about something important."

"Of course. What is it?"

Lena said, "When did you decide to recruit me?"

Jinshan's eyes narrowed.

"Are you not bringing me news of our battle?" For a moment, Lena thought he might get angry, but then he said, "I recruited you when you were at Junxun. You know this. Why are you asking now? What is..."

"Who gave the older boy the key to my room? That night before you recruited me. My door was locked. Who gave him the key?"

Jinshan pulled his head off the pillow and sat up. His mouth hung half-open as he searched for a response. "What are you talking about?"

"An older boy in my Junxun class had a key. He entered my room that night, intending to assault me. I let him have my body. Later that night, when he was asleep in his own bed, I took my revenge on him." Her voice was steady. She felt numb as she recalled the painful memory.

"I remember."

"I changed that night. I have never been able to...to feel things the same way." She was half-talking to Jinshan, half-talking to herself.

Jinshan took the papers off his lap and placed them on his bedside table. He looked concerned. Whether for her or himself, she couldn't tell.

His voice sounded tired. "Lena, you were given certain gifts in life. I only wanted to help you develop them. And it has been a great honor to work with you." Jinshan gave her a soft smile.

Lena acted as if he hadn't spoken. "You made it seem as if you were doing me a favor by helping me get away with an act of violence."

"I was. *I did help you.*" She heard a touch of indignation in his voice as he glanced over her shoulder, and she knew he would call for the guards the moment he suspected a threat. Lena thought she heard Jinshan's chamber door opening, but when she turned in that direction, no one appeared.

The guards would have shown themselves. They were alone. Lena turned back toward the bed.

And took one step closer to her master.

General Chen entered Chairman Jinshan Cheng's personal chamber and closed the door softly behind him. If the old man was asleep, he didn't want to wake him. Things were not going well in the Pacific, and the general would rather not have to report the bad news.

However close to death Jinshan was, he remained the ultimate authority figure in China. He could banish General Chen to the political prison at Qingcheng, or send him to an early retirement. Jinshan might lose a little face at such a move, with all the political clout General Chen had built up in the past few months, but in the end it wouldn't matter. Only the appearance of power mattered.

General Chen just needed to hold his current title until Jinshan was gone. With the right allies in place, General Chen was confident that Secretary Ma could be won over, naming him as vice president and further increasing Chen's power. But none of that would happen if Jinshan fired him, meaning General Chen had to keep giving Jinshan updates. But it also meant that he couldn't give him too much bad news...

General Chen considered this as he stood inside Chairman Jinshan's darkened personal chamber, listening for a beat before he walked around the corner and into sight.

He hoped to hear snoring.

Instead, he heard his daughter's voice.

Lena loomed over Jinshan's frail body.

Fear crept into his eyes. Jinshan knew this was the end. Or he was at least beginning to suspect it.

"What has upset you so, Lena? Someone must have said something." Jinshan was employing the tactics of an old intelligence officer. A quest for information, camouflaged to sound like sympathy.

"Someone did."

She could see his mind working out the problem. Trying to find a solution.

"Your father," Jinshan guessed.

Lena didn't answer.

"Listen to me, Lena. You know that he cannot be trusted. Your father wants your loyalty. He sees the way you and I have worked together and..."

"You still haven't answered my question. That day before you recruited me. Tell me, who gave the boy the key to my room?"

His voice was silent, yet his gaze held her answer.

Jinshan closed his eyes. "Life is a cruel gift..."

Lena felt the old familiar tug inside her. The pull toward violent action. Although this time it wasn't just a bloodlust. It was a craving for revenge. She forced herself to remain disciplined, and continued listening to the old man on his deathbed.

Jinshan opened his eyes and looked at her. "I once had faith in our system. But there came a time, when I was about your age and working for the MSS, that I became disenchanted. I saw the corruption. The failure of governments to perform. Not just ours. My travels showed me that it was the same in every country, under different guises. I was without purpose. But I had skill. I could influence others. I could out-think my opponents. I used my connections to build my net worth and power, just because it felt good. But still, I was without purpose. Until this." He held out his hand for effect. "This war to end all wars. This was my symphony. My purpose. I used my talents to take control of China, to unite the nations around the world. I used whatever means were necessary, because the end result will be worth it." His eyes watered as he spoke.

Lena's lip quivered. This was the siren song that had moved her over the years, but this time with a twist. Jinshan's whispers of truth, his ultimate goal, resonated with her. She too saw the flaws in governments around the world. The endless imperfections. But he had lied to her. From the beginning he had lied.

Jinshan said, "I never married. Never had a child. You were the closest thing…"

Lena shook her head forcefully, a tear streaming down her cheek. "Don't. You chose me as your recruit before the boy entered my room that night. My assault was part of your plan. You selected me for your program based on my performance in your camp. You made a deal with my own father to bring me into your organization. Did he know? Did he know how you were going to do it?"

A tear streamed down Jinshan's own face now.

Lena continued speaking through gritted teeth. "Then you set in motion plans to ruin me. To have that boy ravage my body. To destroy my innocence so I would be broken and vulnerable. You used that vulnerability as leverage to gain my trust and cooperation. So you could rebuild me into your…"

Jinshan began slowly nodding. "Yes." His voice was but a whisper. "An assassin. An intelligence officer. I built you into my greatest asset. Lena, you are my proudest achievement."

She said, "You are not who I thought you were. I used to

believe in you. But everything you've given me, everything you've said...it all started with this unforgivable betrayal."

Jinshan's face went red. "I know what you came here for. I can see it in your eyes. I suppose I deserve it."

"You do."

"Go ahead, then, if you must."

With the quickness of a trained assassin, she removed a razor-sharp knife from the concealed sheath at her waist, then leaned forward and carefully moved the blade across Jinshan's throat.

A dark crimson line appeared.

She had carved a half-inch-deep laceration in his neck, slicing open his carotid artery and windpipe. Blood began pouring down from the gash. Air bubbles spewed from the windpipe.

Jinshan's face morphed in excruciating pain. His eyes widened and his fingers fumbled at his neck, and then Lena watched as the life drained out of him, his eyes staring off into the dark abyss where his soul now resided.

Lena's heart pounded. She looked down at her hand, now covered in dark blood.

She had just killed the most powerful man in the world.

Lena froze as she heard a shuffling behind her. She turned to see her father standing alone in the dark, cavernous room. Her heart beat faster still.

The knife was still in her hand.

"He is dead?" General Chen's mouth was agape as he stared at Jinshan's corpse.

Any moment now he would call in the guards to arrest her.

The sound of the door opening a second time. A single pair of footsteps on the marble floor. Lena expected to see a guard, but then Secretary Ma appeared, standing next to General Chen.

He covered his mouth. "What?" he cried, running over to Jinshan and placing his hands on his neck as he tried in vain to help the dead leader.

Lena looked up at her father, who was staring back at her.

General Chen called out, "Guards!"

29

David heard the commotion as he entered the Silversmith team's tactical operations center. Groups of men and women were high-fiving and hugging each other.

"The war is going to be over!" one analyst cried out.

David saw Susan standing in her office doorway, speaking to one of her operations officers.

"What happened?" David asked.

"We just received word that Jinshan Cheng has died," she replied.

David's eyes widened. "You're kidding?"

One of the younger CIA operations officers said, "I mean, it's over now, right? Ma will be put in charge. He wants peace. That's what our sources tell us."

Someone else said, "Shh. Don't start talking like that. Just be patient."

David followed Susan into her office, and the door shut behind them. He could still hear the jubilation outside.

"Why aren't you celebrating?" David asked.

"I'm cautiously optimistic. The battle at Panama was a stalemate at best."

"We sank three of their carriers and half of their Jiaolong-class ships."

"True, but the Chinese army has weakened our ground forces near the Panama Canal Zone. And half their fleet is missing."

"*Missing?*"

"The troop transports weren't near the Galapagos, where they were expected to be. A good number of their warships are also unaccounted for."

"Maybe they dropped off their troops and cargo and were sent back to China to reload?"

"Probably. Which doesn't bode well for this being an end to the war."

David said, "Jinshan just died. We need to see how Ma behaves. Our agents in China say he will be more favorable than Jinshan. We may be able to strike a peace agreement sooner than previously thought."

"There is still fighting going on. Nothing has changed yet."

David said, "It will take time for new orders to permeate through the ranks. Be patient."

Susan still didn't look happy.

David said, "How did Jinshan's death occur? Natural causes or..."

Susan sat behind her desk. She typed on her computer, then turned the monitor to face David. The screen was polarized so that it could only be seen if someone was facing it directly. When the message came into view, he read it quickly and asked, "That's Tetsuo? Holy shit, how did he get this information?"

Susan didn't answer.

Tetsuo had sent a cable from Beijing saying Lena Chou killed Jinshan. No further details at this time.

Susan turned the screen back around and David sat in the chair across from her. He leaned back, flabbergasted, shaking his head. "It worked. Your plan worked. How did you know she would do it?"

Susan said, "I knew that by allowing Lena to go on the mission with Chase, there was a reasonable likelihood of several positive outcomes. We had several of the world's best psychological operations specialists create an in-depth model of what makes her tick. I knew what triggered her. With her concern for her child, she was in a fragile state, and she's always been capable of inflicting violence. She was allowed inside again because Jinshan trusted her. The NSA hacked into her MSS recruitment records years ago. But only in the past year did we learn that Li Chen was Lena Chou. Her loyalty to Jinshan was her driving force. With that removed..."

David said, "So the PSYOPS specialists said she would kill Jinshan?"

"No. My intention was to have Tetsuo re-establish contact with her in Beijing. I wanted her to work for us there, alongside Dong."

David whistled. "And now Ma will be in power, with Dong as the vice president. Dong has already told Tetsuo that he wants to end the war, right? With Dong influencing Ma, this is exactly what we've been hoping for."

A knock at the door.

Susan said, "Come in."

One of the CIA operations officers stuck his head in. "Susan, you better come see this." He looked worried.

Susan and David got up and walked out onto the operations floor.

The celebrations had stopped. Now everyone was looking up at a TV screen. The woman who had been celebrating when David entered the office was now covering her mouth in horror. Someone else swore.

Susan said, "What's going on?"

A woman in an Air Force uniform answered. "We've been attempting to establish communications with Dong or members of his team for the past two hours through backchannels. We're in contact with the State Department, and they're doing the same through official and unofficial channels. No replies."

David whispered, "What are we watching? Why's everyone so upset?"

"CNN is piping in a live feed of China's politburo. They've been called in for an emergency session following Jinshan's death."

David read the ticker tape on the bottom of the screen.

GENERAL CHEN TO BE NAMED NEW CHINESE LEADER

"Someone please turn up the volume."

David could hear a voice on the TV. A newswoman with a British accent.

"And we are hearing now that General Chen, formerly the highest-ranking military officer in China, has assumed the leadership role after Jinshan Cheng's death. General Chen was...."

The voice droned on, giving Chen's biographical information.

David turned to Susan. "How is this possible? I thought all of our analysts said that Ma was named successor?"

Susan didn't respond. She was staring at the screen.

The newscaster came on again.

"And now you can see General Chen, in full dress uniform as he proceeds down the main aisle of the grand auditorium. There are thousands standing and clapping. General Chen is flanked by his senior staffers and, we are told, by his daughter."

David watched General Chen march up the auditorium stairs and stand behind the podium. The thousands of Chinese politicians and leaders sat, and the room went silent. When

General Chen began speaking, his voice was animated, his hand moving like he was giving a show. David couldn't understand what he was saying, and no translation was given. But it reminded him very much of old black-and-white footage of another leader, that one from a dark period in European history.

General Chen's voice grew stronger. His words faster. His pitch higher. Rising to a crescendo. The audience fed off his energy, working themselves into a frenzy. They were giving him a standing ovation now. Then he marched off the stage and back down the aisle, his staff following him.

The auditorium began emptying, the audience members following him as his entourage passed.

"What are they doing? Why are they all following him?"

The CIA analyst said, "They're going to the courtyard outside."

"Why?" David noticed that the most disturbed people in the Silversmith office were the Mandarin-speakers.

The TV footage changed to a view of an expansive courtyard, which at first appeared to be mostly empty. Two tanks were set up before a row of soldiers.

The newscaster said, "*We are being told that these are...prisoners. They have prisoners lined up.*"

The prisoners were bound at their wrists as they stood shoulder to shoulder, facing the tanks. Now the men and women from the auditorium, led by General Chen, entered the screen's view. The politburo members funneled around, gathering near the tanks. Soon thousands of audience members joined them, surrounding the row of prisoners.

Awaiting the public execution.

General Chen walked over to stand in front of the group. He began speaking into a microphone as two soldiers escorted a prisoner toward him. The prisoner also began speaking, his voice carried by outdoor megaphones.

"That's Dong. Holy shit. That guy speaking now is Dong."

"What's he saying?"

"That the men standing here have committed crimes against the state...he and all of his countrymen should be grateful that General Chen will provide excellent leadership for their future...Something like that. Dong is basically pledging allegiance to Chen, publicly."

One of the analysts said, "I think those prisoners are Dong's staff. Damn. Actually, I think some are politburo members, known to be aligned with Dong. General Chen is publicly executing Dong's allies. And he just made Dong pledge loyalty to him."

"Wait, who's that one?"

"Oh, holy shit. That's Ma. That's Secretary Ma."

"He just said that Secretary Ma led a coup d'état attempt. That Ma is the one who killed Jinshan."

"I thought it was Lena Chou?"

"It was."

".... and that the punishment for such treason is death. He's saying Ma is going to..."

General Chen raised his hand, pointing at the row of prisoners. Two chain guns on top of the tanks unleashed a stream of yellow tracers, cutting down the men in a horrific spray of red. Limbs and bodies flew dozens of meters.

David glanced at Susan, who looked like she'd been punched in the gut. Her carefully laid plans to insert Dong into a position of influence had been wiped out in a flash of violence. "This is bad," she said, shaking her head.

On the TV, the audience who had just witnessed the executions were now applauding like crazed fanatics as General Chen continued speaking into his microphone. Huge banners were released from the rooftop of the government building behind him. Giant red propaganda banners with yellow stars in the center.

"What's he saying? He keeps saying the same thing over and over. What is he saying?"

One of the Mandarin speakers said, "It's a Chinese saying that effectively means 'the gloves will come off.' Now he is saying that 'our progress in the war against our American enemies continues. We will invade their country and crush our enemies.'"

David watched as General Chen gained energy from the crowd, spittle flying from his mouth, his animated motions and crazed eyes reminiscent of dictators past. David couldn't help but think that Lena's actions had allowed this to happen.

That they had empowered a monster.

30

SOUTHCOM Headquarters
Doral, Florida

David and Susan were in General Schwartz's SOUTHCOM morning war brief, listening from their seats in the back of the room.

"How many ships are in that fleet?" the general asked.

"We think as many as fifty, sir. At least two dozen dock landing ships. The newest Chinese variants."

The display near the front of the room showed a map of the Americas. The missing Chinese ships were missing no more, the fleet having circled around the southern tip of South America before turning north into the Atlantic.

"The Chinese unloaded the shipboard PLA ground personnel and equipment at the major Pacific ports of Callao, Peru, and Buenaventura, Colombia, several weeks ago. That was the last time we had eyes on these ships. Our HUMINT sources provided video and photos while they were in port. However, within the past forty-eight hours, several of these same transport ships have begun showing up in ones and twos in Chile and Argentina."

"So the Chinese are sending empty troop transports into the Atlantic?" General Schwartz asked.

The one-star Marine general giving the brief nodded. "That's correct, sir. We believe the ground troops were unloaded near the Panama combat zone to provide the PLA commanders with reinforcements if they need it."

The screen changed to show the aerial image of the Chinese ships, reminding David of a picture his father used to hang on his office wall. All of the ships were grouped close together, long tails of white water streaking behind them.

The briefer said, "This was taken from a Triton surveillance drone six hours ago. About six hundred miles northeast of Rio de Janeiro, Brazil."

The group of military men and women began talking worriedly.

"We think this is the northernmost group, sir."

General Schwartz said, "If they're moving this Chinese fleet into the Atlantic, then General Chen doesn't intend on keeping those troop transports empty. Where would he use them?"

"Chinese ground forces are massing in Venezuela. Our best guess is that this PLA Navy Atlantic fleet is headed there. The PLA Air Force is already engaged in daily battles with US planes over the Caribbean and Gulf of Mexico. Until now, we believed their strategy was denying us the ability to support war operations in Panama. But they may be trying to establish air superiority. To support their own naval operations and amphibious landings in the region."

Another general said, "If they were able to stage a landing somewhere like Nicaragua, that could effectively cut off the US supply lines to Panama, allowing their main forces to break through the geographical bottleneck."

General Schwartz lifted his head, blowing out a breath. "It appears that our naval victory in the Pacific was only a partial success." He turned to face the lone admiral sitting at the table. "What are your thoughts, Scott?"

The two-star admiral said, "Sir, fifty ships, and only half of them warships? The fact that they are headed into the Atlantic is significant, but this is not an insurmountable challenge. Atlantic fleet will be ready. We've begun to considerably ramp up production of the Long Range Anti-Ship Missiles, as well as air-dropped mines and electronic attack drones, the kind we used at Johnston Atoll. Our ships are prepping in Norfolk, Kings Bay, and Mayport for a large-scale sortie. We've gathered just about every airborne asset capable of carrying the LRASM at the three main air bases near Norfolk. They're undergoing maintenance and training before we redeploy them to bases throughout the southeast and to our Atlantic carriers. We'll have a strong joint air attack plan ready to go."

David leaned over and whispered to Susan, "The Chinese know that our Atlantic forces outnumber their fifty-ship Atlantic fleet. Something seems off about this."

General Schwartz was looking right at him. "Something you'd like to add, Mr. Manning?"

David felt his face get hot as all eyes turned toward him. "Sir, the Chinese must be aware of the strength of our Atlantic fleet, and of our CONUS-based air assets."

"What's your point, David?"

"They must have a plan...to attack them...sir."

The two-star admiral said, "With what? Their closest PLA Air Force base is several thousand miles away. We have sunk all but a handful of their submarines in the Atlantic. The ones that remain don't have enough firepower to..."

General Schwartz held up his hand. "David, see me afterwards."

"Yes, sir."

"Admiral, by the end of the day, I want to see our plan to attack the Chinese Atlantic fleet."

General Schwartz met with Susan and David privately after his briefing. David couldn't help but glance at the five stars he now wore. He remembered having to memorize the names of the five-star American admirals when he was a midshipman at the Naval Academy.

"What have you got?" General Schwartz asked.

Susan said, "Rojas. The hypersonic weapons expert. We're getting closer to identifying where the Chinese are holding him. The SF teams have narrowed it down to three camps."

The general nodded. "Good. Will it make a difference?"

David said, "If we can bring him back to the States and have him show us how to create the coating, it would be a matter of weeks to implement. My team has already solved how to scale it. We're working with STRATCOM on updating their hypersonic glide vehicles and warheads."

"We'll need you to speak with STRATCOM actual today." David handed him a single-page document in a folder. "Here's a list of things we need approved. That will need to be destroyed as soon as it's completed. The moment we get Rojas in the States, we're sending him out to them for implementation."

A knock at the door.

"Enter," the general called out.

His secretary stuck her head in. "General, you asked me to remind you that you've got five minutes until your two o'clock call with POTUS."

"Thank you." After the secretary disappeared out the door,

the general looked at David. "I'm going to need to tell him about our break-glass-in-case-of-emergency plan."

"Yes, sir, I thought you might."

"He may not take it well. Politicians don't like risks."

David bit his lip. "Sir, given the current status, I think we need to execute the contingency plans you and I spoke about. I believe General Chen's ascendance to power, and recent Chinese military movements, constitute an emergency."

General Schwartz stood. "Agreed."

"So do we need to wait for presidential approval first?"

"What's the point of having a fifth star if you don't get to piss off the president? You have my approval. Set things in motion. Any calls you need me to make, keep feeding me the information, like you have been doing."

"Yes, sir."

31

Lena sat next to her father as tanks rolled through the streets of Beijing. The military parade was his idea. A way to increase morale and patriotism. The military had been preparing for over a week, and the event went on for an hour. Rows of soldiers in dress uniform goose-stepping at right-shoulder-arms. Gleaming bayonets on modern black rifles. Newly designed mobile ICBM launchers. Squadrons of attack helicopters.

Crowds of underfed civilians waved red flags like their lives depended on it. And the all-seeing eyes of MSS-monitored CCTV cameras used facial-recognition software to identify each and every one.

Lena was numb to it all. But the endless display of military hardware delighted General Chen, who sat in an elevated box seat, surrounded by rows of fawning politicians and military commanders. Some of them were replacements of the recently executed.

Jinshan had been a powerful figure. But General Chen was something else. Lena was surprised how he had consolidated power so quickly, wiping out his enemies and instilling fear in everyone around him. China was now an authoritarian military dictatorship, with her father as its supreme leader.

During the middle of the ceremony, the parade of soldiers suddenly stopped and turned to face him. An aide whispered something in General Chen's ear, and he rose, nodding and grinning with excitement. He hobbled his bulky frame down the stairs, escorted by soldiers, to receive a medal from the unit commander.

Minister Dong leaned over to her and whispered, "It is the Order of August First. The highest military award. Only ten people have ever received it."

Lena looked at Dong. The neutered head of the MSS had kept his title, but he was now only a figurehead. General Chen had installed one of his loyalists next to Dong, and he was making all of the Ministry of State Security decisions now.

Lena said, "What has he done to deserve it?"

Dong replied, "Does that matter?"

They watched as the medal was placed around General Chen's neck. Lena could practically feel his pulse pounding, the endorphins filling his bloodstream as his lifetime quest for power and affirmation was realized. He walked back up the stone steps to his elevated perch and waved to the masses. Hundreds of thousands of Chinese citizens cheered. Lena's father beamed.

Hours later, after a lavish lunch with senior military officers and their social-climber wives, it was finally time for business. General Chen sat at the head of the long conference table as his senior leaders poured praise onto him until finally he frowned and demanded they begin updating him on the status of the war.

A PLA general leaned forward and began giving updates. Lena recognized him as one of her father's former subordinate unit commanders. It looked like he had pinned a few more stars onto his collar in the past week. She wondered what her father did with the former general in that position. Loyalty was all that mattered to General Chen, she knew.

"We are locked in a stalemate in Central America, General. Our forces are making progress, but the Americans have dug into their positions north of the Panama Canal. With our recent naval defeat..."

A PLA Navy officer bristled. "We were hardly defeated. We sank five American ships and shot down nearly one hundred aircraft."

Lena knew that was an exaggeration. She had read the raw intelligence reports. Only a few dozen American planes were destroyed, not the astronomical figure that the PLA Air Force had claimed. And four of the five American ships were *damaged*, not sunk. But these were facts no one in this group dared bring up.

There was nothing like a public execution to start the good news flowing.

"We expect to break through the American lines within the next week, General."

General Chen looked at the map. Bright red arrows plowed through the blue American positions.

"How?" he asked.

"Sir, we intend to use..."

General Chen stood. "You have had weeks with the same soldiers, the same equipment."

"Yes, sir, but..."

"The Americans are holding us back. What did I say during my speech to the politburo? We must be stronger."

"Yes, sir."

General Chen widened his eyes and used his hands to emphasize the importance of his words. "We must use all of our resources. It is crucial to our victory efforts that we break through. Our naval fleet is now transiting up the east coast of South America. They will be in Venezuela by...by when, Admiral?"

"Next week, sir."

"Next week." General Chen snorted. "Hmph. I want action *now.*"

"Our men are short-handed after the recent attacks. We are waiting for reinforcements..."

"You have an inordinate number of troops in the vicinity. What are they doing, if not fighting?"

"Sir, there are many things they must do..." The officer answering the question was caught off guard. "Logistics. They must drive fuel and ordnance north to the front lines. And some are being used to guard prisoners...we have several POW camps. They must..."

General Chen shook his head. "No. That is a waste of resources. Close the prison camps."

"Who will guard the prisoners?"

He shrugged. "Terminate all of the prisoners."

The officer's mouth dropped open. "Sir...that is...*illegal.*"

General Chen rose from his seat, his chair falling backward behind him. "Do not dare to tell me what I can and can't do. I told you to terminate the prisoners. We must use all of our soldiers for fighting. We must put forth maximum effort!"

He turned to another general and said, "What of the unconventional weapons programs we are developing. Could we use those to break through the stalemate?"

Most of the faces looked horrified.

Someone had the good sense to placate him with, "We will look into it, sir."

General Chen said, "The Americans wouldn't expect a chemical attack. It worked well in Korea. We could use gas to break through Central American land mass."

Lena looked at the men around the table. They were fearful for their lives. Despite the irrational things he said, no one would dare contradict him.

General Chen continued, "It is imperative that we break through those lines and start moving northward by the time the naval fleet arrives in Venezuela. We must force the Americans to deploy their resources to Central America. This will relieve pressure on our naval fleet in the Atlantic. Once our naval fleet reaches Venezuela, our Atlantic fleet will allow us to execute an amphibious landing on the American homeland. This will be a crushing blow. We must break through Panama before then."

Several of the generals and admirals in the room began offering suggestions. Lena thought they sounded like children playing a game. These generals had risen through the military ranks during a career of peace. And now they were moving hundreds of combat divisions half a world away, in the largest war the world had ever known.

General Chen said, "Lena, what do you think?"

The room went silent as all eyes fell on her.

Lena kept her chin up as she spoke. "The Americans have enough aerial range to attack our naval fleet as it moves north. The latest MSS intelligence report suggests that the Americans are gathering their strike aircraft together on a few specific military bases. They are using these bases as hubs to increase their Long Range Anti-Ship Missile capability. An amphibious landing would require Chinese air and naval superiority."

"We will have it!" shouted one of the PLA generals.

Lena was unimpressed, and it must have shown on her face.

"You think we will not succeed?" her father asked.

"Not unless we are able to damage the American air and naval forces that would be used to counterattack our naval movements."

One of the generals said, "We have moved many of our air assets into the region. We can launch an attack..."

Lena interrupted him. "Your forces are busy maintaining a stalemate in Central America. Any reallocation of those air and ground forces would damage your ability to fight the ground war. And an attack on targets near the continental United States would be very costly to our attacking force."

"That is not true!" said the same general, no doubt trying to save face in front of her father. "We attacked an American base during the Panama battle last week and hit eighty-five percent of our targets with only ten percent losses."

Lena said, "You had surveillance support. You knew where the targets were and could use a mass satellite launch to gain precious targeting and communications capability. Our next mass satellite launch won't be ready for weeks. You would be flying blind, General. Hoping that your targets were where they were supposed to be. Hoping that the Americans didn't wipe out your air force. The same air force that is needed to provide air support over Central America."

The room went quiet. The PLA Air Force general went red with anger.

General Chen looked amused. "What would you suggest, Lena?"

"General, allow me to speak with my Russian contact. They have a significant submarine presence near military bases on the east coast of America. Those submarines could gain reconnaissance—targeting information on the naval positions. And it is possible the Russians have a number of cruise missiles that could be used to severely damage critical air force installations. The same installations that are at this very moment improving the American anti-ship missile capability."

General Chen nodded. "I like this idea. Let the Russians lose some of their submarines and help soften up American forces. It would save ours for when they are truly needed."

Lena said, "If the Russians agree to this, they will likely want to keep plausible deniability, for political reasons."

"What does that mean?"

Lena said, "We will need to tell the world it was us."

"Even better." General Chen smiled.

Lena said, "Then I will speak with my Russian contact."

32

Victoria expected to die tonight. But she had to try something.

Over the past couple of weeks, the number of Chinese guards at the camp was reduced to support the war effort. The American prisoners had been used more and more for manual labor. Under the guards' supervision, the Americans had, in small numbers, been made to participate in more cooking, cleaning, and construction efforts. Most of these duties had previously gone to what Victoria's men called the "locals."

Victoria had now met with the scientist's wife several times. During their conversations, she revealed that her husband had been recruited by the CIA. He was an expert on some type of materials science processes that made hypersonic weapons more effective. But the Chinese had captured him the day they landed in Peru, and he was now being forced to work at the research facility next to the POW camp. He knew that his wife was talking to the Americans, and Victoria was doing everything she could to send a signal back to the US.

They had sent Morse code transmissions from the local military jeep twice more. But when Chinese military personnel finally tracked down the source of the transmission, they killed the fat local soldier. Victoria was thankful it was just him.

Plug had been put to work in the laundry room, where he received regular updates on the outside world from Rojas's wife, also working there. The "local" prisoners had occasional access to outside information that Plug would then pass on to the prisoner network using tap code, where it would be relayed to Victoria.

One such contact was the food supply truck driver, who traveled to the camp weekly from a nearby town. He had informed them of General Chen's brutal actions.

"The truck driver said that executions have already begun in other prison camps," Plug said. "They've been shooting the prisoners and then burning the bodies in pits. Burn pits that never stop burning. Ash falling on the nearby towns. The truck driver said that yesterday a group of Chinese soldiers began using diggers to create a big pit about a mile down the road from here."

Victoria could feel the hair on the back of her neck rise as she watched Captain Tao from their position in the prison yard. The Chinese PLA officer, visible sitting in his second-floor office, was speaking with several of the guards. All of them wore serious expressions. Tao didn't normally meet with so many guards in his office. In fact, Victoria couldn't remember ever seeing that many in there at once.

"Your escape plan," she said. "Can the timeline be moved up?"

Plug said, "We don't have everything ready yet, but how soon were you thinking?"

"Tonight. It's got to be tonight."

They started after midnight. The only guard on duty was asleep. Victoria could hear him snoring. Plug had received the key from Rojas's wife, who had it specially made by a metalsmith in town. He unlocked his cell door first, then began working on the others. It was slow going, and every sound caused them to stop. Each footstep or sniff. Every metallic slide of a prison cell door was excruciatingly loud to her oversensitive ears.

Then came the hard part. Killing the guard.

Victoria selected the chief and Plug to do it. The chief had rolled out of BUDS years ago due to an injury, but even after weeks in prison, he was heavily muscled. Plug was also athletic, a former football player. She just prayed that they would be quick and quiet so as not to alert the other guards.

Nearly one hundred prisoners of war were hunched down at the foot of their cells, waiting in darkness. If the guard towers turned on their spotlights, they would illuminate the rows of emaciated Americans kneeling in the gravel.

Plug and the chief crept toward the sleeping guard. They had only minutes until the two laundry trucks were supposed to break through the main gate. Victoria tried not to think about the probability of success. She knew the plan was flawed, but returning to US soil wasn't her only goal. They needed to do everything possible to help win the war. Even if they could escape for a few hours and force Chinese troops to search for them for a few days...that would help the war effort. And if they died tonight, it was better to go down fighting.

It was honorable.

It was her duty.

But it still frightened the shit out of her.

The rumble of a diesel engine echoed through the jungle. She peered at the dimly lit clock barely visible through the mess hall window. If that was their truck, it was early.

One of the tower lights turned on, illuminating the dirt road in front of the camp's main entrance. Victoria looked at Plug and the chief, only feet away from the snoring guard.

The diesel engine grew louder. It was their truck. She could see two men in the front seat, each wearing a mask. One of the search lights came on.

A whistle sounded, and Victoria snapped her head to look at the snoring guard.

Only he wasn't snoring now. The whistle had woken him.

Even in the dark, she could see his wide, horrified eyes as he took in the prisoners making their way toward him.

The guard began screaming something that sounded like, "HOW-YEE! HOW-YEE!" Now more tower searchlights came on and more whistles sounded, this time from the towers. Then a gunshot, and one of the prisoners fell to the ground, dead. The others hit the deck, seeking cover. More gunshots. Victoria could see Chinese soldiers aiming rifles at the laundry truck, now parked, a spider web of cracked glass covering the windshield.

More guards ran to the prison cells, training their weapons on the retreating prisoners. Plug and the chief were backtracking, holding up their hands.

Captain Tao had them all lined up in the center courtyard within minutes. The guards did a count. Captain Tao screamed something, and the guards stuffed them all back in their cells.

All except for the chief.

They took him away, and out of sight. Captain Tao stood over her cell as it happened. The crack of a rifle shot. And then another. The American prisoners were screaming bloody murder, hands clenched on metal bars, shaking their locked cell doors. Even holding rifles, the prison guards looked nervous.

Captain Tao stared down Victoria, who, jaw clenching, stared right back at him. He motioned at her, and the guards began to head toward her cell.

Here it was.

Her end.

The other prisoners were howling as they watched the guards approach her. Swearing. Spitting and throwing dirt and human excrement. Anything to stop another brother from being murdered. Anything to stop Victoria's execution.

But as she heard keys jingling, a siren began wailing from the pole-mounted megaphones.

The guards began screaming at each other in Chinese. Captain Tao looked worried, pointing and shouting. He began barking orders and the guards dispersed, leaving the prisoners in their locked cells as they ran out of the prison yard and into their barracks.

Then the lights went out, one at a time.

"What were they saying?" someone whispered from a cell nearby.

"Some sort of air raid," someone else replied.

Victoria leaned back into the cell's concrete wall, holding her knees tight, thinking about the chief. Another man who had perished under her command. Her thoughts flashed to images of shipmates being pulled under after she'd abandoned ship. The same sick feeling of helplessness. She had failed to save her men.

In the silent darkness, Victoria let the pain wash over her. She thought of her own father's death, his carrier struck by a missile as she watched from her circling helicopter.

She gritted her teeth, not allowing herself to cry, as her emotions stirred into anger. Where was God in all of this? What was the point of it all? Why was she put here, if she couldn't control the outcome of these events? She became numb as she gazed up at the misty clouds partially covering a half-moon.

Then two familiar shapes moved across the moon.

She sat upright in her cell, listening...

An unworldly noise rose over the calls of jungle insects and animals. The beating of helicopter rotors unlike any Victoria had heard before.

She glanced up at the guard towers. In the moonlight she could make out a few faces in the nearest tower. Young Chinese men, sweating while holding their rifles, waiting in fear, slapping mosquitos.

Wham.

One of the guard's heads snapped back, and his body fell to the floor.

Wham.

Another guard flew off the tower backwards, falling forty feet and slamming into the dirt with a thud.

Then the night air erupted with the rattles of automatic rifle fire from multiple locations. Silent figures weaved through the camp. Special ops, Victoria knew. Dark shadows with four-tube night vision devices clipped to their cranial gear. They operated as one, spread out from each other, moving with quick precision. Every few seconds, the rapid bursts of suppressed gunfire emanated from their rifles.

The noise level increased as one of the aircraft landed in the prison yard. Victoria could see it better now. It was one of the stealth helicopters special forces pilots had flown in the raid that killed Osama bin Laden.

One of the American special operators appeared in front of her cell. "Commander Manning?"

"Yes."

"How many prisoners are here?"

"Ninety-eight." She shook her head. "Ninety-seven, I mean."

"You know where this man is?"

The soldier used a dim light to illuminate a picture of Rojas.

She pointed. "They keep the scientists in a building one hundred yards over there."

As the soldier spoke into his lip microphone, Victoria could see the Chinese guard barracks. The windows were lit up with gunfire like a thunderstorm. Up and down her row of cells, other American special forces soldiers used bolt cutters to open the locks.

Victoria heard the soldier say, "Affirm, ninety-seven. Roger." They cut the lock, opened her cell, and she was free. Just like that.

"Ma'am, you'll come with us."

She followed two of the soldiers, who firmly guided her into a waiting stealth helicopter. The scientist and his wife were brought in seconds later.

"Wait, what about the other prisoners?" she said.

"Not enough room," one of the crewmen replied.

Victoria's eyes widened and she started to get out. "I can't leave."

One of the special forces men easily pressed her back down into her seat.

"Ma'am, please sit down. We've got two Chinooks en route. They've got room for the others. You're going in here." The aircrewman strapped her in. She was moving and thinking slow, still in shock from how quick the rescue had unfolded. Then she felt the familiar sensation of a helicopter lifting off from the deck and nosing over, and a moment later they were moving low and fast over a dark jungle.

33

Norfolk, Virginia

Norfolk had always been one of the largest military centers in the world, but its military presence had increased tenfold since the war began. The city was home to several huge bases, all located within a twenty-mile radius of each other. Norfolk Naval Station was home to the Atlantic fleet, and nearby were Langley Air Force Base, FTC Dam Neck, Naval Air Station Oceana, and Naval Amphibious Base Little Creek.

Chase had never seen Norfolk like this. With the reinstitution of the draft, millions were put into uniform and trained in various military occupational specialties. The highways were crowded with convoys of Humvees and transport vehicles, and the roar of military jets was ever-present overhead.

Chase remained assigned to DEVGRU, also known as SEAL Team Six. The unit was one of the most elite teams in the world. Having spent the past few years with the CIA's special operations group, returning to the military training regimen was an adjustment. He secretly hated much of the training, but

Chase was getting in the best shape of his life, mentally and physically.

The High Altitude Low Opening (HALO) jumps were exhausting and dangerous. The unit was requalifying everyone, making sure that new members of the team wouldn't hesitate to follow procedures when it came time to execute.

After a few days of overland training, they began doing nighttime drops out of C-17 transports over the cold Atlantic. The paradrops transitioned into underwater operations, where the team swam with advanced gear and trained on the newest version of the SEAL delivery vehicle. They joined up with a Virginia-class submarine, and practiced entering and exiting through its specialized locks.

Chase and the team spent days on end in urban warfare training centers, practicing raids on buildings in the remote North Carolina woods. They also practiced confined area assaults, and operations both with and without the use of their high-speed comms equipment.

"Slide this sleeve on."

Chase was in one of the urban warfare training centers, where a weapons instructor was training them on a new toy.

Chase placed the black sleeve over his left forearm. It reminded him of an NFL quarterback's play-calling sleeve, although probably a bit heavier.

"What's this for?"

"You'll see," said the instructor, handing him a set of clear goggles that looked like an expensive set of ski goggles. Chase and two other SEALs placed them on.

"Comfortable," he noted.

"Ready?" asked the instructor.

"Yup."

"Press the power button on the top left of your wrist device."

The wrist device and his goggles came alive. The goggles

allowed him a complete field of view but now fed in extra information and video projections.

"Damn. This is shit hot."

"You haven't seen the good part yet. Press this button, and select UAS One."

Chase used his wrist-mounted control set to toggle through the choices painted onto the screen in front of him. He could still see the outside world clearly, and it was a bit uncomfortable switching to the text displayed up close.

"You'll get used to it. Trust me, you're going to like this thing…"

Chase selected the UAS One on his screen and a square video feed appeared on his heads-up display. Below it was an aerial map.

Chase whistled. "This is from a drone?"

"Correct. You'll be able to control up to three of them at a time. They're small quad-copters. They can give you real-time battlefield intelligence, increasing your situational awareness. Or…you can select attack mode."

He demonstrated, commanding one of the overhead drones to attack a target twenty-five yards away. Chase and the other SEALs glanced up as they heard buzzing overhead, and then the target—a wooden post in the middle of an empty field—exploded in red smoke.

"Oh shit. This is crazy."

They spent the next few days training on how to use the drones in combat situations.

The unit was the cream of the crop. It was professionally satisfying to be assigned to them, but also maddening to be here INCONUS while a war was going on in Central America. Every few days the unit's intelligence officer would provide a TS-level brief on the status of the war. Today's information was grim.

"Russian military forces are on high alert. Their strategic

bombers at Engels-2 have been forward deployed to northern Russia. There are also indications that several of their submarines have increased their activity level off the US east coast. They may be providing intel to the Chinese."

"They're probably listening to this meeting," quipped one of the SEALs.

Another said, "Hey, tell the Russians to send over Kournikova and Sharapova, and I'll give them whatever they want."

"Da, comrade," said the first.

The intel officer rolled her eyes. "The northernmost ships in the Chinese Atlantic fleet are now east of Brazil. Their Atlantic fleet is divided into several different surface action groups and spread out over more than one thousand nautical miles. Most of their high-value units are clustered around the three Jiaolong-class nuclear battleships that are providing air defense and ASW protection to the SAGs."

"ETA to destination?" asked the DEVGRU's commanding officer.

"They are expected to reach Venezuela within two weeks."

The commanding officer said, "I am assuming that's why all of our jets are now parked at NAS Oceana and Langley AFB? In preparation for our attack on that Chinese fleet?"

"Sir, my understanding is that Norfolk is one of the logistics hubs we are using to arm and train all of our air assets in LRASM tactics. Long Range Anti-Ship Missile. Almost all Air Force attack aircraft and just about every Navy air wing aircraft that isn't fighting in the Pacific is here, either getting maintenance or training on the use of those missiles. They should be scattered to a number of bases and carriers soon."

The CO said, "So it sounds like there's going to be a big naval battle in the Caribbean."

"That would be my guess, sir."

The CO looked between Chase and the intel officer. "Either of you two know what *our* target will be?"

Both shrugged. "Negative, sir."

"Very well. Keep going."

The intel officer continued the brief, but Chase could feel the frustration in the room. Later, when Chase and the team were checking their gear for yet another day of urban warfare exercises, a younger SEAL approached him.

"How much longer are we going to be doing this? Why aren't we downrange, man?"

"Wish I had a good answer." It was all he could say.

"The Chinese are moving north through Costa Rica now. This special project isn't gonna do us much good if we're still here training when the Chinese arrive."

Chase could only shrug and agree. He would say the same thing to his brother later that day.

Once per week, Chase flew to Pensacola to give and receive updates at the Silversmith HQ. The mission he and the DEVGRU operators were training for was so sensitive, the Pentagon didn't trust its system of classified electronic communications to pass along the information. Instead, Chase and the unit intelligence officer received weekly face-to-face briefs in a Sensitive Compartmented Information Facility at NAS Pensacola.

It was past midnight by the time Chase drove from their base to Naval Station Norfolk, where he would catch an 0200 military airlift command flight to Pensacola. One of several small aircraft running almost around the clock between Florida, Norfolk, and DC military bases.

The drive was peaceful, even if his ears were still ringing from the live fire training earlier that day. Now he enjoyed the empty road, and a dark sky filled with stars. He rejoiced at the thought of his sister, recently freed from a POW camp. David had arranged for them to see her in Pensacola, and Chase was grateful for that gift.

His mind turned to his other unexpected gift. His son. During downtime, instincts Chase never knew he had were now overwhelming his thoughts. His saving grace was that he had so little downtime. But now, on this long drive, he decided that he would speak with David about the boy and plan a visit, when he could. Who knew when that would be...?

Oceana Boulevard connected with 264 westbound up ahead, the highway empty this time of night. He glanced to his left as he passed Naval Air Station Oceana. Even in the dark, he could make out the rows of jets parked on the flight line. More F-18s and F-35s than he'd ever seen in one place. It was amazing so many were here, considering all of the ones that must have been deployed in the Pacific, supporting the war in Central America.

He glanced between the road and the naval air base. The grounded jets' dark silhouettes were far from the perimeter road, but there looked to be a decent amount of activity on the flight line. Dozens—no, hundreds—of tiny LED wands were moving around the jets. Chase shook his head. The maintenance personnel must be working around the clock. The Chinese didn't care if you had time to sleep.

Sleep. Chase rubbed his eyes and looked back to the road. He was going to sleep well on his flight to Pensacola.

A white-yellow flash lit up the sky in the direction of the naval air station.

Then another. Followed by a series of thunderous booms.

Chase stopped his car on the highway shoulder and looked toward the explosions. Yellow balls of flame mushroomed fire and smoke into the sky above the airfield. Two explosions. Then four. Then they were almost continuous. A Fourth of July grand finale.

It was sickening. Fireball after fireball. Booming echoes thundering from more than a mile away.

Right in the vicinity of the aircraft.

Chase watched the explosions for more than a minute, his mouth hanging open in horror. He was about to unbuckle and get out of his car when the flashing blue lights of a military security force truck appeared behind him.

The explosions had stopped now. Three men with rifles surrounded Chase's car, and one indicated for him to roll down his window.

"Sir, please show us your ID."

Chase produced his military ID, and the man looked at it before handing it back. The security men were alert, shifting their scan between Chase and their surroundings.

"Sir, we're going to need you to move along. The highway's going to be shut down for security reasons."

Chase nodded. He started his car, then drove away. The military vehicle remained in the middle of the road, lights flashing. Chase thought he could hear the thunder of jet afterburners as he drove away. Maybe it was the sound of a continued attack? Driving away felt wrong, but there was nothing he could do.

Chase realized he was white-knuckling the wheel. His mind was racing, thinking about the implications of losing God knows how many advanced jets. Shit, the LRASM anti-ship missiles were there too. This was going to be bad.

Only when Chase arrived at the Naval Station Norfolk airfield did he realize the full scope of the devastation. Even in the darkness, he could see the flames and smoke rising from the Navy piers. Dozens of fires were still burning. Sirens and emergency vehicle flashing lights were everywhere, and helicopters had search lights pointed over the base.

"What happened?" Chase asked the petty officer on duty at the air terminal.

"We don't know. About half an hour ago, we just started hearing explosions coming from the naval station."

"What's the damage?"

"Nobody knows yet. They shut down access to the base. No phones. No one gets in or out. I'm surprised they let you pass. Anyway, sir, your flight's delayed. All air traffic has been shut down. You're first on the list when it resumes."

Chase slept on a couch in the air terminal, rising with the sun. Sipping coffee, he looked in the direction of the pier. Black smoke still rose from the wreckage.

The morning news showed intense and disturbing footage. Chase was surprised that the military had cleared the video for release. Rows of damaged ships, many with blackened, charred holes in their hulls and superstructures. One destroyer had been hit, and both aircraft carriers looked to be out of commission.

Then the newscaster said, "Reports of similar attacks at other east coast military bases have been coming in this morning. Both Naval Air Station Oceana and Langley Air Force Base were attacked. No word yet on how enemy forces were able to carry out the attack, but the Pentagon expects to give a public briefing later today."

The news channels didn't show the video footage again. Chase was certain that Chinese agents would pass it on to Beijing. Valuable battle damage assessment information on an incredibly successful attack.

Chase thought about what this meant for the war. A Chinese Atlantic fleet was heading north, and America's anti-ship capability had just been gutted.

34

"Our collaboration with the Russians is working well," General Chen said.

Lena and her father stood with a few of his senior military and intelligence leaders as one of the men showed them a summary of international news headlines from the past twenty-four hours. Every global news organization outside the United States was plastering coverage of the surprise Chinese attack on American east coast military installations.

They watched mobile-phone videos of post-attack damage. Originally broadcast on American TV, they were now continuously shown by international news agencies and shared on social media. The footage was incredible. Both for the damage it showed and its value to the Chinese intelligence organization.

Lena said, "I am very pleased with the overwhelming success of the operation, Chairman General." Watching as the monitors showed rows of destroyed American fighters, bombers, and missiles, she found herself wondering where the Americans were keeping her child.

Minister Dong said, "The Americans had consolidated their air forces to load them with advanced new anti-ship missiles.

These jets were to deploy to the Pacific and begin attacking our supply lines. This priority shifted when they discovered our Atlantic fleet movements. Most American Atlantic ships were also in port, getting final loads of stores, fuel, and weapons before setting sail to meet our fleet."

General Chen said, "Our timing was very good."

One of the main screens changed to a satellite picture of Norfolk Naval Station, showing cruisers and destroyers burning in the night. General Chen grinned.

Minister Dong said, "Our analysts say that at least seventy-five percent of their ships and upwards of ninety percent of their aircraft at those bases are now out of commission."

At first Lena was surprised that her father had allowed Minister Dong to continue participating in these meetings. But then she understood that having a defeated rival remain in his inner circle fed into his narcissistic personality. A constant reminder of his greatness, and a warning to anyone who might try to unseat him in the future.

General Chen turned to a PLA colonel waiting behind the inner circle of leaders whom Lena recognized as the slithering man from China's unconventional weapons program.

The colonel placed a tablet computer on the table in front of the general, pointing to the data it displayed.

"Our chemical weapons will be deployed to Panama and Hawaii in the coming days."

One of the politburo members said, "Is that prudent?"

"Strength is the only language an enemy understands," responded General Chen.

Out of the corner of her eye, Lena saw Minister Dong shift his weight. He looked uncomfortable with the conversation.

General Chen said, "And what of our strategic deterrence program? Has the Russian biological weapons research improved our progress?"

"Indeed, General. While the Russians would not share all of their secrets, what they did share allowed us to reverse engineer one of their most powerful bioweapons." The PLA unconventional weapons officer began to describe the biological weapons breakthrough. "The warhead contains a single dose of the agent. Airborne transfer between those infected is very rapid. The virus stays alive in the harshest weather conditions. It affects animals of all kinds. Birds and mosquitoes will both carry it and spread it to humans."

General Chen watched the reactions of those around him. "What happens to those infected?"

"It starts like a harsh flu strain. Those infected seem sick, but the virus is not discernible from most other illnesses in the flu family. After a few weeks, their condition gets progressively worse. This timeframe is important. If it kills too quickly, the virus won't spread. But the weeks of incubation will allow a substantial number of people to become carriers. If launched in a large population center like New York City, we estimate at least one-hundred million people could become infected."

Minister Dong said, "What is the mortality rate?"

"Once infected, over ninety percent die, usually in week three to four."

Lena felt sick. No amount of discipline could hide her distaste. She looked at her father. "What would be our objective in using such a weapon? The Russians have pledged to act on our behalf if the Americans launch nuclear weapons."

"The Russians can't be trusted with such a vital role. Minister Dong said so himself, when we spoke with Jinshan."

Minister Dong looked down at the floor. "I worry about the instability of such a dangerous biological weapon."

General Chen frowned. "Obviously the biological weapon would be used only as a deterrent. Equal in devastation to an American nuclear attack on China. Jinshan carelessly allowed our nuclear warheads to be diminished. This gives us a weapon so deadly, no country would consider taking advantage of our weakened nuclear ability, for this biological weapon would wipe out..."

"Everyone," said Dong.

General Chen glared at him. "It would wipe out any enemies that would dare launch nuclear weapons at us. An organic deterrent freeing us from reliance on fickle allies."

Minister Dong said, "General Chen, with respect, our plans call for massive deployments of Chinese troops and eventually Chinese civilian personnel into the US after we conquer it. While I can see the value in using *some* of these unconventional weapons to overcome tactical obstacles, do you think it wise to deploy such weapons at scale?"

"I think it is wise to win, Mr. Dong. I think it is wise to win." General Chen looked over the small group until his eyes met Lena's.

"What do you say, daughter?"

Lena could hear her own heart beating as she tried to suppress thoughts of her child being gassed or dying of some synthetic variation of the bubonic plague.

"General, your strategic vision and your talent for commanding our great military is unrivaled. But with the success of the Russian attack..."

"You mean *our* attack..."

The Russians, as Lena had predicted, denied involvement in the attack on Norfolk. Fanned by MSS information operations teams, news agencies around the world were reporting that Chinese submarines and long-range hypersonic cruise missiles had conducted the attack. This was preposterous, Lena knew. The Russian submarine force and a sizable contingent of Russian aircraft were the only ones in a position to make it happen. But the comically uninformed world media didn't know that, which suited the Russian president's diplomatic aspirations to deny involvement. And it suited her father's ego to accept credit.

"Of course, General. *Our* attack." A respectful bow of her head. "With the current state of play, I am confident we can achieve victory without the deployment of unconventional weapons."

General Chen contorted his face into an ugly expression. "You have a woman's gentle disposition, Lena. But an ultimate victory demands supreme fortitude. We will use our chemical weapons to break through tactical barriers in the Pacific theater. And we will use the biological weapon as a deterrent. I plan to inform the Americans of our new capability as soon as possible."

The meeting broke up and Lena went back to her apartment. She looked out over the Beijing skyscrapers as the sun set, thinking of her son.

She thought about Jinshan and his motivation for conquering the world. He had believed it stupid for democracies to give decision-making power to the masses. Democracy allowed for ignorance to rule, he argued. Jinshan had envisioned an enlightened leader.

Instead, her father had taken the throne. Lena thought about what her father said of the chemical and biological weapons. General Chen wanted total victory, whatever the cost. He would destroy everything in his path, if victory required it.

Lena had seen the bloodlust in his eyes when he ordered the execution of his political rivals. She now suspected that her own penchant for violence might have been inherited from her father. Some sort of sick genetic curse. While her own desire to kill had subsided since giving birth, she still felt it there, beneath the surface.

As Jinshan's assassin, Lena had an outlet for these dark desires. But she was also a scholar and an intellectual. Her father had none of these redeeming qualities.

And he had none of the qualities that made her admire Jinshan.

At least Jinshan had been motivated by utopian goals. He had made decisions with careful thought and strategy. Her father believed in using brute force and scorched earth. She thought of what might happen to her child under such a ruler.

And she thought about her own role in her father's success. Was she not responsible for putting him in power? Had her murder of Jinshan not made this possible? She was the one to suggest that the Russians attack the American anti-ship missile hubs near Norfolk. Without her advice, China might not be in such an advantageous position.

Duty and loyalty tore her in opposite directions.

She placed her drink on the table and rose to her feet, then walked out her door and headed onto the streets of Beijing.

Tetsuo fought to keep his composure as he watched her enter the restaurant, a small place owned by Japanese immigrants. He ate in the restaurant every few days, but never held meetings with an asset here. It was a place he went to think. To decompress from the intensely stressful life as a non-official cover spy living in enemy territory.

So when Lena, a woman who had killed for that enemy country, took a seat across from him, he was understandably concerned.

Lena said, "We need to talk."

Tetsuo attempted to keep some semblance of professional-ism. She was unlikely to have started off with that if he was about to get rolled up by the MSS. But even if she was here on good faith, that didn't mean they weren't being watched.

"Sure." He placed his chopsticks down and took a sip of water. "I have a place we can..."

She shook her head. "We are black. I wouldn't have come here if they were following me. And they don't know about you." She whispered, "I'm the only one who does. And I destroyed the only evidence."

Tetsuo felt the color drain from his face. Whatever she said, he was burned. He would need to start making arrangements to get out of the country. He would...

"Stop thinking about yourself and listen. I want to speak with someone. I think you worked with him once before. Chase Manning."

Tetsuo could feel his body temperature rising. He needed to make a decision. His training told him to slow things down, make sure both of them were safe, and then start extracting information. But his instincts—hell, her clenched fist on the table—told him that he needed to throw the training out the window. Start talking to her here, in an almost-empty Japanese restaurant that may or may not be free of listening devices. Shit.

"You can talk to him in a week, after we come up with a plan to do so, or you can give me a message to pass on now. You can't talk to him quickly, and you know that."

"I know who your highly-placed agent was. I saw you two meet. I went to him and confronted him about it, which was why he broke off contact with you. Not just because my father has him under surveillance."

Tetsuo blinked. He hadn't heard anything from Dong since Jinshan's death. Just like Lena said, he had assumed it was because the situation had become too risky. "Then why hasn't anyone approached me?" he said. He could have easily replaced the word "approached" with arrested. Or shot.

"Because I haven't told anyone what I know." She didn't need to mention the cyber operations specialist who helped her with the facial recognition ID. He wouldn't talk. And she had destroyed the evidence anyway.

"Tell Susan that I know the recent attacks on American Atlantic military bases didn't come from the Chinese. And tell her that I am the single point of contact between Russian and Chinese leadership."

Tetsuo's face remained impassive, but Lena could see his pupils dilate.

She took out a pen and wrote down a username and the name of an encrypted social media service on a napkin. From her insider knowledge of MSS cyber operations, she knew that it was one of the few encrypted messenger services that, with some software help, could get around most of the Chinese cyber surveillance nets.

"Use this to contact me. You are familiar?"

He nodded.

"You have this username memorized?"

He nodded again. She touched the napkin to the candle flame and tucked it in the candle glass to burn.

"Just tell me the day minus three and the hour plus four. I'll meet you here. Bring CovCom. Soon."

Tetsuo nodded. He had covert communications equipment in a safehouse near the Japanese embassy. Meeting her there would be risky, and riskier still bringing CovCom. But if she was really going to start working for them, and she had the access she claimed, it would be well worth it.

The paper finished burning in the candle. Lena rose from her seat and left the restaurant without looking back.

35

NAS Pensacola

The three siblings grabbed food from an on-base burger joint and took it to the beach. David laid out a white sheet and they sat. It was warm. Turquoise waves washed ashore. A light summer breeze almost counterbalanced the oppressive humidity.

"No air conditioning around here?" Victoria said.

David said, "It is a little warm, isn't it?"

She placed her hand over her heart in a momentary gesture of compassion. "I'm fine. This is nice. Thanks for putting this together."

Victoria was about to ship off to her next assignment, and Chase was only in for a few hours. They might not see each other for quite a while.

Chase said, "I thought you'd be used to the heat now." An easy smile. Victoria could tell they were treating her with kid gloves, the normal banter softened due to her months-long stay in a Chinese prison camp.

David said, "How are you adjusting?"

Both of her brothers were watching her closely. She said, "I'm not going to lie. It sucked. But a lot of things have sucked about the past year."

Chase looked at David. "Any predictions on the next year?"

David reddened. He was always the Boy Scout. The one not wanting to break any rules. Victoria understood that he had fallen into this incredibly important role, an assignment that allowed him to see some of the nation's most vital secrets. David wouldn't do anything to jeopardize their country's success.

She punched Chase on the shoulder. "Leave him alone."

Chase rubbed his shoulder, feigning severe injury. Victoria rolled her eyes.

David said, "Everyone's working hard on different projects. It's...complex. That's all I can really say right now."

Victoria looked at David with sympathy in her eyes. "You seem frustrated."

Chase picked up a small rock and chucked it into the water. "He is."

Victoria said, "Is it about the scientist? Rojas? That was the reason they took us here, right? The scientist in my camp was important."

David cleared his throat, then shook his head. "We can't talk about that."

"Sorry," said Victoria.

David waved it off. "No, it's fine. Just, you know. OPSEC and all..."

Chase wiped ketchup from his mouth. "Loose lips..." Then he seemed to realize that Victoria had actually *been* on a sinking ship...and went silent. Both brothers took the opportunity to take a few extra bites of their meal. Nothing but the sound of chewing.

David said, "So you're going to Jax?"

Victoria nodded. "Yup. Flight doc wanted to make me med down, but I talked to the admiral and greased the skids there. I'll be joining up with a reserve unit, if you can believe it. They're stashing all of the helo pilots they don't know what else to do with in that squadron, then deploying us on whatever still floats."

Chase said, "I heard they took some ships out of mothballs in Philadelphia and refitted them."

Victoria said, "You heard right."

"Is that really faster than making new ones? Doesn't seem like the right way to go about it."

Victoria did an impression of their father's voice. "Son, there's the right way, the wrong way, and the Navy way."

The brothers chuckled.

"I miss the old man."

They all went silent again. This time not even the sound of chewing.

Chase said, "So are you in charge of the squadron, then?"

Victoria said, "No, actually, I'll be thrown in the wardroom with about fifty other pilots. Most of them are reservists, but a few active-duty types like me. My XO took command of my former squadron once I was captured. And apparently going back there wasn't an option. So, I get to just fly...which, aside from the threat of death, should be pretty nice."

Chase nodded approval.

David looked more worried. "Please make sure you are careful."

"I know, David." She turned to Chase. "Is that what's bothering you? You know what's coming and it scares you?"

David said, "No one knows what's coming. And we're all scared."

"So what are you worried about?"

David said, "I work on puzzles and chess games all day. Trying to think three moves ahead of my opponents."

"And?" Victoria said.

David finally relented. "Our opponents have too many pieces. And we can't use all of ours. We can't even use all of our moves, and some of them I don't want us to use..."

Victoria said, "What did Dad used to say, when he was teaching us chess as kids?"

Chase grimaced. "He told me that I should take up lacrosse."

The siblings laughed.

Victoria said, "Sometimes your best move is to let your opponent defeat themselves. Any way you can do that?"

David nodded. "We're working on it."

"You'll get there. Keep studying the board."

David looked at his watch. "Oh crap. I've gotta run."

"Already?"

They rose and David hugged his sister goodbye. "You guys all right getting out of here?"

Chase nodded. "I know where we're going."

Then it was just her and Chase.

"Is David always like that now?"

Chase nodded. "He has become a spook. Or a boss. Or a spook boss. I don't even know how to describe it. But it's really annoying. He's privy to all of the information that nobody else is. And he's always stressed and everything, just like we all are, but..."

"But what?"

"But he's not. China is on the verge of breaking through our lines in Central America, of taking over Hawaii. They've got a giant fleet headed to fight us, and David is pulling the strings for General Schwartz, and he's just..."

"What?"

"It's like he's *okay* with losing."

Victoria cocked her head, giving her brother the most disapproving look she could muster.

"Well you see him all the time now, right?"

"Once per week I fly here and get a half-day brief, then fly back to my new unit." Chase lowered his voice. "They've got us doing some crazy training, but we don't even know what we're going to be doing. It's freaking SEAL Team Six, and they still don't tell us anything about this mission. It's like they've got us prepping for every different scenario."

"Well what does David say when you raise your concerns about where the war is headed?"

"He says he can't talk about it. Just like he did with you now. The one time I got him to say a little more, he said something to the effect of 'we're choosing our battles.'"

Victoria punched him on the shoulder. "Don't be an idiot. David's one of the smartest people I know. And he doesn't give up. If he's doing it this way, there's a reason. So, buck up and have faith."

David returned to the Silversmith building and found Susan waiting in his office.

"We just got a cable from Beijing. Guess who contacted Tetsuo? Lena."

David walked over to his chair and sat, rubbing his chin and looking at the floor while his mind spun into gear. "It's not a counter-intelligence op?"

Susan shook her head. "No. Tetsuo is too high of a risk for that. They would have taken him in for interrogation and tortured him until they found out who else he was running over there."

She was right. David said, "Did she offer us anything?"

"She just asked for CovCom gear."

"What do you think did it?"

Susan said, "You've heard about this bioweapon thing?"

"Yes, of course."

"I think she's spooked about her kid again. She felt it was safe before. But not now. Her father has given her new motivation."

"We need to figure out a way to work this into our existing plans."

"Already working on it."

Victoria's initiation into the HSM-60 Jaguars wardroom took place in a darkened pub near Jacksonville Beach. Over fifty pilots, all wearing their flight suits, filled just about every seat in the place. Two female bartenders were busy filling pitchers nonstop.

The walls were lined with aviation relics. Squadron patches and propellers. The door of an old helicopter. An inflatable female doll of questionable proportions hung from the ceiling.

Victoria could see this from a window just outside the bar. She stood there with six other "newbie" pilots, Plug included. While a commander and a lieutenant commander with thousands of flight hours between them were hardly new aviators, they were new to the squadron and thus being initiated accordingly.

Whap! Whap! Whap!

Inside the bar, all of the pilots began pounding the tables in unison.

Whap! Whap! Whap!

Plug was smiling ear to ear. He had pregamed with a few shots of tequila, until the squadron pilots inside playfully kicked him out of the bar once the ceremony was about to begin. Now he looked at the ensign and two LTJGs who were also in this group. They had come straight from flight school and looked more scared of this initiation ceremony than they were of facing the Chinese.

The bar door slammed open, and a six-foot-five, very wide man wearing a Polynesian tribal headdress and modified flight suit, the arms cut off to look like football coach Bill Belichick, stood towering over them.

"Get in here, rookies!" The big guy looked at Victoria and gave her an impish grin. "And you, ma'am...*please*..."

Victoria laughed and rolled her eyes, then followed the line of new pilots as they entered the dark bar. The sound of pilots pounding their chairs echoed throughout the pub. Hooting and hollering. The sour smell of beer on the floor. On a lit stage off to the left, Victoria saw the squadron's commanding officer and a few of the more senior lieutenants in chairs decorated to look like thrones. The senior officers, who all knew her, smiled apologetically.

For the next thirty minutes, the new pilots were put through a series of playful and humorous hazing rituals. Jokes were told. Insults were thrown. One junior pilot, after consuming an inordinate amount of liquor, ran to the tattoo parlor next door and got his call sign tattooed on his rear end. Large quantities of alcohol were consumed by most, although Victoria, never a big drinker, just nursed a single beer.

When it was over, the new pilots were recognized and those without call signs were awarded them.

The squadron's CO came up and shook Victoria's hand as people were leaving. "Thanks for playing along."

She laughed. "I haven't had this much fun since I was in prison."

He smiled awkwardly and they discussed her ship assignment.

The party continued as the night went on, and the junior officers got progressively rowdier and more intoxicated.

As darkness fell, a shortened school bus, painted gray and given all the markings of a Navy aircraft, pulled up outside the bar. A young ensign fresh out of flight school, who hadn't partaken in the festivities, was on duty that night. Instead of manning the squadron phones, his job was to drive the bus up and down Jacksonville Beach, taking the pilots from bar to bar and, eventually, their homes.

An inebriated Plug stood on a bar stool and exclaimed, "Jaguars! Uniform change! All those participating in bar golf, meet on the bus, in proper attire, in five minutes! Your score-cards are here."

One of the lieutenants began handing out pieces of paper and pencils. "Hey! Hey! Listen up... okay... okay... This will be a nine-hole course. Each bar is one hole. Each sip from your drink is considered one shot. Like, one golf shot."

"One swing!" someone said.

"Right. Right. One swing. Okay...We'll be at each pub hole for thirty minutes. Some of the pubs are marked as sand traps. That means you can't use your right hand. Some are marked as water hazards. That means you can't go to the bathroom at that hole."

"What if it's number two?"

"Shut up, Trainwreck!"

Plug said, "If it's a par five, you get five sips to finish your drink. Par three, you get three sips. Everyone get it?"

"YEAH!" the group yelled.

"Okay, if you're going to wear golf attire, go change. The bus leaves in five."

The group scattered, and the real party was on. Soon the

squadron's more adventurous members headed from pub to pub, and the night became a blur of laughs, beer, and flight suits.

Victoria had one more beer at the next bar, where Plug found her. He was in rare form, but he seemed more subdued than he'd been prior to their time in a POW camp. They spoke loud over the sound of a second-floor band.

Plug said, "You been going to the shrink?" All of the POWs were made to visit a therapist.

She nodded.

"It helping?"

She shrugged.

"Yeah. Me neither."

"Is this helping?" She held up her beer and nodded toward his own.

"Kind of." He smiled.

Victoria said, "Lotta Chinese ships coming. This'll probably be the last one of these outings before we're underway."

"Yup. What do you think our chances are?"

Victoria knew what he was asking. The approaching Chinese fleet was larger and more capable than the remaining US Atlantic fleet, after the damage of last month's attack on east coast bases. When she was a CO, she would have said what needed to be heard. A positive, upbeat message. But here, to Plug, she just said what was on her mind.

"It'll probably be rough."

Plug squinted at her. "Well shit, boss, going out in a blaze of glory is what I've always dreamed of. We're gonna be like the last starfighters..."

They finished talking and Plug went up to the top floor to listen to the band and get another drink. Victoria finished hers and slipped out with an Irish goodbye.

The next morning, she arose with the sun. She took a long

run on the hard-packed sand of Jax Beach. It felt great to sweat. And there was no better feeling of freedom than exercising next to the ocean.

She came to a rest near the Lemon Bar and chuckled to herself as she saw Plug's familiar frame lying face up on a small sand dune.

She nudged his foot with her sneaker. "Hey, you alive?"

"Head hurts..."

"You get all that drinking out of your system?"

"Yes, ma'am. I think I did." He opened his eyes and peered up at her. "You seem like you got all the bad stuff sweated out of you."

Victoria said, "I think maybe I have..."

———

David entered the west wing of the White House and was led to the Situation Room.

"You can go on in, sir," said one of the staffers waiting outside. The US Secret Serviceman held the door for him.

General Schwartz, wearing his Army Green service uniform, caught his eye with a nod, indicating for David to sit in the empty seat to his right. David walked over and sat as the members of the National Security Council spoke.

David felt the tension in the room. President Roberts sat at the head of the Situation Room conference table. He looked five years older than the last time David had seen him. The members of the National Security Council sat around the table. They were some of the most senior members of US government: the Secretaries of State, Treasury, Defense, Energy, and Homeland Security, as well as the Attorney General, the White House Chief of Staff, the Director of National Intelligence, the Chairman of the Joint Chiefs of Staff, the Director of the CIA, the Homeland Security Advisor, and the Ambassador to the UN. It was clear from the looks around the table that none of them were pleased with what they were hearing.

The Chairman of the Joint Chiefs of Staff said, "We anticipate that the Chinese Atlantic fleet will reach port in Venezuela by early next week. By that time, most of the Caribbean and Gulf of Mexico will be within striking distance of the PLA."

The Secretary of State, who David heard was privately urging the president to resign, said, "So let me summarize, General. The Chinese Navy has re-focused its Pacific fleet on protecting its supply lines to Asia in the South Pacific, and they continue to control the South American littorals. The Chinese Atlantic fleet is beginning to arrive in Venezuela. China's South America-based army and air force are strengthening each day, readying for what we assume will be a major push northward. Meanwhile, our military in Central America is getting pounded, and our east coast naval and air assets were decimated in an unforeseen attack. Is that about right?"

The Chairman of the Joint Chiefs said, "Mr. Secretary, I would add that American forces fought valiantly to hold off a Chinese advance in Panama. And..."

The Secretary of State said, "I don't question the valiance of our military members, General. But it sounds like the Chinese have taken South America, and the situation is only getting grimmer." He turned to the president. "Our president recently received a lovely note from the Chinese leader, General Chen, informing us of their new biological weapons program and their intent to use it as a nuclear deterrent. They apparently weren't concerned about the ban on such weapons."

The door opened, and heads turned toward an Air Force officer who delivered a note to the president. President Roberts looked up. "Tell them."

The Air Force officer cleared his throat. "The PLA has begun using chemical weapons in Panama. The reports are still preliminary, but it looks like they've broken through our lines and are now moving north toward Costa Rica."

The president nodded to the Air Force officer. "Thank you, that will be all."

"Those poor souls," said the Secretary of Energy.

The Secretary of State said, "Mr. President, with all due respect, our strategy is clearly not working..."

The president looked at David and General Schwartz. "Gentlemen, I think it's about time you shared our strategy."

General Schwartz nodded to David, who stood.

David said, "Ladies and gentlemen, my name is David Manning. I work for Joint Task Force Silversmith. How many of you are familiar with Operation Bodyguard, the Allied deception plan during World War Two?"

Beijing

Lena knocked on the door of Minister Dong's private residence after hours. His wife eyed Lena with disapproval, but Dong shooed her away and guided Lena into his private study. He opened a gray box resting near his bookshelf and flipped a switch. Lena recognized it as an anti-electronic eavesdropping device.

Lena said, "I wished to speak with you about the strategic deterrence program."

Dong said, "The bioweapon, you mean. What about it?"

"You seemed concerned."

"I am."

Lena said, "Our nuclear launch process has very strong

safeties involved to ensure no mistakes are made. I worry that this biological weapon doesn't have the same safeguards installed. A weapon of this power should not be easy to release."

Minister Dong said, "Neither the biological weapons program nor our strategic missile program is under my purview."

"True. But the satellite launch facility *is*. You still control what happens on that island."

Minister Dong narrowed his eyes. "What does that matter?"

"The military has broken through the American lines in Central America. Our Atlantic forces will soon open up a second front on the American homeland. The final push is coming. If the Americans get desperate, General Chen might be tempted to use his strategic weapons. He has ordered the Strategic Missile Commander to make both nuclear and biological strategic weapons ready for this final stage in the war. Our nuclear missile submarines have clear safety procedures. But the Strategic Missile Commander won't be able to use our nuclear missile submarines to deliver this biological weapon. They are already waiting off the American coast. He needs a missile launch system that will be ready immediately. I believe your space launch facility has an appropriate launch system, does it not? You could offer this. Then you would have influence over the safety protocol. I am very interested in the design of the safety procedures for this weapon."

"This is most interesting." Dong met her eyes with a knowing look. "Who gave you this idea? A new friend? Or an old one, perhaps?"

Lena said, "You once asked me to support you when your moment came. That moment can still come, if we work together. But we must move quickly."

36

Chase returned to the Norfolk Naval Station airport and waited in the base ops building for the rest of the DEVGRU team to arrive. An Air Force jet was scheduled to pick them up in a few hours, and the SEALs were only starting to get here. Hurry up and wait.

Norfolk was as busy as ever, despite the immense damage from weeks earlier. There were signs of the attack, for sure. Lots of scaffolding on superstructures. Remains of sunken ships. But the sailors, Marines, and airmen were everywhere, hustling to and fro, like things were accelerating. Most weren't allowed to leave their ships and bases. A new operational security rule. They were to be ready to set sail, or hop on a transport, the moment they received the order.

On the waiting area near the airfield, the TV was playing local news. Another story on the looming naval battle in the Atlantic. The talking heads were predicting the worst, with most American ships still under repairs and in port. The few seaworthy ones had already been sortied. But the experts felt they would be little match for the approaching Chinese armada.

When the newscasters finished that discussion, they moved on to how bad the economy had gotten.

"C-17's arriving in ten," said one of the unit's senior chiefs who had called up to the control tower to get an estimate. Chase walked out to the flight line, his green sea bag hung over his shoulder.

"You gonna tell us what we're doing yet?" one of them asked Chase.

"Soon." He smiled.

Twenty minutes later, the elite special operations team was loaded on an Air Force transport. The rear door closed, and the aircraft began rolling down the taxiway. Eight hours earlier, David and the Silversmith folks had given Chase the biggest surprise of his professional career when they informed him of DEVGRU's mission.

Now it was Chase's turn to pass that news on to the team. His first stop was the cockpit, where he informed the pilots that they would be changing their destination in flight.

They let him remain up front during takeoff. The view was spectacular.

"Hey, man," one of the pilots called to Chase over the internal comms. "You see this?"

The port at NS Norfolk was emptying out. A line of destroyers steamed out of the channel and into the Atlantic. The two aircraft carriers—both covered with construction tents and scaffolding earlier that day—were now in various stages of departure, one with tugs attached, just leaving the pier, the other plowing east through the water just outside the final channel marker. Their flight decks were clear, and they appeared undamaged.

"I thought all those ships were out of commission?" the pilot said.

Chase put a finger over his lips and made a shushing noise.

As the C-17 Globemaster III leveled off at altitude, Chase headed back to the cargo bay where the DEVGRU team was waiting, sitting in rows of passenger seats. The unit's intelligence officer was connecting her computer to a monitor.

Seeing Chase approach, one of the SEALS yelled to him over the whine of jet engines.

"Hey, Chase, spill it, man. Where are we headed, Costa Rica? There's money riding on this, brother. What's the deal? We going to need to put on our chem gear?"

Chase shook his head and handed the intel officer an encrypted drive, which she slid into her computer.

"We're not going to Central America."

He pressed the button on the computer and a map appeared, showing their flight path. An arrow heading halfway across the world.

"We'll be headed to the Western Pacific."

A few whistles from the crowd.

"Our orders have us HALO dropping at these coordinates..."

Chase glanced at the screen, now showing a blue submarine icon northwest of the Philippines.

"...where we will meet up with the *USS Jimmy Carter*, already on station."

The *Jimmy Carter* was a Seawolf-class submarine, one of the most advanced submarines on the planet.

"Once aboard, the *Carter* will get us within range of the Chinese space warfare launch facility near Hainan."

The room went quiet. Some wore looks of disbelief. Others were shaking their heads.

"Sweet," said one of the SEALs.

"To do this, we're going to have to fly through heavily guarded airspace. We'll be escorted by electronic warfare UAVs

—which will jam enemy radars—and a section of F-22s. Our flight path and the electronic attack package are designed to allow us to arrive on station undetected. But the good news is if anything goes wrong, we should know pretty quick."

"Yeah, we'll be a fucking fireball."

"Pretty much." Chase depressed a button and the screen switched to their mission brief. "All right, this is what we've been training for. Let me take you through it once without interruption. Then I'll take you through it a second time and you can ask any questions you want."

The briefing took about two hours. There were plenty of questions. When they were finished, most of them slept, knowing it would be their last rest for a while.

Twelve hours later, with two Air Force electronic attack drones jamming every radar within two hundred miles, the C-17's rear door opened, revealing the black abyss below. Dim red lights lined the cargo bay floor.

Wearing their masks and pressurized jump suits, the SEALs looked like futuristic warriors from a science fiction film. Weapons and gear were secured tightly to their bodies.

The cargo was dropped first. A series of water-tight trunk-sized containers, each parachute triggered by a twin set of radar altimeters.

Chase stepped forward, his heart pounding as he watched the elite soldiers in front of him jump out into the night sky, their limbs extended.

Then it was his turn.

His stomach was in his throat.

The sound of his breathing through the oxygen mask echoed in his ears.

He jogged forward. The roar of jet engines and hurricane-force winds and sub-zero temperatures enveloped him as he leapt.

Then the feeling of falling...

Falling into the black night sky.

Eventually he reached terminal velocity, small IR lights on each suit visible through his augmented vision device. A heads-up display showed a digital countdown as his altitude dropped from thirty-five thousand feet to less than a thousand. His chute deployed. Chase steered toward the IR buoy the submarine had enabled, a floating beacon only they could see.

Then he landed in the water with a splash and began unclipping himself from his chute before swimming toward the other SEALs already in the inflatable boat they'd brought with them.

It took less than five minutes from splashdown until the submarine surfaced. Soon they were aboard, getting dry and checking their gear. Then the *USS Jimmy Carter* submerged again, quietly heading into enemy waters.

37

Port of La Guaira
Venezuela

PLA Air Force fighter jets circled high overhead as Admiral
Song watched the port fill with Chinese warships and cargo
vessels. Cranes moved the ballistic missiles first. While several
of the hypersonic cruise missiles had been flown in, these larger
medium-range ballistic missiles were not suitable for air
transport.

A young communications officer entered the admiral's
observation tower. "Admiral, General Chen wants to know when
the hypersonic weapons will be operational." The communications officer could see the distaste on the admiral's face. "I apologize, sir. Would you like me to delay our response?"

"No. Tell him we estimate forty-eight hours."

"Yes, sir."

Admiral Song despised General Chen. He thought him an
idiot, although he had to admit it was impressive how rapidly
the man had consolidated power.

The rumbling of tanks and armored fighting vehicles could be heard outside. Admiral Song looked through his binoculars, watching the heavy vehicles load onto the transport ships on the pier. Rows and rows of PLA military vehicles were lined up, preparing to roll onto the dock landing ships. These tanks had been dropped off on the Pacific coast of Colombia. They had been held in reserve in case they were needed for the push north, but General Chen had other plans. Using chemical weapons, he had broken through the American lines in Panama, and so these reserve armor units were sent to Venezuela.

Admiral Song was instructed to load up the reserve troops and armor and sail north to ports on the American Gulf Coast. Russian and Chinese attack submarines—which were now entering the Caribbean—would target American surface ships and submarines to clear his path.

But first, the American air defenses must be destroyed. That's where these hypersonic missiles would be used. Once that happened, Admiral Song's bombers could begin large-scale strikes on American soil, softening coastal defenses prior to the PLA's landing on the US mainland.

Admiral Song hoped to use the port of New Orleans, but that would depend on the battlefield conditions. With any luck, in a few weeks' time, he would be watching Chinese ships offload just like this, but in an American port.

"Sir, General Chen has responded. He said forty-eight hours is not good enough. He wants our ships moving north within twenty-four hours."

Admiral Song nodded. "You see, Lieutenant? Even at the highest levels, it is the same. Why do they ask questions when they already have your answer? Very well. Tell the general that we will change our plans and intend to have our fleet moving north within the next day."

"Yes, sir. Do you want me to tell our operations team?"

Admiral Song frowned. "No. Allow them to do their work. General Chen's whining won't change the physics of how long it takes to move a tank onto a ship."

"Yes, sir."

Admiral Song left the port via helicopter, heading to the tactical operations center at their base near Caracas. Once there, he studied the upcoming plans with his staff. He was nervous. Twenty destroyers and a handful of submarines would escort nearly two dozen transports through American-controlled waters. It would take at least a week for his ships to travel the distance without delays. But he expected delays.

One of the intelligence officers said, "Admiral, we have received some alarming reports of a large number of American ships and submarines leaving port during the past few days."

Admiral Song frowned. "How is that possible? Those vessels are supposed to be out of commission. Show me."

The intelligence officer snapped his fingers, and one of the analysts brought up images on a computer screen.

"Our surveillance personnel located near America's naval bases take note of all activity. This all occurred very recently. A large sortie of many units. Twenty-two destroyers. Two carriers. Several cruisers, frigates, supply ships, and submarines. The numbers are here. But I urge caution. This is new information, and unsubstantiated. It may be that our human assets have been compromised, and the Americans are sending us false information."

Admiral Song had heard of such treachery. The deception of spies. Some of their intelligence could be part of an American misinformation campaign. The Chinese MSS did the same thing, he knew. The MSS was trying to get the Americans to believe that his unit would be conducting its amphibious landing on Costa Rica when they were actually headed to the American Gulf Coast.

"Do we have surveillance imagery on the American military strength at Norfolk?"

"Sir, PLA space command has begun their mass satellite launch this morning. They have just begun providing us with updated satellite imagery."

"Show it to me now."

The intelligence officer brought up a series of images of the large American naval base. The damage on display was tremendous. Even on infrared, he could see a sunken ship in the harbor. That couldn't be faked. Holes in the flight decks of two carriers still in port. The Russians had really outdone themselves.

"Their military airfields?"

"No change, sir. Our pre-attack intelligence was correct. We caught them at their most vulnerable. The majority of their advanced fighters and bomber aircraft were located together to onload their anti-ship missiles."

The intelligence officer brought up a series of satellite images showing damaged aircraft in rows. Some of the damage seemed to have been cleaned up. But in other areas, wings and engine parts were strewn about like trash in an alleyway.

He nodded. "This is good." He turned to his staff. "I believe the reports of ships leaving their harbors must be an American deception campaign. We start our journey north tomorrow."

Susan was on the phone when David entered her office. Her second-in-command was sitting on her couch. She motioned for David to shut the door.

Susan spoke into the phone. "Yes, sir. We just received the

information. I understand." She hung up the phone without saying goodbye.

David said, "That was General Schwartz?"

Susan nodded. "You saw the flash intel report from our friend in Beijing?"

"I did. The balloon is going up."

"Yes. Admiral Song's amphibious fleet is now sailing out of Venezuela. Medium-range conventional ballistic missiles and hypersonic cruise missiles will be launched on US targets within the next few days."

David said, "That part about the bioweapon scares the shit out of me."

Susan said, "Me too. We need to be sure everything is ready."

David said, "The NSA team is finished writing the code. They're doing QA now and will transmit when we give the order."

The phone rang. Susan flung it to her ear. "Yes, sir. Understood. ARCHANGEL is a go."

———

David ran down the linoleum hallway, swinging into one of the rooms where his team worked.

"Is it ready? Tell me it's ready."

Henry and two NSA programmers blinked at him.

"We'd like to test it once more, but..."

"No time. Send it."

One of the programmers fixed his glasses and began typing. "Okay. It's ready for transfer."

Henry walked over to David. "Did we get the okay?"

David nodded. "ARCHANGEL is a go."

Within minutes, a team of NSA technical experts took the

ten-pound black box into the Blue Angel hangar, which was adjacent to the squadron spaces where David's team now resided. The hangar was under heavy guard, not just because the Silversmith team was nearby.

Inside the hangar was a drone capable of hypersonic flight. An unmanned version of the SR-72. The NSA experts physically uploaded the program Henry and his team had designed into the drone's on-board computer. Twenty minutes later, the drone took off in broad daylight, going supersonic over Mobile, Alabama, shattering windows with its sonic boom. Within six hours, it had reached the East China Sea, where it transmitted fourteen gigabytes of code to the waiting antenna of the *USS Jimmy Carter* before self-destructing and crashing into the Pacific.

38

The Chinese military space launch facility was located on a small island base just northeast of Hainan. The Chinese had transformed a few square kilometers of rock jutting out of the South China Sea into a substantial island military facility. The island now contained multiple large runways for landing military transport aircraft, as well as dozens of man-made peninsulars used as rocket launching sites. Each peninsular was capped with a launch pad. The entire island base was surrounded by a man-made sandbar, turning it into an atoll. The outer sandbar ring protected the inner islands from weather and waves.

The SEALs were in their scuba gear when the drone transmission came with their execute order.

The captain of the *USS Jimmy Carter* told Chase and the SEAL team commander, "Our UAV picked up surveillance footage of their crews making preparations for the next mass launch. Swim fast."

The special operations team headed into the airlock chamber, and the hatch was closed behind them. Shortly after, the compartment began filling with water. Once filled, the team opened the outer compartment and swam into the cold, dark ocean.

The SEALs used handheld propulsion devices to cut their journey down to ten minutes. Reaching the island's outer sandbar, they staged and anchored their equipment close enough that it wouldn't be pulled away by the current, but far enough from shore that it wouldn't be uncovered by a receding tide.

It was dusk when the seven-man team emerged from the water and quietly stepped onto the atoll's outer beach carrying silenced MP submachine guns and wearing black wetsuits. Their footsteps in the sand were washed away by the lapping waves.

Fifty yards to the team's east, a security vehicle was parked on the same sandbar.

Two passengers sat in the security vehicle. One was a CIA asset—one of the deep cover operatives Susan had been running for nearly a decade. The other passenger was a Chinese military guard who was now convulsing in the passenger seat, a syringe in his neck, its plunger depressed.

The Chinese agent stepped out of the vehicle and motioned to the SEALs. "We must hurry. The launch is in minutes."

The SOF team climbed into the back of the security vehicle, which sped along the sandy beach and onto a paved road. Through the rear cutout in the drab green truck bed cover, Chase and the SEALs could see other Chinese military personnel, along with missile transport trucks, helicopters parked on the flight line, and technicians working on satellite antennas.

The security vehicle stopped outside an unmarked rectangular building and the guard led them around the back. "This way."

The Chinese agent swiped a keycard in a digital lock and typed in a code. After a beep, the metal door opened, and the

American special forces team followed the Chinese agent into the building.

They hurried down an empty hallway until the agent stopped at a door marked with large red Chinese characters. He signaled for them to wait in the hallway, then typed on the keypad next to the door and entered. Chase heard a thud, and then the agent reappeared, motioning for them to follow. Inside was a dark room filled with security monitors. A Chinese woman lay on the floor, a syringe sticking out of her neck, convulsing just like the other man.

"Close and lock the door," the agent whispered, and the men complied. Chase looked at the monitors. Dozens of launching pads were arranged on the center of the island, steam rising from most.

The team's NSA man said, "Is this the computer I should use?"

The Chinese agent shook his head. "No."

"Which one, then?"

"We will need to get in there." The agent pointed at one of the screens.

"You're shitting me," said Chase. The agent was indicating a screen that showed at least a dozen Chinese men and women sitting in what looked like a NASA operations floor. Multiple armed guards were clearly visible throughout the space.

The DEVGRU team leader said, "Lead the way."

"First I need to disable security communications." The agent began typing on a computer. Several screens on the wall went black. He then walked over to a radio control box and began changing frequencies.

He looked at Chase and the SEALs. "The room is two doors down on the left. About twenty men are inside, at least half of them armed. I have made sure they will not know we are coming. But some of them could still cause problems for our mission. It would be best to disable them all quickly. As soon as we enter."

Chase and the men nodded.

The group left the security room and jogged down the hallway, weapons at the ready. The SEALs led the way, with Chase and the NSA guy following. Adrenaline surged through Chase's veins.

Two of the SEALs took station on either side of the door. One of them held a flashbang. The Chinese agent grabbed his wrist. "No. It could damage the equipment."

Chase wondered what this guy thought the bullets were going to do.

Then the Chinese agent was swiping his keycard and typing in another code, and the door opened with a hiss. The SEALs raced in, one after another.

And the shooting began.

Chase had never seen men move so fast. Five DEVGRU SEALs sped through the room like men possessed, their weapons spouting off suppressed rattles as they went. The air smelled of gunfire, and Chase could actually hear the thumps of bullets hitting bodies.

Within seconds, every Chinese target in the room was on the floor, covered in blood.

Chase forced away any contemplations of who these people were, or whether they deserved this ending to their lives. Those haunting thoughts would have to wait.

As the SEALs began yelling "Clear," Chase looked at the Chinese agent. "Which computer?"

He pointed to one in a row of terminals in the front of the room. Chase removed a gray laptop from his water-tight backpack and placed it on the desk next to the computer. The NSA man took a seat at the terminal and they both went to work, Chase acting as a sort of surgeon's assistant while the NSA man performed the meticulous work of cyber-hacking. Like surgery, it was a life-or-death matter.

Two miles away, the *USS Jimmy Carter* had just finished connecting an NSA-owned undersea fiber communications cable to a trio of nearly invisible communications buoys.

"Line-of-sight connectivity achieved," the NSA cyber expert announced. A laser-communications signal was now beaming to the building's roof, transferring vast amounts of data back and forth to the NSA's fiber communications cable via the buoys.

This allowed a small army of NSA cyber warriors in Fort Meade, Maryland, who had been training for this mission for the past two months, to get to work. Chase could just imagine them sitting there, high on caffeine, looking at the clock, waiting for the indication that connectivity had been achieved like hungry stock traders waiting for the opening bell.

Chase felt a tremor in his feet.

A loud rumbling noise outside shook the building.

"It's begun," said the Chinese agent. Another rumbling sound. Chase glanced through the high slit of a window from his seat. He could see the rockets firing into the sky, one after another, each carrying dozens of mini satellites that would be deployed and operational within minutes.

The mass satellite launch had begun.

The SEAL commander tapped the NSA man sitting at the computer terminal on the shoulder. "Did we make the connection on time?"

The NSA man looked at his screen while he typed. "Good up and down links...Yeah. I think we're good. *Son of a bitch*...I can't believe this actually worked."

David was on a secure video call with the president, Silversmith, and the two five-star generals in charge of SOUTHCOM and NORTHCOM, General Schwartz and General Mike Lowres, respectively.

Susan sat behind David, allowing him to speak.

"Mr. President, gentlemen, I have good news. Operation ARCHANGEL appears successful so far. The software overlay is operational."

The president said, "What does that mean, David?"

"Mr. President, now that the software is operational, the NSA is able to access all of the data going in and out of the Chinese space launch facility, which, for security reasons, was the central hub by which all of the PLA's satellite data had to flow."

"So they won't have access to their satellites when the attack begins?" the president asked.

"Sir, the Chinese will still see data from their satellites. But now the NSA can manipulate it. Within a few minutes, US Cyber Command will swap the data they receive. Think of it like robbers swapping the security feed of a bank vault. The new information the Chinese military and intelligence units receive from their satellites will be filtered through the NSA's ARCHANGEL program. Except this isn't just video feed to a bank vault. This is all of China's surveillance, communications, targeting, and GPS location data. Crucial information needed for their imminent attack."

General Schwartz said, "David, when will US units be able to access the datalink?"

"General, you can start putting out orders to all units to make the link connection immediately. Cyber Command has updated all crypto codes and software."

The president said, "What impact will this have for us?"

"Sir, China will now see only what we want them to see. We

have essentially hijacked China's satellite network. Our military units will be able to use this network for targeting, communications, and datalink capability. We now have our own GPS and surveillance system, courtesy of the PLA."

"Won't they shoot it down, just like they've shot down our own satellites?"

"Eventually, yes, sir, they probably will. But because the Chinese don't yet know this has occurred, there won't be anyone trying to shoot these satellite constellations out of the sky."

The president looked relieved. "Gentlemen, this is pure brilliance."

39

Lena stood next to General Chen as they watched the Atlantic battle unfold from the Central Military Commission's strategic operations command center. The next twenty-four to forty-eight hours might determine the fate of the war. And perhaps the fate of her child.

The PLA colonel standing duty greeted General Chen and said, "Our fleet travels north, General. The mass satellite launch is complete. Soon our GPS and datalink will sync up with all Venezuela-based weapons systems. Short-range missile attacks will commence as we target all air defense units along the American coast."

The general pointed at the map of the region. "Take me through the rest of the plan."

"Certainly, General. Our aircraft based in Colombia and Venezuela are standing by. The first units launched will be our fighters and airborne early-warning aircraft. The fighters will destroy any American aircraft that attempt to impede our progress. Then our airborne troops will begin parachuting into landing zones inside the continental US. We will deploy several thousand troops deep in the American countryside, gaining control of airfields and fuel depots. Our bombers will destroy military targets inside the US that had previously been protected by surface-to-air missiles."

"And what of Central America, while this is going on?"

"Our Pacific naval fleet is moving north along the coast. PLA forces are fighting in Costa Rica. But we will launch simultaneous strikes on the American ground forces in Central America and Mexico."

General Chen listened a while longer and then waved off the officer. "Fine, fine. How much longer until we begin launching our missiles?"

One of the senior officers announced, "Sir, the first strike is about to begin."

Admiral Song could taste the salt spray on his tongue as a steady wind carried the sea up to the bridge wing of his Jiaolong-class battleship. All around him, he could see Chinese ships on the horizon, spread far enough apart to not be easily targeted by a single enemy submarine but close enough to reap the benefits of the mighty Jiaolong-directed energy air defense and anti-submarine capability.

"Global positioning system is online, Admiral. Our hypersonic batteries in Venezuela are loading their targeting data now, cross-checking with the updated reconnaissance imagery."

Admiral Song nodded. "Good. Any changes to the American defensive posture?"

The two officers glanced at each other.

Admiral Song said, "What is it?"

"There is no change to the satellite data, sir, but..."

The other officer said, "Some of our organic drones are now sending back information from the US mainland."

"Already?"

That was good news. The ships were still more than a day away from reaching the US mainland.

"Why is this a problem?"

"Sir, there was a discrepancy in some of the reconnaissance data."

"Well what do the satellites show? Those are over us now, providing real-time feed."

"The satellites show the same images they did during the *last* mass satellite launch, Admiral."

Admiral Song was losing his patience. "I don't see the problem. What the hell are you saying?"

The admiral's phone rang, and he picked up, annoyed with these stuttering fools. "Go ahead."

The voice on the other line was the Central Committee Liaison Officer. Similar to the political officers that all Soviet vessels used to embark, this man reported directly to the politburo. "General Chen would like an update, Admiral."

Admiral Song exhaled, willing himself not to curse. "Tell the general that our ships are now sailing north of Cuba. Air coverage is overhead. And the first wave of hypersonic missiles is about to shoot off the rails. And don't call me again. That last part was for you."

He hung up the phone. The two bumbling junior officers were still standing there, looking nervous.

"*What?*"

"The drone imagery, sir..."

"*What about it?*"

"Sir, it does not *match* the satellite imagery. Our organic reconnaissance drones use a different communications channel. It is very reliable."

Admiral Song narrowed his eyes. "Show me."

They walked into the intelligence cell, located behind

multiple airtight doors and an armed security guard. Once they were inside, an analyst showed a series of images on the large flat screen in the center console. Half a dozen intelligence analysts were in the room, all watching the admiral. An unusual nervousness permeated the room. They weren't being quiet because he was the highest-ranking officer in the fleet. There was something wrong, and they were waiting for him to see it.

The intelligence officer said, "Admiral, this was the image from the satellites last week. And this is the image coming from the satellites right now. And here...this one we just got from our drone now flying over Norfolk naval base."

Admiral Song's face went white as he remembered the intelligence report they'd discounted a few days earlier.

"Sir, the Norfolk ships aren't damaged...they're *gone*..."

"What do you mean, the American carriers have been *deployed*?" General Chen rose from his seat, the veins in his neck pulsating. Lena watched as his quivering minion reported unexpected movements from the American Atlantic fleet.

"Sir, two carriers and their escorts. Our reconnaissance aircraft spotted them just now. Their location is inconsistent with the satellite data we have received."

General Chen narrowed his eyes, looking left and right along the row of senior advisors.

"Minister Dong. What does this mean?"

Lena thought it was interesting that her father picked the one man in the group who wasn't considered a loyalist. Even General Chen was forced to recognize true competence when it mattered.

"It appears that we have been deceived, General. Either the

Americans have hacked into our drones, and want us to believe they have a stronger fleet, or..."

"Or what?" General Chen looked worried now.

Minister Dong paused in thought. "Our mass satellite launch occurred less than twelve hours ago. My sources tell me that the Americans have not yet attempted to shoot down our satellites."

"That is unusual."

"Yes. It is possible that our attacks on American anti-satellite systems are bearing fruit. Or it is possible the Americans have corrupted the data we are receiving from those satellites."

"Why would they do this?"

"They may have wanted to appear *weaker* than they really are..."

Lena looked at the tactical display. The digital image showed the Chinese fleet's location northwest of Cuba. Dangerously close to America, if the US military was trying to lure them in.

General Chen said, "But...you say it is still possible that our drones have been corrupted? The satellite data *could be* accurate?"

The hopeful words of a frightened leader.

A PLA admiral approached General Chen. "Sir, our submarines are now tracking several groups of American ships entering the Florida Straits." He looked uneasy. "I believe the American fleet was not as damaged as previously assessed."

General Chen's face grew red. He snapped his gaze toward Lena. "The Russians failed us. Was that on purpose?"

Lena shook her head. "I don't think so, General. But the Americans have many spies. It is possible that they were made aware of the Russian operation."

General Chen looked toward his military advisors. "What is the impact?"

The PLA admiral said, "Sir, it is hard to be certain. We are receiving many conflicting reports."

"What is the worst-case scenario?"

The admiral said, "Worst case is that the Americans have two carrier strike groups headed to meet our fleet in the Gulf of Mexico and Caribbean. They are already within attack range with their aircraft, if they have any on board."

The general looked confused. Then the confusion turned to fury. "How was I not made aware of this!" He slammed his fists down on the table.

Lena said, "The American air bases. Was that a ploy as well?"

"Both our organic drone recon imagery and the potentially corrupt satellite imagery continue to show significant damage to American air bases. Hundreds of aircraft were destroyed." The speaker, a PLA general, glanced at Minister Dong.

Minister Dong said, "In light of the naval deception, is it not possible that the Americans are only making it appear as if their aircraft are destroyed?"

"How would they do that?" General Chen said.

"Decoys, sir. We have used similar tactics in training. We would need to examine the aircraft closely to be sure. But our drones can't get close to those air bases without the risk of getting shot down."

The PLA admiral said, "That is unlikely. If these images of destroyed aircraft are actually decoys, the Americans would have had to move the real aircraft to another base. Our agents have been monitoring all American military bases. We would have seen this occur."

General Chen wrung his hands together. "How does this change our attack strategy?"

The PLA admiral said, "We should modify some of our

targets. Attack the approaching American strike groups before they reach Admiral Song's Atlantic fleet."

"What about our submarine force?"

The PLA admiral said, "Admiral Song has only a handful of attack submarines, and those are protecting his capital ships, the Jiaolongs. Even if they were detached, it would take them more than a day to reach the American fleet. The real threat is of air and missile attacks. And the Jiaolongs are more than capable of defending against these."

General Chen raised his voice, making a decision. "Reallocate our targets. Defeat the American naval fleet. But make sure we also destroy the land-based air defense threats. Our second wave relies upon this."

Lena watched as the general's command was relayed among a handful of officers in the command center. They communicated the information in different ways. Via voice, wearing high-tech headsets that transferred the information directly to Admiral Song's combat information center. And via secure chat messages being transmitted to missile battery commanders, the PLA Air Force commanders preparing their jets to launch from South America, and the ship and submarine commanders of Admiral Song's fleet.

All of these communications would transit through the multi-billion-dollar constellation of Chinese mini-satellites recently launched from the South China Sea.

But first, the commands and associated targeting data made a quick stop in Fort Meade, where they received instant analysis.

And a few modifications.

David and Henry watched from the Silversmith operations

center as an NSA tech provided them with the play-by-play from his computer.

"The NSA has received updated command information from Beijing. GPS overlays and distance corrections are being uploaded into the Chinese targeting and navigational computers."

Henry leaned over to David and said, "Can you tell me now?"

David shook his head. "Not yet."

The NSA tech said, "The PLA Navy and Air Force datalink and GPS are now controlled by Fort Meade."

A muffled cheer from several of the workstations. Everyone in the room was monitoring their consoles with rapt attention, watching secure messages travel back and forth from various ultra-secret command centers in the United States. The war had given the best American computer programmers a great incentive to work for the NSA. No one was going to get rich creating the next social network during World War Three. But the same drive and ingenuity that built Silicon Valley was put to work in other ways. The NSA and other American agencies recruited and trained these men and women to become lethal cyber warriors.

Now came the payoff.

An Air Force technical sergeant rotated in his swivel chair and announced to the group, "The first Chinese hypersonic missiles are launching from Venezuela now."

Henry said, "So this is it, right? The attack is starting?"

Outside the building, an air raid siren began wailing.

Henry looked nervous. "Should we seek shelter?"

David kept watching the digital display that showed locations of ships and aircraft. Very few air tracks were flying yet. Some Chinese radar planes, and a modest combat air patrol. No American aircraft had launched.

Then several red air tracks appeared over Venezuela, each with a velocity vector jutting out from its center. The length of that vector symbolized its speed. These were the first of the Chinese hypersonic cruise missiles. Their speed vectors quickly lengthened until they spanned the Caribbean.

"Holy hell," David said, looking at them. "That's at least twenty, and they're just getting started. This had better work."

Henry said, "If it doesn't, we should probably listen to that air raid siren and seek shelter."

"If it doesn't, we won't have enough time."

"Will you tell me now?"

David looked at him. "Fine. What do you want to know?"

"Start with the hypersonic weapons."

David continued watching the digital air tracks as he spoke. "After the scientist, Rojas, was captured by the Chinese, we realized that even in the best-case scenario, both the US and the Chinese were going to have the Rojas hypersonic technology. But we could choose to differentiate how we used it. The Chinese had a distinct advantage with their mass satellite launch capability. We wanted them to be overly reliant on that capability. We've been grooming them to believe it was effective for the past year. Lulling them into a false sense of security. But as you know from your work, that network wasn't secure."

Susan walked over. "Is this an unauthorized briefing?"

David said, "You said he could come in here."

Susan shrugged. "At this point, what does it matter? Win or lose, everyone will know what we did tomorrow."

Henry said, "So the Chinese satellite communication and datalink..."

David said, "That was a major advantage for the Chinese in all of the battles they've fought over the past year. We let them think that their superior anti-satellite capability was shooting down our own satellites. But we let them. We purposely made it

easier for them to do. We allowed them to become overconfi-
dent, and now they are. The PLA linked their biggest, most
important weapons systems into a satellite network. But with
your code, we now control it. We can now read their communications. The NSA has hundreds of personnel who have been
working nonstop on how to offset the digital navigation and
targeting data the Chinese are using. We now control their
targeting."

Admiral Song stood in the ship's combat information center.
One of his best officers had just reported more errors showing
up in their satellite communications and datalink network.

"Admiral, our ships are preparing to launch cruise missiles
on land-based targets. During their pre-launch checks, they
have detected severe inaccuracies. But they were ordered to
launch anyway."

"What were the inaccuracies?"

"They think the GPS targeting data is wrong."

A gasp from some of his men caused Admiral Song to turn
around. One of the video monitors showed the nearby escort
ships. Destroyers and frigates.

One of the destroyers looked like it had been cut in half.

The ship's bow and stern were jutting out of the water at odd
angles while the area amidships sank below the sea.

The sailors in combat began shouting.

Then the screen flashed white. When the image returned, a
second ship was hit, a geyser of whitish-gray seawater rising up
hundreds of feet from its center.

Admiral Song felt a chill run down his spine.

The junior officer next to him yelled, "Sir, the missile

commander has issued an alert! We are under attack from our own hypersonic missiles."

A hundred miles away, the Chinese missile battery had just finished launching several dozen hypersonic cruise missiles. They reached Mach six within seconds, and took mere minutes to travel north over the Caribbean and reach their targets. Both before launch and during their flight, the missiles received updates from the constellation of Chinese mini-satellites now orbiting the earth. From ground control stations in Venezuela, Chinese missile men eagerly watched their screens. The missiles had been programmed to destroy American land and sea targets. Error messages began appearing on the Chinese ground control station computers immediately after launch. But there was nothing they could do.

The hypersonic cruise missile that hit Admiral Song's escorts was supposed to destroy US Army air defense radars near the Everglades.

It was approximately 942 nautical miles off target.

Or just twenty-five feet, if you were one of the programmers sitting in the NSA's ultra-secure operations center in Fort Meade.

On board Admiral Song's Jiaolong-class ship, the room suddenly went dark as a missile tore through the center of the superstructure. Admiral Song felt the floor sink and then rise upward again, collapsing everyone to the floor, breaking bones and knocking several unconscious.

When the dim emergency lights illuminated the room, he couldn't hear anything. But he could see sailors scrambling around inoperative computer terminals. Sparks spewed from an open gash in the electrical wiring on the bulkhead. A sickening feeling washed over the admiral as the deck began pitching up at a steeper and steeper angle.

As his hearing came back, fire and flood alarms rang

throughout the ship. He climbed out of the combat information center and hobbled up a ladder to the bridge to look out at his fleet. Plumes of black smoke rose from at least half of the ships within view. Some were missing altogether.

Then another hypersonic missile slammed into his ship, incinerating him and everyone nearby.

40

David watched as General Schwartz was piped into the Silversmith operations center via secure video conference.

"Susan, David, you've got exactly two minutes. What information do you need to pass?"

"Sir, we're reading communications between PLA battlefield commanders and the Chinese military high command. General Chen and his leadership are now aware that their satellite networks are unreliable. They've ordered all Chinese military units to disconnect from satellite-based datalink."

General Schwartz was surrounded by men in various versions of camouflage utility uniforms. Behind him was the massive tactical operations floor at SOUTHCOM.

"This was expected."

"Yes, sir. Soon we'll stop being privy to Chinese military comms. But you need to know that the Chinese military has received orders to begin a large-scale air attack on American units. Chinese fighters and bombers are being scrambled, and all remaining Chinese naval forces are being moved in toward the littorals to support."

"Understood."

"One more thing, sir. The Chinese have sent word to their Russian military counterparts. Russian strategic forces are on high alert."

General Schwartz was like a machine processing information. He spoke to someone off camera. All David could hear was "Recommended COA?"

Someone David couldn't see replied, "Those targets in Costa Rica are still critical to defeat. We could divert some air assets to..." David couldn't hear the rest. Military generals hatching out plans and deciding where to move their pieces.

General Schwartz looked up at the screen. "We're setting ARCHANGEL Phase Two in motion."

The video call ended.

Immediately after the video call with David, General Schwartz's air operations staff contacted the strike warfare commander for Operation ARCHANGEL. In the last-minute scramble that always took place during important military operations, screaming men and women in various military operations centers began bargaining with their counterparts in other services and intelligence organizations. Not the least of which was the NSA's ultra-secret cell filled with cyber operations specialists who had tapped into the Chinese datalink. They were now providing new, last-minute targeting information to American and allied air assets.

The targeting data and mission orders were transmitted to US military units at bases around the world.

This included several remote airfields in Canada.

Gander, Newfoundland

"A moose! Hightower, check it out, man. I finally saw a moose!"

"That's great, Jack." Major Chuck "Hightower" Mason taxied his B-1 to the hold short line of runway three-one at Gander International Airport.

For weeks they had been waiting here in the Canadian wilderness, sleeping in camouflaged trailer barracks that the US Army had set up. Tarps covered their aircraft to make them invisible to overhead surveillance.

Hundreds of jets had been sent here the night of the faux attack on US military bases. Fighters and bombers. Transports filled with maintenance personnel, equipment, and parts. All communication to and from Gander had been cut off for security reasons. No one had spoken to their families since arrival. Their location was classified.

Half the US Air Force had been hidden away in places like Gander, Newfoundland, and a half-dozen other remote locations throughout Canada. Gander, the same place where thirty-eight commercial aircraft were diverted to on September 11, 2001, now held over four hundred American fighters and several squadrons of bombers.

Tonight, they were finally leaving.

Hightower looked out through his cockpit window as hundreds of aircraft performed the elephant walk, the slow taxi toward the runway that was normally used to train for massive sorties. But this wasn't training. This was a colossal, simultaneous alert launch.

"I got to tell you, Hightower, I'm sure glad I saw a moose before we left. I mean, if we get sent to Canada, I better see some wildlife, you know? Aside from these dumb fighter pilots that we got stuck with."

Hightower allowed himself a glance. The antlered animal strolled down a nearby road, seemingly oblivious to the thunderous engine noise erupting from the runway every few seconds as the jets took off.

Soon entire squadrons were blasting into the night sky, led by F-35s from the 4th Fighter Squadron, the Fighting Fuujins. Then F-15Es from the 336th Fighter Squadron, the Rocketeers. Hundreds of others followed, including Hightower's B-1. Canadian air force aircraft also thundered upward, joining their American partners in the transit south. The same thing was occurring at several other airfields across Canada, as well as US bases that hadn't been part of the deception.

USS Michael Monsoor

Victoria and Plug had gone from rags to riches. Three days earlier, they had been told that the Navy was reactivating old frigates and refitting them after being in mothballs for so long. Instead, the helicopter squadrons waiting at NAS Jacksonville and NS Mayport were told to join up with the sortied ships of the Atlantic fleet. Ships that, until recently, had been thought damaged or destroyed.

Now they were on DDG-1001, the *USS Michael Monsoor*. One of the three Zumwalt-class destroyers, the sleek and modern ship cut through the deep blue waters north of Cuba. The *USS Michael Monsoor*, after traveling through the Panama Canal to the Atlantic several months ago, was one of the ships reportedly damaged beyond repair during the submarine attack on Norfolk.

But that, like so much else, was a ruse.

Plug made the radio call. "MONSOOR control, good morning, Jaguar 600 with you twenty miles to your east at angels one, one dipper, ten difars, two torpedoes, and a partridge in a pear tree."

"Jaguar, *Monsoor* control, kick channel four."

"Roger."

Plug switched them to a secure communications channel, and they began working with the ship's tactical airborne controller to help visually identify all of the unknown contacts nearby.

"Jaguar 600, *Monsoor* control, we've just received a one-hour time-late location on a possible submarine. Standby for coordinates."

The data was transmitted from the ship to the helicopter, and Plug immediately set up their navigational information to direct them there.

"Coming left," said Victoria, and she banked the aircraft hard left. "Dropping to five hundred feet."

"Roger five hundred."

She lowered the collective power lever with her left hand and felt a flutter as the rotor angle changed and they began losing altitude, flying toward an enemy submarine. Victoria tried to keep her thoughts clear, but flashes of her dark past once again crept into her mind's eye. The submarine attack that had sunk the *Stockdale*. The submarine attack that had killed her father on the *Ford*. She began breathing heavier.

"Boss." Plug was looking at her, his visor up. "You good?"

Victoria glanced over at her copilot and nodded quickly. "Yup."

Just keep flying.

41

David and his team ate and slept in the Silversmith building for the next few days, on call in case Susan or anyone else needed their expertise as their plans were executed. Most of the team remained in the huddle rooms, reading or talking. Trying not to worry as the clock ticked away. David and Henry, the only ones authorized to be in the Silversmith operations center, returned to give the larger group updates every few hours. But now they had returned to observe.

It was a front row seat to history, and to the results of their work. They tried to remain out of the way, sitting in the back of the room. Dozens of men and women from various military and intelligence organizations typed on terminals and spoke into headsets.

A senior enlisted Air Force woman wearing a headset called out, "Chinese aircraft are taking off in large numbers from their bases in Venezuela and Colombia."

Susan and the operations officer next to her nodded, acknowledging the update. On the large digital map display, dozens of red air tracks began appearing, their speed vectors stretching north.

Susan said, "Do they have any indication of the American air tracks to the north?"

"Negative. We think not yet, anyway. They're still pretty far off. Won't show up on organic Chinese radar planes for another hour or so."

Henry leaned over to David. "What are they talking about?"

David said, "You are starting to hear about some of the other missions that we planned. You were in one compartmentalized team whose job was to help us gain access to the Chinese satellite network. It was crucial, but we were also working on several other programs that, when combined, should bear significant fruit."

Henry motioned toward the screen. "And those blue symbols up top...those are one of your programs?"

David nodded. "Remember during the Chinese submarine attack, how a lot of news agencies were immediately showing footage of our military bases under fire?"

"Of course. Some idiots with cell phone cameras gave it to the news, who put out vital intelligence. They showed all of our destroyed ships and aircraft."

David didn't blink. "We distributed them. Those videos were staged. Produced by some very talented folks—who, interestingly enough, used to work in Hollywood and now work for the CIA. You're familiar with the term Deep Fakes?"

"Of course. It's when they use modern technology to manipulate videos to show something false. The Chinese used it during the opening stages of the war. They put out a false video on all of our major news networks showing our president announcing that he was nuking China."

"That's right. They wanted to confuse us. And to trick the world into believing that the United States launched nuclear missiles at North Korea. But in actuality, China did that. Chinese submarines fired on North Korea, and then China convinced the world it was us. That gave them enormous political leverage."

Henry said, "So you are saying that the submarine attack on our bases...that was faked? By us? And that all of those videos that went out over the news...those were..."

"Created by us. Delivered to the US media by anonymous assets. Once the videos were picked up by the global media, where we had no authority, the US government officially demanded that US media organizations stop showing the false attack imagery. This further solidified its veracity, in the eyes of any foreign intelligence operatives."

Henry said, "So what actually happened?"

"We closed off access to all of those bases. The night of the attack, we flew as many of those jets as possible to a few remote airfields in Canada for safekeeping. With only limited ISR capability, the Chinese—and the Russians, for that matter—can't look at everything. From our agents in China and Russia, we knew both countries were spending all of their resources scouring every inch of US air bases. They saw what we wanted them to see. Destroyed decoys mostly. We sank one ship on purpose. A few aircraft. We needed to make it look real. But with the increased security around our bases, we were able to minimize the cameras. We covered our ships with scaffolding and fake damage. Every so often, we would leak images to suspected Chinese agents operating in the US. Susan is still running some Chinese agents."

"Are you supposed to be telling me this?"

David shrugged, looking at the digital map. The red aircraft were separating into groups, some heading west over Central America and others north toward the approaching American fleet. "All of our cards are on the table now."

Henry shook his head. "So, let me get this straight. We have a full-strength US Navy Atlantic fleet and a healthy Air Force headed into battle, and the Chinese don't know about it? Am I understanding that correctly?"

"They'll know about it soon." David smiled.

"But what about Russia?"

"What about them?"

"Wouldn't they tell China that they didn't launch the attack? Wouldn't they deny involvement?"

"They did deny it."

"Yeah, but...that was like a non-denial denial, right? Weren't they winking at China when they denied it?"

David said, "We have some people who helped with the winking."

"Holy shit." Henry frowned. "Wait. I'm still missing something. The hypersonic weapons."

"Ah, yes."

"You used the Chinese's own hypersonic weapons to inflict massive damages on their own ships..."

David pointed to the screen showing live drone video of smoking Chinese tank formations. "And some of their ground assets in Central America..."

"Right."

"But..."

"But why did you need Rojas at all, then? You've been trying to get access to his technology for months now. If you were planning to just hijack the Chinese hypersonic weapons, why did you need to make your own? Or was that fake too, just to throw the Chinese off track?"

David shook his head. "Oh, no. Henry, there are a few ways to manage the navigation of long-range weaponry. I mean really-long-range weaponry. Like intercontinental ballistic missiles. The inertial navigation systems inside ICBMs cost a ton of money and take a very long time to make. If you are trying to build up a fleet of hypersonic weapons, and you can use GPS targeting data instead, it's much more efficient to do so."

"Which is what the Chinese did?"

"Yes. They went for the quicker, cheaper, and more vulnerable option, using their supposedly secure satellite technology to guide their weapons. But the American military, like it always has, went for the higher-cost, higher-quality option. The hypersonic weapons we have been working on aren't short- or medium-range cruise missiles. We already have those. But we felt we needed something that could achieve a prompt global strike on demand while not relying on a satellite network that could be hacked."

"Our ICBMs...that's why you had all the Air Force missile men locked away by themselves, and why Rojas went to STRATCOM?"

David nodded as Susan walked up to them. "He's sharp."

David said, "We used the reliable weapons we already had. Our ICBMs have inertial guidance systems that are incredibly accurate. They have to be. If the Russians launched a nuclear attack, one of the first things they would do is take out our GPS networks. We've been training for this for decades."

"But our ICBMs are nuclear weapons..."

"They *were* nuclear weapons. The Air Force has been working on its hypersonic glide vehicles for years. One of the variants was designed to be a direct substitute for all of our ICBM warheads."

Henry's eyes flickered back and forth as he thought. "So, you took out our nuclear warheads? We have no nukes?"

"A lot fewer, that's for sure. But don't tell anyone..." He winked.

"And you replaced them with hypersonic glide vehicles..."

"Right. Our HGVs are now installed in our intercontinental

ballistic missiles. A reliable, pre-existing way to get them in orbit and on a programmable trajectory of our choosing."

"Where does Rojas fit in?"

"He had to help us master the new heat-resistant coating that we used to cover all of the hypersonic glide vehicles. Now they are able to keep a much higher speed upon reentry into the earth's atmosphere without overheating their inner navigational computers. That means we now have hundreds of incredibly powerful hypersonic weapons that can hit targets with pinpoint accuracy, anywhere on the world, within thirty minutes."

Henry said, "Holy crap."

David smiled. "Yeah."

"Well when do we launch those?"

One of the Air Force officers manning a terminal near Susan called out, "STRATCOM reporting in. Standing by for launch."

David looked at Henry. "Soon."

Hightower and the six other B-1s departed north out of Gander, not south like the other aircraft. They went supersonic shortly thereafter, covering as much ground as possible before slowing to refuel with a KC-10 tanker orbiting near Iceland.

After refueling, the bombers headed east at high speed, where they met up with a flight of five Royal Air Force jets circling over the Norwegian Sea after launching from RAF Marham in Norfolk, England. Four UK F-35 Lightning IIs, the newest-generation fighter recently acquired from the US, escorted an ultra-secret RAF RC-135 Rivet Joint electronic surveillance aircraft. Inside the RC-135 were, among others, two members of the Government Communications Headquarters, or GCHQ, the UK counterpart to the American NSA. Both men sat at computer terminals on the aircraft with black curtains surrounding their station. They were operating the latest in offensive cyber weaponry, tetrabytes of code painstakingly crafted to demolish Russian defensive networks. The GCHQ chaps were excited to finally put it to use.

As the American B-1s approached the RAF planes, a pair of F-35s broke off and took up station on Hightower's wing. Dawn was breaking, and the B-1 crew watched as one of the RAF pilots pressed a handwritten note against the gold-tinted cockpit glass. The mission had called for complete external radio silence, so this must have been important.

"What's it say?" asked Hightower from the left seat.

His copilot sounded out the words. "Y-O-U-R-E. W-E-L-C-O-M-E. It says 'You're welcome, treasonous colonials.'" His copilot turned, grinning. "Ha. That's hilarious. Brit's got a sense of humor."

"Wonderful. If we don't die from Russian missiles we'll die from British humor."

Hightower gave the RAF pilot a thumbs up, which he returned, before banking right and climbing.

They flew for another two hours, skimming a layer of cirrus clouds as the night sky turned into morning. Both pilots knew that cyber and electronic attacks were now being launched on a variety of Russian networks, including electrical grids, communications networks, and, most importantly, air defense computers. The gentlemen from GCHQ were tapping into Russian military communications, taking over the message traffic of some commanders, and telling the few air defense radars still online to stand down until further notice.

Now over the Baltic Sea, the B-1s separated, dropping low to the deck as they made their weapons runs, still thousands of miles from target.

"Coming up on the outer range line," called the weapons systems officer. "Configure for weapons release."

"Roger, airspeed coming back. Bay doors opening."

Beneath each B-1, massive bomb bay doors opened, the air whipping by at hundreds of knots. One by one, the bombers launched the newest variant of the Hypersonic Conventional Strike Weapon.

Each missile's nose was angled down sharply like a doorstop and widened at the base into a cylinder. Four metal tail fins made microscopic adjustments to control its flight path.

Upon release, the missiles momentarily floated below their aircraft, seemingly suspended in mid-air before their scramjet engines ignited. Then the hypersonic weapons zoomed off toward the horizon, their engines pulsating, the missiles reaching speeds in excess of one thousand feet per second.

The hypersonic cruise missiles headed toward separate targets spread out over thousands of miles. The closest target was the Volga radar at Baranavichy, Belarus. Other radar stations were targeted near St. Petersburg, Kaliningrad, and Armavir, Russia. Two of the missiles struck command and control centers for the Russian ICBM strategic missiles while others destroyed naval Extreme Low Frequency communications facilities so they couldn't provide launch orders to Russian nuclear missile submarines. Lastly, one of the hypersonic cruise missiles targeted Russia's "Doomsday" plane, the newly built command and control aircraft based on the IL-96 airframe. With all other strategic nuclear command and control facilities destroyed, this plane was supposed to provide survivability.

That wouldn't happen.

Without warning, each of the American hypersonic missiles drove into their targets at over six thousand miles per hour. The kinetic energy negated the need for warheads. Each impact was the equivalent of three tons of TNT. The damage was catastrophic.

When it was over, Russia still had hundreds of nuclear

weapons. Missiles on mobile launchers. Warheads in bunkers near strategic bombers. A handful of nuclear missile submarines. But the American hypersonic attack wasn't meant for them. This was only the first step, and it was very effective.

The Russian nuclear early warning radar centers, and short-fused nuclear launch mechanism, was destroyed.

In the Silversmith tactical operations center, David witnessed an Air Force officer pounding his desk in jubilation.

"Russian early warning radars are offline. MQ-180 data confirms the BDA."

Henry said, "What's that mean?"

David whispered, "We've just taken out Russia's ability to detect a nuclear missile launch."

"That's great."

"That's good and bad. Russia won't know if we launch our ICBMs. That's good. But destroying those systems is also a possible indication of an imminent nuclear strike."

Henry's eyes widened. "So they might get trigger happy and launch on us just because we took out their radars?"

David said, "We've made that difficult. We destroyed some of their communications networks that would slow down the kill chain. And we have agents and allies working to influence their decision process. But ultimately, the Russian president could end the world right now. This might be the riskiest part of the operation."

Henry looked horror-stricken.

"I know. But it's the only way."

"The only way to what?"

David said, "We need to take out both China's and Russia's ability to launch nuclear weapons."

Henry said, "That's how you're using Rojas's technology? Our hypersonic glide vehicles in the ICBMs?"

David nodded.

Susan said, "What's the status at STRATCOM?"

An Air Force officer replied, "They just started the launch, ma'am."

For ARCHANGEL Phase Two, Pentagon planners had provided a list of no less than five hundred targets in Russia and two hundred in China, all of which needed to be destroyed within thirty minutes of taking out the Russian early warning systems.

Cruise missiles, even hypersonic ones, wouldn't do. The strike aircraft launching them would have to travel too far over enemy terrain, which posed too great a risk.

So, David's team settled on a different solution: a conventional global strike using ICBMs. Before the war began, America had four hundred and fifty LGM-30G ICBM missiles deployed at F.E. Warren Air Force Base in Wyoming, Minot Air Force Base in North Dakota, and Malmstrom Air Force Base in Montana.

After the war began, these missiles were modified to include Multiple Independent Reentry Vehicles. Each MIRV warhead now contained a newly updated Hypersonic Glide Vehicle.

Almost immediately after the Russian and Chinese early warning radars were destroyed, the American ICBMs began launching from their silos. In remote farmland and mountainous countrysides across the US, streaks of thick white smoke rose up into the night sky and arced to the northwest.

Hundreds of missiles were launched. America was moving all of its chips into the pot. The HGV-carrying missiles stabilized in a vertical climb, each rolling about its longitudinal axis to the target azimuth and pitching over toward the target. At precise moments, various engines ignited on each missile, making fine corrections in pitch, roll, and yaw axes. Their inertial guidance system used stars in space as a reference backup, cross-checking its position with the on-board computer's expected location and then making tiny corrections to improve accuracy.

After a few minutes, three stages of engine burnout and jettisons occurred. Then the rocket thrust terminated, and hundreds of delivery vehicles coasted in space, hurtling around the globe.

"Wow. Look at that," said Lt. Suggs, piloting his F-18 Superhornet south over the American heartland. His squadron, along with a handful of others, had been stashed at CFB Cold Lake in Alberta, Canada, "hidden" next to a few Canadian F-18 squadrons and stuffed in surveillance-proof hangars until last night.

Outside the cockpit, he and his weapons systems officer watched as dozens of ballistic missiles separated from their boosters in the night sky.

"Those are ICBMs, brother."

"Yeah. See the way the gas is expanding like that? That's the sunlight hitting the exhaust. They look like phosphorescent sea creatures from the deep."

"There's another. Wow, look at all of them," said his copilot. "Didn't the Russians say they would fire on us if we launched any more nukes?"

Suggs's body temperature rose and he felt numb watching the missiles' white exhaust gasses expanding into long balloon shapes.

"Let's just focus on the mission," he said. "How far out is the tanker?"

"Twenty minutes."

The nose cone of the lead Multiple Independent Reentry Vehicles "bus" opened to reveal five sleek hypersonic glide vehicles. Now over the northern Pacific Ocean, the individual HGVs began separating from their "bus," each maneuvered to a precise trajectory and then released. The individual HGVs now aimed for separate targets, each within a few hundred kilometers of their fellow passengers.

The hypersonic glide vehicles "surfed" on the outer reaches of the earth's atmosphere at over fifteen thousand miles per hour. Gradually, the metallic vehicles were pulled toward the earth by gravity and encountered atmospheric drag.

The effects were violent. Each HGV experienced aerodynamic heating and braking, but the Rojas coating protected its insides from the fifteen-thousand-degree shockwave near its nose.

The hypersonic glide vehicles continued to slow considerably but maintained a sizzling-hot temperature and a velocity of over Mach 8 when they made impact on their targets.

The Russian ICBMs were the first to go.

From the ground, the approaching HGVs looked like meteors travelling in precise geometric patterns. Observers witnessed the bright white objects racing across the sky in distant groups of five before collectively descending at a slightly steeper angle, and thus arriving almost simultaneously at targets dozens of kilometers apart. Sonic booms followed the glide vehicles as they cut through the atmosphere and rained down destruction on the missile fields of Kozelsk and Novosibirsk. The weapons destroyed mobile launchers in the Siberian pine forests, and three submarines in their pens in Yagelnaya Bay and Zapadnaya Litsa. Soon hundreds of targets were being hit in rapid succession.

Similar attacks were occurring in China, a simultaneous hypersonic missile strike on all known nuclear targets. Operation ARCHANGEL was in full swing.

Pensacola, Florida

In the Silversmith operations center, everyone stood at their stations, several calling out updates while most just waited for news. The tension was palpable.

"Recon drones are flying over targets now, but we won't really know for a while," David said to Henry.

Someone called out, "The first wave of American fighter aircraft is now over the Gulf of Mexico. They're attacking what remains of the Chinese fleet."

A naval officer said, "Our submarines are engaging Chinese and Russian submarines. Priority is sinking the remaining boomers."

Susan walked toward David, looking stern. "It's going well."

David said, "That's what worries me. How will General Chen react?"

"We need to hit those boomers."

Henry furrowed his eyebrows. "The boomers? What are those?"

David said, "Ballistic missile submarines. All of the other targets were easier to keep track of. Our intelligence services have been working for months on getting the exact locations of the ballistic missiles and strategic nuclear bombers. We're hitting those with our HGVs. But the submarines are another matter. They're harder to keep track of. US attack submarines normally trail them from the moment they leave port. But after the war began, we had a supply and demand problem among our fast-attack submarines."

Susan said, "There are two enemy ballistic missile submarines that we're particularly worried about."

One of the CIA operations officers yelled to Susan, "New information coming from Beijing." The man shook his head. "It's not good."

42

Beijing, China

The air raid sirens began wailing throughout the PLA command center as American hypersonic missiles struck their targets. General Chen's security detail moved him quickly out of the building. Lena was evacuated with her father and the other senior leaders onto a pair of waiting presidential helicopters, which took them to the airport. Once there, they were shuffled onto a Boeing 747—the Chinese presidential aircraft. The irony of its American manufacturer was not lost on Lena as she hustled up the stairway. The doors shut, engines running, and soon they were sitting down in the main conference room as the large aircraft began its takeoff roll.

A PLA Air Force general said, "General Chen, we are able to communicate with all of our military forces from this plane. We will provide you with information as it arrives. You shall have full capability to command the war as we ensure your security."

Over the next few minutes, Lena watched her father's deteriorating psyche as the news came in from around the globe.

"All Chinese and Russian nuclear launch systems are down?" General Chen stood hunched over the central conference table, hands on his forehead, staring at the floor. He didn't bother to make eye contact with his subordinates.

"Our navy still has two submarines off the US coast, although each has sent up messages within the past few hours that American naval vessels are actively hunting them."

Lena said, "I have heard from my Russian contacts that their submarine force is under similar threat."

General Chen looked up at his strategic missile force commander. "Tell me what you know of our hypersonic missile attack on the US."

The commander was young for a four-star general. He had been promoted, like many of his fellow senior officers, when General Chen came to power.

"The Americans appear to have sabotaged our hypersonic missiles. Most of them crashed into the Gulf of Mexico."

Minister Dong said, "My sources tell me that some of our hypersonic weapons have hit our own ships."

General Chen slammed the table with his fist and glared at the strategic missile force commander. "Is that true?"

"We are still gathering information, sir."

General Chen collapsed into his seat, rubbing his temples. Lena couldn't remember ever seeing her father appear so afraid. She didn't like it. He was unstable enough already.

General Chen said, "How could they have launched a conventional strike around the globe with such precision?"

A PLA Air Force general offered, "It's possible they used their nuclear ballistic missiles, sir."

The strategic missile commander shook his head. "Don't be a fool. One of our radar stations was hit only ten kilometers from here. If the American strike was nuclear, we would be dead."

Lena watched her father flexing his jaw as he listened. He was furious. She said, "We have many air force jets flying to support our remaining naval vessels in the Caribbean. Surely there must be some good news."

Her father looked up, hope in his eyes.

The PLA Navy admiral was half listening while holding a phone to his ear. His face was ashen. When he placed the phone down, he said, "Our ships and aircraft are involved in heavy fighting with the American Atlantic fleet. There appears to be a large reserve force of American aircraft entering the region from the north."

Captain Ray "Skip" Hagan had just gone feet wet over the Gulf of Mexico in his F-35A. The Air Force fighter was one of four flying in formation down from Canada. Through his four-hundred-thousand-dollar helmet-mounted display system, he was able to look "through" the aircraft's skin and see the hundreds of other American fighters flying in the night sky around him. The world was illuminated by a combination of night vision, infrared, and digital tags. As he turned his head, each aircraft was outlined by a small green reticle. Onboard computers fed information to him, digitally displayed through his helmet. The F-35 improved the situational awareness of pilots tenfold over previous-generation fighters. If anything, the challenge was dealing with the overflow of information while not forgetting the first rule of being a pilot: fly the aircraft.

Hundreds of Air Force and Navy jets had been racing south throughout the night. Tanking with the refueler aircraft was madness, reminding him of Outer Banks gas stations during July. Only it was at night, with hundred-million-dollar fifth-generation fighters.

Skip shifted in his seat as he looked through his helmet and moved his hands along the controls, typing keys and flipping switches as the digital information was displayed on his helmet. Gigabytes of data streamed to and from the other aircraft in silence as they flew on super-cruise toward what Skip hoped was an unsuspecting enemy.

"Black Widow One-Nine-Five and flight, Blue Knight." The Air Force E-3 Sentry airborne air control aircraft, flying over the central Gulf of Mexico, was checking in with each group of fighters and assigning them targets.

Skip spoke into his helmet microphone. "Blue Knight, Black Widow One-Nine-Five and flight, go."

"Black Widow One-Nine-Five and flight come to new heading one-seven-zero. Kill tracks bravo-seven-two through bravo-eight-two. How copy?"

"Black Widow One Nine-Five copies all."

Through their helmets, Skip and the three pilots on his wing could now see the tracks the Air Force radar aircraft had just assigned them flashing to catch their attention.

Skip banked his aircraft left, and his wingmen held formation. They were being fed targeting data from the E-3, and kept their own radars off for now. He increased throttle until the jet was flying at close to seven hundred knots, his hands dancing around the weapons system control keypad as he ensured the correct missile was selected and armed.

When they were in range, he depressed the weapons release button, and four AIM-260 Joint Air Tactical Missiles dropped from his aircraft and rocketed forward. The three other aircraft in his section followed suit.

The missiles traveled one hundred and fifty miles south at five times the speed of sound, where they turned on their active homing radars. The missiles quickly found their targets: a squadron of China's advanced J-20 fighters and a Chinese airborne early warning aircraft.

The targeted Chinese fighters were flying blind. They had just received inexplicable orders to stop using their datalink and GPS. The Chinese J-20 squadron commander had just finished dividing up his squadron onto different radio frequencies so that their radar control aircraft could verbally assign them targets.

Alarms began ringing in his ear and lighting up on his cockpit display. Looking out his cockpit window, the Chinese fighter squadron commander watched in horror as his large radar control aircraft burst into flames and fell into the sea.

This was when Skip's AIM-260 missile burst into the Chinese fighter, sending fragments through the fuel tank and engines. As the other missiles struck their targets in rapid succession, Chinese fighters exploded in the night sky.

Across the Caribbean and Gulf of Mexico, similar scenes unfolded. Hundreds of American fighters were clearing the skies. Creating a path for strikes on the remaining Chinese fleet. And carving the way for the Marine landing that had just begun in Panama.

As the reports came in to the Chinese presidential aircraft, Lena watched her father's psyche progressively deteriorate.

Minister Dong said, "The Americans launched a surprise attack with unexpectedly large reserves of aircraft and naval warships. Our ships and aircraft are engaged in combat throughout the Caribbean and Gulf of Mexico. My analysts tell me that the PLA Navy and Air Force are each taking heavy casualties. American submarines are sinking our destroyers. Our own hypersonic missiles, somehow hijacked by the Americans, have hit our Jiaolong-class battleships, severely depleting our air defense and anti-submarine capability."

One of the PLA generals said, "But our troops are advancing in Central America. We have broken through American lines in Costa Rica. Some of our scout units are as far north as Mexico."

Minister Dong shook his head. "My team tells me that a division of US Marines has just landed in Panama. If that is true, they could cut off our supply lines and flank us."

The PLA general barked, "That is ridiculous! If that were true, I would have heard..."

General Chen clenched his fists, speaking through gritted teeth. "Enough. The Americans have gained the upper hand."

He sounded tired. Lena thought of her child. What if this war ended today? Someday she might be able to travel to America. She had done many bad things, but surely the Americans would value her contributions.

The only thing she was sure of was her motherly instinct to protect her child. She must continue to guide her father to a safe outcome. This was why she had remained after Jinshan's death. She looked at him. He was unstable and surrounded by loyalists who—aside from Dong— would only tell him what he wanted to hear. Her work was almost done, though. She wondered if she would be able to get her father to surrender if...

General Chen turned to the PLA Navy admiral. "Our nuclear ballistic missile submarines."

Lena's heart stopped.

The admiral said, "Yes, sir?"

"You said two of them are still operational and in range of American targets?"

The whispered conversations around the table went silent. The PLA Navy admiral nodded. "Yes, General Chen. I believe..."

"You believe? Confirm, now! I will wait."

The admiral rose and walked to the next room. Through the

large window Lena could see him speaking to one of the plane's communications specialists.

Was her father about to order a nuclear strike? He couldn't possibly think that was a good option. She risked a question while the group waited. "Sir, before we explore whether any of our own missiles are ready, it would be prudent to inquire whether the Russian capabilities..."

"The Russians are inept fools. The blundering idiots have nothing left, according to these reports." He waved in Minister Dong's direction.

Lena could see her father's mind working through a problem.

General Chen said, "The Russians claimed they destroyed those American air and naval bases. But we now know that they did not. Perhaps the Russians are allied with the Americans? Or..." He looked at Lena, and then each member of his inner circle, with suspicion.

Lena realized her father had hit the next stage of crumbling authoritarian leader: paranoia. Although, in this case, he was correct to be distrustful. She and Dong had both been working against him, in their own ways.

Minister Dong said, "My sources tell me that the Russian military—particularly their air and missile forces—have suffered great casualties over the past twelve hours. Respectfully, General, I do not believe the Russians have betrayed us. Perhaps we should engage with them. These new attacks on the Russian military—presumably the work of the Americans—are sure to help our cause."

Dong was seeing the same suspicion forming in General Chen's eyes and trying to head it off before it grew worse.

General Chen narrowed his eyes. He nodded slowly. "Perhaps."

The door opened and the PLA Navy admiral entered. "General Chen, regretfully, one of our two remaining nuclear ballistic missile submarines has been lost. The other, however, is active and able to execute your firing orders."

General Chen stood, clenching his jaw. Lena felt a chill run down her spine as she looked at him.

He said, "Fire our remaining nuclear weapons at American military targets. We must regain the advantage."

43

Lena left the conference room shortly after her father had given the order. It wouldn't be quick. No thirty-minute kill chain, thanks to the American hypersonic strike on Chinese nuclear weapons centers. But the orders had been given, and within a few hours, a Type-094 Jin-class submarine, now hidden off the coast of Florida, would launch its twelve JL-2 nuclear missiles at American military targets.

After giving the order, her father had requested a meal. Plunging the world into nuclear terror had apparently given him an appetite. He was now stuffing his face with gourmet food and a few glasses of wine to ease the tension. Most members of his leadership team ate with him. But not all.

"Minister Dong." Lena called to him in the aircraft passageway. "Do you have a moment?"

"We *all* may have only moments." His stare was deadpan.

She gestured for him to follow, and they slipped into an empty pair of seats in a remote area of the passenger section.

"I'm as concerned as you," she whispered.

Minister Dong frowned. "Well, it's a bit late for regrets. Your father is about to launch a nuclear attack on the United

States. What do you think will happen next? The world will be our enemy. The Russians won't defend us. They can't. They've been castrated. Some of our nuclear weapons will be aimed for American military forces in Mexico, where they are in combat with our own troops. That means our nuclear weapons will likely kill hundreds of thousands of our own men. Millions on both sides will die of radiation poisoning." He paused, holding her stare. "Jinshan never would have approved of this."

Lena said, "I know this. I want to stop it. And don't mention Jinshan again."

"Well your father never would have risen to power if you..."

"*Enough.* Is there a way to get the coordinates of our nuclear missile submarine?"

Minister Dong realized what she was planning and shot her a disapproving look. "What you speak of is treason," he whispered.

"It's a solution..."

"It may be possible."

"How?"

"According to the admiral, they are using backup communications and codes to initiate the nuclear weapons launch. With all of our communications problems, we could ask them to confirm their orders. It's non-standard, but it would mean that the missile submarine would send a transmission. The submarine commander would be forced to emit an electronic signal. They wouldn't outright give their coordinates, but I can probably get that information from the communications specialists."

"We need to make it happen."

"Even if you could get those coordinates, any message out of this aircraft will be scrutinized."

Lena removed a large-screen cell phone from her pocket, showing it to Minister Dong. "I can send a message. But we need to do it soon. Now go get me the coordinates of that submarine."

Silversmith Tactical Operations Center

David was looking over the various reports flooding in from Central America. Marines aboard the *USS Wasp*, *Green Bay*, and *Ashland* had just executed an amphibious landing, re-capturing the Panama Canal Zone. The daring maneuver had cut off Chinese ground forces in Central America and Mexico from their supply lines. With F-22 and F-35 fighters leading the way, the American Air Force had taken control of the skies.

American cruise missiles and special operations forces were now pummeling Chinese air defenses from Mexico down to Panama. And with the Chinese SAM threat removed, US bombers were now hitting the juiciest targets. Tank convoys. Heavy weapons. Helicopter bases. Troop transports. The level of destruction was simultaneously marvelous and sickening.

One of the CIA officers waved to them from the communications room. "Susan, we just got a flash cable. Highest priority, routed through Japan. You need to see this now."

"Japan?" Susan stood from her desk and walked into the secure comms room to read the cable.

"Yes, ma'am. It's got a latitude and longitude, and a timestamp with today's date. A little less than ninety minutes from now."

Susan snapped her fingers for David to come over. He wrote down the position and they headed over to a chart.

Susan said, "David, this is from our new agent in Beijing."

David knew that meant that Tetsuo had received the

message from Lena via her new covert communications. The equipment she was using had the ability to send and receive burst transmissions by piggybacking off any nearby Chinese communications signals. But there was a heavy risk of getting caught. So, if she was sending this message, it must be crucial.

David traced his finger along the chart until he came to the location the coordinates were referencing.

"It's in the ocean. Halfway between Miami and Bimini."

Susan said, "What would be important about..."

David cursed. "Oh my God. We've got one more Chinese boomer unlocated, right?"

Susan's eyes went wide. She yelled out to her Navy rep on the operations floor, "We need to get these coordinates to the Navy ASAP."

Victoria was on her fourth flight in the past eighteen hours. Her muscles ached, and her rear end was sore from sitting so long. Overhead, the air battle explosions had slowed considerably. Last night was epic. Victoria and her copilot had witnessed their own private fireworks show. Tens of thousands of feet above them, and probably thirty miles away, the PLA Air Force had met the US Air Force over the Florida Straits.

Victoria was glad for sunrise. Day landings were always easier, and she was so tired it felt like she was drunk. She lined up her MH-60R Seahawk with the churning white water of the *USS Michael Monsoor's* wake, the warship's sharp angles making it look like she was about to land on a futuristic spacecraft.

"Coming over the flight deck," called her copilot.

"Roger."

Victoria eased the aircraft forward over the large flight deck, steadied, and then lowered the power until the aircraft landed with a jolt. She gave a thumbs up to the plane captain in front of the helicopter, giving permission for the flight deck team to transit the rotor arc. Moments later they were chocked and chained. Her copilot departed the aircraft and Plug got in. He was the aircraft commander on the next crew.

"Hey, boss."

"Good morning." She was about to begin her turnover brief when a radio call interrupted them.

"Jaguar 600, Control, how much fuel do you have right now?"

Victoria frowned, looking at her fuel gauges. "About 1.5 until splash. They're filling us up as we speak."

"600, Captain says you need to take off immediately. We have just received intel of a hostile submarine getting ready to launch missiles. It's last known posit is twenty-five miles to our north. We need an immediate attack. Standby for submarine datum."

Plug waved to get the plane captain's attention and signaled for them to stop refueling.

Victoria said, "Where's your other pilot?"

"I don't know, but I don't think we can wait."

"Agreed."

Victoria felt a vibration in her seat as the ship began speeding up. Then it listed to port as it made a hard turn in the direction of the Chinese submarine. The chocks and chains were removed, and the flight deck was soon empty except for their helicopter, rotors spinning.

Over the radio she heard, "You have green deck."

Victoria said, "Coming up and aft."

She pulled power, stabilized, and then brought the stick aft and pulled more power. The helicopter slowly moved back-ward, suspended in a hover over the back of the flight deck. She kicked the nose out to the right and pulled power right up to the limits. Instead of climbing, she moved the stick forward, bringing the nose down, skillfully transferring all of that increased engine power into airspeed while maintaining a constant altitude.

Plug and their aircrewman began announcing the completion of checklist steps to each other, then worked with the ship's tactical controller to ensure they had the latest information on the Chinese submarine.

"Let's spit a pattern of passive buoys and see if we can triangulate his position. Then we'll dip and go active," Victoria said.

"Roger." Plug relayed the plan to the ship.

Ten minutes later, Victoria felt the vibrations of the speeding aircraft diminish as she slowed.

POP.

"Buoy one away," called the aircrewman. "Good chute. In the water."

POP.

"Buoy two away..."

Her aircrewman continued to make calls from the back of the helicopter, updating them on the status of the sonobuoys. Underneath each one, long strings of acoustic sensors lowered themselves into the deep, sending the data back to the helicopter through a transmitter atop the floating buoy.

The passive buoys they used wouldn't send out active sonar pings. Every ping was a warning to their prey. And once the enemy submarine took evasive maneuvers, her job would become much more difficult.

"We got something, ma'am. All right...there...got a fix. It's about one thousand yards from buoy number two."

Plug passed the information back to the controller on the ship while manipulating his tactical display. "Okay, I got a track. It's going zero-three-zero at five knots."

The aircrewman said, "Signature sure looks like a Type 94. Making some weird noises though."

Victoria looked at the display screen. Plug's fingers raced over the keypad, updating the track and...

"Shit. I think I lost it. It was there a second ago and then...I think he must have gone deeper. Checking. Hold on. Yup, there it is. The submarine changed course and speed too."

Victoria was flying in a racetrack pattern near the buoys, staying close enough that they would be able to attack quickly once they were ready.

"Okay, now we've got him headed two-seven-zero at fifteen knots. Let's make our attack run. Boss, I'm giving you a fly-to point."

"Copy."

Victoria banked hard right and brought her helicopter around to line up for their attack. In the back of her mind, something was bothering her. Memories of the last time she conducted anti-submarine warfare came flooding back.

The submarine that had killed her father. She shook her head, hoping Plug didn't notice as she physically tried to clear her exhausted mind. But the troubling feeling wouldn't leave.

"Okay, I've got you on course. Going through weapons release checklist," Plug said. His hands were still speeding over switches and buttons, setting up for their torpedo drop.

Victoria's pulse raced as a million thoughts flooded her mind.

Just fly the aircraft.

She checked her gauges. Airspeed and altitude were good. Heading was where it needed to be. Fuel was low. Shit, fuel was really low. She wished they could have taken more, but it would only really be a problem if this first torp missed the bastard.

The memory came back.

The submarine that fired a missile at her father. Her brain

was telling her something was wrong. This feeling wasn't just anxiety about her past demons.

This was her mind telling her to wake up. There was a problem in front of her and they weren't seeing it. She frowned at the tactical display.

"One mile until weapons release," Plug said.

The day her father died, she had been hunting a submarine near his aircraft carrier. The tactical problem was just like this.

"Copy," said the aircrewman.

"Roger," replied Victoria, her pulse racing as she watched the distance count down. "Any update on the track?"

The submarine had changed depth and speed, and shortly after, Victoria's aircraft had reacquired it. Just like this.

"Negative, same course and speed, ma'am."

Then the P-8 had killed it with a torpedo. Or at least, everyone thought they did...

Plug said, "All right, .4 miles. Weapons release on my third now." He paused. "Now...now..."

"Stop! Don't press it!"

Plug stopped, looking at Victoria with wide eyes. His finger was suspended one inch over the button, unmoving, as he awaited further command.

Victoria looked at him, flipping up her visor. "I think it's a decoy."

"What?" he said.

"This is the same exact course and speed I saw when we thought we were tracking a submarine near the *Ford*. Same flipping course and speed. It was a decoy. I'm coming left. Take your finger away from that button, please."

Plug did as commanded. "Shit, boss, are you fucking sure about this?"

"Let's prepare to dip right near where you first held contact."

Plug was still looking at her like she was crazy. "You think it's still there?"

"Just do it."

Plug said, "Yes, ma'am." He wiped sweat from his forehead.

"Be ready to drop as soon as we ping. If it's still there, that sub's going to be getting ready to launch missiles. They'll probably be shallow."

"Roger."

Victoria slowed their aircraft to a hover a little more than fifty feet above the ocean, and the multi-million-dollar dipping sonar, the most advanced in the world, lowered from beneath the helicopter. Once in the water, it continued to reel out until it was at Plug's specified depth.

"Going active."

"Roger."

Victoria could hear the loud, high-pitched ping sending a jolt of sound energy out in all directions.

The aircrewman yellowed over the internal comms, "There it is!"

Plug said, "Oh shit, he's right there..."

On the tactical display, they had received an active sonar return exactly where Victoria believed the Chinese submarine to be hiding.

Plug didn't hesitate this time. "Torpedo away, now, now, now."

He depressed the torpedo launch button and the six-hundred-pound MK-50 lightweight torpedo released off the helicopter, slowed by a parachute before plunging into the ocean.

"Torpedo's running. Going active."

Victoria could hear the torpedo's higher-pitched pings growing faster.

"Torpedo has acquired target. Torpedo is homing..."

"This is going to be quick..."

Two hundred feet beneath the ocean's surface, the MK-50 lightweight torpedo continued to ping, using each soundwave to verify its range to target. It raced to a point just next to the hull and exploded. The combination of explosion, high pressure, and temperature ignited much of the air inside the submarine, but the fires were soon out as seawater flooded into multiple compartments.

From the helicopter, Victoria watched as a deep blue patch of ocean half a mile ahead of them turned white before erupting into a geyser of water over one hundred feet in the air.

44

Chinese presidential aircraft

"We have received reports of an emergency beacon in the Atlantic. I'm afraid this was the last remaining ballistic missile submarine, General Chen. I believe it was sunk." The Navy admiral looked at the table as he spoke, too afraid to meet General Chen's eyes.

Silence around the table, until the door opened and another PLA general entered the room. "Sir, I regret to inform you that our forces in Central America are now taking heavy losses. American air strikes are bombarding our troops in Costa Rica and Mexico. And the US Marines have taken back Panama..."

General Chen lifted his water glass and threw it across the room, shattering it on the wall. Lena studied the faces around the table. It had to be over, now. She could see the military men looking toward her father for leadership. She could only hear the white noise of aircraft engines, electronics, and ventilation as he stared back at them, wordless.

Lena glanced at Dong, who said, "General Chen, if I may, we

still operate from a position of strength. If we contact the Americans now, we could negotiate a truce. This would allow us to consolidate our forces in South America. The Americans will be happy to end the fighting. We can bring our ground forces back into protected territory, and go back to starving the American economy. The vast areas of land we now hold in Asia and South America will give us long-term advantage."

General Chen looked at Minister Dong. "Surrender?"

"It would not be surrender, sir. It would merely be a consolidation of our scattered forces."

"Do you really think the Americans will just let us walk away and regain our strength? They have destroyed our nuclear capability. If your own intelligence reports are to be believed, they have destroyed much of the Russian nuclear forces as well. They have..."

The aircraft's conference room door opened, and a PLA Air Force major entered. "Sir, a communication from the American president."

All eyes looked at the sheet of paper in his hand.

General Chen's face was red. "What does it say?"

"The American president wishes to speak with you regarding the terms of our surrender."

Lena winced.

"The terms of our surrender?" General Chen fumed. "Of our *surrender*? You see! They do not want peace. They want victory."

Minister Dong said, "General, we have limited options."

"Perhaps. But we do have options." General Chen turned to the strategic missile commander. "You have loaded the biological weapon onto one of our long-range ballistic missiles, as I commanded?"

"Yes, General Chen."

Lena felt ill. Her nightmare had arrived.

General Chen's face twitched. "Prepare it for launch."

Several of the advisors around the table spoke at once, urging caution.

"Sir, I must warn against…"

"General, perhaps we could…"

General Chen waved off their objections. "Quiet. I said prepare the biological weapon for launch."

Lena thought about telling her father this was a bad idea, but in her judgment, there was no reasoning with a man in his state of mind. She needed to let this play out and evaluate options as they came to her. Right now, she had none.

Minister Dong said, "General Chen, this is madness. The statistics on this weapon are horrifying. It is meant as a deterrent. Not to be used. We would be destroying the world. We would be destroying ourselves."

General Chen glared at him. "I have consulted with my experts. They say we will have time to inoculate many of our citizens."

"Sir, hundreds of millions could die."

General Chen frowned. "And we who remain will be victorious."

The mouths of several officers around the table were hanging open in disbelief.

"I have made my decision. Victory, whatever the cost. If you disagree, speak up now. We'll let you off the plane. Immediately."

The PLA strategic missile commander said, "Sir, I must inform you that due to the nature of this weapons system, the security procedures for this missile are…*unique*."

"Fine. Launch the weapon."

"No, sir, I must explain. We implemented certain safety protocols…"

Lena said, "General, I spoke to you of this a few weeks ago. You approved that the biological weapon would have the highest security protocol. The biological deterrent is not set up for a remote launch. Not yet."

"What are you saying?"

"You and I will need to be at the launch site in person, sir."

General Chen cursed. "Idiocy. How long, then? How long until we can get there?"

"We can be there in one hour, sir. The warhead is kept at the space launch facility, sir."

Lena entered the aircraft bathroom a few moments later, removing her CovCom device. She needed to send one more message. She only hoped it would reach them in time.

USS Jimmy Carter
South China Sea

Chase and the DEVGRU special operations team had completed their mission twenty-four hours ago. They had remained with the Chinese agent inside the PLA Space Operations command center room, surrounded by the bodies of those they had neutralized, while the satellites were launched into orbit. Then they had departed the way they came, bringing the Chinese agent with them.

Now back aboard the *USS Jimmy Carter*, fed and rested, showered and shaved, Chase and the team were unexpectedly activated for a new mission.

"They want us to go *back*?" the SEAL team commander asked the ship's captain. Chase sat next to the two men in the captain's cabin, all three reading the very short mission brief on the computer screen.

"Am I reading this right?" Chase checked his watch. "We gotta roll. This is happening now."

Twenty minutes later, Chase and six SEALs gripped their diver propulsion vehicles, speeding through the dark ocean. He wondered what they would find. They had departed the island undetected, but the dead bodies littering the control center and surrounding area must have been discovered by now.

Chase's mask broke the surface of the water under the cover of darkness. Searchlights scanned the base. Dozens of military vehicles and foot soldiers patrolled the island—many more than yesterday. Chase and the SEALs secured their dive gear and crept onto the beach in a low crawl. The waves lapped them as they moved on their knees and elbows, gripping suppressed rifles.

"Psst. Vehicle approaching."

The island was little more than a few miles of dredged-up sand, along with a big runway and several missile launching platforms positioned on jutted-out peninsulas. Surrounding the island was a man-made sandbar that protected the inner islands from waves and weather. A four-wheel-drive security vehicle was making its way along the outer sandbar, a spotlight from the passenger side scanning the sparse vegetation opposite the water.

Through his night vision goggles, Chase watched as one of the SEALs waited for the security vehicle to drive by his position. The SEAL then crept upward, jogging low behind the vehicle and firing two suppressed rounds through the driver's open window.

In one athletic motion, the SEAL opened the driver's side door, flung out the driver, and jumped in. Two flashes in the window as the SEAL killed the shocked passenger. As the vehicle came to a halt, Chase and the rest of the SEALs hurried over. They picked up the dead driver and passenger and stuffed them into the rear.

The SEALs headed toward the main island, careful not to drive too fast or too close to any observers. They parked in a dark alleyway next to the airfield hangar.

The SEALs got out and scattered. Some took up sniper positions hidden in various locations throughout the base. Chase and the team leader climbed onto the hangar's roof via a fire escape ladder. Chase held an observation scope, monitoring the runway and periodically checking his watch.

"Any minute now."

A giant Boeing 747 appeared out of the low cloud layer, touching down with a skid on the runway. Dozens of security personnel surrounded the aircraft. A mobile stair ladder was rolled up to the passenger door, and Chase watched as two security guards and a PLA general began walking down the stairs.

"Is that him?" Chase heard one of the SEALs say in his earpiece.

"I don't think so."

"He's getting in the car; do I take the shot?"

"Negative."

The SEAL team leader, lying in the prone position on the hangar roof next to him, asked, "Chase? That him?"

Chase's observation scope had a facial recognition computer inside it. The bar at the top of his view ran from left to right and then went red.

"Negative," said Chase. "Not our man." He removed a round watertight case from his backpack, opened it, and removed two quadcopter drones that fit into his palm. He tapped on his wrist pad and the drones whizzed upward into the night air.

He looked through his observation scope again, and this time two small squares of streaming video feed appeared.

Toggling between the different infrared camera views, he began to update his team.

"I count a total of twenty-one personnel on board the aircraft. It looks like most are gathered in a conference room on the second level near the nose. Standby...okay. Yup, I think that's our target. He's getting up now and..."

Distant gunfire erupted from Chase's left. On his observation scope, Chase saw the infrared silhouettes inside the Chinese presidential aircraft stand in alarm.

One of the SEAL's voices came on Chase's earpiece. He sounded like he was running. "Contact in position bravo. I'm going to draw them out to one of the missile launch pads."

The team leader next to Chase responded calmly, "Roger." He repositioned himself, continuing to look through his sniper scope.

Chase said, "It looks like they're staying put. Some of them are coming out, but not our target..."

Several more PLA officers appeared at the jumbo jet's doorway, running down the stairway and into the waiting cars. Chase heard more cracks of gunfire now. Closer.

"Foxtrot is taking fire."

The team leader said, "Fuck this. Open fire on all targets."

Chase heard the simultaneous eruption of gunfire from several sniper positions nearby and watched through the observation scope as the Chinese military men making their way down the stairs were hit with lethal fire.

The vehicles at the bottom of the stairs became riddled with bullet holes, and the tires of the 747 burst as multiple sniper rounds tore through them.

Lena saw the unbridled fear on her father's face as gunfire erupted outside the aircraft.

As soon as they landed, base security had informed them that the base had been attacked yesterday and that they would need to take extra precautions. Now Lena understood how the Americans had gained such an advantage in the Atlantic. They must have used China's own datalink and communications networks against them.

After sending her CovCom message to Tetsuo, she expected them to try something like this. A decapitation strike, assassinating her father. She had assumed the Americans would use one of their advanced weapons, like a cruise missile, but if the US had a team of special forces operatives already here...it made sense to use them instead. They would be more accurate, despite the personal risk.

General Chen paced the room. "Why are we still in here?"

"Sir, there is gunfire outside. You are safe here. Allow us to neutralize the threat. We don't want to risk you getting hit."

"Get me to a vehicle. We must launch the weapon."

Lena said, "What if we use one of the emergency escapes? Move one of your vehicles to the rear of the plane. We could ferry out a handful of security personnel with my father and slide him down there?"

The PLA security officer waivered.

General Chen said, "Do as she says."

The man nodded and relayed the command into his radio. "All units concentrate fire on the attacking positions." More security vehicles took up positions around the jumbo jet, firing automatic weapons in the direction of the aircraft hangars.

Moments later, Lena, her father, the PLA strategic missile commander, and three security personnel were sliding down an inflatable yellow emergency escape on the far side of the aircraft. Several vehicles had been positioned around the tail as a protective barrier.

Chase could hear the clicks and pops of suppressed rifle fire next to him as the SEAL team leader fired at the shadows escaping from the aircraft's rear. Through his observation scope, Chase watched the group of Chinese men rush into the security vehicles and speed away.

One of the shadows rushing into the lead vehicle was a woman with long black hair.

The SEAL team leader spoke into his headset, transmitting to the team. "They're on the move. Heading east. Alpha is in pursuit."

Chase and the SEAL team leader rose from their prone positions, running toward the roof ladder and sliding down. Two Chinese soldiers now stood in the alleyway beside their hijacked vehicle. Chase raised his pistol and placed two rounds in each of them. Their bodies dropped to the dirt. Then he sprinted into the driver's seat, the SEAL team leader taking shotgun, and hit the gas, racing to follow the Chinese presidential convoy. Yellow muzzle flashes and the rattle of automatic weapons erupted all around them.

Chase flipped his clear HUD glasses down. The two small drones he released a few minutes ago were now approximately two hundred feet above, their multi-spectrum cameras quietly observing the action. He used his right hand to tap on his wrist pad while driving with his left.

"You need me to take the wheel?" the SEAL team leader asked.

"Yeah."

He took the wheel while Chase kept his feet on the gas,

glancing down to finish typing on his wrist pad. They were now gaining on the convoy ahead of them.

A few more taps on his wrist pad. Now Chase saw a green rectangle appear around the moving vehicles displayed on his visor's video feed. He toggled which target the rectangle surrounded until it locked on the lead vehicle.

Chase made a radio call into his headset to the command and control team aboard the *USS Jimmy Carter*. "MATCH-STICK, this is Alpha, do you copy my video feed, over?"

"Alpha, MATCHSTICK, roger, over."

"MATCHSTICK, Alpha, confirm target ID, over."

"Alpha, MATCHSTICK, roger, standby. Our analyst says that the lead vehicle contains our target. Target is heading toward the missile launch command and control building. It is mission critical that we stop that from happening, over."

"Roger MATCHSTICK, request air support on target vehicle, over."

"Alpha, MATCHSTICK, we have UCAS lock on the lead vehicle. Time on top, fifteen seconds. Out."

Lena bounced and jostled as they drove, four of them facing each other in the vehicle's back seat. The first rays of morning light now shined over the ocean, illuminating the long, sandy road they traveled on. Ahead was a peninsular, a launch platform at the tip and a two-story rectangular building nearby.

The strategic missile commander said, "That's it. We must get General Chen and me inside. Then our biometric information will unlock our ability to fire the missile."

"Biometrics? My fingerprints?"

"And retina. Yes, General."

Lena watched as the general's head of security placed his

hand on his earpiece and began speaking. "Yes. When? Are you sure? *Who...*" His voice trailed off, and Lena could see him fighting the urge to look her way. Instead he leaned toward her father and whispered something in his ear.

General Chen's pupils dilated. He turned toward her, chest heaving. "Our communications specialists detected a message sent from our aircraft. They believe it was you."

Lena didn't answer.

"Have you betrayed me, daughter?"

Lena now saw the head of security point his pistol at her. He called out to the two security men in the front of the vehicle, and the one in the passenger seat turned to face the rear, drawing his weapon. The strategic missile commander backed away, attempting to melt into his seat.

Lena mentally calculated the distance to her opponents, weighing the probability that she would survive versus the importance of achieving her mission.

She was about to make her move when the earth exploded underneath them.

A third drone circled eight hundred feet overhead, launched directly from the USS *Jimmy Carter*. About the diameter of a kitchen table, it was primarily used for surveillance and reconnaissance. It did, however, have a limited offensive capability.

The drone fired two miniaturized missiles, each armed with a five-pound warhead. The weapons struck the Chinese presidential vehicle in rapid succession. One hit the engine block, destroying it. The other struck the left rear, igniting the fuel tank and causing it to flip the vehicle over.

Chase stopped their vehicle near a small sand dune twenty yards away from the wreckage. Two Chinese escort SUVs skidded to a halt next to the damaged vehicle, the occupants exiting and forming a perimeter around their leader. Some began pulling people out of the burning debris.

Chase tapped on his wrist and saw the video image from his mini drones.

"Seven...no...nine personnel. At least two are injured. One looks dead. They've got about fifteen yards to travel between there and the building. I'm sending in the LMAMs."

"Roger."

The two mini drones Chase controlled could be used as kamikazes. The US military termed them Lethal Miniature Aerial Missile systems, or LMAMs. Chase used his keypad to toggle onto his targets and then gave each an attack command.

Like fragmentation-capable giant hornets, the two LMAM drones flew toward the group of Chinese officers and security personnel now huddled behind the three vehicles. As the first drone approached, its buzzing rotors now audible, some of them looked up.

At a height of ten feet, the fragmentation device underneath the drone exploded, sending shards of hot metal out in a fifteen-foot kill radius. Instantly, the group went down. Some clutching their wounds, others mostly stunned but uninjured. Two were dead.

The second drone exploded seconds later, magnifying the damage.

Chase and the SEAL team leader were already on the move, firing at their targets while they held the advantage. Then gunfire rattled behind the Chinese vehicles and sand kicked up around them, halting their advance.

———

Lena and her father were the only ones still alive in the rear of the overturned vehicle. In the front seat, one of the few remaining security men had squirmed out of his seatbelt and was firing a rifle from the prone position, partially hidden from the approaching American soldiers.

Lena saw that her father was bleeding from the neck. The wound looked very painful, but it wouldn't kill him if he received medical attention.

She, on the other hand...

Lena looked at her hands, which were covered in dark blood flowing from her abdomen. The pain was excruciating. But she knew it wouldn't last long.

She was going to bleed out.

Lena could already feel the energy draining from her body. It took everything she had to stay focused. Her mission wasn't over. She thought about her child again. About her life's work, however misguided. About her own flaws, and her pathetic attempts to overcome them. Did these last efforts even matter? Would anything make up for the sins she had committed?

She didn't know. Life had been cruel to her. But life was cruel to everyone. She could only control her own actions. And she could only act for a few moments more. She could only affect what was in front of her. Lena hoped it would make a difference.

"You betrayed me, daughter," her father whispered, looking at her. "You ungrateful wretch."

"You betrayed me, father."

A pop of gunfire from the driver's seat as the security man took another shot.

One of the few remaining military officers outside the vehicle stuck his head in. "General Chen, we have radioed our troops on the other side of the island. They are sending reinforcements. Only two Americans are here. We will hold them off until our reinforcements arrive and then get you into the building."

Lena looked at him. "You gave away your only child. For what? Promotion and power?"

General Chen said, "You are a naïve fool. Greatness comes only to those who take it. I do whatever it takes."

Lena saw movement in the corner of her eye. She turned and looked out the window, concentrating on a silhouette in the sand a dozen yards away. She squinted, trying to focus...

Impossible.

But it was him. Chase.

He was part of the team that had come to kill her father. To stop his insane act of vengeance upon the world.

He didn't see her yet. It was dark underneath the overturned car, she realized. He wouldn't see any of them, hidden here in the shadows.

She looked at her father, took a deep breath—like it was her last—and screamed Chase's name.

Chase heard the scream and his eyes snapped to the overturned vehicle's dark interior.

"What was that?" asked the SEAL. Sand still kicked up around them as rounds whizzed by.

It was Lena's voice. She had just screamed his name. And then, in English, "He's in here."

"She's telling us where to shoot."

Chase flipped his weapon to three-round burst, took aim, and began firing.

Lena watched as rounds tore through the SUV and its occupants. Her father's face and chest imploded into chunks of red and gray. The security man in the front seat was shot multiple times and killed. And then Lena felt a burst of white-hot pain in her shoulder as a round tore through her, too.

Through the ringing in her ears, she heard more gunfire, and footsteps closing in.

In a daze, she felt herself being dragged out of the vehicle.

Sand on her cheek, she now lay on her side. Cracks of gunfire in the distance. Her eyes open but not seeing much. Then her vision shifted into focus and she saw a white man wearing a black dive suit standing over her father, who lay dead next to her.

They were taking pictures and checking his vitals.

Then Chase's face hovered above her own.

She wanted to say something. That she was sorry. But she didn't have the energy. Her breaths grew short.

He leaned down and whispered into her ear, "I'll take care of our boy. He'll have a good life. I'll make sure of it."

She felt at peace, and closed her eyes for the last time.

45

One year later

Chase stood next to his brother as David turned over the barbeque chicken on his grill. They stood before an expansive view of green lawn and distant Blue Ridge Mountains on a sunny afternoon in rural Virginia. A few colleges were starting to play football again, a first since the war ended. Some of the games would even be televised tonight. The brothers sipped cold beers, smiling as the three kids played on the swing set in the backyard.

"Lindsay, can I help with anything?" Chase asked.

David's wife was setting the outdoor table. A glass jar of lemonade over a red-and-white tablecloth. Paper plates and corn on the cob. Salad and freshly baked bread from the new neighborhood bakery. The stores were opening again, too.

"Just get the kids to the table, please."

Chase called the three children. David's two, and his boy.

"Arthur, come on. Hey, buddy. Come on, you can sit up here in the kids' seat. Want me to chop that up for you?"

David smiled at his brother. "You're getting the hang of this dad thing."

"I kind of have to."

"Yeah...tell me about it."

They sat down and ate. Nothing but the sounds of crickets and cicadas and kids playing and crying. The conversation was light. Victoria was returning to sea next week. Her first command of a ship. Well, the other one didn't count, they figured.

"You gonna apply for that job?" David asked his brother.

"Yeah. I think so. I think being a cop would suit me."

USS Essex

100 nautical miles west of San Diego

Victoria sat in the captain's chair of the *USS Essex*. She had just come up to the bridge to get some fresh air after reading Plug's email to her.

The war was over, and Plug had switched over to the reserves. He had also just accepted a civilian job as a helicopter air ambulance pilot.

"Captain Manning, good evening."

The command master chief stood next to her. He usually didn't come up here. "I happened to see a message from BUPERS just now. Thought you might be interested."

She stood from her chair, nodding for him to join her outside on the bridge wing. "What'd you see, Master Chief?"

"I saw your name on the list for admiral. You'll put it on next year."

Victoria shook her head. It was crazy to think about. "That so?"

"I thought you'd be a bit more excited than that, ma'am. Isn't that every officer's dream?"

She looked at him. "You know me well enough by now, Master Chief."

He nodded. "I guess I do, ma'am." He held out a box of cigars. "Still..."

She rolled her eyes. "You're going to get me in trouble."

She stuck her head into the bridge. "Officer of the Deck. Please announce that the smoking lamp is lighted." The men and women on watch looked on approvingly.

"Aye, ma'am."

The CMC and Victoria smoked their cigars in silence as the ship steamed north. They spoke of life and career. And then a bit about the war.

"Do you think it is really over?" he asked quietly.

She nodded. "I do. But we must never forget it, so it won't happen again."

Firewall

They say it will be our last invention.

Artificial General Intelligence. A machine that is infinitely more intelligent than the smartest human alive...a creation so powerful, it will change everything we know.

Some say it will be the answer to all of our problems. Others call it a weapon of immeasurable strength.

But before this new era of Superintelligence begins...

What would the world's most powerful people do, if the discovery was close at hand?

What would you do, if ultimate power was within your grasp?

With FIREWALL, USA Today bestselling author Andrew Watts takes you to exotic locations around the globe, and keeps you guessing every step of the way. Part spy novel, part tech-nothriller adventure, FIREWALL is a fast-paced, cerebral thriller that's perfect for fans of Dan Brown and Michael Crichton.

Get your copy today at AndrewWattsAuthor.com

ALSO BY ANDREW WATTS

Firewall

The War Planners Series

The War Planners

The War Stage

Pawns of the Pacific

The Elephant Game

Overwhelming Force

Global Strike

Max Fend Series

Glidepath

The Oshkosh Connection

Books available for Kindle, print, and audiobook.

Join former navy pilot and USA Today bestselling author Andrew Watts'
Reader Group and be the first to know about new releases and special offers.

AndrewWattsAuthor.com

ABOUT THE AUTHOR

Andrew Watts graduated from the US Naval Academy in 2003 and served as a naval officer and helicopter pilot until 2013. During that time, he flew counter-narcotic missions in the Eastern Pacific and counter-piracy missions off the Horn of Africa. He was a flight instructor in Pensacola, FL, and helped to run ship and flight operations while embarked on a nuclear aircraft carrier deployed in the Middle East.

Today, he lives with his family in Ohio.

SIGN UP FOR NEW BOOK ALERTS AT
ANDREWWATTSAUTHOR.COM

From Andrew: Thanks so much for reading my books. Be sure to join my Reader List. You'll be the first to know when I release a new book.

You can follow me or find out more here:
AndrewWattsAuthor.com

Made in the USA
Coppell, TX
02 June 2020

26875359R00231